Great mysteries with a medical slant. ᵣ ₑₜₑᵣ ₖₒwₑy weaving credible and realistic clinical scenarios with quirky characters and fast-moving plots. Page-turners across the board!
— **Peter DiBattiste,** MD Former VP, Cardiovascular Development, Janssen R&D

If you look for books that are full of suspense and intrigue you will love the Sarkis series. I can't read them in bed or I end up never falling asleep. Peter Kowey brings his deep knowledge of medicine and his gift for writing together to create a masterful mystery series.
— **Jim DBiasi,** Principal, 3D Communications

Dr. Peter Kowey is a splendid physician, medical lecturer, medical teacher, human being, and medical detective writer and story teller. His previous novels have been wonderful reading and there is no reason to believe that this, his latest one, will not be as well.
— **William C. Roberts, MD,** executive director, Baylor Heart and Vascular Institute, and editor in chief, The American Journal of Cardiology

I love reading Peter Kowey's novels. Easy reading with a surprise twist in all the plots. The characters are easily brought to life. Each book, however, has a message to deliver regarding problems concerning healthcare. Looking forward to the next adventure of Philip Sarkis.
— **David A. Cohen M.D.** Education Coordinator, Department of Medicine, Lankenau Medical Center

To read a Peter Kowey novel is to be educated, entertained and gripped by a thriller - all at the same time. His writing is a feast for both the mind and the imagination. I always crack the pages of a Kowey book with a smile, knowing I'm going to get a lot more than I bargained for.
— **Pete Taft,** Managing Partner, TAFT Communications

Dr. Peter Kowey continues to write his ___ *the Philip Sarkis series. These entertaining* ___ *interested in the medical mystery genre.*
— **Gerald V. Naccarelli** M. ___ *rdiology, Penn* ___ *Medical Center*

Death on the Pole is so different, rich and enjoyable. The plat twists and turns, and we all come away more enlightened in the process. Great formula, Dr. Kowey.

—**John Zogby,** author and founder of the Zogby Poll

I thoroughly enjoyed the latest book in the Sarkis series. The plot was filled with unexpected twist and turns and the ending left you wondering what is next for Philip?

—**Robert Hall,** Publisher Emeritus, Philadelphia Inquirer

Couldn't put it down—great read. Engrossing fast-paced mystery intertwined with cogent medical knowledge.

—**Ralph Brindis, MD, MPH, MACC,** Past President American College of Cardiology

Connie and I became fast friends as I watched her life unfold on your pages. I was sad to say goodbye to this remarkable woman.

—**Paula Thomasson,** Founder, Merevir Strategies, White House Advance Staff, Clinton Administration

Peter Kowey again displays his gifts for telling tales that ask deeper questions like "How can love survive deception?"

—**Richard Verrier, PhD,** Professor of Medicine, Harvard Medical School

Dr. Peter Kowey has clearly described the impact of medical malpractice problem in his excellent books.

—**Joseph Alpert, MD,** Editor, American Journal of Medicine

It held my interest from start to finish and reminded me of Grisham's The Firm. This book deserves a large readership.

—**Mike Morris,** Past Chairman, Board of Trustees, St. Joseph's University

People talk about page turners, and this really is one, combining mystery, suspense and excellent character development.

—**Jack Gelbach,** Financial Consultant, Merrill Lynch

In his novels, Dr. Peter Kowey combines the knowledge of a skilled clinician and scientist with an intriguing writing style that captures the attention of the reader. The combination offers a unique experience of education and entertainment in the context of fictional mysteries. These are must reads.
—Robert Myerburg, MD, FACC, Emeritus Chief of Cardiology, University of Miami School of Medicine

DEATH BY YOUR OWN DEVICE

A PHILIP SARKIS **MYSTERY**

The Philip Sarkis Murder Mystery Series

PETER KOWEY, MD

iUniverse®

DEATH BY YOUR OWN DEVICE
A PHILIP SARKIS MYSTERY

iUniverse books may be ordered through booksellers or by contacting:

iUniverse
1663 Liberty Drive
Bloomington, IN 47403
www.iuniverse.com
1-800-Authors (1-800-288-4677)

Because of the dynamic nature of the Internet, any web addresses or links contained in this book may have changed since publication and may no longer be valid. The views expressed in this work are solely those of the author and do not necessarily reflect the views of the publisher, and the publisher hereby disclaims any responsibility for them.

Any people depicted in stock imagery provided by Getty Images are models, and such images are being used for illustrative purposes only. Certain stock imagery © Getty Images.

ISBN: 978-1-5320-9383-8 (sc)
ISBN: 978-1-5320-9382-1 (e)

Library of Congress Control Number: 2020903426

Print information available on the last page.

iUniverse rev. date: 02/24/2020

To my mother, Edith

She couldn't know how much she inspired me to tell stories as well as she did while I sat on her knee.

To my father, Pete, who did nothing more than support our entire family with all of his might

To our children, Olivia, Jaime, and Susan and our sons-in-law, Mark and Sean

Ours is a "modern family," but Dorothy and I couldn't love and respect all of you more. And our special thanks for the six wonderful souls you have produced and upon whom we dote relentlessly.

CONTENTS

ACKNOWLEDGMENTS

I would like to thank James Kaufmann, PhD, my best friend from high school, for his terrific help with whipping all of my books into shape. Kauf is an esteemed and now-retired medical writer in Minnesota, who not only helped me keep my grammar straight but also helped to improve the story's consistency. Without Kauf, none of my books would have been good enough to publish.

I am deeply indebted to Steve Crane, the owner of Pavilion Press and the publisher of my first four books. Steve gave me my first break for which I will be forever grateful.

Donna Simonds and Roe Wells, my long-term administrative assistants, have provided logistical support, *making available* books for signings and other appearances and to everyone and anyone who asked, and keeping my bewildering schedule straight.

Finally, Dorothy, my wife and *soul mate.* She was the first to suggest that instead of being angry about things I couldn't change, to use my right brain to pursue my dream of telling stories.

1
CHAPTER

He had finally fallen asleep in the on-call room when his beeper restarted its infernal chirping. He had lost track of how often his pager had gone off on this busy night. The frequency and the urgency of the calls might be atypical for the other cardiology fellows but not for Marwan. They didn't call him "Black Cloud Baschri" for nothing. It seemed to Marwan—and his peers—that he got hammered with emergencies just about every time he was on call for the NorthBroad University cardiology service, and that night was no exception.

The evening had started out reasonably placidly. Marwan arrived home to his sparsely furnished bachelor apartment on Twelfth Street around 7:00 p.m. and had concocted some sort of dinner sandwich from the contents of a nearly empty refrigerator. The cheese had a little mold that he dissected with his customary surgical precision, and it sat reasonably well, along with a few slices of turkey breast, on stale rye bread he had bought the previous weekend at a corner deli up the street. A little mustard and a pickle, and Marwan was satisfied. A lot better than his relatives in Iraq would be able to find.

As expected, his meal was interrupted by a couple of calls from nervous residents and medical students whom he quickly discharged with reasonably good humor. Although Marwan was generally known as a good guy, residents knew he could be grumpy on the phone. But it was August, and that meant green interns on service who were taking on their first real clinical responsibilities. And since patients with heart problems frightened them more than anything in medicine, Marwan expected to do a lot of hand-holding until they got their sea legs. Better to answer their questions on the phone now than to have to go in later and pull their balls (and their patients') out of the fire.

Marwan began to relax as only he could, pulling out his laptop and working on his latest cardiology research project. He had arrived in the US with his parents as a child refugee and had worked his way through college, medical school, and then the hopelessly steep internal-medicine residency training pyramid. Not only had he established himself as a competent clinician, but he had published half a dozen papers in high-profile medical journals. His research was the primary reason he had been able to escape low-level training programs to arrive at one of the better academic cardiology fellowship programs in the country.

His latest project had to do with racial and gender bias in clinical trial enrollment, a topic Marwan understood well, having experienced bigotry firsthand during his early days of training. His mentor promised him that if he did a good job, the manuscript might be published in a journal like JAMA, which favored papers with a political bent, and that it would attract wide media attention once in print. All the work had been worth it, Marwan admitted to himself. He was where he wanted to be, on track to be a hot-shot academic cardiologist, just like his parents had dreamed.

Marwan fell to his work and lost track of time. He was still awake at midnight when a fresh heart attack patient hit the NorthBroad ER. He activated the catheterization lab team from home and then took a short ride to the hospital in his beat-up Subaru wagon to meet Tim Weiss, the interventional cardiology attending on call, in the emergency room.

Marwan and Tim took the patient straight to the cath lab, where they placed a balloon catheter and stent in the patient's occluded coronary artery to open the blockage responsible for the heart damage. Despite the lateness of the hour and the severe thunderstorms that were crossing the area in bands, the cath lab team had been assembled and the procedure performed so quickly that only a very small portion of the patient's heart muscle had died. By 4:00 a.m., the patient was in a bed on the cardiology floor, surrounded by his grateful family, who could do nothing but thank Marwan and Tim for their outstanding work. Marwan beamed. This was the reason he had wanted to be a doctor. What else in life could give anyone so much satisfaction?

So now what? Marwan thought as he walked down the deserted hospital corridor toward the elevator. Push the down button and go home, or push the up button and sleep in one of the on-call rooms provided by the hospital. Not an easy a decision. The drive home would be through pouring rain, and upstairs, in the on-call room, there would be at least three other people snoring away. But rounds started early in the cardiac ICU, and even if he couldn't sleep up there, he could at least get a shower and clean scrubs. And so Marwan went to the sleeping room and stretched on a board-like bed, struggling to get a couple of hours' rest, until another call roused him yet again.

Marwan stumbled out into the lighted hallway and was surprised to see that his beeper screen indicated the call was from an exchange he recognized as the Lehigh Valley area of Pennsylvania. He knew it was upstate because he had a few friends from Iraq who had taken jobs there, and he had their numbers in his contact directory. He pulled out his cell and called the number and was greeted by a woman's voice.

"Hello, who is this?" she asked.

"Dr. Marwan Baschri, senior cardiology fellow at NorthBroad. I believe you called our answering service?"

"Yes, this is Liz Gold. I'm a nurse practitioner at Allentown. Dr. Ray Gilbert, one of our electrophysiologists, would like to speak to you, please. Can you hold while I get him on the phone?"

"Sure," Marwan answered sleepily. Although the name wasn't familiar, Marwan had been carefully schooled to be especially polite and to quickly accept calls from doctors who might have patients to refer to NorthBroad. Referrals were the lifeblood of a great cardiology program, and Marwan wanted people to know he had trained at a premier place.

Liz put the phone down, and Marwan could hear her walk away and then quickly back again, repeating Marwan's name as Gilbert came on the line.

"Hi, Marwan, this is Ray Gilbert up in Allentown. You're on call for the NorthBroad cardiology group?"

"Yes, Dr. Gilbert. What can I do for you?"

"We need your help with a patient who was transferred to our hospital last evening with frequent shocks from his ICD."

Marwan snapped to full wakefulness. ICDs, or implantable defibrillators, were designed to save lives by shocking the heart internally when they detected an abnormal and serious heart rhythm, and they usually were highly effective. However, patients who had these devices occasionally developed such frequent episodes of arrhythmia that the devices could begin to deliver shocks too frequently or even incessantly. In even worse cases, the device could begin to sense a fast but normal heart rhythm and falsely shock the patient. Either way, it was bad news. The shocks caused enormous discomfort to the patient, kind of like being kicked in the middle of the chest by a mule. In addition, frequent device shocks could weaken the heart and cause heart failure or even kill the patient it was supposed to be protecting. As such, this was one of the most serious emergencies in medicine and required prompt and expert treatment, starting with potent drugs designed to quell the cardiac arrhythmias.

Marwan's first question, as he pulled out his trusty notebook: "What antiarrhythmic drugs has the patient received, Dr. Gilbert?"

"I started him on intravenous amiodarone," Gilbert answered, "but the damn arrhythmia just got worse and more frequent. I added lidocaine and a beta-blocker, but now he's having it every few minutes."

Marwan asked the next obvious question. "Is the device still activated?"

"I tried to turn it off, but the ventricular tachycardia wouldn't stop, so I had to turn it on to shock him back into normal rhythm, which seems to last for a few minutes before the damn arrhythmia starts again. I don't have any other drugs to offer him, and we don't do VT ablations up here, so I need to get him down to your place as soon as possible."

Marwan didn't have the expertise to get into a detailed discussion of the case with this doctor. And besides, his job was to take the message and call the attending cardiologist on call to see how he or she wanted to proceed.

"Got it, Dr. Gilbert. I just need a few more things before I call my attending and get the ball rolling. What's the patient's name, age, and diagnosis?"

"His name is Nolan Perini, and he's seventy-three. He has a non-ischemic cardiomyopathy and had his ICD put in only two or three months ago for primary prevention. He hadn't used his device until last night, when he went into electrical storm."

Marwan processed all of that to mean that the patient had a weakened heart muscle not caused by a coronary artery problem and that the defibrillator had been placed to prevent sudden death in this person, who was at high risk because of his heart disease. Perini hadn't had any arrhythmias previously but now was apparently having them incessantly.

"So is it OK for us to arrange the helicopter transfer?" Gilbert asked impatiently.

"I'll call the attending on duty for electrophysiology. Once I have his or her permission to accept your patient, I'll get him an ICU bed."

"He's going to need more than that. Somebody has to see him with me when we get there to figure out how to keep him alive."

"You're coming with the patient?" Marwan asked. This was highly unusual.

"You betcha. A nurse and I will be on the helicopter to deal with his arrhythmias. If I don't go, I'm pretty sure you'll be unloading a corpse. Who's the attending on duty?"

"Hold on a minute," Marwan answered. He sprinted back into the on-call room, flicking on the light, eliciting groans from the three house officers who were awakened by the noise and the light. Marwan looked at the on-call roster tacked to the bulletin board, flicked off the light, and ran back to the phone.

"Dr. Sarkis is the attending on duty."

"Really?" Gilbert said. "Philip Sarkis?"

"That's right."

"Wow, I didn't know he was at NorthBroad."

"He's been here a few years, I think."

"I trained under him at Gladwyne Memorial, a few years ago. I thought he was living in the Poconos somewhere and was out of academic medicine."

"I can't help you there, Dr. Gilbert. I'm sure he'll fill you in when you get here. Let me call him and get things in motion," Marwan said, yanking Gilbert back to the case at hand.

"Right. Yes. Call me at this number as soon as you have things arranged. Our helicopter is available so we can be down there within an hour."

Armed with most of the information he needed, Marwan promised to call back in a few minutes, hung up, and immediately asked the answering service operator to call Dr. Sarkis at home, where he probably was soundly asleep.

Which he was trying to be. The problem was that the Sarkis-Deaver family bed was overpopulated. Philip and Dorothy shared space, as usual, with two fairly large dogs, out cold in their customary position at the foot of the bed. In addition, Erin, their three-year-old, had had another nightmare and had come into their room shortly after midnight. She was now sleeping soundly between Philip and Dorothy. Erin, at best a fitful sleeper, had somehow turned herself horizontal, feet on Philip's pillow, head on Dorothy's. Neither even thought about moving their angel for fear of awakening her and eliciting more details about the bad dreams that seemed to occur almost every night. The pediatric psychologist they consulted believed the bad dreams were a by-product of Erin's losing her mother and the rocky adoption process that had finally placed her and her five-year-old sister, Emily, in the warm and loving hands of Philip and Dorothy. "She *will* get better; just be patient and keep loving her, and she'll be fine," he had counseled.

Now, several months and dozens of difficult nights later, Philip and Dorothy weren't so sure. They contemplated getting another opinion, although they had to admit that Erin's daytime life was pretty darn normal, and she seemed like a happy kid most of the time. Her sister Emily's nightmares had finally dissipated, and she now slept soundly every night. Philip and Dorothy were relieved that both the girls had adapted to their new life about as well as they could have hoped.

Philip kept his cell phone on the bedside table when he was on call and had it set loudly so he couldn't ignore it. Marwan's call startled him, the noise almost causing him to fall to the floor from his precarious perch on the edge of the bed. Once upright, Philip grabbed the squawking device and tried to silence it quickly before it awakened his crew. He needn't have worried. He looked over his shoulder as he walked out of the bedroom to converse with whoever was bothering him and saw that none of his bed companions had stirred an inch.

"This is Philip Sarkis. Who's calling?" he asked impatiently.

"Dr. Sarkis, this is Marwan Baschri, the cardiology fellow on call."

"Hi, Marwan. What can I do for you?" Philip asked, now trying to be as cordial as he could. Philip remembered what it had been like to be on the front lines and how difficult and daunting it was to disturb an attending physician in the middle of the night.

"I think we have a hot one for you, Dr. Sarkis." Marwan went on to describe the clinical situation and the patient who was in trouble at Allentown Hospital, trying to be as complete as possible without losing the forest for the trees and holding up the transfer. He depended on Sarkis to ask clarifying questions, which came fast.

"So we don't have any idea why this fairly healthy man suddenly decided to shock his brains out?"

"I haven't seen any of his records yet. I'm sure they'll be coming on the helicopter with him, along with his cardiologist."

"He's flying with the patient to our place?"

"As soon as I give them the word. I told the doc there that I would call him back after I spoke with you. I expect it will be an interesting trip."

"Why?"

"The patient is having a lot of arrhythmia, and the weather is terrible."

Philip hadn't heard the rain and thunder because they had begun to use a white noise machine outside the bedrooms to help Erin sleep through the night. Like other potential remedies, that one had made little difference in her sleep patterns.

"What's the name of the doctor coming with Mr. Perini?"

"Ray Gilbert. He said he knows you."

"Yes. He trained with us years ago. Good guy and pretty smart, overall. If he couldn't figure this one out, then we probably do have a major problem on our hands."

"So I can tell him to bring the patient down?"

"Yes, but if he's already on a lot of drugs and breaking through, we're going to have to alert the electrophysiology lab team to set up to do an ablation procedure."

Marwan agreed, but the prospect made his palms moist. What Philip had referred to was a hopelessly complicated and dangerous procedure in which electrical catheters would be inserted into the bottom chambers of the patient's heart to map the part from which the nasty arrhythmias were originating. Once identified, those same catheters would be hooked up to a radiofrequency generator to heat their tips to effectively cauterize the abnormal tissue. This was one of the most daunting procedures in all of medicine in the best of circumstances. Bringing an unstable patient to the lab for an ablation, off hours, was really scary business that Marwan had successfully avoided so far in his training career.

"Do you want me to call in anyone to help out with the procedure, like one of the electrophysiology fellows?" Marwan asked, hoping to dump the case onto one of his senior colleagues.

"Nah, we can handle it, Marwan. Just tell them to get the patient down to our place as quickly as possible. Tell them to bypass the ER after they land and go directly to the EP lab. I'll meet you and the staff there inside an hour. I just need to get dressed and drive in. At least there won't be any traffic."

"OK, Dr. Sarkis. Drive carefully; the weather is terrible," Marwan said as he hung up. He promptly dialed Gilbert, who answered Marwan's return call himself and was happy to get the green light.

"We'll meet you in the EP lab, Dr. Gilbert," Marwan said. "Dr. Sarkis has asked me to assemble the staff so we can start the ablation case as soon as you get here."

"Excellent, Marwan. Thanks for all your help. I look forward to meeting you very soon."

Marwan spent the next several minutes activating beepers for the EP lab staff on call, taking their calls and informing them of the task at hand.

"A little like assembling a strike force," Marwan mumbled to himself as he took a few minutes for the luxury of a wake-up shower before the onslaught. *I wanted a fellowship experience with a lot of action and sick patients to care for,* he thought as he strained to dry himself with one of the miniature towels that the hospital deigned to make available for the house staff. *I guess that saying is correct: be careful what you wish for.*

2
CHAPTER

While Marwan showered, Dorothy slept, and Philip dressed, Ray Gilbert was scrambling to prepare himself and his patient for the short but exciting ride to NorthBroad. Unlike some large university hospitals, Allentown General couldn't afford its own helicopter, so the hospital had arranged with a local airport to have a chopper and crew available on short notice. It was important to have this capability, even though they didn't use it very often. It was a way of reaching out to their northern neighbors and attracting the referral business that had become so important to their bottom line. They knew that most of their feeder hospitals were able to stabilize almost all of their patients and ship them to Allentown General by ambulance, but the availability of air transport—at Allentown's expense, of course—made the hospitals and doctors in the hinterlands feel secure and confident that their southern neighbor was there when they needed help in a hurry.

Given the cost involved, physicians weren't permitted to order air transport without the authorization of the hospital administrator. So Gilbert had spent the last twenty minutes identifying which of the dozens of hospitals administrators' turn it was to take the call. The person this particular evening had a day job running cafeteria services. Getting her on the phone and then convincing her that there was no other way to save the patient's life was pure torture.

"Dr. Gilbert, can you tell me why we can't just send the patient to NorthBroad by ambulance?" the administrator asked.

"We don't have time for that, Ms. Savitz," Gilbert said, trying to remain civil. "The patient is very sick and might die on the way."

"And do you know if the patient's insurance will pay for the transfer? It's very expensive, you know."

"I have absolutely no idea, and I don't have time to check. We have to leave now. The helicopter is landing on our pad as we speak."

"Dr. Gilbert, you should have cleared this with me before you called for the helicopter."

"I was trying to save time and a life, Ms. Savitz."

"I'm going to have to call the hospital president and get back to you, Dr. Gilbert."

"Fine; you do that, Ms. Savitz. We'll wait."

Gilbert hung up and immediately went to the unit where Mr. Perini had already been transferred to a stretcher. He was scared out of his wits. His wife, Ellen, stood by his bed, holding his hand, trying to overcome her own terror while helping her husband remain calm.

"How much Valium have you given him?" Gilbert asked the nurse who was taking care of Perini.

"He's had twenty milligrams IV over the last few hours, Dr. Gilbert."

"Give him another five, and let's go. Hospital administration has approved the helicopter."

"They did?" the nurse asked. "Do you have the signed forms?"

"Being faxed—on their way. Now let's get Mr. Perini on his way."

The nurse, obviously wary, told Gilbert that she would have to talk to the nursing supervisor on call.

"Go right ahead. Liz Gold, my nurse practitioner, will take over until you get back."

As soon as the nurse was out of sight, Gilbert told Liz to help him push Perini and his IV poles to the elevator and then to the roof. He invited Mrs. Perini to accompany them to the helipad; then he whispered to Liz, "We have to hurry, before the nursing supervisor or the dumb-ass hospital administrator puts the kibosh on this."

While they waited for the elevator, Gilbert realized that he now had to replace the nurse for the transfer. He anticipated, correctly as it turned out, that the patient would need active resuscitation while in the air. Since the helicopter was for civilian and not medical use, Gilbert would have to bring his own people and equipment. A paramedic had been easy to recruit from one of the ambulance teams that hung out at the ER, but he needed somebody with considerably more experience and expertise in handling serious cardiac arrhythmias. The only person he could trust in this situation was his nurse practitioner, Liz Gold.

"Liz, I want you to go on the helicopter with me. Are you willing to do that?"

The decision was complicated. Beyond her concern for her own personal safety, Liz and Gilbert had lots of history, some of it good but most of it bad. Liz had been the nurse in charge of the electrophysiology program when Gilbert arrived to take his staff position. It was a small operation with a limited number of procedures, and Gilbert was charged with modernizing things, bringing in new procedures and techniques, and building referral. Liz found all of this exciting and spent many hours with Gilbert, organizing the program, hiring staff, previewing and buying new equipment, and even working with architects to design a unit to house and monitor the arrhythmia patients they planned to attract.

It didn't take long before Liz and Gilbert started to spend a lot of time together outside the hospital. Sure, they brought along work that they pretended to care about and discuss, but as time went by, the venues became much less amenable to work than to plain old cheating. The affair should have been predictable. Both were good-looking. Liz wouldn't be mistaken for "pretty," but she was a maniacal exerciser who kept her forty-year-old body trim and athletic. Gilbert was younger than Liz and also had a good body, his by genetic default, with boyish good looks that had always gotten him the women he wanted. And Gilbert was a hound, already known to have preyed on several nurses and staff at the hospital, even before his wife, Linda, had died. Liz knew all that and didn't care. She was having some overdue fun.

Their flirting kept heating up until Gilbert leaned over and kissed Liz in a parking lot one night when he was dropping her off at her car. Groping led to petting led to motel rooms led to hot sex that neither could get enough of. And that would have been fine and dandy except for one small detail named Noah Gold.

Noah was Liz's husband, a junior-college professor in Allentown who'd met Liz on a blind date shortly after her arrival from nurse practitioner school in Baltimore. Their courtship had been anything but promising. It wasn't Noah's doing. He was totally convinced that Liz was going to be his wife. Rather, Liz was the vacillator. She just wasn't sure he was the one. She felt comfortable with Noah and lonely without him, and she knew her biological clock was running out of ticks, so after many months of uncertainty, she succumbed and agreed to marriage. Noah was ecstatic and spent the next few years attempting, in any way he could, to prove to Liz that she had made the right decision. They tried to have kids, but Liz couldn't conceive. She was secretly relieved about that and found ways to delay the infertility work-up that Noah wanted so badly.

Which was a good thing, as it turned out, because shortly thereafter, Gilbert came along. Liz had feelings for him she never had for poor Noah. "Is it love," she asked herself several times a day, "or infatuation that will eventually melt away?" It didn't matter; Liz was smitten and had no plans to give up Gilbert for anything or anybody, including Noah.

Easy to say, but Liz was increasingly concerned that Noah was becoming suspicious about her absences. Liz frequently used nurse practitioner–practice meetings for cover, but Noah was now asking more questions about the subject matter of the meetings and who else from Allentown General attended. His questions convinced her that he was on her trail.

Liz knew she was playing a dangerous game. There were plenty of ways that Noah could discover her duplicity. People in Allentown liked to gossip, and Noah was friends with a number of people who worked at Allentown General. True, Noah liked to play the absent-minded professor, but Liz knew it was a ruse. He was keen observer who took everything in and, worse, had a temper that made Liz worry about what he might do to Gilbert and to her if he ever discovered their affair.

Fear of Noah's reprisals and her animal attraction to Gilbert prompted Liz to pressure Gilbert to leave Allentown with her, to start their life together someplace—anyplace—else. Not exactly what Gilbert had in mind. Not only had he grown up in the area, but he liked his job at Allentown General and didn't want to give up the referral practice he had so carefully built. He liked Liz a lot, and they had fun together, but she was not the woman he envisioned spending his life with, not by a long shot. He was enjoying his freedom.

So he made excuse after excuse for why he couldn't take off with her and cohabit. They still saw each other because Ray enjoyed the sex, but Liz was impatient for a commitment of some kind. That they worked together only made things more difficult. His hope tonight was that she wouldn't interpret his asking her to take on this emergency mission as anything more that it was—desperation. Her response worried him.

"If you need me, Ray, of course I'll do it. I would do anything for you."

"It's a little dangerous, Liz. The weather is awful, and I expect that we're going to have to continue to resuscitate Mr. Perini all the way to Philly."

"I'm here for you, Ray."

Crap, Gilbert thought. *This woman has glommed on to me, and it's not going to be easy to scrape her off. I'm going to have to work on that when I get back—if I get back. Right now, I have no choice.*

"OK. Then let's get this show on the road," Gilbert said, trying to sound braver than he felt.

The helicopter was waiting for them. Harry, Gilbert's enlisted EMT, had already assembled a defibrillator and a medical kit. Gilbert and Liz pushed the stretcher to the door of the chopper, with Perini's wife, Ellen, walking briskly behind them.

"I'm sorry, Mrs. Perini, but we can't take you on the chopper," Gilbert turned to tell her. "Our insurance doesn't cover family members, and this is going to be a wild ride with this weather. You can drive down there and meet us at NorthBroad. I'll tell them to expect you. Shouldn't take you more than an hour on the turnpike. Is that OK?"

Ellen was disappointed but relieved since she hated flying, and the helicopter scared her to death. "Whatever you say, Dr. Gilbert. I'll make other arrangements with my family. Just make Nolan better, please!"

"We will, Ellen. I promise," Gilbert said, only half believing it himself.

Gilbert next had to deal with the helicopter pilot, George Blake, a crusty Vietnam War veteran who owned the helicopter and piloted it for his customers. His copilot was his son, recently licensed, following his father into the private flight business.

"How you doin', Dr. Gilbert? I'm your pilot, George, and this is my son, George Junior, or just Junior."

"Nice to meet you," Gilbert said, introducing Liz and Harry. "Thanks for taking us to NorthBroad."

"Happy to do it, but I won't shit you, Doc. We really shouldn't be flying in this weather. I know you need to get this patient down there in a hurry. And if anybody can get you there, we can. I'm just warning you that you're going to have to hold on for dear life. There's a lot of wind and turbulence."

Gilbert nodded and looked over at Liz and Harry, hoping they weren't losing their nerve.

"You got your paperwork, Doc?" Blake asked.

As if on cue, Nolan's heart went out of rhythm, setting off the portable alarm that was on the stretcher between his legs. Fortunately, after just a few seconds and before anyone could react, his defibrillator charged and shocked his heart back into a normal rhythm. It all happened so quickly that Nolan never had time to pass out. Consequently, he felt the shock. Sedated but awake, Nolan groaned, bringing Ellen back to his side to hold his hand and reassure him, tears welling up in her eyes, as they had so many times over the last several hours.

"You see, George, we need to get going right now. Can't wait for the paperwork. My team and I are going to be pretty busy keeping Mr. Perini alive. So whatever you can do to keep our flight smooth will be greatly appreciated."

"Got it, Doc," George said. "Let's get loaded up. We'll deal with the hospital types later."

A few seats had been removed from the passenger helicopter to accommodate the stretcher and to permit Nolan's caregivers to access him from either side. The equipment took up almost all the rest of the space, so Gilbert, Liz, and Harry were forced to squat or kneel on the floor of the copter. George warned them again to hold on as best they could to avoid getting thrown around the cabin. After seeing all of the stuff they had brought on board, George dispensed with the lecture about seat belts and flotation devices that he normally gave to his passengers.

George steered a direct course to NorthBroad, making sure that air traffic in the area was aware of the urgency of the situation. Though clearance was not necessary because of their low altitude, George knew that everyone on his bird would appreciate knowing that the tracks had been cleared and that the NorthBroad staff would be waiting for them with open arms. Though they were bounced around in flight, they managed to avoid lightning strikes and were able to land precisely on target at the NorthBroad helipad. Perini had cooperated and had needed only a couple of shocks for arrhythmia, one with the device and one delivered externally to keep his circulation intact. Liz was liberal with the use of the sedative and narcotic drugs that were being used to keep Perini calm and minimally aware of the mayhem his heart was causing. Harry sampled vital signs every five minutes and sat by the drug box, ready to dispense whatever other medication Gilbert might need.

They were greeted by several members of the NorthBroad staff, including the nursing supervisor and an intensivist and anesthesiologist. Nolan was offloaded carefully, shielded by blankets against the torrents of rain and wind that were sweeping the roof of the NorthBroad hospital facility. They moved quickly and were just about inside the hospital building when all hell broke loose. Nolan's heart went out of rhythm, and this time, when shocked by his implanted device, it decided to go flatline.

"Asystole!" Liz yelled as she looked at the monitor, which was followed by a full-scale cardiac resuscitation. Nolan stopped breathing and had to be intubated in the hallway by the anesthesiologist, who had thoughtfully brought along the required equipment. He used a bag to breathe for Nolan while they continued their sprint down the hallway toward the elevator bank. Gilbert was able to reprogram his device to begin to pace his heart artificially at a more rapid rate, and over the next few seconds, Nolan's rhythm finally returned and with it, his blood pressure and ability to breathe on his own.

"Let's knock him out with narcotics and put him on a ventilator as soon as we get to the EP lab," Gilbert said. "There's no point in having him awake for what they might have to do there."

They maneuvered their way into the oversized elevator car, designed to transport patients with loads of equipment, exiting at the sixth floor. Two turns brought them to the electrophysiology laboratory, where Marwan and Philip were waiting anxiously, along with three members of the lab team who had been summoned from their beds to aid Philip. Two of the staff came out into the hallway, introduced themselves briefly, and then quickly wheeled the stretcher into the lab to begin their preparations.

Gilbert recognized Philip immediately and was impressed with how good he looked—a new beard, a lot more gray hair, but the same athletic body and piercing brown eyes behind stylishly oval spectacles.

"Dr. Sarkis, it's so good to see you again. Thanks for doing all of this."

"Happy to help, Ray," Philip answered

"It's been a long time."

"Yes, it has, Ray. A lot of water over the damn." Philip said, trying to remain polite but feeling deeply stressed as he anticipated getting started on the complex case that would determine whether Mr. Perini would live or die.

"We really need to catch up, Philip," Gilbert said, hoping that Philip wouldn't be offended if he called his old mentor by his preferred first name—not Phil, but Philip.

"That we will, Ray," Philip replied, either ignoring the familiarity or not caring, wondering why Gilbert didn't have the same sense of urgency about saving the patient. "For now, let's focus on what we have to do to keep your patient alive."

3
CHAPTER

S tanding by awkwardly, Liz Gold finally stepped forward to introduce herself. "Dr. Sarkis, I'm Liz Gold, Dr. Gilbert's nurse practitioner."

"Jeez, sorry, Liz," Gilbert said. "Philip, Liz has been with me since I went up to Allentown. Very knowledgeable and helpful. She volunteered to take this nightmare helicopter ride to help me with Mr. Perini."

"Very brave of you, Ms. Gold."

"Oh, please call me Liz. Everybody does. I've heard a lot about you from Dr. Gilbert. You did an excellent job training him at Gladwyne."

"One of our best students, for sure," Philip said, wondering where and how Liz fit into Gilbert's life.

Marwan, always the pragmatist, stepped out of the lab. "Dr. Sarkis, do you want me to talk to Mr. Perini's family and get his wife's consent for our procedure? He's been anesthetized and intubated and can't sign."

Before Philip could answer, Gilbert cut in. "You must be the fellow I spoke with on the phone."

"Yes, and you must be Dr. Gilbert. Nice to meet you," Marwan answered tersely, trying to hide his irritation with being sidetracked.

"We couldn't let Mrs. Perini get on the helicopter," Liz explained. "She said something about having her nephews bring her down in a squad car. One of them is a cop in our area. Even with that, she probably won't be here for another half hour or so."

"I have to talk to her before we start the ablation," Philip said. "I want to make sure she understands the risks."

"She gave her verbal consent," Gilbert said. "I'm pretty sure it would be OK to start."

"I don't think that's a good idea, Ray," Philip insisted, annoyed that Gilbert could be cavalier when it was Philip's neck that would be on the line. Philip had bitter memories of all the trouble he had gotten into the last time he performed a procedure without an informed consent document. "We'll get set up, and I'll start looking through the records," Philip continued. "By the time we're ready to stick the groin, she should be here."

"I'd really like to scrub in on the case, Philip," Gilbert said.

"You're more than welcome to observe and help us with the electrogram recordings in the control room. The hospital has a pretty strict policy about hands-on procedures by doctors who have not formally applied for credentials, so scrubbing in won't be possible, Ray. Sorry."

Gilbert tried to hide his disappointment. "That's OK. The fun part is reading the electrical signals during the catheter mapping. I'm fine with that."

"Marwan will show you and Liz the way into the control room. It's a nonsterile area and lead-lined, so you don't have to put on an apron or scrubs. I'm going to go through the case plan with the EP lab staff so they know what stuff to get out for me. Marwan, tell the front desk to call us as soon as Mrs. Perini gets here."

After his short conversation with the lab staff, Philip grabbed the CD that contained Perini's electronic medical record and retreated to his office, only a few steps down the hall. He flicked on his computer console, inserted the CD, and started to scan through myriad files. As usual, they were in spectacular disarray, carelessly thrown into random documents by a clerk with no medical knowledge to speak of. And compounding the confusion was that records from Perini's original hospitalization in Wilkes-Barre had been thrown into the pile.

Fortunately, Philip was able to dissect through most of the extraneous information rather quickly to focus on the most important elements.

From what he could see, Marwan's patient summary had been mostly correct. Perini had a heart condition in which the left ventricle, the chamber responsible for pumping blood out to the general circulation, was weak and poorly functioning. The problem had been discovered about a year earlier, when Perini had visited his family doctor for shortness of breath on exertion and ankle swelling. Perini was in the waste disposal business, and he had explained that he was simply unable to put in the long hours on his trucks as he had in the past.

As usual, the doctor began with a general physical examination and a set of laboratory tests that had revealed nothing abnormal except for an elevated BNP, a peptide found in the blood in patients who had congestive heart failure. The presence of an abnormal BNP suggested to the family physician that Perini might have a heart problem, a suspicion he acted upon by obtaining a cardiology consultation.

The cardiologist who saw Perini in Wilkes-Barre detected some subtle findings on physical examination and on the electrocardiogram he performed in his office. Not only did he hear fluid-like sounds in Perini's lungs, but he also heard a "gallop," or a heart sound caused by blood rushing into a failing heart chamber. He wasted no time in sending Perini for an echocardiogram that revealed, as expected, that Perini's heart was enlarged and was pumping with roughly half its normal efficiency.

There followed the conventional and almost inevitably negative work-up to try to find a cause for the heart muscle weakness, followed by the unleashing of chemical warfare. Perini was treated with multiple medications designed to make his heart work more efficiently and help him live longer but not necessarily feel better, which was his principal concern. Nothing his doctors did improved his function enough so he could return to full-time employment, and with each passing month, his depression mounted.

After several weeks of frustration, still with no explanation or improvement, his cardiologist finally sent him to Philadelphia for consultation with a specialist in heart failure, intending to prepare Perini for heart transplantation. With just one visit, the heart-failure guru was able to come up with a simplified medicine regimen that Perini tolerated and that improved his symptoms dramatically. His next ultrasound, carried out just a few weeks later, showed marked improvement in cardiac function and his stamina.

Philip continued to comb through the records, now trying to find out why, if his situation was better, Perini had an implanted defibrillator. Such devices weren't considered necessary for patients who had improvement in function, since whatever had damaged the heart had been reversed or mitigated, and the risk of a lethal arrhythmia was much lower. Apparently, the cardiologist caring for Perini decided to seek an arrhythmia consultation from one of his partners because of an electrical disconnection that had been discovered at the time Perini had first become ill. That person, Dr. el-Sheikh, saw Perini and informed him that he was at high risk of dying and needed not only a pacemaker but also a defibrillator. His note read, "Mr. Perini and his wife understand the necessity of having a device implanted as soon as possible to prevent passing out or dying suddenly."

And so a Sterling Medical defibrillator, with the ability to also pace both of Perini's lower chambers in synchrony, had been implanted about ten months after Perini's initial presentation. The implant had gone well, with no complications, and Perini was enrolled in a program in which his device could be monitored regularly at home. Which should have been the end of the story except …

Except three months later, or just two days ago, Perini's device began to detect and to shock what was clearly a disorganized, nasty, rapid, and unstable rhythm coming from the bottom chamber of his heart. El-Sheikh was on call the night Perini presented and was completely overwhelmed. He was only a year out of his training and had no idea how to deal with the tidal wave of arrhythmias that battered his patient. He quickly called Ray Gilbert and told him about the "electrical storms" that Perini was having and requested that the patient be transferred to Allentown. When Gilbert also failed to quell the arrhythmias, the lateral to NorthBroad had occurred.

"And here we are," Philip said to himself. "I guess this is where the buck stops."

Next, Philip scrolled down to the Allentown records, a bit better organized but still a hodgepodge of information entered by various members of the medical staff, mostly in chronological order. It was clear that much of the historical information from Wilkes-Barre had been cut and pasted into the Allentown chart, a practice that was popular among young doctors, who were barraged with work, to save time. But as Ben Franklin University Hospital had learned in the Connie Santangelo case, there was a substantial risk that wrong information would be perpetuated, leading to a bad patient outcome. Philip worried constantly about the reliability of information he was forced to review from outside hospital charts as a consultant.

"Healthy skepticism is a good thing," Philip muttered to himself as he scrolled through the endless nursing, pharmacy, and dietary notes. All formulaic and much of it to justify billing or to cover the hospital's butt, and little of it directly pertinent to patient care, let alone the problem that Philip had been called upon to solve.

Finally, and most important, the electrocardiograms. And there was a slew of them, recorded periodically by protocol and many more generated when Perini decided to show off and have a nasty arrhythmia. But unlike the Wilkes-Barre records, Allentown had managed to obtain some full twelve-lead EKG recordings when Perini was at rest and not having storms of arrhythmia. There were only a few tracings during which Perini's pacemaker was dormant. The demand feature meant that when Perini's intrinsic heart rate was greater than sixty beats per minute, the pacemaker would deactivate and allow his own sinus node to control the heart rhythm. Philip increased the magnification on his computer so he could examine the sinus rhythm tracings in greater detail.

The abnormality wasn't at all easy to see. Philip had to print out several of the tracings and use a magnifying glass to be doubly sure that what he was seeing wasn't an artifact. But the more he examined the tracings, the more convinced he was that a sentinel finding was not only present but that it had developed recently. It certainly had not been there when he had his device implanted at Wilkes-Barre. He wondered if it were findable on EKGs taken during Perini's outpatient follow-up. He made a mental note to ask Gilbert to procure those tracings.

Philip continued his rampage through the records, now anxious to finish his search and get back to the case that was facing him head-on. He did take the time to carefully examine the medications that Perini had been given at Wilkes-Barre and at Allentown. They were essentially the same, except for intravenous amiodarone that Gilbert had started at Allentown to replace the lidocaine that el-Sheikh had used in Wilkes-Barre to try to shut down Perini's arrhythmia. Both lists had medications for heart failure and hypertension and high cholesterol, many of which Perini had been taking for a long time, and an antibiotic started by Perini's family doctor a few days before for an apparent upper respiratory infection.

Most important now was a few minutes with Mrs. Perini for her consent and to ask her a few questions, and then to the lab, where Perini was hopefully resting peacefully on a ventilator. Philip closed down his computer and put the CD that contained Perini's records into his lab coat pocket. He sped down the hall to the visitors' waiting room, his Keds sneakers giving him a little added traction as he zoomed around corners. Through the window of the waiting room, Philip was able to see three people seated with their coats on, looking glum. Given the hour of the morning and their sullen appearance, Philip was pretty sure Ellen Perini had arrived with her nephews.

Philip zeroed in on the plainly dressed woman with pretty eyes and graying blonde hair tied back into a ponytail. She held Kleenex in her hand and periodically dabbed at her moist and reddened nose, looking down at the floor forlornly.

This is a no-frills kind of person, Philip surmised, as he strode through the waiting room door and stuck out his hand to greet her.

"You must be Mrs. Perini," Philip began. With Ellen's nod, he continued. "I'm Dr. Philip Sarkis. I don't know if Dr. Gilbert told you about me."

"He did, Dr. Sarkis, and he spoke very highly of you. He told me if anyone could save Nolan's life, it was you."

Philip smiled and looked down at his feet. "Ray is too generous, Mrs. Perini. But we'll do everything we can to get your husband better. I just want to go over a few things and ask you some questions. Is that OK?"

"Doc, do whatever you need to do," answered a baritone voice from behind Philip. One of the two men who had accompanied Ellen had risen from his seat and was on his way over to shake Philip's hand. "Nice to meet you, Doc. I'm Ned Perini, Nolan's nephew. I work in the family business with him, and so does Jake over there."

A wave from another well-fed and very large seated family member, stained baseball cap in place.

"Terrific," said Philip. "Glad you're all here. One of my fellows, Marwan Baschri—"

"He was already here, Doc, and explained what you're going to do. We signed them papers."

"Good," Philip answered, making a mental note to commend Marwan for his efficiency at his next evaluation. Settling himself into a seat across from Ellen, Philip began. "Then let me make sure you understand that we're going to be putting catheters in your husband's heart to see if we can locate the area where the arrhythmia is coming from. If we can, we'll try to cauterize that area to make the arrhythmias go away. There's a chance we won't be able to find the arrhythmia source—"

"Why not, Doc?" Ned interrupted, standing over Philip and Ellen.

"Because the arrhythmias may not be coming from a single source. There might be something that is making the heart generally irritable, in which case, we won't be able to do the cautery or ablation."

"Your Marwan person said there's a chance that Nolan could die from this procedure," Ellen said.

Philip made another mental note for a second entry into Marwan's file, this one not flattering. Getting consent was hard enough without emphasizing the bad stuff.

"Young doctors sometimes think they need to stress the potential negative outcomes so you won't be surprised. And he's right to do that. Except I've been doing these procedures for a very long time and rarely have had severe complications. You need to know they're possible, but I wouldn't focus on them too much."

Ellen sighed, obviously relieved. "What are the chances you'll be able to control Nolan's heart rhythms, Dr. Sarkis?"

"I would say they're pretty high," Philip said with as much modesty as he could. "I'm not sure what the solution will be yet, but I've been dealing with this kind of problem for most of my career." *Except when I got my ass sued so badly that I almost went crazy and ended up practicing Mickey Mouse cardiology in the Poconos for a few years*, Philip thought. Ellen didn't need those details if she didn't already have them. "I do have a couple of questions, though. Was your husband ill with a cold or flu before he had the heart failure problem?"

"I don't recall anything out of the ordinary, Doctor," Ellen answered. "Do either of you remember your uncle being sick?"

Ned and Jake shook their heads. "Just that shortness of breath thing that put him in the hospital."

"Nolan does get bad colds, though. I will say that. He was just getting over one when all this hit a couple days ago," Ellen said.

"Yes, I was going to ask you about that. Did he see his family doctor?"

"He did. The doctor told Nolan to call him right away if he got sicker because things could get bad fast with his weak heart and all."

"What did the doc do for his cold?"

"Gave him an antibiotic."

"Erythromycin?"

"I think so. Why?

"How many days ago was that, Mrs. Perini?"

"Let me see. About five because he was supposed to get ten total."

"It looks like they continued it after he was admitted. Is that right, Mrs. Perini?"

"Yes, I told them he needed another five days, and they said they would take care of it. Except ..."

"Yes?"

"Well, the nurse told me that Nolan wasn't awake enough in the ICU to take pills so the doctor on call told them to give it to him through a vein."

"And it looks like they continued the IV erythromycin at Allentown?"

"I guess so. The nurse did ask me why he was getting it, and I told her that he needed a few more days to clear his lungs."

"So Allentown thought they were treating a pneumonia?"

"They didn't say one way or another. Why is this so important, Dr. Sarkis?"

"Just gathering information so we can give him our best care here, Mrs. Perini."

"Doc, we're so grateful," Ned interjected. "How long do you think this here procedure is going to take? I figure Jake and I are goin' to want to sit with Aunt Ellen until it's over and Uncle Nolan is in the clear."

"A lot depends on what I find. I don't think it'll be more than three or four hours. I'll come out and talk to you as soon as we're finished."

With that, Philip stood, shook hands with the three, and left the waiting room. He stopped in the men's room to empty his bladder and headed for the lab where the team had Nolan sedated, prepped, draped, and ready to go. Marwan was scrubbed, gowned, and gloved, standing on the left side of the table. Philip put on a cap and mask before he pulled on a lead apron while he beckoned to Marwan.

"You're on the wrong side of the table, my man. If you're going to do this groin stick, you need to be over here with me."

Marwan nodded nervously and walked around the foot of the table to stand next to Sarkis.

"Arterial puncture first, right, Dr. Sarkis?" Marwan asked, anticipating that Philip would want to thread the first mapping catheter up the aorta and into the left ventricle, the most likely site of origin of the arrhythmia.

"No, Marwan, we're going into the femoral vein first and take that baby up the IVC into the right ventricle. I want to do some electrical stimulation before we go into the arterial circulation."

"Philip, do you want to scrub and glove up?" the EP lab head nurse asked by convention.

"No. We're going to let Marwan take the shot first. I'll stand right next to him and watch carefully; I promise."

Marwan did not disappoint. Having rotated several times in the catheterization laboratory during his first fellowship year, he was able to gauge the anatomical landmarks perfectly and puncture the femoral vein on the first try. In went the guide wire, over which a sheath was placed

that would allow easy entry and withdrawal of catheters that would be used for various purposes during the case, including measuring electrical activity and stimulating the heart.

"Ray, can you and Liz hear me in the control room?" Philip asked.

"Sure can," Gilbert replied over the speaker system in the lab.

"Great. Before I do any voltage mapping or ablation, I want to do some right ventricular stimulation to see if I can induce an arrhythmia."

"Do you think you'll be able to get it started?" Gilbert asked.

"We'll see," Philip answered.

Once Marwan had stationed the catheter in the apex of the right ventricle, Philip walked over to the stimulation box that was part of a console of electrical equipment on a cart sitting next to the patient. Philip began to pace the heart rapidly and at intervals timed by the millisecond and then delivered premature beats to determine the stability of Nolan's heart.

Gilbert was not surprised that this form of stimulation yielded nothing. Perini's heart disease was such that programmed stimulation, the technique Philip was using, would have a low yield in reproducing the arrhythmia that Nolan had been having spontaneously.

"I want to try some different stimulation methods, Ray," Philip said, anticipating his skepticism. "I think we may be able to bring out an arrhythmia with short-long-short sequences."

Only Gilbert understood what that meant. "Really, Philip? Are you sure that's going to work?"

"Never sure, Ray, but that's why they call this a laboratory."

Deftly, with only a few spins of the dials on the stimulator, Philip began to introduce stimulation sequences that progressively rendered Nolan's heart less stable until the heart went totally out of rhythm.

"That's what he was doing at our hospital," Liz blurted out as soon as she saw the recordings on the screens she was watching in the control room.

"As I suspected," Philip announced. "He's snowed, so we can let Nolan's defibrillator shock his heart to stop this thing."

The technician in the lab monitoring Nolan's device through a radiofrequency wand said, "The device is charging. A shock will be delivered in a couple of seconds."

Which it was. Nolan's body jumped a little but the device had effectively terminated his arrhythmia, restoring calm to the laboratory.

"So what do you think, Ray?"

"I can't believe that he's been having torsades all along."

"Torsades?" Marwan chimed in, sounding incredulous. "He's been having torsades?"

"Yes, torsades, Marwan."

"But we gave him a lot of magnesium at Allentown, just in case," Gilbert explained. "Why didn't it work?"

"Because sometimes it doesn't. And don't forget—you were also giving him amiodarone."

"Oh, yeah," Gilbert muttered, barely audible, realizing what a colossal mistake he had made. Amiodarone not only wouldn't stop the arrhythmia, but it could actually make it worse.

"OK, Marwan, we're done with stimulation. This is what I want you to do. Stop the IV amiodarone, put an NG tube down, and start Mr. Perini on 150 milligrams of mexiletine every six hours, and get him to the unit. Got it? Oh, and make sure that he doesn't get any more erythromycin."

Philip turned to see Gilbert turn beet red when he heard the last few words of Philip's charge.

"Ray, I'm going to talk to the family. How about if you and I plan to meet in the cafeteria in about a half hour for breakfast, and we can break down the case."

Gilbert's throat was so dry that he could only nod as Philip passed by the control room window on his way to the waiting area.

"Wow, Doc, that was fast," Ned said as Philip sat down among the three family members. "Is Uncle Nolan OK?"

"Not only is he OK, but I think I can tell you with a fair amount of certainty that he's going to be just fine."

"You found the problem?" Ellen asked with tears in her eyes. "I can't believe it!"

"I had a pretty good idea of what was going on before I went into the lab. Let's just say that one of the medicines Nolan was receiving made his heart irritable. Now that we stopped it, his heart should settle down. I also gave him some medicine that acts like an antidote. As soon as that drug kicks in, his heart should go quiet, and we can begin to wake him up and get him back on his feet."

"That's great news, Doc," Ned said.

"I'm just sorry that he had to go through all of this suffering. I know Allentown Hospital will regret they had to send you down here and should pay for the added expenses. You know, anything insurance doesn't cover."

Ned smiled at Jake and Ellen. "No worries there, Doc. We don't care about the money."

"I'm just saying, you know, the insurance company might give you a hard time about payment for the helicopter and the bill our hospital will send out. It could be a lot of money, and it was avoidable."

"Doc, I hate to argue with you, but if we hadn't come down here, Uncle Nolan might have died. So this was money well spent."

"And Dr. Sarkis," Ellen said, finally choking back her tears. "Money is not a problem for our family."

"I'm sorry if I offended you, Mrs. Perini. I thought Nolan was in the waste management business and was having trouble working on the trucks."

"That's right, Dr. Gilbert. Our family owns and operates just about every landfill in the state of Pennsylvania."

"You do?"

"The reason why Nolan told the doctors he can't work as hard is because he's old school and insists on sharing a lot of the tough jobs with his men. He loves to roll up his sleeves and operate forklifts or load and unload trucks. He's a tough guy."

"I see."

"So we ain't going to sue nobody or ask for money, Doc. We're just glad Uncle Nolan is going to get better quick. That's the main thing."

Philip could only nod, overwhelmed by the goodness of these people, their gratitude, and their common sense. *Hugh Hamlin and Bonnie Romano turned me inside out after I tried to help them*, he thought. *What a difference.*

He walked wearily back to his office, preparing what he would say when he met with Ray Gilbert for what was likely to be a lively clinical discussion.

4

CHAPTER

Philip cut through the clinical labs to the hallway that would take him out to the main lobby, one floor down from which was the NorthBroad Hospital cafeteria, a huge circular expanse where the entire staff, including physicians, found nourishment. *A term used loosely*, Philip thought, as he looked around at the various food stations. NorthBroad, like almost all hospitals, hadn't connected the part of the dietary department that made recommendations about healthy foods to patients with the part that was responsible for serving food to employees. In his most cynical moments, Philip would surmise that the deplorably unhealthy foods the staff was forced to eat weren't chosen through stupidity but instead represented a plot to foster more heart disease among their well-insured staff, as a way of recovering some of the money NorthBroad was forced to invest in employee health benefits. Even Philip had to wonder if his scorn of hospital administration was rational or simply a byproduct of his constant irritation with the people who ran the place but didn't understand the core business that they had effectively ruined.

It didn't really matter because Philip almost never visited the cafeteria, except when he was meeting someone, and even then, he would insist on taking whatever they purchased back to his office to consume, while he ate his own food from home. Too much noise and distraction during a busy workday, and too many nosey people to have an intimate conversation. This early morning was an exception. There were only a few people sitting, half awake, bent over their coffee cups, trying to rouse themselves. Among them were Gilbert and Liz Gold, sitting a little too close for Philip's comfort, having an intense conversation that Philip was pretty sure wasn't about medicine.

Philip grabbed a cup of black coffee and headed over to their table. When Gilbert and Liz saw Philip, they stopped talking, sat back in their chairs, and welcomed him. Philip stood awkwardly next to their table before finally sitting down.

"This is some place, Philip," Gilbert started, trying to make conversation. "I've never been in this hospital before."

"Yeah, big place," Philip answered, obviously distracted and not in the mood for small talk. "Liz, would you mind if I spoke to Ray ... alone?"

"Certainly, Dr. Sarkis. Ray, text me when you're done. I'm going back over to the EP lab area. We're going to have to figure out how we're getting back to Allentown."

"Sure," Ray said, dreading his now-private conversation with Philip.

Philip waited until Liz was out of earshot. "You hittin' that, Ray?"

"Huh?"

"C'mon, Ray. I figure something has to be distracting you to make you miss Nolan's diagnosis. Just thought that maybe Liz was the diversion."

"Philip, I really respect you, but that isn't any of your business."

"Right. So you *are* doing her. Is she married?"

Gilbert looked down and sighed, trying to decide if he wanted to be interrogated. "Not happily."

"But you are?"

"I was. My wife, Linda, died suddenly after I got to Allentown. I thought you knew. Most of the people at Gladwyne did."

"Jeez, I'm sorry, Ray. If I heard it, I forgot. I guess I was a little distracted back then myself. You know about the malpractice case that took me down."

"Yeah, I heard you were sued and out of medicine for a while. Then you were practicing general cardiology in the Poconos."

"I was until my significant other and I moved down here. NorthBroad had a full-time faculty job. I'd had enough of private practice, so here I am."

Philip wondered how much of the backstory of the Hamlin and Romano murders Gilbert actually had heard and whether he knew that it was Dorothy who had left *him* in the Poconos and had moved to Philly after he narrowly escaped prosecution for the attack on a malpractice lawyer in Boston. He decided to skip the sordid details but to offer a little of the wisdom he had gained through the process.

"Look, Ray, I'm not going to candy-coat this thing. The Perini case was a real bad miss."

"I still don't understand. How can you be so sure that he had torsades?"

Torsades de pointes is a rhythm abnormality from the bottom chamber of the heart that can be inherited but in most cases is caused by a drug that has a specific effect on the ECG. Gilbert was blown away that Philip had suspected and then proven the diagnosis.

"All right, let's deal with the medicines first," Philip began. "Perini was doing fine until he went to his family doctor for a cold and got a prescription for erythromycin."

"It wasn't on his med list on admission. I know. I checked when I worked him up."

"That's correct. It wasn't. Ellen picked up on the fact that the resident didn't order it after he came in, and she hounded him until he wrote the order. She was afraid to death that Nolan would get pneumonia on top of his heart problem."

"But he couldn't take erythromycin. He couldn't get anything by mouth. He wasn't awake enough to swallow the capsules."

"I know, so your idiot resident ordered it intravenously."

"He did what?"

"He threw gasoline on the fire, Ray. The oral erythromycin was bad enough, but the increased levels he got with the IV really stretched his QT interval."

"And caused all of those awful arrhythmias."

"When I went back through his chart, before I came to the lab, I saw that Perini had periods when things were pretty quiet. Turned out it was when his pacemaker was on and his heart rate was not slow. But when the pacemaker was turned down, his QT interval was a yard long, and the arrhythmias would start firing off."

"And you were able to replicate that sequence in the lab?"

"Exactly."

"Which means that the IV amiodarone they gave him up there and that I continued was just making things a lot worse?"

"Afraid so," Philip answered.

"Why didn't the magnesium work?"

"Too little, too late, I think. That's where the mexiletine comes in. Once we get enough of it into him, he should quiet down."

"What did the family have to say when you met with them?"

"Not much. They're just happy the guy is OK."

"And you think I blew the diagnosis and almost killed him because I've been having an affair with a married woman?" Gilbert asked.

Philip took a sip of his coffee, contemplating how much of his soul he should bare to this suffering young doctor, and decided that telling Gilbert his story wouldn't help. "Ray, I won't get into the specifics, but a lot of the troubles I had back at Gladwyne were self-inflicted. Let's just say I fell off the marriage train. It was a horrible experience, believe me."

Gilbert looked off into the distance, measuring his response. "I appreciate your concern, Philip, and as a matter of fact, I *have* been distracted. But it's not because I'm obsessed with Liz. If anything, the affair is winding down. She tells me that her husband has a temper, and I don't need the aggravation."

Philip nodded, not sure he believed Gilbert but willing to listen to his explanation.

"My worry, Philip, is that we've had a rash of cases from upstate that I can't figure out."

"You mean you don't know why they have arrhythmia problems?"

"Sort of. Well, actually, it's simpler than that. I don't even know *why* they're getting devices."

"They don't meet guideline criteria? You know that's not a big deal, Ray. We're talking about our professional organizations setting arbitrary rules. You know how I feel about that crap."

Indeed, Philip's disdain for guidelines was well known among his trainees and the profession in general. He had written several scathing editorials and papers outlining their limitations, his most important point being that over half of what was contained in guideline recommendations for practitioners was based on conjecture and opinion and not on high-grade scientific studies. Furthermore, for fear of conflict of interest, anyone with industry relationships of any kind was excluded from the guidelines-writing committees, which meant that the people who participated were not the most senior or knowledgeable people.

Nevertheless, guidelines were accepted by payers, hospital administrators, and the naïve patient public as the absolute truth upon which all clinical decisions were to be grounded. Most dangerous was their use by lawyers who routinely roasted defendant physicians who dared to stray from the guidelines to treat an individual patient problem differently. What made the situation even more frustrating for doctors was that any given disease state might have dozens of guidelines, published by competing professional organizations trying to sell their own medical journal, and recommendations among these documents were never uniform or consistent.

Gilbert had anticipated Sarkis's legendary ire. "I know all of that, Philip. And I agree that they're flawed. But I'm not talking about subtle interpretations of the guidelines. There have been several cases in which I flat out couldn't figure why the patient had received a pacemaker or a defibrillator in the first place."

"Give me an example."

"Well, Nolan is one of the most obvious. You saw his history. His ejection fraction was bad at the beginning, but they waited several months, as they should have, to see if he would get better. And he did, but they went ahead with the defibrillator anyway."

"Did you call the doctor up there and ask why they did that?"

Gilbert dropped his head. "No, but I should have."

"And you have a lot of other examples?"

"I do. Some aren't as blatant, and most of the patients weren't harmed."

"Then how did you discover them?"

"Calls from primary care doctors up in that area who were concerned and weren't getting straight answers. Some of them even sent the patients down to me for a second-opinion consultation, so I had a chance to go through the records."

"Were there cases that were guideline-adherent but your clinical judgment was different?"

"Yes."

"For example?"

"In a couple of cases, the patients were pretty old. I would've left them alone."

"That's a tough one, Ray. You know it's not about chronological age. Biology is the most important thing."

"I know that, Philip, and I always try to take that into account. But we're talking about demented people in their nineties getting defibrillators. That's just not right."

"Ray, unless you get a lot more specific information about what's going on up there in the boonies, I'm not sure there's much you'll be able to do about it."

"I know, and what makes it even worse is that our hospital has built a strong relationship with the doctors in that area. They send a lot of their cardiac surgery and tough coronary artery cases to us. If we start making noise and accusing them of inappropriate things, they'll send their patients elsewhere, like Penn State Hershey or Geisinger."

"I understand, Ray. It puts you in a tough spot. Have you been able to focus on any particular hospital or doctor? Maybe you could get a little glimpse behind the scenes."

"I haven't been able to identify an individual, but most of the problems seem to come from the farthest northern areas. And there's one other thing I noticed. I hesitate to bring it up because it sounds pretty stupid, but a number of questionable implants have been Sterling devices."

"You mean the new device company that just came online?"

"Have you had a chance to see their stuff?"

Philip winced. He almost never entertained device representatives in his office. But every once in a while, his young and inexperienced NorthBroad secretary would put one on his calendar. Since he had left his treasured Rhonda at Gladwyne, Philip had gone through several secretaries and had been told by his chief to lighten up on them. So when appointments he disliked were scheduled, he usually held his tongue and gave the people a few minutes to explain what they had for sale.

The visits were pleasant enough. After all, most of the representatives had been selected because of their outgoing personalities and good looks, and they were eager to impress. Unfortunately, what they had to offer to the medical profession—and to Philip's patients, in particular—usually fell short. Most of the new things that pharma or device reps were given to "promote" in doctors' offices were me-too products that added marginally to what was already out there and frequently did so with no real economic advantage.

Such had been the case with Sterling, who descended on his office several weeks earlier and had a chance to tell Philip about their products. In preparation for their meeting, Philip had learned that a number of executives and engineers had become unhappy and frustrated with the market leaders and eventually colluded to leave and form their own device company. They had been careful to use technology that was no longer patent-protected by the three companies that shared the cardiology rhythm-control device market and to change the hardware and software to be able to skirt allegations of patent infringement. They jazzed up the devices just enough to make them look good and did whatever they could to provide better prices and service.

"I remember meeting with a couple of their people a few months ago. Their devices seemed OK but nothing special."

"Agreed. That was my take. They were pretty aggressive with the people in my group, getting in our faces. When they didn't make much headway with us, they went to the hospital bean counters and made a case for a lower price point. Next thing we knew, the devices were on our shelves, and our department managers kept asking us if we wanted to give them a try."

"Did you?"

"I put in a couple of them in low-risk cases, just to shut them up."

"How'd they work out?"

"Fine, as I recollect. Their implant equipment is not quite as refined as the stuff we usually use, but it was passable. The programmers were nothing like anything we've been used to, so it took a while to become familiar with them. And of course, we had to send some of the nurses away to Saint Paul for a few days so they could get educated on how to use them."

"When are these companies going to get together and make a universal programmer so we don't have to waste so much time?" Philip muttered.

Gilbert could only shake his head, acknowledging the Tower of Babel that device technology had become. Each manufacturer had its own equipment to activate and inactivate and to program implanted devices. Since so many different parameters could be interrogated and then changed, learning how to use the devices had become a full-time job for the staff who supported the electrophysiology program. The worst nightmare was the patient who appeared in the emergency department with frequent shocks that sent the ER team scurrying to find someone who could help them take care of the patient. Philip and other senior arrhythmia physicians had lobbied for a "universal programmer" that could be used with any pacemaker or defibrillator to perform the most basic functions, most importantly just turning the damn thing off. But as had become typical in the wonderful world of capitalism, companies dug in, refusing to cooperate for fear that any technology advantage would be unearthed and copied by their competition. With no statute to compel the few manufacturers to collaborate, nothing had been done.

"But you don't suspect that Sterling has done anything to divert cases or to encourage doctors to do inappropriate things, do you?"

"Not really. It could all just be a coincidence."

"My thought, exactly." Philip paused and looked at his former student, realizing that Gilbert was truly unhappy, and figured he was in need of some brotherly advice. "Ray, I suggest you try to put this Sterling stuff aside, and get back to work. Exercise regularly again, and for Christ's sake, get yourself a girlfriend. I'm sure there are a lot of good-looking, single women in your hospital looking for a stud like you. Stop playing the field, and settle into a real relationship."

"I think that's good advice, Philip, and I appreciate your candor."

"Candor has never been a problem for me, Ray, as you know well. Tell you what—if you can put aside some time, we should look into doing some joint research projects. I don't have a ton of stuff going on like I used to, but we do participate in some cool multicenter trials. They're always looking for high-volume centers to help recruitment, and if you do a good job with that, we can get you on some of the manuscripts and steering committees. That should help you kick your career into a higher gear. What do you think?"

"That sounds wonderful, Philip. I feel intellectually isolated up there, and it would be great to do something exciting at work for a change."

"Exactly. Diversification helps quell the boredom. And I guarantee that everything will go better once you get your private life straightened out too. It really makes a big difference when you have a good relationship. I know it did for me."

There had been plenty of rumors about how Philip and Dorothy had begun their relationship, and Philip thought about sharing more of the details but thought better of it. Better to stay upbeat than to conjure up unpleasant memories.

"Thanks for spending some time with me, Philip. I promise to keep in touch, and I'll definitely take you up on that offer to collaborate."

"Good, Ray," Philip said, rising from his chair. The last thing he wanted was to make small talk. Now that his message had been delivered, he was anxious to get on with his day and, if he planned things right, make an early departure to spend some quality after-school time with his girls.

After they discarded their empty cups and ascended the circular stairway to the main lobby, Philip put his arm around Gilbert. "I meant what I said, Ray. I think you have a good mind and a bright future. I regret that I haven't been very good at keeping up with the people who trained with me, and I want to make it up to you, as best I can. Call me if I can ever be of help."

"Thanks, Philip. I appreciate that. I have a lot of things to work on myself, but your mentorship would be terrific."

They found Liz in the lobby area, waiting impatiently. "I don't know how to get us back to Allentown, Ray," she said, sounding too much like a scolding wife for Philip's taste.

"I can help," Philip said. It took him only a few moments to call his secretary and have her arrange a Lyft driver to meet Gilbert and Liz at the ER entrance. He shook hands with both of them, said his goodbyes, and walked briskly toward his office.

"Quite a doctor," Liz remarked, as Philip retreated.

"Yes. Actually, quite a guy. He offered to help me get back into doing some clinical research. He thinks it will be helpful to my psyche. He had a lot of good ideas."

"He did, did he? Care to share any specifics?"

"Nothing special, Liz," Gilbert answered, quite sure that she wouldn't be at all happy with the most important thing Philip Sarkis had recommended he do to improve his life.

5

CHAPTER

hilip's arms were hurting like they were going to fall off. But his father had preached that a parent's promise was sacred. And Philip had told Emily and Erin that they would finally have a chance to ride their new bikes down the sidewalk along Kelly Drive, just like the big people. After all, Philip and Dorothy had watched adults and kids having fun on the river drive ever since they had moved back to the city from the Poconos. They had waited patiently until Emily and Erin were old enough to have tricycles that could move along fast enough to stay out of the way of the crazy people who zipped up and down the path that bordered the Schuylkill River. And now the time had come.

Philip and Dorothy had moved out of the city to Narberth, a sweet residential village at the top of the Main Line, complete with a shopping village and playground. It was situated west of the city, only a short drive from Boathouse Row and Kelly Drive. Once they arrived at Kelly Drive, Philip didn't want the girls to ride in the parking lot or across the few streets they needed to navigate to get to the bike path, so, besides his lunch-laden backpack, he carried their riding equipment, no petty task. Not only did those sturdy tricycles weigh a ton, but he had to carry both with the same arm, leaving his other hand free to hold on to the hounds. Rocky and Meeko strained at their leashes, as excited as the girls to begin their jaunt. Philip was almost prostrate before making it to their starting point. But now, finally, the fun could begin.

And it did, the girls jumping on their pretty pink tricycles and scurrying off much faster than Philip thought possible. He and the dogs were forced to run to keep up as they wove their way around and through the pedestrians, runners, and riders who populated the walkway. But as hectic as it was, Philip had to admit he was having some of his best fun in a long time. And he not-so-secretly enjoyed the adulation of passersby, who had to be jealous of the father of such gorgeous and sweet children who worshipped Philip for being the most wonderful dad in the world.

It was an afternoon of perfection, a day of unusually low humidity with a perfect blue sky dotted with puffy white clouds. But sadly, a day that Dorothy couldn't share with her family. Though she had vowed to cut back on her work to be with the girls, difficult cases had come across her desk recently that demanded extra time in the office on weekends. As much as Philip hated being without her, he reveled in the opportunity to have the girls all to himself, to carefully lay plans for a splendid day, including a lunch packed with everything they loved to eat. So when the angels had finally tired themselves out, Philip found a place on the lawn next to the river to lay a picnic blanket and begin to unpack the peanut butter and jelly sandwiches, nectarines, dried fruit and nuts, and cupcakes that the girls would scarf up as they recharged their batteries and prepared themselves for the next leg of their mini-adventure. And treats for the dogs, of course, who could never be left out of any culinary adventure.

"This is probably too good to be true," Philip mused, as he sipped on a juice box and lay back on his elbows, watching the two children who had transformed not only his life but his relationship with Dorothy. Never before had they related so well to each other, ever vying to prove to the other and to themselves that the decisions they had made years ago—to leave their old lives and be with each other—had been necessary to land them where they were at that moment: in love with each other and their girls and their two hounds. Yes, only two now, fourteen-year-old Buffy having died just a few weeks earlier, leaving Dorothy and the rest of the family inconsolable for days. The girls were devastated; Philip and Dorothy were anxious to convince them that Buffy was waiting for them at the Rainbow Bridge and would see them all again one day soon.

But Philip had been right. The moment of perfection couldn't go on interrupted. His cell phone *had* to ring at precisely that moment, jolting him back to reality.

"Dr. Sarkis?" started the party at the other end.

"Yes?"

"This is your answering service."

"That's nice. But I'm not on call this weekend."

"I know, Dr. Sarkis. We tried to reach you on your pager several times before we got your cell number from the hospital operator. I apologize, but I have a call from a Dr. Ray Gilbert, and he says it's urgent that he speak with you."

Philip grimaced. "I guess I asked for this when I told him I would be there for him whenever he needed me," he muttered to himself. "Did he give you any details?" Philip asked the operator.

"No, Dr. Sarkis. I'm sorry. He only left a number where you can reach him. He sounded pretty desperate to speak with you, though."

Now what the hell am I going to do? Philip thought, closing his eyes, anticipating a headache. "Please call Dr. Gilbert back and tell him that I'm in the middle of something and will have to phone him back in about an hour."

"Yes, Dr. Sarkis. I can do that."

"Apologize for me, but tell him I can't talk right now."

Philip hung up, realizing that whatever he did from that point on, his afternoon had been effectively ruined. He was now under time pressure to get home, and when he arrived, there would be no gradual unwind and pleasant evening preparation but rather a headlong dive into another urgent medical problem. This was what the public didn't understand about being a doctor. It wasn't just the long hours he had to spend at work but, even more significant, the personal cost of dealing with problems off hours, problems that literally could mean life or death.

And so, the forced march back to the car with children, dogs, and equipment. The drive back to Narberth was extra-long because of traffic, although the girls clearly enjoyed themselves and had fun with Meeko and Rocky, who always appreciated human attention. It was Philip who was knocked off kilter. But as agitated as he was, he realized that his pique was more his fault than Gilbert's, even though his former pupil had deigned to infringe on his weekend.

Philip ushered the girls into his bedroom, situated them in bed with some milk and cookies on the bedside table, and turned on Cartoon Network. The girls had become expert in deflecting the hounds, who wanted to know which of the cookies they were entitled to. They giggled as Meeko and Rocky climbed on top of them, eager to pilfer whatever they could of the forbidden treats.

Philip retreated from what he knew would be a chaotic scene to his den, where he dialed the number Gilbert had left for him. He looked at his watch. Two hours had elapsed since his answering service had called him, which meant that Gilbert had been wrestling with his emergency for nearly three hours. Hopefully, he had resolved it.

Gilbert answered, almost instantly, words spilling out quickly. "Philip, thanks for calling back. Sorry to interrupt your weekend. It's that damn Sterling thing again. Big problem with a patient."

"OK, Ray, slow down and start from the beginning."

"Last night, the guys up north sent me another patient who was having frequent shocks from her device. Fifty-five-year-old who had a heart attack about a month ago. Young, but she was a smoker and had a terrible family history. She did fine after they opened her arteries, but she got a defibrillator implant last week. She was readmitted yesterday when she arrived in their ER after getting a bunch of shocks. They weren't able to get her rate controlled, so they loaded her into our helicopter and flew her here in no time. I told the flight crew to hold on the pad while I got a look at her, suspecting that we were going to have to ship her down to you for an ablation—a real one this time—if she was having VT."

"Wait a minute, Ray. She shouldn't have gotten a defibrillator that soon after a heart attack. They're supposed to wait at least a few weeks to see if her cardiac function comes back."

"Tell me about it, Philip. I was already pissed off when I found that out, but I was really frosted when I reviewed the electrograms they sent, and I saw the patient. It wasn't VT, Philip. It was AF with a rapid rate that triggered the device."

Silence as Philip seethed. The patient had experienced an arrhythmia coming from her upper heart chambers, not the bottom, which would cause her to die suddenly. The defibrillator had sensed a rapid rate and decided to try to shock the rhythm back to normal, which was simply not possible since her shocking electrodes had been placed in the bottom chamber. The device was never intended to stop atrial arrhythmia. A terrible scenario for the patient but one that could usually be handled by simply turning off the device and giving drugs to control the heart rate.

"Thank goodness you figured it out, Ray," Philip finally said. "You saved the patient a lot of trouble."

Silence once again, this time as Gilbert gathered himself.

"But if that were all there was to the case, you wouldn't have put in an urgent call to me, would you?" Philip continued.

"No, Philip. The story doesn't end there," Gilbert answered, obviously having a difficult time continuing the conversation.

"Deep breath, Ray."

"Right, deep breath. OK, so I took the woman off the helicopter and admitted her to our unit, where she proceeded to have several more episodes of rapid AF. By that time, I had turned the damn defibrillator off, but she dropped the crap out of her blood pressure with heart rates that went up to 220. She was on a lot of medication to slow her heart rate, and they weren't touching her."

"You're sure it was coming from the atrium."

"Yeah, definitely from the top chamber. But then I began to suspect that something else was going on."

"Did she have normal thyroid tests, Ray?" Philip asked, hoping that Gilbert hadn't forgotten that high thyroid levels could accelerate the heart rate with atrial arrhythmias and be resistant to drugs.

"Normal T4 and TSH."

"Good," Philip said, trying hard not to sound relieved. "What drugs did you have her on?"

"The kitchen sink, including amiodarone, but they were knocking the hell out of her blood pressure without touching her heart rate. I was beginning to think that she had another problem."

"Pre-excitation, I'll bet," Philip concluded. A congenital heart condition in which impulses from the top heart chamber go directly to the bottom of the heart, driving it to dangerously high heart rates that could be lethal.

"Right, a bypass tract!" Gilbert answered excitedly. "Thank goodness you came to the same diagnosis. Otherwise, I wouldn't be able to live with myself."

"What next, Ray?" Philip said through clenched teeth, anxious to find out what had happened to the poor patient.

"I decided to take her to the lab to find out if she had a bypass tract. It was going to have to be pretty close to the septum to give her a narrow QRS, but she already had a pacemaker device so I didn't have to worry about interfering with her normal conduction system."

"Good," Philip confirmed. He suspected that Gilbert would have had a hard time burning an abnormal fiber without damaging the wires that sent normal impulses to the bottom chamber. "So were you successful."

"Yes, but I perforated her heart."

"You did what?"

"Come on, Philip. You have to know how nuts the situation was. The woman was crashing, and I couldn't make her heart rate go down. I was so focused on finding and ablating the pathway that I lost track of one of my pacing catheters, and it ended up in her pericardium."

"Damn. Not good, Ray."

"I know, I know. The pathway was a bitch. It was right next to the His bundle, and it was a miracle I didn't cause heart block. Anyhow, I recognized the perforation right away and drained the effusion, and she's fine. She wasn't on any blood thinners so the bleeding sealed up pretty quick. Her heart rate and blood pressure are perfect now, and she's waking up nicely from the anesthesia. So all's well that ends well, I guess."

"I'm sorry I didn't call you back sooner, Ray. But I doubt I would have told you to do anything different."

"I was calling mainly for hand holding. There was no time to send any recordings, and the patient was definitely not going to survive a transfer."

"I agree. You handled it well, Ray."

"Thanks, Philip. I appreciate that. But it does bring up the same problem we talked about a few weeks ago."

"Yes, it does."

"Not only was the device put in too early, but the implant had to have had something to do with provoking that bypass tract to become active. They damn near killed her, Philip. What do you think we should do?"

"Not sure, Ray. I do agree that you have to do something if patients are getting hurt."

"That's what I think."

"But you can't come down on the docs up there too hard, or they'll just blow you off."

"I understand that, Philip. I've been racking my brain and can't come up with a reasonable solution."

"Tell you what, Ray. Let me talk to Dorothy. She knows a lot about issues like this and has a lot of common sense and excellent judgment. I would love to hear what she has to say. How about if I get back to you on Monday?"

"Philip, that would be great. I really appreciate your help with this."

After they hung up, Philip put into play the late-afternoon ritual of pet care and childcare that was now a regular part of his existence, being especially attentive to the details so when Dorothy came home, they would have time for brain picking over their favorite cocktails.

The dogs heard the garage door go up long before Philip, who had just parked his butt on one of the kitchen stools at the island that had rapidly become the center of their family life. The marble counter was their first destination whenever they returned home and the place all family members and visitors placed their belongings on arrival, before they had a chance to distribute them or put them away. Philip, the neatnik, struggled to keep the counter in order, while Dorothy and the girls seemed hell-bent on recluttering the space at every opportunity. So Philip wasn't surprised when Dorothy staggered into the kitchen and began to throw the many bags she had lugged in from her car onto the surface, the contents spewing this way and that. His head shaking, Philip began to sort through the stuff, all the while exhorting Rocky, counter-surfer extraordinaire, to keep his paws down and his nose out of the fragrant food bags.

"Philip, I really need a glass of wine," Dorothy said, while planting a light kiss on his cheek as encouragement.

Enjoying being manipulated by his partner, Philip smiled, pulled an opened bottle of Chardonnay from the refrigerator, and poured a generous portion into a wine glass, engraved with the profile of a Portuguese water dog.

"It was tough being at work today. I wish I could have been outside. Did you guys have fun at the river?"

"We did. The kids had a blast, and the doggies were well exercised. They should sleep well, especially after all the food they scarfed up for dinner."

"Good."

"We did have a minor interruption that I need to talk to you about."

"Something bad happen to the girls?" was Dorothy's first thought.

"No, they're fine, and so are the hounds. It was a phone call from Ray Gilbert."

"Who?"

"Remember a few weeks ago I had to go into the hospital to help Marwan with a helicopter transfer?"

"Yeah. Gilbert is the guy who rode with the patient in the chopper?"

"Right. I told you he was worried about some patients up in the Carbon County area getting defibrillators inappropriately."

"Vaguely. You told him to cool it, right?"

"Yeah, and to clean up his private life."

"So he called you today. Why? You told me you weren't on call."

"Yes. He called to ask my advice and to hear that he had done the right thing with one of his patients."

"And had he?"

"I guess so, although his procedure very nearly bumped her off."

"So what did he want from you?"

"This woman came from the same area, and her device was unnecessary too, according to him. He wanted advice about how to deal with it."

"Without pissing off the universe."

"Especially the people who send him cases from up there."

"But he feels like he has to do something to ease his conscience," Dorothy surmised.

"Precisely. I love problem-solving with you. You cut to the chase aster than anyone."

"Stop buttering me up. Let me think on it while the wine seeps into my brain, and we get our dinner ready."

Philip readily agreed, confident that Dorothy would do exactly as she said. However, he began to wonder when Dorothy still hadn't returned to the subject through dinner prep and consumption, cleanup, and the protracted childcare necessary to get "E squared," as they referred collectively to the two girls, properly prepared for bed. It wasn't until they had both landed in bed themselves, switched on their bedside lamps, and prepared to pursue their customary reading that Dorothy finally returned to the Gilbert conundrum.

"When we've had problems with people who refer to our firm, we've been most successful with the education thing."

"How do you do that?"

"Frame it carefully, and look for the proper venue. Maybe you and Gilbert can make yourselves available to do a symposium of some kind."

"They love case conferences."

"Perfect. The great Dr. Sarkis agrees to do a seminar where you'll discuss complex cases. Gilbert can be the host, and you and he will pick cases that illustrate the issues you're most concerned about."

"Without identifying any of them, so none of the docs who attend will be embarrassed."

"Exactly. He'll have to be careful to disguise the perpetrators, but the facts will be clear."

"And I'll present treatment options."

"Based on the best science and guideline recommendations, of course."

"Brilliant," Philip concluded.

"Maybe. Depends on how well Gilbert sells it and how receptive the docs up there might be."

"Ray's pretty savvy and knows the territory well. I'm sure he can slant this well to get the right people in the room and in a receptive mood."

"Pick a good restaurant, and don't spare the alcohol. You'll be surprised how much easier that will make your task."

"Done. I'll call Ray on Monday and lay this all out for him."

"That's fine. Let him take the lead, but stay hands-on, Philip, if you want to make sure this will work and not waste your time."

"Good advice."

"And now, this oracle is closed for business. I want to read the next installment of *Outlander*. Jamie and Claire are on a new adventure, and I have to see how it works out."

"Wait a minute. I've seen that series with you. I thought you only watched it for the soft porn."

"And what's wrong with that? Might give me some new ideas."

"If only," Philip teased, opening his Hamilton tome, finally starting to feel relaxed. Rocky and Meeko jumped on the bed and spun around two or three times before stretching out at the bottom, obliterating any free space there had been for Philip's legs. "I guess it's all about the hounds," he said, not expecting any reply from Dorothy, now escaped from reality and fully immersed in her own personal time machine.

6
CHAPTER

Philip called Gilbert as soon as he got to his desk on Monday morning.

"A case conference, Philip?" Gilbert asked. "Are you sure that's a good idea? Wouldn't it look like we were rubbing it in?"

"Not if we pick the cases carefully and present them anonymously."

"Anonymous won't work. They'll recognize the cases and get pissed off. This isn't doing it for me, Philip. Did Dorothy agree?"

"Wholeheartedly. In fact, it was her idea. She's used a similar approach in her law practice and has gotten good results."

"I'm not opposed to the idea of educating the sons of bitches. I just want to be careful that we don't set them off. And if they suspect we're going to give them a hard time, they won't even show up."

"All right. I get it. How about if we do it this way? You put together three or four major topic areas that reflect the bogus cases they've sent to you. I'll make up a case around each of those topics. All fictional, so they won't recognize any of the facts, but hammering away on the issues we want them to understand. What do you think about that approach?"

"Yeah, I guess that might work," Gilbert admitted.

"Good. Think about it the next couple of days, and send me a list by Wednesday or Thursday. Next weekend, when I have some time, I'll put the cases together, and if you like them, we can start the process of setting up a dinner conference."

"I want to have the final word, Philip."

"No worries. I'll send the cases to you in draft form, and you can edit the hell out of them."

Silence while Gilbert weighed the idea.

"OK, while I work on the list, I'll talk to Liz about the best way to put the seminar together."

"That should be fine. I'll leave the logistics to you. But remember, we need to make it very convenient for those docs so they'll attend. If they don't show up, the idea is shot."

"Liz has been here a long time, Philip. She knows a lot of the people who work in their offices. I'm sure she can get some inside information that will help us entice them."

Philip was torn between accepting Gilbert's story about using Liz Gold for her organizational skills and wondering whether planning a conference was just another way to get her alone so he could get into her pants. At this point, he had little choice but to concur and move on.

"Email me your subject list and whatever background information you think I'll need, and we'll get this show on the road."

"Literally *on the road*, Philip, because one of the things that I know about the docs up there is that the program will have to be in their backyard. They won't travel far."

"I understand," Philip answered with as much enthusiasm as he could muster. The thought of having to drive at least a couple of hours after a long day at work was not his idea of a good time. Unless he could parlay it into something pleasant. "Let's see if we can do this program on a Thursday or Friday, and I'll just stay up there and go to our house in the Poconos for a long weekend."

"I'll let you know if we can manage that once I hear back from the docs. There are at least a half dozen arrhythmia people who have to be there. When I have the date, I'll call each of them personally."

They ended the conversation by agreeing to talk in a week. Philip took his phone out and quickly scanned his calendar for the following weekend. The girls had a birthday party and Dorothy a luncheon date with an old friend. Nothing that would interfere with Philip's working on a case conference. "Shouldn't take more than a couple hours," Philip muttered to himself as he sat back in his desk chair. "It's not like I haven't done case conferences before." He chuckled, considering how grossly understated that remark truly was.

What Philip had not considered was how tired he might be the following weekend, after what was going to be an action-packed week. Every single night was booked and would allow Philip almost no downtime at home, something that he had come to covet and even depend on.

Monday evening would feature a practice meeting at NorthBroad that Philip hated with a particular passion. This was a forum in which the practicing physicians would be berated by penny-pinching, parasitic administrators for not keeping up their practice volumes, losing money, squandering referrals, and using staff foolishly—like having the temerity to ask nursing assistants to use their time to help frail patients get into and out of their clothes in examination rooms.

Their most recent squawk was the amount of time it was taking physicians to complete outpatient charts. The administrators could not have cared less about how this might negatively influence patient care. Their main concern was that incomplete charts retarded billing patients and insurance companies, which meant that the hospital couldn't collect. And what was that money to be used for? More administrators, of course, and lavish buildings in which their offices would be housed.

"We simply have no control over how we practice medicine," Philip would remind his colleagues frequently. But they all conceded that the situation would never change significantly. The physicians and the impotent medical societies that represented them had lost the war to determine who would ultimately control how medicine was practiced. With the victory of the bean counters had come the undoing of medicine as a profession. Philip and his colleagues were "employees," their patients were "clients," and their staff was indentured and made to spend more time making sure patients were billed than cared for and comforted.

"I hate those meetings," Philip would complain to Dorothy as the date approached.

"I know you do, Philip," she would answer, trying her best to sound empathetic and not weary of Philip's whining. "Why don't you say something?"

"I'm afraid I'll lose my temper and beat somebody to a bloody pulp." Though this was a reply that most people would consider hyperbole, given Philip's track record of the people he didn't like having ended up dead, Dorothy was not inclined to dismiss the remark lightly.

"Well, then, don't go."

"It's a requirement. Technically, they could dock my salary if I miss over half of the meetings. I know that sounds ridiculous, but I wouldn't put it past them. So I go and just sit there and listen to the drivel."

"Get home as soon as you can, and I'll have a scotch waiting for you," was the best Dorothy could do.

Tuesday evening was a school function. Emily and Erin were both enrolled at the Narberth Elementary School, just a few blocks from the comfortable ranch-style home that Philip and Dorothy had purchased when they departed the confines of Philadelphia. Though they thought they would hate not being near the central part of the city, the move to the western suburbs had been a terrific idea. They loved everything about the village in which they lived, especially the girls' school. It was housed in an old brick building that had been extensively renovated just a few years before to improve the movement of students and teachers, to provide better heat and air conditioning, and to enhance the recreational facilities.

On Tuesday evening, the girls were scheduled to perform in a pageant, an attempt by the teachers to have every student perform with his or her class—acting, singing, dancing, or whatever they enjoyed and had confidence doing, individually or in a group. It would be a long evening, with no child left behind, but Philip looked forward to it, surely not for the performance skills but for the opportunity to witness the sheer joy that it brought to Dorothy, who beamed whenever one of her girls was in view.

Wednesday was a black-tie affair. A very special night for Dick Deaver, who was being honored by his cronies for twenty-five years of service to the Union League. Dick had joined the organization years before to provide a place to entertain clients and to meet influential people in Philadelphia. Dick quickly realized that in addition to the networking aspect, the organization had tremendous untapped potential for advancing the public good. He convinced the governing body to fund projects to benefit the growing population of homeless in Center City, pointing out how unpleasant it was to step over smelly people lying in the street on the way to the League's lavish function. His ideas had brought forth a few successful and high-profile projects that had begun to transform the Union League's image from a stodgy, reactionary organization of wealthy and entitled old men to a paragon for public good.

The key to success had been Dick's tireless fund-raising, not only among the membership but also across several constituencies who understood and sympathized with the plight of the homeless. Many were persuaded by the blight the homeless placed on a city that was ever more interested in attracting tourists to the historical sites and businesses to the newly expanded convention center. Even the most conservative among the Urban League membership had to admit that Dick's projects had been successful beyond anyone's expectations and that his energy and commitment had been the key element. This week, Dick would be feted, and the highlight for Philip would be Dorothy's speech. Though she detested public speaking, Dorothy had agreed that her remarks would be essential to the event, and she had been preparing for weeks. Though she had not divulged the contents entirely, Dorothy's inquiries of Philip as she made her preparations made Philip as sure as he could be that his soulmate would hit the right note with brevity and wit.

Thursday evening was the cardiology fellows' journal club. Philip would host about twelve of the cardiac fellows at his home, serving pizza, soft drinks, and beer, while they worked their way through a couple of contemporary articles from the literature. Philip selected the papers carefully and used them to teach the fellows about cardiology and the science of clinical investigation.

"It's important that you learn how to be critical of what's in the literature," he liked to remind the young physicians, "especially if the article is an important one and likely to influence the way you intend to treat patients." And so the group would spend the bulk of the evening pointing out the strengths and the weaknesses of what they had read, what they might have done differently to improve the experiments, and how to place the results in the context of clinical care.

Though endorsing the idea of hosting the fellows, Dorothy made it a practice to greet all of them warmly and then absent herself from the festivities. When they lived in closer quarters, this meant getting out of Dodge entirely. But now, with a larger home, she could sequester herself in the bedroom they had turned into an office, working away while the hounds lounged on *their* chairs that, not by coincidence, happened to be the most comfortable in the house.

Friday evening activities had become a recurring joke between Philip and Dorothy. Each week, they would make plans to get a babysitter and venture out, just the two of them, to explore a new bistro or restaurant in the area. The Main Line was blessed with dozens of good eateries, many of which were small BYOs, relatively inexpensive, and with good food of various fare. Almost all of them also subscribed to a delivery service, which, for a relatively small fee, would pick up food that was ordered on the internet and deliver it to the customer's home. Thus, despite their best intention, after each arrived at home after a long week and had a glass of wine or a cocktail, they would succumb and agree to stay home with the hounds, order in, and watch something on television before collapsing into bed and falling into a restful sleep.

During this active week, Philip did notice that Gilbert had faxed over a few pages that contained the subject matter of the cases Philip would eventually discuss at the case conference. However, it took Philip until Saturday afternoon, after a long walk in the woods with the dogs and a small lunch with Dorothy, to finally settle into his den and review Gilbert's outline. What he read should have disturbed him, but, after years in practice, Philip's cynicism had gotten the better of him. The truth was that Philip had observed the same tendencies among his own colleagues and referring physicians.

For reasons that *no one* had ever adequately elucidated, doctors tended to overtreat and to overuse technology. That's not to say that all kinds of supposed experts hadn't expressed a "learned" opinion on the topic. The literature was rife with articles, surveys, editorials, and op-ed pieces that intended to explain the practice. Philip's favorites came from the bioethicists. He scoffed at the notion that a PhD, who had never practiced medicine in the trenches and wouldn't know a patient if he tripped over one, would have the audacity to suggest why doctors did what they did. One of their most cited reasons was "defensive medicine," an issue that Philip agreed was important. The fear of getting sued drove doctors to order unnecessary tests, but how much of that influenced doctor behavior was debatable. Other explanations included shameless profit-making, ignorance of the literature, and, of course, pressure from patients who were frequently anxious to leave no stone unturned in their quest for absolutely perfect health. The latter issue was a particularly large problem on the Main Line, where the wealthy spent an inordinate amount of time worrying about aches and pains that were rarely serious but a source of constant concern.

Gilbert's issues were, thus, all familiar to Philip. Gilbert described patients like Perini, who had cardiac disease but not of sufficient severity or intensity to have required a procedure or an expensive device. There were others for whom a relatively simple device was warranted, but a much more complicated implant procedure had been recommended and carried out. Gilbert was also quite concerned about supposedly missed diagnoses, cases in which an arrhythmia had actually occurred, but the site or mechanism had not been correctly pinpointed. And then, several examples in which arrhythmias had been discovered incidentally, perhaps during a routine visit to a general practitioner, but were attacked in a most aggressive and unwarranted fashion, many times leaving the patient worse off than he or she had been at the beginning of the process.

Philip perused Gilbert's list and constructed a list of five overarching themes that he addressed with fictional cases. For each, the facts of the case would be followed by a list of questions he would ask of the audience to engage them in the process. At work on Monday, he combed through his extensive files and selected a few figures and tables that would help to emphasize the learnings from each case and, hopefully, drive his point home. This Socratic method of teaching and audience interaction had served Philip well throughout his teaching career. If Dorothy was right and the problems Gilbert had identified were caused by a lack of understanding, Philip was confident he could remediate.

By midweek, Philip had compiled the cases into a PowerPoint presentation that he emailed to Gilbert, inviting comments. Within an hour, while in the middle of reviewing a manuscript, Philip's cell phone rang. He hated when that happened, but he had a pretty good idea of who was phoning him before he even looked at the screen.

"Hi, Philip. This is Ray Gilbert."

"Hi, Ray." Philip tried to keep the agitation out of his voice. "So you received the file with the material, right?"

"I sure did. Just calling to thank you. The cases are on point, and the questions are perfect. I'll do a couple of minor edits, and we should be all set."

Edits? Really? Philip thought, choking back his irritation. "What are the logistics for the meeting, Ray?"

"Not sure yet. I have to meet with Liz tomorrow afternoon to see how much progress she's made, and I'll get back to you. Like I told you, we'll aim to place the meeting up north somewhere, at a nice restaurant that the EPs might be attracted to."

"Right, Ray. It's all about the food and wine."

"Don't know how much booze we'll be able to provide. I'm pretty sure I can get our hospital to pay for a dinner for doctors who refer patients, but they have a policy about alcohol. We'll see."

"I'll leave the particulars to you, Ray. Just get me the date as soon as you can, and I'll block my calendar."

They hung up, promising to keep in touch by email. Gilbert was pleased with their progress, but Philip was still feeling uneasy. *No time to explore that now*, he thought. Better to wait to talk to the oracle about his concerns, preferably over cocktails, Philip concluded, as he plunged back into his desk work.

That evening, Philip sat at the kitchen island with Dorothy, sipping their wine and whiskey, while waiting for the pasta water to boil. From their stools, they could observe the girls, perched on the great-room sofa, watching a video, while petting the dogs, who were lying on their laps.

"I finished the cases for Ray Gilbert's conference and sent them to him today."

"I'm sure he was grateful."

"Quite so. He's excited about the conference idea now, but I don't think he understands how dangerous his situation might become."

"How?" Dorothy asked.

"If this isn't just a simple case of a 'knowledge gap,' and somebody up there is playing fast and loose for profit motives, they could come down real hard on Ray."

"Like they did on you in the old days?"

"Exactly."

"You didn't go into that with Ray today, did you?"

"Of course not. It's way too early. I'm hoping we can resolve this matter to everyone's satisfaction and move on, but—"

"But if you can't?"

"Then I'll have to tell him my story and warn him about the repercussions of becoming a caped crusader. How people get pretty whacked out when they are criticized and blamed."

"Be careful with that, Philip. Ray is a big boy. He has to make his own decisions."

"You're right. I just want to make sure he doesn't behave as naively and ineptly as I did back then. It could mean serious trouble for him and maybe even for Liz, for all I know."

"I'm sure you'll give him good advice, Philip. Now let's get this dinner going. The girls are going to come charging in here any minute to tell us they're starving."

The rest of the evening was pro forma: Philip and Dorothy trying to enjoy their dinner, while the girls played with their food and looked for any excuse to giggle and be silly. Parental admonitions took them back to their meals for a few minutes, until they once again lost their concentration. And so it went until they had consumed enough food to satisfy Philip and Dorothy that they wouldn't starve to death, followed by the piteous pleading for the dessert they really didn't deserve but always received. Once the girls were tucked into bed, Philip and Dorothy themselves collapsed, watching a mindless television show before lights went out.

But this night, as he lay in bed, Philip's mind wouldn't shut down. He was concerned about Ray Gilbert but wasn't sure why. Could it be that he wanted Gilbert to avoid what Philip had endured? The event that had both energized and frightened him and had almost ruined his academic career? He tossed and turned until he finally went out to the living room and decided to let that memory replay in his head like an old movie.

7

CHAPTER

I t had begun innocently enough. His fellowship mentor in Boston had several times evaluated patients who had come to him after a pacemaker implantation. A few had had a procedural complication, but most were relatively young and uncomfortable with the idea of having a device in their bodies for the rest of their lives. Bernard Lowenstein had become convinced that many of the patients who had been referred to him for a second opinion regarding their cardiac rhythm problem not only didn't need the pacemaker that had been implanted by their prior physician but that it was in their best interest to have the hardware removed.

This issue was brought into bold relief a few months into Philip's fellowship. Lowenstein presided over what had become a famous and well-attended Friday afternoon case conference. He used the seminar as an opportunity to illustrate cases in which his strong recommendations had proven beneficial to a recent patient. It was during one such discussion, packed with medical students, residents, and fellows, that Lowenstein presented a particularly disturbing case, followed by a suggestion that would change Philip's life.

"How many people in this room had an opportunity to see Mr. Arbuckle in the hospital last month?" Lowenstein began.

As expected, only a few hands went up; the vast majority of the people who filled the conference room were unaware of Mr. Arbuckle's saga—the ideal opportunity for Lowenstein to hold forth.

"Dr. DiBona, you're familiar with this patient, are you not?"

"I am, Dr. Lowenstein," replied the junior faculty member.

"Would you like to present his case to our audience?" Lowenstein asked rhetorically, as if DiBona had any choice.

But he clearly didn't mind and, in fact, craved the spotlight. Reggie DiBona had recently joined Lowenstein's staff after a spectacular two years of fellowship in England. He was considered a rising star, and he was anxious to make his mark. His British accent, acquired at Cambridge after immigration from the Philippines, made him sound even smarter than he was, and he used that illusion to its fullest extent, in his very best king's English and enunciation.

"Mr. Arbuckle is a seventy-eight-year-old gentleman with a history of hypertension and high cholesterol who was taking a diuretic and niacin for those conditions. He had no other significant past medical history and has no family history of cardiac disease. He reported to his doctor that he occasionally would become lightheaded after standing for a prolonged period of time. The worst was an episode during which he became intensely lightheaded when he was standing with his wife in a queue waiting to enter a show—"

"Where was the show, Reggie?" Lowenstein interrupted.

"Broadway. In New York," DiBona answered without missing a step.

"And why do I ask, Mr. Wicks?" Lowenstein asked, addressing his question to a redheaded and usually cocky Harvard medical student who was rotating on the cardiology service. The student stammered, stymied, as Lowenstein knew he would be—an opportunity for a dramatic answer from the chief. "Because you must know *every* detail of the patient's history if you hope to unravel his problem and construct a treatment plan that will work," Lowenstein pronounced triumphantly. "Reggie, why did you need to know the answer to my question?"

"The patient is from Chicago. He and his wife were visiting New York when he nearly passed out."

"And so ..." Lowenstein coaxed, knowing the answers but wanting to play the professor.

"He was taken to New York Medical Center."

"Where the doctors were strangers, correct?"

"Yes."

"And the unfamiliarity created even more anxiety for the patient. So what happened next, Reggie?"

"They admitted him and did a number of tests, most of which came back normal. However, in the early hours of the morning, while Mr. Arbuckle was asleep, they observed a four-second sinus pause on his telemetry monitor. The next morning, he was visited by a cardiologist, who told him they had discovered the cause of his 'blackout.'"

"What is wrong with this diagnosis? What is missing, Mr. Wicks?"

The medical student perked up, anxious to make up for his previous miss. "He didn't black out when his heart slowed down?" Wicks answered tentatively.

"Precisely," Lowenstein pronounced. "And the cardiologist didn't bother to obtain a full history of the event. What were the extenuating circumstances, Reggie?"

"Mr. Arbuckle had been touring New York with his wife all day and hadn't had anything to eat and little to drink. He had forgotten his diuretic medication in the morning and decided to take it later in the afternoon. And though it was a warm evening, Mr. Arbuckle had insisted on dressing in a suit and tie for the performance and had been standing in line for several minutes before he became pre-syncopal."

"Precisely and well summarized. This man's blood pressure was low, and that is why he nearly passed out. But what about the four-second pause on the monitor? Dr. Greenfield, I believe you may be able to enlighten us on this point."

Michael Greenfield was another of Lowenstein's fellows and Philip's peer, a Californian who was pursuing his studies at Harvard after completing his basic cardiology training at UCLA. He had already conducted some high-level research projects, including an ingenious study to which Lowenstein referred. Only too happy to recite his findings, Greenfield started in.

"We wanted to find out if normal people have cardiac rhythm variations and how severe they might be. We needed some volunteers who would be willing to carry a recording device, called a Holter monitor, for a day or two while they pursued normal activity. The plan was to observe their heart rhythms continuously for twenty-four hours. We had a hard time finding people who would do it until I started asking some of my classmates, who thought it would be cool. So we monitored fifty healthy medical students."

"Normal medical students? Is there such a thing?" Lowenstein asked, fishing for a few laughs. "And your findings were remarkable."

"Yes, we published our results in the *American Journal of Cardiology.* We were surprised to see that nearly everyone, almost 90 percent, had something that we might call abnormal if we saw it in a patient, including skipped beats, rate slowing, and pauses."

"Were any of those pauses as long as four seconds, Dr. Greenfield?"

"They certainly were, Dr. Lowenstein. They were actually pretty common when people were asleep."

"Remarkable. And what did your study teach us, Dr. Greenfield?"

"Just because you see a rhythm abnormality, you can't assume that it needs to be treated because it could be a normal variant."

"Precisely. So, Reggie, what happened to Mr. Arbuckle?"

"They told him at the hospital in New York that he needed a pacemaker to prevent more episodes."

"Which they implanted that very day."

"Yes, they did. They discharged Mr. Arbuckle the next day, and he went back to Chicago where—"

"Wait a second, Reggie. Let's see if anyone here who doesn't know the case can tell us what happened."

Philip had been sitting in the back of the room taking it all in. Although he should have known better, before he realized it, his right hand went up in the air, just as Lowenstein turned in his chair to survey his sector of the conference room.

"Ah, Dr. Sarkis. You're awake after all."

Nervous titters around the room.

"Quite so, Dr. Lowenstein," Philip said, smiling, trying to handle his mentor's taunt in good humor.

"And your prognostication, Dr. Sarkis?"

"I suspect that Mr. Arbuckle had another lightheaded episode."

"Spot on, Philip. Actually, several—am I correct, Reggie?"

"Yes, Dr. Lowenstein. The spells became more frequent and more intense. After he returned to Chicago, he nearly passed out three or four times. He was readmitted to the hospital, but they said they couldn't find anything wrong with his heart or his pacemaker. They suggested a psychiatric evaluation."

"So typical of weak doctors. Call the patient crazy when you can't figure out the clinical problem," Lowenstein said.

"Their recommendation didn't sit well at all with Mr. Arbuckle. He talked to some friends who knew about our program here in Boston and recommended that he see us. I evaluated him in the office and recommended that he come into Brigham for some testing and so the entire team would have a chance to opine."

"And what did we find, Reggie?"

"Mr. Arbuckle had an obvious problem with controlling his blood pressure. It measured high when he was lying down but would fall dramatically if we had him stand for a few minutes, especially after he took his water pill."

"And the pacemaker?"

"We did two things. When we turned the pacemaker rate down to a very low rate, Mr. Arbuckle's intrinsic electrical system functioned just fine. And when we turned the rate up and paced the lower chamber continuously, Mr. Arbuckle's blood pressure went even lower when he stood up."

"So not only was the pacemaker not helping, but it was actually hurting," Lowenstein concluded.

"Yes, the artificial stimulation from the pacemaker actually caused the heart to contract abnormally, which made his blood pressure lower. It aggravated the problem."

"Which made our recommendation even easier."

"Yes. Pacemaker extraction. That, coupled with some adjustments of his medicines and making sure he drank enough water, made for a remarkable improvement. We're now about three months out, and he hasn't had any more of the severe episodes. He still has some minor events, but he says he can live with those."

"Simple solutions are always the best," Lowenstein commented. "And important to emphasize that we should never raise patient expectations past what is achievable. We don't cure very much of anything. Our goal is to palliate and improve symptoms so patients can remain functional. Nevertheless, Mr. Arbuckle's case is a remarkable example of how good clinical principles can make all the difference in a patient's outcome. Any questions or comments?"

Philip couldn't resist the temptation to ask the question he knew was on everyone's mind, but no one else dared broach: "Dr. Lowenstein, why take the pacemaker out? Why not just turn the rate down and leave it in place?"

Lowenstein smiled, not only anticipating the question but relishing the response. "I think it was good for the patient's psyche," Lowenstein said. "It will make it easier for him to put the trauma behind him so he can move on."

"But extraction carries risk," Philip pushed on, "especially if you try to take the lead out as well."

"Point taken, Dr. Sarkis," Lowenstein answered, enjoying the exchange. "And doctors are always more persuaded by the potential for physical than emotional or psychological harm. I would say that in most cases, patients do better and feel better when they no longer have the pacemaker in their bodies. Which is why we've extracted dozens of pacemaker generators over the last several years, and why, I suspect, we'll continue to do so. And if the lead comes out of the vein easily, we get that out as well. If not, we cap the lead and leave it."

The room was quiet as the participants absorbed Lowenstein's message and until Lowenstein called for the next case. But by then, Philip was distracted and anxious to speak with his professor about an idea that was taking shape in his brain. He waited until the conference concluded and Lowenstein was walking down the corridor toward his office. Philip caught up to him in stride.

"Dr. Lowenstein, I found the pacemaker case we discussed to be intriguing. Would it be possible to review the cases in which you have recommended pacemaker extraction and publish the experience?"

Lowenstein stopped to think and to answer. "It's possible but difficult. Someone would have to go back through the files and find the patients. We haven't kept a list that I know of."

"Who does the extractions?"

"Our cardiac surgeons have done them all."

"If they keep a list of patients you have referred, I might be able to find the patients in their records."

"You could, Philip. But keep in mind that this is a hot issue. Anything you say will be contested by those people who profit from the pacemaker business."

But Philip was undaunted. He identified over thirty patients similar to Mr. Arbuckle, who had extractions over the preceding ten years. Philip pulled records, contacted the patients and their private physicians, and discovered that almost all had done well after extraction, with only a handful requiring further treatment. The manuscript he fashioned was reviewed and edited several times by Lowenstein and Reggie DiBona, until they agreed it was suitable for coauthorship and submission. Several journals rejected the article as anecdotal and unscientific with much bias, until it was finally accepted and published by a mid-level cardiology journal. Nevertheless, the paper attracted media attention; reporters always were eager to uncover misdeeds, especially by physicians.

Philip was able to expand the project into larger databases, working collaboratively with public interest groups that were concerned about the overuse of technology, particularly in elderly and susceptible patients. With the publication of more articles, the issue eventually caught the attention of headline-hungry politicians. A Senate subcommittee on aging, wanting to know how unnecessary pacemakers might influence Medicare spending, summoned Philip, now in his first faculty job, to testify about his project.

Philip's testimony before the subcommittee was compelling and led Congress to pass legislation that would require a prospective review of all pacemaker implants in Medicare patients. Their recommendation stunned the scientific community and brought the ire of senior physicians down on Philip and his colleagues. Doctors were angered that they would have to go through administrative hoops to implant a simple pacemaker. Professional societies issued statements decrying the decision, pointing out the dearth of hard scientific data that had been presented in support of a proposition that physicians were not doing the right thing for their patients.

Philip was attacked at nearly every meeting he attended. His superiors at Gladwyne Memorial, his first faculty job, were concerned about the negative publicity they were receiving and warned Philip that his career there was at stake if the furor didn't die down. Philip even received a few threatening letters that stopped just short of bodily harm but made it clear that he was a pariah in the cardiology community. Though intimidated, Philip refused to recant. And he was supported by many honest practitioners, especially Dr. Lowenstein, who heartily agreed with his position and encouraged him to stick to his guns.

It was a tough several months that might have gone on even longer, if not for a *New England Journal of Medicine* paper, published by another group from Philadelphia. With no input from Philip, they reviewed a sample of Medicare patients who had received pacemakers prior to the prospective review decision and documented that in at least a third of patients, a number consistent with Philip's estimates, a reason for the implant couldn't be discerned. The article was pivotal, corroborating Philip's findings and finally convincing the medical community that doctors weren't helping patients with a profligate pacemaker implantation philosophy. In addition, precious resources were being wasted, while the price of health care escalated under the pressure of rising device costs.

Philip regained his stature in the academic community. His alignment with public advocacy groups helped him gain his first appointment to a prestigious advisory committee at the FDA that launched his career as a clinical trialist. He earned the grudging respect of those who had been critical of his early work. Things had come together for Philip in a way he could not have foreseen, and he was in his ascendency to academic greatness until ... until Bonnie Romano and Hugh Hamlin sued him, and he lost everything.

Philip was determined not to let Gilbert risk his nascent career. Things might not work out as well for his young colleague as it had for Philip. He resolved to do whatever he could to guide Gilbert through a difficult situation.

But Philip should not have been worried because at that very moment, the man he was worried about was doing everything he could to ruin his life. Crawling out of the covers after his latest sexual adventure with Liz, hunting for his underwear, which had been tossed across the room during their passion, Gilbert tried to remember how he had gotten to his apartment.

What had started as a meeting to plan the educational program for referring doctors had morphed into plans for dinner and drinks to refine an agenda that, Gilbert knew, had been all but completed. Gilbert drove himself to the restaurant to meet Liz, who had insisted on getting into something more *appropriate* after work. Sitting in traffic, Gilbert reviewed how he would finally tell Liz that their affair was over. It was the best thing for both of them, as he hoped she would see. They might still be able to work together. Liz was an integral part of his practice and was very knowledgeable. But he had already resigned himself to the possibility that Liz might choose to walk away if she couldn't have him. As painful as it would be to retrain an associate, Gilbert understood Philip's admonition and agreed that getting over Liz was the first step in cleaning up his act and getting back to being a better doctor and person. Tonight was the night he would confront Liz and end their affair. Liz showed up looking as seductive as ever, having taken the time to redo her hair and change into a dress that revealed just enough of her curvaceous body to be alluring. Gilbert knew when she ordered him a second martini that he was headed for trouble, but he didn't demur. Liz told Gilbert not to worry about the agenda; she was pretty sure she would be able to put the meeting together, based on their conversation and the material Philip had sent. They should take a break and enjoy dinner and their time together.

The rest of the evening was a blur. They had discussed their future and its challenges before Liz offered to drive Philip home and help him to his door. He remembered flailing with his keys at the threshold and Liz laughing at his clumsiness. They finally got the door open and stumbled into the apartment, falling over the living room sofa, landing on top of each other on the floor. In his altered state, Liz pushing against him was too much for Gilbert, who rolled over on top of her and began to kiss her hard. Clothes began to fly, and their lovemaking began. Their "unplanned" sexual adventure eventually landed them in Gilbert's bed, where Liz now slept peacefully.

Gilbert staggered into the living room in his underwear and plopped onto the sofa, trying hard to remember the dinner conversation that came back to him in bits and pieces. He remembered telling Liz that he was uncomfortable with his adulterous affair, and Liz reassured him that she had no feelings for Noah and that she planned to leave him when the time was right. Gilbert tried to tell Liz that he needed to move on and that he didn't see their relationship becoming permanent, but Liz thwarted each of his arguments, desperate to keep him at all costs, willing to put aside plans for a long-term future if that was what Gilbert wanted. And when Gilbert expressed concern about her husband's temper and his strong desire to keep her, Liz countered with reassurances that she could control Noah and that Gilbert needn't worry about him.

Back and forth they went until Gilbert had finally given up, and Liz ordered the third martini, knowing that it would guarantee no further meaningful discussion but rather lead directly, as it had, to a tumultuous night of sex that she hoped would convince Gilbert to put aside his reservations, all the while strengthening her hold on the man she loved.

8

CHAPTER

The day of the clinical seminar finally arrived. As Philip had feared, Liz and Gilbert had selected an evening that followed a long outpatient schedule, so when Philip climbed into his car for the trip north, he was already exhausted. Even worse, since it was midweek, he would not be able to bail out and stay in his Pocono home after the meeting but would have to head all the way back to Philly to prepare for the next workday. But this was an arrangement with which Philip was highly familiar, having presided over hundreds of regional dinner programs for referring doctors over the years to stay in touch with them and to stimulate consultation. With the arrival of E squared, he had stopped giving up his evenings for such things, and Dorothy and he were glad for it.

"Do you miss it, Philip?" Dorothy had asked the previous evening over cocktails.

"It had its moments," Philip admitted. "It's fun to play the expert, and I do think I helped the docs get through some complicated issues. But it was definitely a long run for a short slide. I gave up a tremendous amount of time with my first set of kids to keep patients flowing into

Gladwyne, and look what it got me. They're gone and not coming back. I'm not making the same mistake with you and our babies."

To make matters worse, Liz and Gilbert insisted on convening the meeting at 6:30 p.m. so that the doctors could come directly from work and wouldn't be out too late. But they had also selected a restaurant considerably north of Wilkes-Barre, all of which meant that Philip would have the pleasure of slogging through rush-hour traffic pretty much the entire way to the meeting.

As he traveled north on the turnpike, he reviewed in his mind the topics he wanted to cover and the best way to get his points across without angering the participants. No easy task, as most doctors— cardiologists, in particular—were cocky and averse to having someone tell them they had erred in any way. Dorothy had exhorted him to stay positive. Start with the things that had been done correctly, and gently steer the discussion to the aspects that could be improved.

Despite his misgivings, Philip's journey was smooth. When he pulled up in front of the restaurant a few minutes after 6:30, he had to chuckle. Each time he did one of these restaurant programs, he was assured that the venue was one of the preferred eateries in the area. Each might have had its charm, like this old tavern, but rarely delivered anything better than a mediocre meal.

Philip's timing allowed him to make a grand entrance and be greeted graciously by Gilbert and a few other physicians who knew him personally or by reputation. While he mingled, Philip decided on a glass of the house cab, which he planned to nurse as long as possible. Important to be social but mentally crystal clear to take on the task at hand.

A few of the doctors had brought along their nurse practitioners or physician assistants, who had taken a table and were conferring among themselves. Philip immediately recognized Liz, clearly the most attractive and well-dressed of the group. As he turned from the bar, she rose from her table and walked over to him.

"Dr. Sarkis, great to see you again. I'm Liz Gold. We met at NorthBroad. Thanks for doing this program for us."

Philip surveyed the woman, having little difficulty understanding Gilbert's attraction. Liz was a stunning redhead with blue eyes, high cheekbones, and full lips that curled easily into a welcoming smile. He could see that if Liz turned on the charm, most men would be toast.

"Nice of you to invite me, Liz. Looks like you have a great turnout."

"Your reputation precedes you, Dr. Sarkis. People up here are eager to hear what you have to say about any topic."

"I'm sure the restaurant selection also helps."

Liz looked around. "Let's be honest, Dr. Sarkis. This place is OK but not what you're used to in Philly. The docs like it because the drinks and food portions are generous, and it's easy access from the hospital and their offices."

"And it's free."

"Yeah. Our hospital helped with the restaurant, and we got a few of the drug and device companies to throw in some money to pay for the drinks—and for you, of course."

"I'm not worried about getting paid, Liz. This is a favor for Ray."

"We know and appreciate that, Dr. Sarkis," Liz said, using the first-person plural to emphasize that she and Gilbert were a team. "But we can provide at least a modest stipend for your time and travel expenses."

"Yeah, turnpike tolls are pricey these days," Philip said with a laugh. "But I do appreciate that. When do you want to get started?"

"We thought we would get everybody's dinners in front of them and then start the discussion that can carry over through dessert and coffee."

"That's fine."

"You can either have something now, or you can eat after, or—"

"How about if you just package up my dinner, and I'll take it home with me?"

This was Philip's routine. He had never gotten over pre-lecture jitters that made early dining impossible, and he hated eating after the talk when all he wanted to do was get on the road. Better to wait until his stomach settled down on the ride home, and then he could eat uninterrupted in front of the late news with doggies by his side.

Dinner was announced a few minutes later. Philip sat at one of the four tables that had been set up in front of a podium and screen. He tried to chat with the participants he didn't know, shy men and women who, when they spoke did so self-consciously and with thick accents. The wait staff moved fairly quickly to take orders and bring out the salads. Liz came over to summon Philip to the podium, where Gilbert was preparing to make introductions.

"Hi, everyone," he started. "I'm Ray Gilbert, and I want to welcome all of you to our program this evening. Let me explain how we'll proceed. We've put together a few cases that we believe illustrate some important diagnostic points and management decisions. I'll present the cases, and we've invited Dr. Philip Sarkis to comment about each of them before opening the floor for discussion. We encourage each of you to be vocal and to ask a lot of questions. I would emphasize that these cases aren't real. We used elements from many cases to put together hypotheticals. I think you'll enjoy the opportunity to pick the brain of a person who has led the field of electrophysiology for several years."

Used to lead the field, Philip thought, *before I was deballed by a couple of scheming assholes.* He wondered how many people in the audience knew the backstory of his downfall, near suicide, and resurrection years ago. Or how he had spent the last few years trying to put the pieces of his life back together, finally finding redemption in the arms of his former lover and, more recently, in dedicated parenthood.

Philip's attention returned to the meeting just as Gilbert finished Philip's introduction. "And now, a professor of medicine and member of the cardiology faculty at NorthBroad; it gives me great pleasure to introduce my mentor, Dr. Philip Sarkis."

Polite applause as Philip rose to walk to the podium, where he shook Gilbert's hand and gave him the perfunctory hug. "I'm delighted to be here. It's always pleasant to see old friends and to interact with the very fine cardiology community in this region. As Ray said, we really want all of you to participate in the case discussions and to offer your opinions. There are no right or wrong answers; there are always multiple ways to approach complex cases. My goal is simply to point out what we know from trials and guidelines and to focus the discussion. The rest of it's up to you. So let's go ahead and get started. Ray?"

Philip stepped back so Gilbert could retake the podium.

"The first case involves a sixty-eight-year-old man who presented to the hospital in heart failure. He was treated and stabilized. Testing showed normal coronary arteries but greatly reduced cardiac function. His ejection fraction was less than 20 percent, and he had global dysfunction. No specific cause for this cardiomyopathy was uncovered. While on an extended external cardiac monitor, he had a lot of arrhythmia, including some short runs of ventricular tachycardia and, surprisingly, didn't cause symptoms. Questions about the case?"

From table two, a young physician asked, "Did he have a family history of heart disease?"

"Good question," Gilbert acknowledged. "His father had a heart problem and was found dead in his bathroom when he was in his fifties. And he also has a brother with heart failure."

"So this could be a familial problem, right?" the eager young doctor persisted. "Would genetic testing be of any help?"

"Let's have our expert answer that," Gilbert said, anxious to turn things over to Philip.

"Worth a try," Philip began. "Realizing that there's a high chance that a characteristic mutation is unlikely in this case. But if one were found, it would help to counsel the man's family, especially any male children or grandchildren. But there are some very compelling issues here we need to deal with. First, what are we going to do to protect this patient against dying suddenly like his relatives?"

One of the senior doctors at table three said, "He needs a defibrillator, right?"

Philip suppressed a smile. Someone had taken the bait. "He may eventually, but what about the timing?"

"I think he should get it right away. He had ventricular arrhythmia. I would hesitate to send him home without protection."

"You have hit on the reason we presented this case. Does anyone know what the guidelines recommend?" Philip asked. He had to keep from wincing. He was hardly a guideline fanatic, but in this case, they would make a useful point.

The answer came from the physician assistants' table. "They recommend that you wait several months before putting a defibrillator in a person like this."

"Why?"

Silence. *This is working perfectly*, Philip thought as he provided the answer. "Because a substantial percentage of people like this will have a significant improvement in cardiac function over time."

"How does that happen?" came a question from the back of the room.

"Many of these patients have a viral cause for their deterioration. When they clear the infection, the heart recovers. So you have to give them some time. What else can you do to protect this guy?"

From the nurse practitioners' table: "Optimize his medicines."

Philip smiled. He figured that the people who really take care of the patients would come up with the most appropriate answer. "Absolutely. We all want to provide protection with devices, but let's not forget that there are many drugs that can treat worsened heart failure and that actually reduce the chances of dying."

"Some of us have experience with the wearable defibrillator," said one of the young doctors in the audience, whom Philip didn't recognize. "What do you think about that idea, Dr. Sarkis?"

Philip had started out opposed to the idea of patients wearing a vest with electrodes that were attached to a defibrillator. Though bulky and sometimes uncomfortable, it had the ability to shock patients, just like an implantable device, if their heart went out of rhythm. It wasn't a long-term solution but Philip had to admit that it was useful as a bridge in specific clinical circumstances.

"I agree that this patient is at risk, so making sure he has a safety net could be important," Philip said as he prepared to deliver the most important message. "But it *is* too early to implant an ICD in this particular patient. Placing devices outside of guideline indications will just get you into trouble. First of all, it might not get paid for, and if something happens to the patient, you could be held negligent."

"Are there exceptions, Philip?" Gilbert asked, playing the diplomat.

"Of course there are. There could be several reasons to go out of guidelines. I do it myself, not infrequently. However, the most important thing to remember is to document everything you do. And make sure you talk to the patient and his or her family, and note that discussion in the chart so you can defend whatever decisions you make."

"Shared decision-making is an important concept; do you agree, Philip?" Gilbert asked the leading question.

"In every respect. But it's not a new idea. Patients and their families have always expected to participate in decision-making, especially when there's a lot at stake, like here." Philip waited for the lesson to sink in before turning to Gilbert. "I know this is a hypothetical case, but what do you think would have happened to this patient, Ray?"

"He could have gone home without a device, if that is what he and his family chose. If his cardiac function came back to normal on a good medical program, he likely would have been event-free."

Gilbert and Philip had decided that they would take the high road and not present cases with bad outcomes to castigate the audience. Happy endings sank in better and resonated with a clinical crowd such as this. But Philip couldn't resist the temptation to raise one more important issue.

"I agree with you fully, Ray. Even though devices protect, remember that most patients, maybe as many as eleven out of twelve, will be just fine with medication alone. The device provides added protection but is not an absolute necessity. So it's a good idea to be prudent in the way you present options to your patients. Don't insist on anything that doesn't make people feel a lot better unless the mortality effect is large. An example is putting in a defibrillator after a cardiac arrest, where the rate of recurrence is very high, and therefore the treatment effect is significant." Philip let his message sink in before asking, "Shall we move on to the second case?"

And so it went—Gilbert presenting the cases; the audience stumbling through their answers, in some cases completely unaware of pivotal trials upon which firm guideline recommendations had been fashioned. Philip did his best to pretend that some of the inane answers weren't so far off base, being as careful as he could not to slip and disclose his surprise at how little the audience seemed to know about the literature.

By the end of the fourth case, Philip had had enough. He gave Gilbert the cut-off sign, and fortunately, Gilbert was able to wrap things up just as the guests finished their coffee and dessert. Despite being famished and wanting to depart for home, Philip felt the need to ventilate. He restrained himself until he said his goodbyes to the attendees and the room had emptied out.

"Ray, do you have time for a nightcap before I shove off?"

"Sure, Philip. Let me say good night to Liz, and I'll join you in a minute. Order me a Balvenie on the rocks."

Philip gathered up his packaged dinner and found his way to the almost completely empty bar. He was halfway into his cognac when Gilbert appeared, shaking his head.

"That didn't go well, did it, Philip?" Gilbert asked, lifting his scotch glass and swallowing half in one gulp.

"Depends on what you mean by *well*," Philip answered. "If you mean, did we make progress and teach them something, the answer is yes. Did we elevate them to a real, good level of knowledge? The answer is no. It would take months of work to get those guys up to speed across all of the areas we know are important."

"So you think the reason for all of the unnecessary implants and inappropriate care up there is because they don't know any better?"

"Looks that way, but we can't exclude other motives."

"Like making more money by doing more procedures."

"Unfortunately, that's the way fee-for-service works, Ray. We're all piece workers, like it or not. And it won't change unless we figure out a better way to pay doctors."

"But what if they were getting kickbacks?" Gilbert posed.

"You mean from the device companies?"

"If you were the new kid on the block, like Sterling, why not provide, you know, an incentive?"

"That's pretty cynical, Ray. You're alleging criminal behavior. People go to jail for stuff like that."

"I'm not alleging. Just wondering."

"And how would you ever prove it?"

"I don't have to prove anything. All I have to do is be suspicious enough to report what I've observed."

"To whom?"

"I don't know. One of our professional organizations, maybe?"

Philip hunched over the bar, shaking his head. "Ray, that's a very dangerous idea. You better be damn sure you know what you're talking about before you start pointing fingers."

"Look, Philip. I don't know what the fuck is going on, but I've had at least a dozen cases sent down to me from the wilderness that stink to high heaven. I agreed to do this seminar tonight to help me figure out why, and you and I both have to admit that we still don't know. I'm not a detective, and I don't live with one, so either I hold my nose and put up with it, or I go to somebody and ask them to investigate the cases systematically."

Philip elected to ignore the oblique reference to Dorothy's skills and Philip's unique access to her expertise, not to mention her father's. Ray had done some homework.

"I understand your frustration, Ray. And what you're suggesting isn't outrageous. All I ask is that you think it through carefully. And, if you do go to someone, that you find out first how much you can trust him or her to keep your revelation confidential so you aren't pilloried by the doctors you rely on for referral."

Gilbert nodded. "Good advice, Philip. I promise to give this more thought and to be discreet."

"That's all I can ask, Ray. There are a lot of people who like to rake the muck. Making doctors look like a bunch of damned idiots sells newspapers and commercial time. Our profession used to be untouchable. Doctors were royalty, and no one dared question them. But the worm has turned. It's open season on the medical profession, and everybody is taking shots."

"How did it happen, Philip?"

"It was the perfect storm, Ray. First of all, we got greedy. With health insurance and especially with Medicare and Medicaid, our patients weren't paying the entire bill, so why not optimize payments? Medicine, with all of its well-intentioned technology, turned into a big business. That attracted snakes who saw a way to make a lot of money, and the doctors went along with it. Drug companies get a boatload of adverse publicity for their pricing policy, but that's only the tip of the iceberg. Medical insurance companies put feel-good commercials on TV and then suck billions out of the health care system, money that comes right out of the patients' pockets. And then we stupidly depersonalized medicine. We spend more time looking at the computer screen than talking and caring for patients, who are no longer cared for by a single doctor. Hell, when patients get admitted to the hospital or go to the ER, they have no idea who's taking care of them, so it's hard to hold anybody accountable. When the bills pour in, patients get angry, especially now with their ridiculously high deductible plans."

Gilbert just looked down and shook his head.

"OK, enough bitching," Philip said. "I could go on for hours about the demise of our profession, but it won't do either of us any good. All I suggest, Ray, is that you think this over carefully before you do or say anything to anyone who has an ax to grind. And remember, you can always bounce ideas off me. I want to be helpful."

"You already have, Philip."

"I hear my stomach growling, Ray, so I'm going to head home and have my dinner. Another long day of patients tomorrow."

Gilbert rose with Philip and gave him another man hug, this time like he meant it.

"Thanks, Philip. I really appreciate your advice. And I'm glad we hooked up again after so many years."

"Me too, Ray. Let's just hope that our little session tonight bears fruit, and those docs heed our advice," Philip said before walking to his car to begin his long journey.

9
CHAPTER

ut it didn't take more than a few weeks before the case arrived that broke Gilbert's back. It was a typical Wednesday afternoon in the clinic. Gilbert was seeing his own patients, while Liz tended to hers. Every hour or so, they would evaluate one together, usually a new patient to the practice or one with a particularly thorny problem, or both. Gilbert usually got the call from a referring doctor or the patient, reviewed the records cursorily, and then had Liz do the initial interview to ascertain the facts of the case and perform a preliminary physical examination, after which she would tell Gilbert about the case before he saw the patient with her. This particular day, she sashayed into Gilbert's office, closed the door, and slowly sank into one of Gilbert's desk chairs, making certain that Gilbert, who was dictating into the phone receiver, would notice her short skirt and low-cut blouse, covered not so well with her white lab coat.

"What do you have for us next, Lizzy?" Gilbert asked. He looked Liz up and down as he hung up the phone on which he had dictated his last follow-up note.

"You're not going to like this one, Ray," Liz warned as she arranged papers on her lap.

"Try me," Gilbert replied.

"We'll do that after work, Ray," Liz said flirtatiously, anticipating their weekly rendezvous.

"Your place or mine?"

"Noah's teaching night school this week—so I'm open for business. Literally."

"You must be horny."

"It's been a while, Ray."

"I've had a lot on my mind. And you do have a husband. If you would wear outfits like that at home, he'd be all over you."

"If he were sober enough to see me. When's he's not drunk, he's asleep, or he can't get it up, so I have to take care of myself ... myself. If you know what I mean."

"Stop it, Liz. We have to get our work done first."

"OK, Dr. Slave Driver. Work before pleasure. Like I said, this one is going to get your dander up. From what I can see, this thirty-one-year-old woman presented to her family doctor about ten years ago with palpitations."

"Who doesn't have palpitations?" Gilbert asked sardonically.

"I do, at certain times, as you well know."

"Come on, Liz. Quit fooling around. I want to get out of here before your husband gets home."

"OK, OK. She got them mostly at night, and they would wake her up from sleep."

"Then she made the mistake of telling her doctor about them, I bet."

"Precisely."

"And he, in turn, referred her to a cardiologist."

"Who made her sick with drugs."

"Let me guess what he gave her. Propranolol?"

"Well, actually, he tried several different beta-blockers before he finally gave up and referred her to an electrophysiologist."

"But not before he scared the living hell out of her."

"Yeah, she was pretty worked up by the time she got to Dr. Pescatora."

"The EP in Hazelton?" Ray asked.

"One and the same. He told her that drugs were a waste of time and recommended an ablation procedure."

"What kind of ablation?"

"He told her she had inappropriately high heat rates, and he would need to cauterize her normal heart pacemaker."

"That's a tough diagnosis, Liz. What proof did he have that her sinus node was firing too rapidly and needed to be ablated? That's pretty extreme, and it usually doesn't work so well."

"They put some monitors on her that apparently showed heart rates at rest that went up to 140 to 150 beats per minute when she was just sitting around, but I don't have the actual recordings."

"Did she have the ablation?"

"Hell yeah. Actually, she had three of them," Liz answered.

"And none of them worked."

"Right. After the last one, the patient was climbing the walls, so Dr. P. decided it was time to up the ante."

"I'm afraid to ask what *that* means," Gilbert said.

"Not much of this is reflected in the records—had to get it from the patient. But Dr. P. told her she had a very serious rhythm problem that would require ablating her normal conduction system and then putting in a pacemaker."

"Don't tell me he took out her AV node and caused heart block. Please!" Gilbert said, hoping he wouldn't have to deal with a young woman whose normal electrical system had been harmed beyond repair and who would need a pacemaker for the rest of her life.

Liz didn't respond to Gilbert's exclamation and continued her commentary, head down to read the handwritten notes she had made in the examination room.

"Dr. P. told her that he had spoken to a pacemaker company that assured him they had a wonderful device that could be implanted easily and that would control her heart rhythm perfectly, better than her own electrical system, and that she would feel much better."

"And she believed him."

"Apparently, because she went along with the plan and had the procedure about three months ago."

"And now she feels worse."

"Much worse. Her palpitations are now completely intolerable. They keep her awake at night. If she tries to exercise, she gets heart pounding, and she's nearly passed out a couple of times, including while she was driving a car."

Gilbert leaned forward, elbows on desk, head in hands. "What did you find when you interrogated the pacemaker, Liz?"

"I need you to look at the recordings I pulled up."

Liz came around the desk and placed the paper tracings in front of Gilbert for his perusal, standing close enough to give Gilbert a dose of her scent. The effect wasn't lost on Gilbert, who had to fight back his inclination to reach out and pull her down on top of him.

"I was afraid of this," Gilbert finally said, taking several seconds to examine the signals from the pacemaker. "She has an atrial tachycardia."

"Not coming from the sinus node?"

"Could be close to the sinus node, but it's behaving like it's coming from the atrial tissue itself."

"Which means?" Liz asked.

"That Dr. P. had the wrong diagnosis in the first place, or he actually caused this tachycardia with all of the burns he placed in this girl's atrium."

"It sounds like he was desperate to help her."

"Agree, which excuses some of his behavior. What I'm really worried about is his conversation with a pacemaker salesperson. Do you think that person may have convinced him to implant the device?"

"Don't know," Liz said. "The patient did say that the rep spent a lot of time with her and the doctor before and after the implant and was teaching Dr. P. how to program the pacemaker. What are you worried about?"

"I'm just worried that this is another example of a pacemaker company pushing docs to implant devices that aren't necessary."

"But what should Dr. P. have done when she wasn't getting better, Ray?"

"Call somebody for advice or refer her out to a center that sees a lot of this kind of thing. Not put in a permanent pacemaker."

"What should we do?"

"First of all, we need to take care of this patient," Gilbert answered. "Let's go talk to her and take a look at her medications and pacemaker programming and see if we can at least make her feel better."

"I suspect that getting some reassurance from you will go a long way," Liz said.

"Then I have to be a good actor because I'm not sure what happened myself. But yeah, I agree that a lot of her problem at this point has to be psychological after all she's been through."

Liz followed Gilbert down the hall and into the examination room. Once again, she was impressed with how much his demeanor changed when he was with a patient. He exuded patience and kindness and, after making a few minor adjustments to her drugs and her device, was able to reassure the patient she would improve, albeit slowly. They agreed to a follow-up appointment in a month to monitor her progress and to determine what would be required next.

Gilbert hacked his way through the rest of his schedule that afternoon, anxious to finish so he could spend some time snooping around on the internet before his rendezvous with Liz. What he eventually found satisfied his curiosity and made him anxious at the same time.

Following the scandals of the 1970s, during which several cases of unnecessary pacemaker implants had been discovered, professional organizations began to put into place registries by which they could at least track implant volumes for the most common devices and leads. At one point, there had been an attempt to track those devices to determine how long they remained in service, functioning normally. When funding to support those registries dried up, device companies continued to report their business volumes by region, and it was those data that Gilbert was anxious to examine. In essence, he was looking for objective evidence that what he suspected about device business in central Pennsylvania was actually true.

Gilbert started with the overall numbers and was not surprised to see that over the last several years, since statistics had been collected by professional organizations, the absolute number of device implants had increased everywhere in the US. There were several reasons for this growth: the aging of the population, the advent of interventional cardiology and new medicines that kept people with heart disease alive longer, and the aggressiveness of doctors who had been trained in the field of cardiac electrophysiology. Most important, a number of clinical trials had been completed that showed that implanting a device prophylactically in patients with advanced heart disease might save lives, which led to a profound proliferation in the number of implants.

Not so in other countries, Gilbert thought. Who else was willing to pump tens of billions of dollars into devices that saved a few lives? What other economy had that much money to burn? And despite their outrageous expenditure, no one had ever been able to prove that Americans got better health care or had better outcomes. *Capitalism run amok, it seems. Technology for technology sake*, Gilbert thought cynically.

But back to the task at hand. Despite the explosion in numbers, three major manufacturers continued to dominate the market, and although no one would ever be able to prove that they fixed prices, device costs were relatively similar among the vendors. That is, until about two years ago when a new manufacturer came online.

Sterling had been heavily financed by venture capitalists who reasoned that an alternative to the big three might be able to win over business, especially if they offered their devices at a reduced cost. Using the bait of equity interest, they were able to lure key people away from the established companies, who were able to kick-start the enterprise into a competitive position within just a few months of launch. Sterling made no secret of their intentions. They had little interest in research and development. They didn't plan to advance the technology significantly. Their game was market competition: enter a new market with a reliable product that was at least as good as state-of-the-art, entice business with better prices, maintain the business with impeccable customer service, and grow market share gradually and conservatively. Stay low on the radar screen for as long as possible, at least until the client base had grown to sustainability, and, above all, maintain modesty and sound business judgment.

Gilbert thumbed through business journal articles that at first had disrespected Sterling and even mocked their attempt to make it to the big time. How quickly the pundits had changed their tune, as the business strategy put forth by Sterling, simple enough for an MBA student to understand, proved to be highly effective, raising their market share in multiple regions of the country.

Their strategy was business keen. Rather than trying to persuade the so-called thought leaders of the value of their proposition, they focused their attention on ordinary practitioners, people who implanted a fair number of devices but usually weren't invited to the consultants' meetings or symposia put on by the big three. Sterling counted on getting their attention with a little TLC and a lot of time spent making them feel important. And it had worked. Despite the restrictions on gifts and payments that industry could dole out to doctors, and the Sunshine Act that made all of those payments public, Sterling figured out ways to make the local physicians feel good about what they were doing and motivated to implant Sterling devices.

A particularly popular tactic was to invite a young, newly minted electrophysiologist to be an investigator on a late-stage clinical trial. These were studies in which an already approved device was further evaluated to prove that some minor modification would provide a treatment advantage for patients. The results, of marginal clinical importance, would be presented by one of the young investigators at a third-rate scientific meeting, underwritten by Sterling in many cases. The company would help the physician write a paper, coauthored by similarly motivated colleagues, to be published in an obscure journal. The arcane process would move the needle on patient care by a scintilla, but the article reprints would be shared by company representatives, advising physicians of the "great advance," while pointing out that similar scientific opportunities existed for them as well.

Gilbert was close enough to the average docs to understand their desire to be courted but sensible enough to understand why their work was just a lot of wheel spinning. He may have been disappointed that they were so easily duped, but the question that remained on his mind as he left his office that evening was what to do about it. The afternoon case of the young woman with a new pacemaker had convinced him that doing nothing was no longer an option. He had to bring his suspicions to someone, and his late afternoon on the internet finally persuaded him to call the local medical society. The hour was late and the office closed, so he jotted down contact information and left the information on his desk blotter, intending to renew his charge the next day, after early morning rounds and before procedures.

Gilbert had all of this on his mind while he drove to Liz's house. It was a route he knew only too well. Despite the security of his empty apartment, Liz had insisted on having him to her bed regularly. A territorial issue, he suspected, and a chance for her to show off the vast array of lingerie that she had acquired just for him.

Husband Noah supplemented his meager salary by teaching night school courses at the community college. "Algebra for Morons," he would call his curriculum to anybody within earshot at the Sneaky Pete bar he liked to visit on his way home. "What the fuck are they going to do with algebraic equations while they're serving time for doing dope?" Noah would go on, ignored by just about everybody sober enough to realize what a loudmouth he was. Noah's after-class visits to the bar extended his nights out enough to provide Gilbert and Liz with their window of opportunity.

Their routine was perfected. Gilbert would park far enough up the street to deflect neighbor interest and come in through the back door. He would be greeted by Liz, two glasses in hand, always dressed seductively for the occasion, making sure that whatever she wore could be pulled off easily by Gilbert, who usually arrived more than ready to entertain. After a long sip of whatever wine Liz had selected, they would attack each other, staggering into the main-floor master bedroom in a twisted dance before collapsing on top of each other on the bed that Liz had carefully prepared with silk sheets, which would be removed and carefully laundered after their tryst. Liz never ceased to be amazed that Noah had never discovered hard evidence of her dalliances with Gilbert, despite the fact that she had violated their marital bed dozens of times.

Despite his obsession with the device situation, Gilbert's performance in bed this particular evening was no different from any other. He ravaged Liz, who reveled in Gilbert's passion. After satisfying himself in minutes flat, he proceeded to pleasure Liz with his mouth. Liz was at the height of orgasm when she heard a familiar sound that shut her down in milliseconds.

"Ray, did you hear that?"

"What?" Gilbert answered, coming up for air. "I didn't hear anything, but then, your legs were—"

"I'm not kidding, Ray. I heard our garage door go up."

Gilbert's love fog lifted quickly. "Are you fucking serious?"

"Get up. Get dressed. And hurry up!" Liz admonished as she grabbed a robe from the closet and made for the door.

"Where are you going?"

"To the living room. If that's Noah, I'll hold him off until you get out of here."

"What about the sheets?" Philip asked, as worried about what Noah might do to Liz as to himself.

"Take them off and throw them in my closet. I'll make up some story about doing the laundry and remaking the bed."

Gilbert nodded and scurried about the room, fetching his underwear and clothing, dressing himself, stripping the bed, and then making for a window exit. The window opened easily but the screen proved resistant to his attempts to unlatch it. He finally resorted to poking a hole and crawling through it, hoping that Liz could come up with another creative excuse for a busted screen. It didn't matter: Gilbert needed to get out of there at all costs to avoid a scene neither he nor Liz was prepared to handle.

Through the backyard, up the alley, Gilbert moved quickly until he was convinced that he had avoided Noah's mayhem. When he emerged farther up the street, he walked slowly to his car, trying to appear calm to any prying neighbors, while his heart was exploding in his chest. Just a few more steps and he would be safely away.

Fortunately, Gilbert had plenty of warning. He clearly heard Liz's voice, pleading with Noah to come back to the house. Then he saw Noah, running like a wild man toward his car, his face contorted with maniacal anger, screaming obscenities at Gilbert, making it clear that he was going to slaughter him on the spot for making him a cuckold. Gilbert fumbled for his keys, realizing that he had only a few seconds to get into his car and lock the door, which he managed to do, just as Noah came up on him.

Furious, Noah beat on Gilbert's windshield with his bare fists until, realizing the futility of using his hands, began to look about for a weapon. He found and hefted a rock that was one of several decorating a neighbor's garden. By this time, Gilbert had his car started and, with Noah out of the way, began to pull away from the curb, forcing Noah to hurl the stone at Gilbert's back window, which exploded on impact.

As much as he cared about Liz's welfare, Gilbert quickly decided that he had had a full dose of the Noah-and-Liz disaster of a marriage. His adrenaline rush finally subsiding, Gilbert was not inclined to return to extract revenge for his car damage or to witness any part of the ugly Gold household fallout, except for what he could see through his now highly transparent rear window.

10

CHAPTER

Gilbert arrived at work the next day, groggy after a night of worry. He had texted Liz several times with no reply. When he finally got to sleep, he was awash in nightmares, most of which ended with Liz's murder, the methods ranging from strangulation to vehicular homicide, always with Noah's contorted face featured in the grisly scenes. Gilbert was more than relieved to see Liz's Volvo parked in its usual place when he arrived at the hospital, and although it would be several hours until he saw her in the hospital, he was also happy to receive a text message from her, reassuring him that she had not been harmed by the rampaging Noah.

When they finally met for a coffee in the midafternoon, between Gilbert's lab cases, Liz provided a full explanation. Apparently, Noah had decided to cut short his usual stay at Sneaky Pete. After loading up with a few shots of Jim Beam, Noah decided it was a good time to see if he could score off of his sexy wife. But seeing his wife's car in the driveway with almost all of the house lights off had set him to suspecting that something sinister was going on and prompted him to walk around the outside of the house before entering. From Noah's angry account,

Liz and Gilbert were noisy enough that Noah could hear them easily from outside the bedroom window. He raised the garage door to flush whoever was in his bedroom and then followed Gilbert to his car. Liz wasn't able to stop Noah before he intercepted Gilbert, and the rest was obvious.

"I'm sorry that happened, Ray. I had no idea Noah would get home early."

"We should have figured it was going to happen eventually and been a little better prepared. Anyhow, I'm just glad he didn't clobber you."

"He threatened to. I was barely able to talk him out of it."

"He certainly wanted a piece of me. Fortunately, no harm."

"Except for your car."

"I'm insured. Just need to come up with some story to get the insurance company to pay for the damage. That's the least of my worries right now."

"Don't fret about Noah. He's pretty harmless when sober. I doubt he'll come looking for you any time soon."

"That's not what I meant. I called the state medical society today and registered a complaint."

"You did? I thought Sarkis talked you out of that idea."

"Fuck Sarkis. He's in his ivory tower and doesn't have to deal with this bullshit every day."

"So what did they say?"

"It wasn't a 'they.' It was a she—a clerk who took down my information and my complaint and promised that one of their physicians would call me back by the end of the day."

"To do what?"

"Not entirely sure. I think they'll review the case list I gave them and then decide if my charge has merit. If so, they'll refer it on to one of their committees. Maybe ethics. I went to their website and read some stuff, but it didn't make a lot of sense."

"Are you sorry you called them?"

"Yes and no. I had to do something, but I'm not sure this was the best thing. I guess I'll see what they have to say when they call back and then decide if I want to push on with the complaint."

But the call back from the medical society wasn't that day or even that week. Eight days later, Gilbert's office paged him for a call from a Dr. Norman Sage, whom Gilbert assumed was a doctor making a referral, but he was quickly corrected.

"No, Dr. Gilbert, you can't help me with a patient, but I may be able to help you. I'm a case officer with the state medical society. I believe you called our office with a complaint?"

"That was last week."

"Yeah, uh, right," Sage stammered. "Sorry about the delay in getting back to you. We're up to our elbows, as they say, so it took us a little longer to return your call. But here I am, at your disposal. What can we do for you?"

"Did the person I talked to relay any part of the problem I called about?"

"Clerks, Dr. Gilbert. Only clerks. All I got was some kind of problem with pacemakers."

"Then I guess I'd better start from the beginning."

For the next fifteen minutes, Gilbert reviewed the problem area, his suspicions, and why he thought an investigation of device implantation by the northern Pennsylvania electrophysiology community was in order. According to Gilbert, physicians in that area were implanting devices in patients who not only didn't need them but who were being harmed by unnecessary procedures. Gilbert tried to be as cut-and-dried as possible, providing a few examples, leaving out any reference to Philip Sarkis but mentioning the evening seminar as proof of his diligence in trying to get to the bottom of things himself.

Sage interrupted only a couple of times for questions while he took notes. At the end of Gilbert's exposition, Sage grunted. "There's a lot of stuff here, Dr. Gilbert. These cases sound complicated. I'll do the best I can with them, but I may need to get some outside help with my review. Is that OK with you?"

"What kind of help?"

"A cardiac electrophysiologist, if I can find one, or a cardiologist at least. I'm a retired baby doctor. This stuff is pretty foreign to me."

"My main concern is that this all stays confidential. If anyone up there suspects that I'm looking over their shoulders or criticizing their work to a professional organization, I'm afraid they would be angry and vengeful. I'd be in hot water at my hospital as well."

"We understand that here at the medical society, Dr. Gilbert. We want to hear from doctors, and we know that if they can't trust us, they won't speak up and tell us about their concerns. Now, that doesn't mean we can always take action. In many cases, we conclude that there was no improper behavior. Lots of times, it's just a misunderstanding that causes everyone to get their panties in a twist."

Panties in a twist? Strange way to refer to a legitimate medical issue with patients getting harmed, Gilbert thought. Sage sounded cavalier, but there was no going back now.

"All right, Dr. Sage. I understand, and I'll look forward to what you have to say. When do you think you'll have something for me?"

"Normally I'd say four to six weeks, but this one is a little more complicated, and, like I said, I'm going to need outside help. Figure no more than two months."

"Jeez, Dr. Sage. That's a big chunk of time in my world. If what I suspect is true, a lot of people could get hurt."

"Can't be helped. We only have a small staff here, and we get a lot of complaints and things to research. I'll try to expedite things, but I can't make any promises. I assume that you won't mind if we call you during the investigation for questions?"

"Of course not. I'm happy to help in any way, especially if it speeds things up."

Gilbert thanked Sage but was far from satisfied when he hung up. He talked about the situation with Liz. She told him that he needed to keep his mouth shut and wait for the medical society to offer its opinion.

Fortunately, despite his heightened sensitivity, Gilbert wasn't directly confronted with more than just a couple of concerning cases over the several weeks that followed, and in those he was able to make some kind of excuse for what may have been sub-ethical behavior. And as the weeks stretched into months, Gilbert's calls to Sage's office to inquire as to the status of the investigation became less frequent, as Sage's assistant's excuses became less plausible. Gilbert and Liz continued their dalliance, albeit with much more circumspection.

Sage's phone call to advise Gilbert that the medical society's investigation had concluded, after six months of delay, was anticlimactic. But Gilbert was still curious to see if his suspicions were validated by an impartial—if borderline competent—reviewer. Gilbert was told that he should schedule an appointment to meet with Sage and his staff at the medical society's office in Harrisburg. The meeting would take about an hour, after which the society would take appropriate action, if indicated. Sage reminded Philip that the deliberations would be closed and the documents sealed, if the society concluded that Gilbert's complaint was without merit.

Gilbert was able to clear his calendar and arrange the meeting for the next week. Liz offered to accompany him, but Gilbert decided that he didn't need the baggage. He had made up his mind that he would take no for an answer, that he wouldn't pursue the case further if the medical society found no wrongdoing. He didn't have the time or the inclination to play the caped crusader any longer, and Liz agreed fully.

But what Gilbert had not figured on—or even remotely anticipated—was what a mess the medical society investigation turned out to be. Whatever could be screwed up, was, including a clueless expert consultant who didn't understand the first thing about clinical electrophysiology. Clueless was bad enough, but the consultant was also imperious. He told Gilbert he decided to ignore the list of cases Gilbert had supplied, citing bias in the selection process, and audited a completely different list, almost all of which were not relevant to Gilbert's complaint. Sage himself was completely hopeless, demonstrating an almost epic ignorance of the issues that Gilbert was most concerned about and interpreting events in a way that a first-year medical student would find suspect.

Bottom line from Sage: "After months of intensive review, the medical society concluded that there was no impropriety." Less than 5 percent of implants in the region of interest were possibly unnecessary, about 15 percent were questionable but probably OK, and the rest were fine. Remarkably, implants of Sterling devices were the most pristine of all, achieving appropriateness ratings approaching 100 percent. Gilbert was informed that the medical society was so proud of their findings and thought they were so important that they had decided to inform the doctors and hospitals involved in their audit, to reassure them that they were doing the right thing. Gilbert needn't be concerned about the confidentiality breach. Sage was sure that all parties would understand why Gilbert had brought his concerns to the society—after all, he was only trying to do the right thing.

"So you're going to do nothing to stop the abuse?" Gilbert finally said.

"We may choose to continue to monitor the situation, Dr. Gilbert," Sage answered, obviously eager to move on to his next task. "But for now, there's no obvious abuse to stop. We'll decide about surveillance later, but we won't need your input further. Now, if you'll excuse us."

Sage and his minions filed out of the conference room, leaving Gilbert sitting alone on his side of the table, dumbfounded. He was so numb that he failed to become angry or hostile. He was like the belligerent Randle McMurphy, rendered placid with an electric shock to the brain in *One Flew Over the Cuckoo's Nest*, staring straight ahead, hardly aware of the staff he passed as he made his way out of the building. He staggered out into the sunny late morning and shuffled to his car for the ride home and his expected report to Liz.

"Ray, you need to forget about this investigation," Liz advised at the end of his unemotional recounting of the hearing outcome in his office later that afternoon. "You did what you could. They screwed it up and then screwed you over. It's time to get on with things."

"They informed the doctors and the hospitals about how their audit got started. They will be able to figure out thatI ratted them out. What do you think our administration is going to think about that?"

"We'll weather it, Ray. You and me together. We'll get through this."

"*We'll* get through this?" Gilbert asked sarcastically. "Is that you and me, or you and me and Noah?"

"Don't be an asshole. Noah isn't a consideration for me anymore, Ray."

"You'd better tell Noah that. I don't think he got the memo."

"Are you seriously thinking about taking this further, Ray?"

"I wasn't before, but I'm starting to change my mind."

"Why on earth?"

"For one thing, I have less to lose. Those assholes blew my cover, so my referral from that area is a goner. I hate it when somebody puts something over on me. This was a hatchet job. Sage and his henchmen wanted to defend the docs up there—for whatever reason—so they never gave my allegations a chance. They promised confidentiality, and now they're going to be broadcasting the news. Do you understand why I can't let this go?"

"So what are you going to do—call the *New York Times*?"

"Maybe."

"Before you do anything rash, I suggest you talk to Dr. Sarkis."

"Philip? Why would I do that?"

"Let's see. He was your mentor and is now your friend. You trust him. What other reasons do you need?"

Gilbert stopped talking. Liz was making sense, and he needed to stop being obstinate. "OK, you have a point. I'll call him and see what he thinks before I decide what to do."

"Excellent, Ray. Get a fresh take, and it will make whatever you decide easier to swallow—for everybody."

But Gilbert didn't have a chance to talk to Philip and ponder his alternatives. News of the medical society investigation and Gilbert's slap-down circulated like wildfire within the Pennsylvania medical community. When Philip heard the news from one of his techs at the hospital, he shared it with Dorothy over cocktails that evening, while Emily and Erin enjoyed their SpaghettiOs dinner, with red sauce that splattered their bibs, thoughtfully provided by Mom.

Dorothy was her usual level-headed self. "Ray needs to back off, Philip. I know you like him, and what he says may have some truth to it, but if he isn't careful, he's going to ruin his career—if he hasn't already."

Philip only nodded, slowly sipping a scotch on the rocks.

"Listen to me carefully, Philip. He can pull you into the mud with him, if he chooses. You need to distance yourself from him and his suspicions."

"I'm listening. He's on his own. I haven't spoken with him in months, and this appeal to the medical society was his idea entirely."

"The problem is that not everybody knows he contacted the medical society on his own. You helped him with that dinner meeting, and now he's drowning. Don't let him pull you down with him."

Dorothy's admonition was timely because the call from Gilbert came the very next day. But Gilbert sounded nothing like a desperate drowning victim to Philip.

"Hi, Philip. How are you?" Gilbert started, cheerfully enough.

"I'm fine, Ray. How about you?"

"Been better, I guess. I need to run something by you, Philip. Something's worrying me."

"Does it relate to the medical society's report, Ray?

"So you heard."

"Some of it. What's your take?"

"I was bushwhacked, Philip. Not only did they do a crappy job, but I think they wanted to hurt me, hanging me out there like that. Not sure why, but I suspect it may have been an 'old boy' kind of thing."

"That's possible, Ray."

"They blew my cover, Philip, after I asked them to be careful."

"Do you have any recourse?"

"I guess I could appeal their findings, but I feel like that's a waste of time."

"So what are you asking me, Ray?"

"What would you do at this point?"

Philip harkened back to Dorothy's advice. Not only was Gilbert's battle futile, but the struggle had the potential to pull Philip into the muck as well. Philip wasn't sure if his answer to Gilbert wasn't selfishly motivated, but out of his mouth it came. "Drop it, Ray. You've done enough."

"That's it? That's all you have to say?"

"What else do you want me to say? This thing has turned into a fucking mess, and you're not going to make it better."

"So I just let the assholes go on putting in pacemakers that aren't necessary and doing business as usual?"

"Ray, you don't know how many of those pacemakers and procedures were needless. You asked a reputable organization to do an audit, and they did. Now you want to reject their findings. I understand your skepticism, but without more evidence, I think you need to put this away."

"My reputation is screwed now—you know that."

"Go to your chief, explain what happened, plead your case, and ask them to keep you on. You're an attractive practitioner, Ray. I'm sure you can cultivate referral from other places. You need to make them know that. And remind them that there are a lot of people who think you're a good person for speaking up."

Silence as Gilbert processed what he had heard.

"Ray, I'm not abandoning you. You're my friend, and I'm happy to help you. I just don't think that pursuing this case is going to work, and I know it's not in your best interest."

"OK. Thanks for talking to me, Philip."

"Sure, Ray. Call me any time. In fact, why don't you plan to come down here to NorthBroad soon? I'd love to have you do a fellow seminar, and we can do lunch afterward and catch up. What do you say?"

"Great idea, Philip," Gilbert answered without a speck of sincerity.

"Shoot me some dates when you're available," Philip continued, undeterred by Gilbert's obvious disinterest.

They hung up shortly thereafter, each knowing that the other's message had not been well received. Gilbert was disappointed in Philip's lack of direction. And Philip was afraid that he—and the rest of the world, for that matter—had not heard the last of the Ray Gilbert crusade.

11
CHAPTER

The next few months of Gilbert's life resembled a neoclassical tale of descent into hell. Liz continued to pursue him, but he was so preoccupied with his job and Noah's threats that when they did manage to find the time and place to get into the sack, he couldn't perform. Liz pretended it was no big deal, but he knew that she wasn't particularly interested in sparkling conversation. And as word spread that Gilbert had turned on fellow physicians, his colleagues became less inclined to get together to grab a beer. He had to smile at the ridiculous excuses his friends came up with to keep him at arm's length. He had become the social pariah of the Lehigh Valley.

So Gilbert started hanging out at bars by himself and drinking too much. With no one to monitor him, he got behind the wheel and drove home too many nights in an impaired state. Fortunately, he got away with it—until one night when he fell asleep, swerved off a street in Bethlehem, and took out a mailbox and fence. He woke up quickly enough to realize what had happened and to confirm that there were no witnesses. After seeing there was minimal damage to his car, he knocked on the door, apologized for the damage, and paid off the owner with two or three times the cost of repairs in exchange for keeping the incident from the authorities and his insurance company.

Though that was the end of bar visits for Gilbert, it didn't stop his drinking. He now had the good sense to imbibe in the privacy of his apartment, which began to look like a tornado had torn through it. He surveyed the increasing mayhem each morning, vowed to clean it all up after work, only to succumb to the temptation of the spirits pretty much when he came through the door every evening. The cycle continued, day after day, interrupted only when he was on call, when he knew that his drinking could cost a patient her life. On those evenings, he was able to still the jitteriness with a small dose of Xanax, just enough to get him to sleep but not too much to keep him from answering "the bell."

Gilbert had almost completely severed contact with his family and talked to his parents only under duress. Neither approved of his career-wrecking behavior or anything else that he decided for himself, and they had no desire to see him. His sister, the parental favorite by far, lived with her husband in Wyoming. Darlene had been in the habit of calling him once or twice a month but was now completely dissuaded from this practice by recent events, most notably Linda's death, whom Darlene had adored. The long periods of phone silence now served to remind them both how far apart they had grown.

When his personal life had been ravaged in the past, he had found solace in his work. But now, the hospital was his principal source of misery. Whereas Gilbert had previously enjoyed a rich referral practice, most of the cardiologists and internists in the area now actively shunned him. Doctors hated criticism, and they now harbored a mostly irrational fear that Gilbert would not only disparage their practice decisions but look for ways to shut them down if he disagreed with the way they did things. Gilbert was a demanding type, and he hadn't been averse to reminding doctors of their mistakes. But he had always been careful to remain friendly and diplomatic for practical reasons.

But all of that didn't matter a whit because as far as the medical community in the Lehigh Valley was concerned, putting up with Gilbert was not only risky but totally unnecessary. Gilbert was far from the only electrophysiology resource in the middle of Pennsylvania, where the number of arrhythmia experts was easily in double digits. Better, the referring doctors opined, to move on to other consultants, many of whom provided service at the same hospital where Gilbert worked.

Gilbert's outpatient and procedure calendars began to look like plain white wrapping paper, a situation he hated for a number of reasons.

Yes, it gave him some time to do other things, like teach and conduct research, but, as with almost all medical centers, clinical revenue was the currency of power. Since a large percentage of Gilbert's salary was based on patient billings, he was making less money. Perhaps as important, his ability to request and build laboratories, to buy new equipment, and to hire staff was seriously curtailed. There was a reason why cardiologists wielded so much power at medical centers—and that reason was green.

Nevertheless, despite watching his life come apart, Gilbert didn't sit still. Determined not to fail, he actively sought new referral sources and came up with a number of ideas for unique programs, designed to entice patients from other regions to visit his hospital. He used his own money to buy time on the radio to advertise for patients to join new clinical trials that he was supervising. He made himself available for any public gathering that would lend itself to a discussion of health-related topics. People liked to learn new things about heart disease. After all, cardiovascular disease was the most common cause of death and disability in the US, and the public was continually reminded of that in the barrage of hospital advertising for cardiology products and services on radio and television.

Though a few new patients trickled into his clinic as a result of his efforts, his patient numbers remained grossly deflated. Those who did come to see him usually didn't need a procedure, and procedures generated money. With his revenue generation in free fall, he correctly figured that it was only a matter of time before the hammer came down. It struck in the form of a dreaded invitation from the head of the hospital to attend an "informal" meeting in the executive office.

Though he was not given the courtesy of being informed of the purpose of the meeting, Gilbert expected it would be about his falling revenue. After all, hospital administrators dedicated most of their time to revenue generation and how best to optimize it. What Gilbert didn't know and couldn't have expected was that the hospital CEO, James Baldwin III, had invited the chair of the Department of Medicine, the chief medical officer, the chief of the Division of Cardiology, the chief financial officer, and the head of the legal department to join the slugfest. Gilbert walked in and almost starting laughing as he looked about the room, trying to figure out the best place to sit to avoid getting caught in the inevitable crossfire.

"Thanks for joining us, Ray," Baldwin started.

Gilbert just stared back and grinned, thinking, *What choice did I have, asshole?*

"I believe everybody knows everybody in the room, so let's get started, shall we?" Baldwin opened his notebook and, with a flourish, took out a fountain pen, the cost of which could have supported the daily economy of a small African nation.

What's the hurry? Gilbert thought as he found a vacant chair. *Got nothing better to do than to sit here with you tight-asses.* Looking around the table, he noted how similar they all were. All men, all graying, decked out in their pinstriped suits and silk ties. *When did doctors start looking like and acting like administrators? And when did administrators become the doctors' bosses? When did medicine get off track and let the financial world rule the clinic? Can doctors ever get their profession back from the moneychangers?* he asked himself—idle rumination because he knew what the outcome of the meeting was going to be, and so did everyone else in the room. The proceedings were pro forma.

"As you probably know, Dr. Gilbert, several of us have been keeping a close watch on your clinical activity over the past several months, and we're concerned," Baldwin said.

If he keeps using first-person plural pronouns, like we *and* us, *I'm going to smack him upside his head,* Gilbert thought. *Who does he think he is, the fucking Queen?*

"Concerned with what aspect, Jim?" Gilbert asked, using Baldwin's first name to deflate his importance.

"There are several things we wanted to discuss. First of all, that messy business with the medical society."

"I explained to Ben Gault, my chief, what happened. The inquiry was supposed to be confidential. I had no idea they would divulge my identity to doctors and hospitals up there."

"You should have talked to one of us or to our legal department *before* you registered the complaint, Ray. That was a big mistake."

"Why? Would you have counseled me not to lodge the complaint?"

"I don't know, Ray. You didn't give us a chance to help you with that decision. You went off on your own."

"Because I felt—no, because I *knew* it was the right thing to do."

"Understandable, but maybe we could have helped you navigate to a reviewer with a tad more sophistication. Somebody who wouldn't be stupid enough to expose the identity of the person making the inquiry."

Gilbert was silent. Baldwin had a point.

"But that's all water over the dam, isn't it? The question now is how to deal with the repercussions," Baldwin continued.

"You mean the fall off in referral."

"And revenue," chimed in the CFO, who said the words while keeping his eyes on the laptop computer screen in front of him, as if it contained up-to-date information on how much money the medical center was losing because of Ray Gilbert's big mouth.

"I'm doing everything I can to get things back up to where they were," Gilbert said, realizing he sounded like a child who was trying to piece together a glass window shattered by his baseball. Eager to succeed but destined to fail. Nevertheless, Gilbert went on to list the measures he had taken to get his patient numbers up. But his words hardly registered and were received with ennui by just about everyone at the table, who felt they had better things to do with their time than listen to a grown man whimper about his business failures.

Baldwin allowed Gilbert to finish his whining and then closed the notebook he brought to every meeting. Nobody knew what he did with the copious notes he took, but closing the book was the signal to the underlings that His Royal Highness was finished with the proceedings and about to depart with a few pithy closing words.

"Ray, we're very grateful for all of your hard work here at our hospital. You have been an asset to our cardiology program. I really mean that. And I understand why you petitioned the medical society about the possibility of unnecessary pacemaker implants, and I'm sorry that it all turned to muck. But we have to get past that incident, and you have to rebuild your program. I know you can do it, Ray. This meeting is just to let you know that we understand, and we're ready to help you in any way we can ... over the next six months."

Nods around the table.

"I suggest you and Ben Gault meet again in a few weeks to see how you've progressed, and Ben can give the rest of us an update. Is that OK with everyone?"

If it's not, I can go screw myself—right, JB, old boy? Gilbert thought.

"Anything else?" Baldwin asked. "If not, I have to move on to another meeting."

Baldwin rose and left the room swiftly, followed in close sequence by the others, each trying to reach the door without getting engaged in conversation and avoiding eye contact with Gilbert. Only Ben Gault, the chief of cardiology, stayed behind. He waited until the room had emptied, closed the door, and took a seat next to Gilbert.

"That was one of the most uncomfortable meetings I've ever attended," Gault said with a sigh.

"Really? It wasn't as bad as I thought it was going to be. At least they didn't flog me."

"You realize what just happened?"

"Yeah. Baldwin pretended that he gives a shit about me and wants to help me out. What a load of crap."

"Much worse than that, Ray. Did you hear that six-month deadline thing? What that means is you have six months to right the ship, or you're a goner."

"As in, out of here? They can't do that. I have a contract."

"They also have a shitload of lawyers who will find some way to cashier you for cause. They might have to give you a payout of some kind, but it'll be paltry, and you'll be history."

"You're my section chief, Ben. Can't you do something about this? Baldwin just told you to monitor my clinical activity. Tell him I'm making progress."

"Are you naïve or in denial? First of all, Baldwin isn't going to depend on me to judge your progress. He'll sic his drones on it, and believe me, they'll know what you generate in revenue down to the penny. Second, I don't have any real authority around here, Ray. Doctors lost that war long ago. You know that. Suits rule; docs drool."

"Docs generate the revenue, Ben. We make the money that keeps the lights on."

"And administrators suck our blood. They have it wired, Ray. First of all, they own us. We sold our practices to them. Read the fine print; they get to do with us whatever they want. And they have stacked the hospital boards with their cronies who rubber-stamp any fly-by-night idea they come up with. They rake in profits, pay no taxes, dole out a pittance to doctors and nurses, assume no liability, and pad their salaries and decorate their offices using money we make with our sweat."

"So we're screwed?"

"Pretty much. Most of us, anyway. A few very large groups in specialties, like orthopedics and GI, have been able to build their own surgery and endoscopy centers, but they're the exception. Cardiac surgeons tried too, but they fell flat on their faces."

"What do you suggest I do now?"

"Ray, time to reality check. You're not getting your referral back, and you aren't going to be able to make up for what you lost with frigging radio ads for dumb-ass clinical studies."

"Wait a minute, Ben—"

"Shut up and listen, Ray. You're finished here in the Lehigh Valley.

Face it. If you want to continue practicing medicine, you're going to have to leave the area and start over. The Southwest would be a good place to look. The population is growing there, and no one will care if you dissed a bunch of docs in Butt-Fuck, Pennsylvania. I'd be happy to write you a letter of reference, for whatever that's worth."

"Worth a lot, Ben."

"Maybe. Depends on where you look. Anyhow, that's my advice, Ray."

"Get out of Dodge. Thanks for the advice, Ben. Definitely something to think about over the next—"

"Six months, Ray. And don't assume they'll give you five minutes more." Gault stood and patted Gilbert on the shoulder. "I like you, Ray; always have. I think you're a principled guy, trying to do the right thing for patients. That's why we all went to medical school. The problem is that no one in a position of power in health care truly gives a shit about the patients. They say they do, but they're fucking hypocrites, Ray. All they care about is money and profits. The sooner you understand that, the less frustrated you'll be. Not happy, just not furious."

Gault left Gilbert alone with his thoughts. Thoughts that continued through the evening and the Big Mac dinner that he got at the local drive-through. As bad as the day was, at least it was finally over. Until Noah Gold decided to pay him a visit.

Gilbert stumbled his way into his bedroom at about 10 p.m. The six beers he used to wash down his three Big Macs had prepared him for a reasonable night's sleep. He maintained consciousness long enough to change into scrubs that he used for bedclothes, to brush his teeth, and to feed his goldfish before collapsing into bed. How long he had slept before the screaming outside his window commenced in earnest was unclear, but it awakened him from a hard slumber.

The first word Gilbert could make out was *cocksucker*. Figuring that he could not possibly be the object of such scorn, he rolled over and tried to go back to sleep. But more profanities floated up to his window, now clearly directed at him, in a voice scarily familiar.

Gilbert leaned out his window. "Noah, you sick fucking drunk. What do you want from me?"

The answer was somewhat predictable. "I want to cut off your dick, and stuff it down your throat."

The day's frustrations boiled over as Gilbert decided to let it all out, the neighbors' sensibilities notwithstanding. "Why? Because I screwed your wife? Oh, wait a minute. Wrong tense, Noah. I should have said, because I've *been* doing her for months? Is that what's pissing you off, Noah?"

"I'm going to kill you, Gilbert. I swear to God."

"Bring it on, Noah. Any time you think you're man enough. And sober enough."

Back and forth they went until one of the neighbors leaned out his window and threatened to call the police, something neither wanted. Gilbert slammed his window shut as Noah retreated to his car, stumbling through foliage.

Gilbert lay on his bed, breathing heavily. Sleep was only moments away, thanks to the beers, but first, a moment of lucidity, afforded occasionally to drunken souls—insights rarely made in a sober state but appearing to the drunk as clear as day. Truth at the bottom of the bottle, some called it. Ben had been spot-on, and Noah had simply put the icing on the cake. He wasn't going to win a war with Baldwin and his henchmen, and Noah was going to continue to harass him. He would have to leave Pennsylvania and soon, without Liz. The only question that remained was how much scorched earth he was going to leave behind on the way out, before pursuing his fractured profession and lonely life somewhere new in the good ol' U. S. of A.

12

CHAPTER

Between Gault's frank assessment of his work situation and impending termination and his Noah-induced Liz problems, Gilbert felt like he had hit rock bottom. And when that happened, he generally found his way to the bottom of liquor bottles on an increasingly frequent basis. When he felt like he needed serious anesthesia, he drank alone at home, where he could guzzle as much as he wanted without worrying about a bartender keeping count or getting behind the wheel of a car. Gilbert liked the taste of beer but realized he needed hard stuff to do the job in a reasonable period and without inducing a massive diuresis that kept him standing over the toilet bowl for half the evening. Single malt scotch whiskey was his favorite, but with his newly reduced salary, he couldn't afford to buy enough of that stuff to get his high. Although Gilbert hadn't yet resorted to Ripple, he made it a point to look for bargains at the liquor store where he purchased his spirits.

This particular week, he had stocked up on a bourbon that tasted OK, had a high enough alcohol content, and wouldn't break the bank. His routine was to sit in front of the TV screenwith a bowl of chips and a glass with ice and just go to town on the hooch. He favored sporting events because they required no thought, so there was less chance his brain would activate and slow his descent into unconsciousness, which, after all, was the goal of the exercise.

But as easy as it was to escape by drinking heavily at home, Gilbert's progressively pickled brain realized that he couldn't sustain solo drinking over the long term. It made him feel even more lonely and depressed, in addition to causing a hell of a hangover. So he returned to visiting a couple of local bars, most of them better termed "meat markets," where he could at least indulge in some socializing. He got to know the bartenders at each place and quickly learned enough about them to know what they liked to talk about. In turn, they would set him up with his customary shots and beer, throwing in the occasional freebie. If he happened to meet another customer at the bar, he would start to chat. With women, he was careful not to put out sexual signals unless he was truly impressed, which he occasionally was.

Gilbert had also become savvy enough to take an Uber or Lyft from his apartment because he was never in shape to drive himself home on nights when he didn't get lucky. And it was pretty easy to summon a ride home when he happened to wake up in the middle of the night in a strange bed. There were a few occasions when he couldn't figure out where he was, which necessitated waking up the sweet young thing to help him. But because heavy drinking was always the goal, Gilbert didn't score very often. He was a good-looking guy and could have done better if he hadn't slurred his words or unleashed a spray of spittle in the middle of introducing himself to likely prey.

It was on one such evening that Gilbert met Tiffany Springer. He had just arrived at Twisty's, a pretty good local eatery with a bar that was generally packed with people looking to meet people. He had to elbow his way up to the bar and wait until he could catch the attention of one of the bartenders. Gail, his favorite, saw him, smiled, put two fingers up in the air, and returned a few minutes later with a shot of Jim Beam and a bottle of Yuengling, which he took away with him in search of a place to drink it. The few stand-up tables around the bar were heavily occupied, though one was being held solely by a pretty woman, elbows propped, sipping from the straw of a multicolored drink that was covered in an umbrella.

Gilbert walked over. "Mind if I share your table?" he asked.

"Help yourself," she said, turning her shoulders away from Gilbert— certain body language for *Not interested, pal*.

Gilbert decided to push. "Come here often?"

"Who me?" the woman answered, shifting back toward Gilbert slightly.

"I don't see anyone else at this table."

"Sorry." She smiled. "I come in now and then. I was supposed to meet a friend, but she texted me a few minutes ago that she can't make it."

"So you're out of here?"

"Soon as I finish this drink. Why?"

"You're cute and seem nice. I'm single and thought we could get acquainted."

"I like your honesty. I'm Tiffany Springer. And you are?"

"Ray Gilbert," he answered, sticking out his hand, which she grasped firmly. "Nice to meet you."

"Same here. And what does Ray Gilbert do for a living, if I may ask?"

"Ray is a cardiologist at Allentown Hospital."

"Well, is he now?" Tiffany said with a smirk. "Ray wouldn't be making that up to impress me, would he?"

"Ray would do a lot of things to impress such a beautiful and bright woman, but fortunately, he doesn't have to lie about his profession."

"Hmmm, I see."

"Which leads to the question, what about Tiffany? I assume she's single as well."

"Yes. Divorced, actually. I'm a journalist." She pushed her long hair back, sipped from her straw, and peeked over the edge of the umbrella to gauge Gilbert's response.

"Wow, what kind of journalist?"

"Newspaper reporter and columnist."

"Local paper?"

"*Allentown Times Herald.*"

"Yes, know it well."

"Then perhaps you've seen my column. I specialize in medical issues. Try to help the public understand what's going on in the medical world and how it relates to them."

"Sure. In fact, I think you interviewed me over the phone a few years ago. A piece on implantable defibrillators."

"Right. I remember your name now."

"Too bad we didn't do the interview in person. That photo at the top of your column does you no justice."

"Thank you, Dr. Gilbert."

"Ray, please. Can I get you another one of the things you're drinking?"

"Sure."

"You'll have to tell me the name of that concoction."

"Just tell Gail to give you one of her special drinks."

They stood talking at the table for almost an hour, nursing their refills, until Gilbert suggested that they find a real table and he buy her dinner. At first, Tiffany demurred, but it only took a little coaxing to change her mind. They spent their time over their meals getting to know each other, reviewing their lives to date, focusing on how each had found their way to where they were, and what they were doing.

They lingered over coffee, each unwilling to call it an evening until Tiffany finally said, "Ray, I really gotta go. I have an early day tomorrow, and I don't like leaving my dog at home too long by himself. He's a rascal, and I suspect he's already munching on something in my closet."

"I understand," Gilbert said. "Could I see you again?"

Tiffany opened her purse, took out one of her business cards, and handed it to Gilbert. "Call me, and we'll see." She leaned over and gave him a peck on the cheek before swiftly making her way to the door. He thought about going back to the bar to get hammered, but for one of the first times in weeks, he chose relative sobriety. After arriving home, he was able to fall asleep and stay asleep, waking without the hangover that had become a regular part of his new existence.

There was no question that he was going to call Tiffany and try to see her again. The question was, when? Soon enough to prove he was truly interested, but not too soon so as to appear eager or even desperate. And which venue to propose for next time? He finally decided on an upscale restaurant in Bethlehem. Tiffany sounded pleased to hear from him, agreed with his suggested time and place, and their first real date was set.

Gilbert decided to drive this time to make it easy for Tiffany and to put a brake on his drinking. He wanted to get to know Tiffany before he invested in a relationship, and he knew he would learn more and put on a better front himself if he didn't get shit-faced. Dressed up, Tiffany really was an attractive woman. Soft brown hair that she wore up on this occasion, a pair of sparkling blue eyes, with a heart-shaped face and soft white skin. *Cherubic* was the word that came to Gilbert's mind as he watched her walk toward his car.

Dinner was a success. They went through the ordinary small talk while ordering cocktails and appetizers. Gilbert felt comfortable talking to Tiffany, who seemed genuinely interested in what he did for a living and his personal life so far. Gilbert described how he had lost Amelia and lied about how much he missed her. He made up stories about his first marriage, making it sound as if it were matrimonial bliss instead of the torture it had become. Tiffany admitted that she no longer liked her former husband but chose her words carefully to avoid sounding spiteful. Better to gloss over the tough parts and try to conjure up at least a few pleasant memories. Both were happy that they hadn't had children, understanding how complicated that would have made their lives. "I'm just happy not to be tied to my ex," Tiffany remarked.

Finally, after a little red wine, the conversation got more serious.

"So, Ray, tell me a little about your work."

"Funny you should ask. Things at work have been rough lately."

"Do you want to talk about it?"

Gilbert smiled. "Off the record, Tiffany?"

"Seriously, Ray. What kind of person do you think I am?"

"The stuff I have been dealing with has the potential to blow a lot of people out of the water."

Tiffany tried to alleviate Gilbert's concern. "We're here as friends, Ray. This is not an interview. Nothing you say will ever be repeated. You have my word."

Gilbert was silent, head down, while he considered unburdening himself to Tiffany. There was no question that he needed someone to talk to—someone who would understand his predicament. Liz served that purpose, but he had decided that leaving her was probably the best way to keep Noah from making good on his threats. On the other hand, this was a reporter who had an interest in health issues, and he barely knew her. What would keep her from using what he told her and going forward with an exposé?

"I could use a sounding board, Tiffany. I really could. This thing has been eating me up."

"I don't know how to convince you, but you can trust me, Ray. I promise."

"Then I need to start at the beginning," Gilbert said as he launched into his story, starting with the first few cases that had roused his suspicion, through the Sarkis intervention, and all the way to the medical society debacle. Tiffany listened closely, occasionally asking questions, intent on letting Gilbert get it all out before reacting.

"Quite a story, Ray; I must agree. How sure are you that those doctors up there are doing bad things to patients for money?"

"At first, I wasn't convinced. But I've seen too many cases to ignore the possibility. There's a lot of money in medical devices, and enough people in the industry who only care about making more of it."

"What are your options at this point?" Tiffany asked, already pretty sure of the answer.

"Not too many. I suck it up and try to stay, or I leave and go somewhere else to practice. What irks me is that if I do either of those things, the people who may be hurting patients are going to get away with it."

"What about going public with your case?"

"That would just throw gasoline on the fire, wouldn't it?"

"Not if you do it correctly."

Ray rolled his eyes. "And should I assume that you know how to do it 'correctly'?"

"Look, Ray. I'm trying to be helpful here. I'm not bird-dogging a story. Just trying to be your friend."

"I'm sorry. It's just that I've had so many people try to take advantage of me recently. I guess I don't know who to trust."

"Well, I know you don't trust me fully yet, Ray, but maybe you should think about what I've suggested. What are the pros and cons?"

"If I decide I'm going to leave Allentown no matter what, then telling the story to the public probably won't make a difference in my career. But could I get sued for it?"

"Not if it's handled properly and it's the truth, which is the best defense against a libel claim. And don't forget that there may be a reward for the person who blows the whistle on a corruption case."

"I don't care about that, but do you really think going public would help patients and doctors?"

"Anything that increases their understanding of their disease will help patients. Some doctors will immediately hate you for exposing your brothers, but if you're right, most will come around eventually. It might be rough on you for a while, but I think you can handle it."

"I don't have much time. If my boss is right, they'll cashier me in six months, regardless."

"Tell you what. Give it some thought over the next few days, and we'll talk about it again. For tonight, let's just concentrate on having a nice dinner and maybe a nightcap at my place."

"Sounds like a plan. Thanks for understanding my reticence. I really want to do the right thing for patients. That's my principal motivation."

"Mine too, Ray."

The rest of the evening was as pleasant as Tiffany predicted. After dinner, Gilbert drove Tiffany back to her apartment and was invited up for a drink and to meet her frisky pup. Though the evening ended with a longish good night kiss, things progressed no further, although Gilbert sensed that Tiffany was definitely interested.

What Gilbert didn't know was that Tiffany was *very* interested but not in Gilbert as much as the story he had to tell. Tiffany marched directly to her senior editor's office on arrival at the newspaper office the next morning. She was so excited to talk to Ned Armbruster that she could barely get her words out.

"Ned, you aren't going to believe who I stumbled into at one of the local bars."

"I told you they're good places to meet interesting people," Armbruster said.

"This was just pure luck. The schmuck came on to me at Twisty's last week. I looked him up when I got home and was intrigued. I kept my fingers crossed, and sure enough, he called for a date. Last night at dinner, he recited his story like a schoolboy."

Tiffany proceeded to summarize Gilbert's saga, emphasizing the issues that were inflammatory and likely to attract the interest of the readership. Armbruster sat quietly, gently massaging his scraggly beard, not wanting to interrupt Tiffany, who, judging from her bloodshot eyes, had obviously been up most of the night, trying to come up with the best way to configure the scandal for an article. She concluded with the most important question: "What do you think, Ned?"

"I agree," Armbruster said. "You're onto something, but the story is going to depend on this guy Gilbert working pretty closely with you and coming up with as many details as he can remember. He's going to have to point you at specific physicians, who hopefully will talk to you, so you can get their sides of the story. There's a lot here. If you play your cards right, we might be able to make it a multipart series."

Tiffany was excited. "If we can substantiate that a pacemaker company was incentivizing physicians to put in unnecessary devices here in Pennsylvania, it's likely that it happened in a lot of other places. This story could easily go national and be Pulitzer material, don't you think, Ed?"

"Let's not get carried away, Tiffany. There's a lot of work to do here. Like I said, it's all about keeping this guy on the chain. Without him, you got nothin'."

Tiffany bit her lip, lost in thought. "I think I can keep him interested. I just have a little work to do."

"I don't want to know what you're thinking, Tiffany."

"Understood, Ned. You don't need to know. I just have to keep Dr.

Ray Gilbert interested in me and make him understand how important it is for the world to hear his story."

"And that you're his mouthpiece."

"Among other things, Ned. But yes, I'll be the conduit for his story, told his way—or sort of. Gilbert has been put on notice that his job is going away in a few months, so I don't think I'll have to pressure him to move along, once he's convinced."

Tiffany spent the next few weeks working Gilbert like he had never been manipulated before. Though not a sex siren, Tiffany was more than competent in the sack. From her ex-husband, she had acquired the skill of using recreational drugs to enhance the experience, something Gilbert knew little about but which intrigued him almost as much as Tiffany herself. Whether it was the coke or the sex, Gilbert couldn't get enough, spending almost all of his free time—and some work time as well—with Tiffany, at her apartment or his.

Liz picked up on the new relationship quickly, eavesdropping on Gilbert's phone conversations and keeping track of his nighttime activity. She waited a few weeks and finally confronted Gilbert with her suspicions.

"So you have a new squeeze, Ray?" she asked testily, sitting in his office one afternoon during patient hours.

"Yes, I'm seeing someone who isn't married for a change."

"I told you I'm ready to leave Noah. Just say the word, and we'll get out of Allentown together."

"Ain't happening, Liz, and you know it. Noah is in the way, and he isn't stepping aside."

"Fuck Noah."

"Look, Liz, I care for you; I really do, but I'm not willing to put my life on the line to have an affair with you. It's just too messy."

"And you're having too much fun with your new whore. Who is she, Ray?"

"Liz, you know that's none of your business." Gilbert ended the conversation by walking into the hallway on his way to his next patient.

Gilbert didn't want to continue the argument because Liz was right. Tiffany was getting to be a very important part of his life, not only in bed but in his head. With her persuasion, he progressively came over to her idea that helping her write an exposé would be a good way to resolve the mess he had made in Allentown and—more important—allow him to move on to a new life with a clear conscience.

13

CHAPTER

What Ned Armbruster knew and Gilbert did not was that for all of her experience and sophistication as a journalist, Tiffany knew precious little about cardiology and even less about the medical device industry. She had learned some medical vocabulary while pursuing stories on cancer and autism and the like, but she had rarely ventured into the complex world of heart disease, let alone the vast industrial enterprise, which manufactured drugs and devices that doctors used to treat it. But she had always proven to be a quick study. Ned and Tiffany knew that Gilbert would be doubly important to them, not only to finger potentially scandalous doctors but also to educate Tiffany about relevant aspects of cardiovascular medicine. She would need this background to give texture to her stories and to help her emphasize the parts that would titillate the reading public the most.

Gilbert and Tiffany's routine was to meet for dinner, followed by lovemaking, and then pillow talk, which Gilbert would use for his teachings. Tiffany sometimes had a hard time staying awake if Gilbert became too technical, so he tried, as best he could, to dumb down his lessons. Gilbert decided that Tiffany would benefit from a historical perspective and started her off with some general background information about how patients with heart disease were treated.

Only a century before, uncertified doctors who chose to care for heart patients were equipped with a stethoscope, an electrocardiogram, and a chest radiograph. As for treatment, it was all about ancient medicinals used in imprecise amounts for a variety of maladies without rigorous proof of benefit or firm knowledge of potential harm. Over the course of only a few decades, the field of cardiovascular medicine had exploded. By the dawn of the twenty-first century, cardiovascular medicine was practiced by board-certified doctors who were equipped with hundreds of drugs and devices to diagnose and treat a host of diseases, many of which had been unsuspected and unrecognized in the bygone era. The most remarkable achievement of all had been the ability to open up the chest, place a patient on a bypass machine, and stop the heart to allow new vessels or valves to be implanted. In the modern era, clinician scientists were discovering and implementing ways to do the same things through catheters and using robots, obviating the risks and the morbidity of cracking ribs.

Gilbert's particular area of cardiology was heart rhythm disorders. Here too, advances had come fast and furious. The first frontier was pharmacology, as drug companies looked for better ways to suppress fast heart rhythms. Although they were successful, large clinical trials pointed out the hazards of drugs that had a direct effect on the cardiac electrical system, dampening enthusiasm for drug therapy and stimulating the search for alternatives. Surgery was the first likely option but was also hazardous and difficult to apply to the vast majority of patients with common but dangerous rhythm disorders.

The most important breakthrough in Gilbert's field came in the 1960s, when doctors discovered that an artificial electrical generator could be hooked up to a catheter that delivered miniscule amounts of electrical current to keep the heart beating when the intrinsic conduction system of the heart failed, as it frequently did in the elderly. Within twenty years of the advent of cardiac pacemakers, a concentration camp survivor named Michel Mirowski single-handedly pioneered the development of a device that could sense when the heart went wildly out of rhythm and deliver an internal shock to abort cardiac arrest. The ability to protect patients from dying suddenly, the most common form of death in the United States, led to unbridled enthusiasm that was fueled by trials, which proved that implanting the device in high-risk individuals prophylactically, before they ever experienced a cardiac arrest, saved lives.

While the statistics proved a difference in outcomes between those who received a device and those who didn't, the cost of doing so was enormous. Since clinical tools to predict which patients were at highest risk were imprecise, only one in fifteen people who had implants would then have an arrhythmia that would require a life-saving shock. Hundreds of thousands of unnecessary devices would add up to an enormous expense to the health care system, but, under immense pressure from the medical community and an unwitting public, the FDA granted regulatory approval. When insurance companies and Medicare finally agreed to pay for these "prophylactic" defibrillators, the gold rush was on.

Three companies jockeyed for preeminent position in the market, all successful in maintaining the price line and marketing their devices to a new specialty of cardiology, men and women who called themselves electrophysiologists. Gilbert was a card-carrying member of his professional organization, not only training for an extra two years with Philip Sarkis to acquire the expertise but also sitting for a board examination that allowed him to put another certificate on his wall and to market his expertise far and wide.

The economic success of cardiac rhythm devices and the advent of techniques that simplified their implantation led to a rapid proliferation in the number of hospitals that offered the services and the number of doctors who chose to train to do the work. Large teaching hospitals that had been the usual referral point for patients with complex rhythm abnormalities developed fellowship programs. They merrily trained young cardiologists who, predictably, migrated not far from the mothership to establish programs in middle-sized and even small hospitals in the community, to siphon off the referral that their mentors had previously enjoyed.

Competition for patients became fierce; hospitals were greedy to gain revenue without the need for large capital expenditures. After all, the procedures could be carried out in coronary artery catheterization laboratories that most of these hospitals had and underutilized because of the overproliferation of those facilities. Heart attacks, especially in young patients, were decreasing in frequency as the effects of better lifestyle and better drugs to lower cholesterol and to treat high blood pressure began to reduce the burden of coronary artery disease.

As the number of rhythm disorder physicians exploded, the

industry responded by funding clinical trials that were designed to expand indications and, thus, device volume. But there was a limit to the number of patients, and declining volumes at all-sized hospitals led administrators to pressure their physicians to keep pace with their competitors, to justify the cost of the infrastructure they had foolishly erected, and to meet their inflated budget projections.

Adding to the device crisis was publication of clinical trial results that began to question the need for such a widespread proliferation of expensive devices, especially in the elderly. And drug therapy, dismissed by the technocrats who relished procedural medicine, advanced as well, albeit with cost concerns. Insurance companies wanted to preserve their profits and began to institute prior authorization programs, in which doctors and hospitals had to justify and explain the need for a test or a device before the patient could get it.

Gilbert explained to Tiffany how the arrival of a fourth device company, one that was willing to simplify the technology and drop prices, had affected his field. Hospitals that were paid by the case were only too happy to purchase the newcomer's devices at a lower cost and tell their doctors to implant them to increase their profit margins. Since a large percentage of doctors were employed by health care systems, they had to obey the hospital's marching orders or suffer the consequences. Electrophysiologists were warned that declining volumes without price control would certainly lead to pay erosion, if not physician layoffs. Since head-to-head device comparisons had rarely been pursued in the scientific literature, physicians, despite their intuition or assumptions, had a difficult time arguing that one company's defibrillator was inferior or superior to another's. It was all about the money, a wonderful milieu for corruption.

This particular night, Gilbert and Tiffany decided to share a post-dinner hot bath at her apartment. They were propped up at either end of the tub, providing a foot massage, one for the other, foreplay for the inevitable coupling that was soon to come. Tiffany had been meeting with Ned regularly, sharing Gilbert's intelligence and learnings, deciding which questions she might ask to lead her to the juicy issues that would sell newspapers. Tiffany felt that Gilbert had provided enough background information for her plunge into the corruption story that Ned and she strongly wanted to pursue. Time to start asking the tough questions.

"It sounds like the device industry became a monster," Tiffany offered from her perch in the tub, trying to sound innocently ignorant.

"If you go to a cardiology meeting anywhere in the world, especially in the US, all you need to do to understand the magnitude of the problem is walk through the technical exhibit area. There are literally acres of booths put up by dozens of device companies, showing off their latest technology, trying to seduce doctors and hospitals into adopting the newest and most expensive equipment and medicines."

"But aren't they justified? They're spending a lot of money to improve patient care and come up with lifesaving treatments, aren't they?" Tiffany asked, hoping for the answer she anticipated.

"Of course. That's what they say their purpose is, and in many respects, it's true. But there's a fine line between developing a truly innovative device or drug and making minor modifications and improvements to leapfrog the competition, simply to sell more product at a higher price."

"Doesn't the manufacturer have to prove to regulatory agencies that the new treatment is advantageous and safe?"

"That's true for drugs, but devices have had a loophole they've exploited for years. If the FDA perceives that the alteration is not substantial and that the new device is roughly equivalent to an existing device, the sponsor can get it approved with minimal, if any, clinical data. Then they're allowed to promote the improvement to convince doctors to use the new and usually more expensive device."

"So competing technology at higher cost, more implanting doctors and hospitals, studies that question medical necessity, and new companies trying to gain market share. Sounds like the perfect storm."

"Yup. Because in the scenario you just outlined, there's only one solution, and that is to pump up the volume."

"Most of these smaller hospitals can't attract more patients, can they?"

"Some of them can, depending on their demographic. For example, as the baby boomers get to the age when you would expect them to start getting heart disease, the number of device candidates will go up. But a lot of these hospitals are in suburban and rural areas, where the population growth is millennials and their children."

"Hardly heart disease–prone."

"Exactly. So the only other thing to do is put more devices in patients you already have in your practices."

"Arm twisting?"

"Let's call it one-sided thinking. Instead of presenting the device as an option, the procedure-hungry doctor makes it sound like there's no choice. And that's the best case."

"What do you mean by 'best case,' Ray?"

"My fear is that some of these desperate people are actually bending the rules to put in more devices."

"How can they do that?" Tiffany asked, practically drooling.

"There are lots of ways. Probably the most popular is fudging the ejection fraction."

"Huh?"

"OK. The most important criterion for putting a defibrillator in a patient who's had a heart attack in the past, for example, is how well the left ventricle, the main pumping chamber, is ejecting blood. Under normal conditions, the fraction of ejected blood is between 50 and 70 percent."

"Not 100 percent?"

"No, some blood is always retained in the heart after it contracts so it doesn't collapse."

"How do you measure such a thing?"

"The most common way is with ultrasound."

"An echocardiogram?"

"Very good, Tiffany. You're learning quickly. By bouncing sound waves off the heart, you can see structures like the chambers and valves. The problem is that the measurement of the left ventricular ejection fraction is semi-quantitative at best."

"You mean that it's estimated."

"Yes, for the most part. Based on the outcomes studies that have been conducted, it's recommended that defibrillators be offered to heart attack patients whose ejection fraction is less than 30 to 35 percent."

"So if someone was motivated to put in a lot of devices …"

"It wouldn't be difficult to come up with a number to justify the recommendation."

"And you think this happens frequently?"

"Yes, I think that's exactly what some doctors are doing. I've seen several cases coming from the northern parts of the state. But how could you know for sure how many unless you went out to these centers and demanded to see the actual echocardiogram images and measured them yourself."

"And nobody does that."

"No excuse for it."

"And you're afraid that as the pressure to maintain volume grows—"

"More doctors will succumb to the temptation to find more patients."

"Are there any other ways to increase the number of cases?"

"Unfortunately, there are. For example, all of the studies that proved the benefit of device therapy stipulated that all of the patients in the studies have maximal medical therapy. That means they had to be receiving recommended doses of the four or five medications that have been proven to be beneficial in optimizing cardiac performance."

"And that doesn't always happen in clinical practice?"

"It doesn't. How much of that is intentional and how much is sloppiness or patient pushback is impossible to say. But underuse of drugs like beta-blockers could clearly increase the number of patients who would be device candidates. Not only underuse but also under-dosing."

"So doctors don't have to lie to patients, but they can manipulate the circumstances so that more of them get devices."

"That's my fear, and I think it's pervasive. There are pockets in this country where the number of implants is way higher than most others, especially in our state. Hard to believe that it's caused by a congregation of particularly sick individuals. I think some doctors are just plain taking advantage."

Tiffany filed as much of Gilbert's information away, doing her best without the benefit of having taken notes. Hard to jot things down while engaged with an ardent lover. Nevertheless, Tiffany's education continued for several weeks until she thought she could start to structure the story.

Tiffany finally scheduled a meeting with Ned to vet her story idea. She decided to ask for an hour in his office at the end of the day, over a beer, and after the next day's paper had been put to bed. She wanted his full attention.

"OK, Tiffany," Ned began, feet up on his desk, Miller Lite in hand. "Let's start from the beginning. What's your angle?"

"Pretty simple, I think. It's all about unnecessary cardiac device implantation."

"Caused by what?"

"The vice that sells the most newspapers: greed."

"Not sure greed outdoes lust in the public's mind, Tiffany."

"It does when ordinary people are run over by people who get rich by taking advantage of them."

"And who is more sympathetic to the reading public than a sick person?"

"Especially a sick person with a serious but treatable disease."

"So, greed is good for us, so to speak. Who are these greedy people, Tiffany?"

"I plan to show a conspiracy between the evil device-manufacturing companies and the doctors."

"Do you have enough evidence to support that approach?"

"After milking Gilbert, I called all of the device companies. None of the higher-ups would talk to me, and they managed to extend the cone of silence to all of their sales people and technical people. I must have hit a nerve because several of their lawyers called and emailed me, warning me to stand down, or there would be hell to pay."

"All of them?"

"Yep, although most of the pushback came from Sterling."

"The one you suspect the most."

"Yes. They were adamant about not influencing doctors and keeping hands off and all that bullshit, even though I never got to ask them specific questions."

"Sounds like they may have something to hide."

"That's what I figured. I had the same problem with the doctors. Almost all of them are hospital employees who were instructed not to speak with the media without permission. None of them was stupid enough to open their mouths."

"So what's your source?"

"Nurses and nurse practitioners who work with the doctors. My friend is a nurse and works up in that area. I asked her to have a social event at her house and invite the people who work with the doctors in the area that Gilbert targeted when he was trying to 'educate' the heathens. The excuse was a stupid Tupperware party. I made sure she served plenty of booze and, as I expected, the crap flowed freely."

"What did they say?"

"Nothing I didn't expect. They freely admitted that their doctors had been putting in a lot more devices this year as compared with past years and that Sterling was the vendor that had picked up most of the surplus."

"Did they say how it happened?"

"Not directly, but it's pretty clear that Sterling was being more generous than the other vendors."

"How so? Kickbacks?"

"If there were direct money exchanges, these nurses weren't privy to them. But they did note that their doctors were going away for weekend 'educational' trips a lot more frequently and dining at nice restaurants on a regular basis, most times without the spouses."

"What does that mean?"

"A lot of the Sterling reps are very good-looking gals and guys."

"Seriously? They were pandering sex?"

"You know how catty nurses can be. It's possible their imaginations were getting the best of them, especially when they were tipsy, but they said the doctors were always in a very good mood whenever the reps would come by. You know what they say about standing a little too close."

"So physicians were willing to put their careers in jeopardy for a tasty dinner and a little pussy on the side?"

"There was more meat on the bone, Ned. Sterling was also using these meetings to help the docs expand their indications for device implants. Since they're almost all compensated based on what's called clinical productivity, they've also been seeing an increase in their paychecks."

"So you're convinced that doctors have been doing the wrong thing for patients to line their own pockets?"

"Yes. I think the evidence is strong and that we can make a good story out of it."

"All right, Tiffany. Start writing and give me stuff to look at as you go through the process."

"How much room are you going to give me, boss?" Tiffany asked.

"Not sure yet. I talked to our publisher, Phineas, last week, and he was pretty excited about the scandal potential, especially if we can in any way imply that what happened upstate in Pennsylvania has happened in other parts of the country."

"My nurses told me that Sterling reps coming into this area from other places seem to understand how things work from the get-go. How solid do we have to make that case?"

"I said *imply* on purpose. It isn't our job to investigate the entire country. We don't have the resources. What will make this story go viral is the implication that it could be happening in other peoples' neighborhoods. I'll help you make sure that angle is well developed in your piece."

"Are we talking a possible series here, Ned?"

"Maybe, and maybe even a Sunday start to kick off the story. Like I said, let's see how well you can tease it all out."

"I think Ray Gilbert is the key to this, Ned."

"Yes, he is, Tiffany," Ned said, as she sashayed out of his office on her way to her next seminar with Dr. Gilbert.

14

CHAPTER

Tiffany's cell phone sat precariously on one of the bedside tables next to Gilbert. Though she had thoughtfully set it on vibrate mode so as not to interrupt their lovemaking, the buzzing noise it made on the wooden table top was jarring, and the vibrations were so violent that the phone fell to the floor, making another loud sound. Gilbert rolled away from Tiffany, with whom he had been comfortably spooning, to pursue the source of the interruption of his pleasant slumber, eventually swinging his legs over the side of the bed before standing on the cold wooden floor. Fortunately for the phone, his big toe found it before his heel. Gilbert bent over to pick it up, answering the call without paying much attention to the 212 area code from which the call originated.

"Hello," he said, trying to clear his head. Not an easy matter after the load of drugs and alcohol he had consumed the night before.

"Hello, Ms. Springer?" the caller asked, seemingly oblivious to the fact that she was talking to someone with a deep voice.

"No, this is not Ms. Springer. Who's calling?"

"I'm terribly sorry. I must have the wrong number," the caller said with a striking British accent.

"You don't have the wrong number," Gilbert replied testily. "If you simply tell me who you are, I'll see if I can find her for you."

"Oh, that would be brilliant. My name is Naomi Jenkins, and I'm an associate producer at CBS Television."

Naomi had Gilbert's attention and a better attitude. "Oh, hi, Ms. Jenkins. Can I tell Tiffany what this is about?"

"I work on one of the network programs. You may have heard of it. *60 Minutes.*"

Is this woman pulling my leg, or is she just off the boat? Gilbert thought. *Have I heard of 60 Minutes? Really?* "Yes, I've heard of *60 Minutes*, Ms. Jenkins. Let me see if I can find Ms. Springer for you."

Which wasn't at all difficult because Tiffany, excited by the source of the call, was now wide awake and grabbing at her cell phone. Gilbert held it over his shoulder, enjoying the tease, while Tiffany threw her naked body at him.

"Give me the goddamn phone, Ray," she hissed before he gave up and tossed it on the bed. "This is Tiffany Springer. What can I do for you?"

Gilbert stood up and searched for his underwear while Tiffany began her conversation, kneeling on the bed, in her nothing-on-at-all.

She ought to be getting used to this, Gilbert thought. Because in the last two weeks, following publication of her first article, Tiffany Springer had become one of the most famous journalists in the region, if not the entire country. She had been contacted for interviews by numerous news networks and newspapers about her scintillating exposé of the evil side of the medical device industry, and she had turned down none of them. She had reveled in her trips to New York and Washington for in-person interviews and didn't hesitate to accept invitations from other countries for phone interviews, obliging her to speak with anybody and everybody through the night due to time zone differences. Never before in the history of the *Allentown Times Herald* had the world's attention been as focused on the region's newspaper, and Tiffany was taking full advantage of her newfound fame.

And the bonus for Tiffany and her newspaper was that she had become the darling of her fellow journalists. No one, not even Tiffany, was sure why or how it had happened, but reporters seemed to be as interested in Tiffany's rags-to-riches story as they were in her exposé. Raised in a poor neighborhood in Pittsburgh. Educated at a community college before a degree from a backwater university. Ascending at the *Times Herald*—from gofer to cub reporter to feature writer to columnist— in only a few years by dint of hard work. The fact that she was attractive hadn't hurt her chances of being noticed by her superiors. But there was something about the way Tiffany answered interview questions that had turned the spotlight on her as much as it had on Sterling and the other medical device companies. She had become adept at innuendo: implying wrongdoing without actually making accusations, teasing her readers so that they couldn't wait to read her next installment. Ned called it journalistic instinct, something that couldn't be taught; reporters either had or didn't have it. And Tiffany definitely had it.

Over the past few days, Tiffany and Ned had many opportunities to sit in his office, savoring their initial success, plotting how best to sustain the feeding frenzy during the succeeding parts of Tiffany's series. They knew they had been lucky with the first installment. There had been little in the news that week except for yet another round of congressional debate about health care legislation. Stalled in Senate committees were various measures to increase revenue to feed the beast that health care had become. Included were provisions to tax the pharmaceutical and medical device industries, which were seeing windfall profits as the boomers hit middle age and required more intensive and expensive health care. Tiffany's article, emphasizing unnecessary device implantation, was timely in that it provided legislators with the ammunition they needed to overcome the industry lobbyists and push forward higher taxes on medical devices.

In the next installment of the series, Tiffany planned to explore the relationships that device companies had forged with physicians over the years. Despite the implementation of strict guidelines from various professional organizations and public reporting of industry support on government websites, payments and perks for physicians continued. It just took a little more effort to make them happen. Instead of inviting physicians and their spouses to lavish social events, companies put on "consultant meetings," to which they invited their best customers under the guise of providing scientific advice. Tiffany would point out in her article that these meetings served the company's purpose of payment, while at the same time stroking physicians who wanted to believe they had valuable scientific information to share—when they really had no clue.

Tiffany also planned to spend time explaining the complex interactions of the device companies themselves. Through extravagant patent protection schemes and clever marketing, three companies had cornered the cardiac-rhythm device market until the arrival of Sterling. It was only with their own schemes that Sterling was able to pierce the armor the other companies had constructed around their business models. That and aggressive pricing had established Sterling in pockets around the country, such as northern Pennsylvania. Here again, without accusation or libelous exposure, Tiffany would imply rule bending and manipulation sufficient to accomplish Sterling's goal of advancing their product line.

Tiffany and Ned had anticipated that her articles, once completed, would prompt other reporters and journalists to conduct their own regional investigations. Tiffany's very first article had already inspired a few investigative reporters to examine their local scene. The result was a smattering of articles that not only corroborated Tiffany's superficial treatment of the scandal but expanded the treatment to include other companies that manufactured a broad range of medical equipment and drugs. The common thread? The willingness of companies to spend money to convince doctors to use their products, sometimes off label and certainly more liberally than anyone had anticipated or guideline committees recommended. Aggressive promotion to physicians was also used to explain how narcotic use had gotten out of control, a topic that had been a feature in the news for months.

"I have to admit how surprised I am by how common this behavior seems to be," Ned observed one rainy afternoon over a coffee with Tiffany in his office. "I thought they enacted legislation to restrict what companies could do for doctors, and whatever doctors did receive had to be registered on a website."

Tiffany observed Ned on the other side of his desk. He wasn't a bad-looking guy but dressing well and looking kempt didn't seem to be on his priority list. Were corduroy pants and cardigan sweaters a costume that city editors were supposed to wear, or were they what Ned chose?

"It's like anything else, Ned," Tiffany replied. "People put rules into place, and other people look for ways to circumvent them. Here's a popular example that I have in my second article. Guidelines say that you can't bring your spouse to these so-called consultants' meetings that companies set up all the time. However, there's nothing to say that you can't have your spouse share the very nice hotel room the company provides for you. Since most of the meetings are regional, it's a drive, so no airfare to worry about. And if you give the company a nominal amount, your spouse can sit in on the lavish meals they serve to the participants."

"What about the Sunshine Law and the website?"

"A joke. Nobody looks at it except for a few watchdog groups. They like to publish a list of high-earning doctors, but it usually ends up on page six of the third section of the paper because no one, including us, really gives a rip. Grassley and the other senile senators who advocated public disclosure thought that patients would want to know if their doctors were profiting from the companies who charge so much money for their pills and devices. Turns out patients don't care about companies paying for lunch or dinner, as long as they like their doctors. Some of the patients think that doctors who don't get paid much aren't worth much anyway. And they may have a point."

"Really?"

"Think about it. If you were a device manufacturer, wouldn't you consult doctors in the community who were busy and influential? And those people are usually the most skilled, if not the most principled."

"I guess you have a point."

"There's a lot of stuff like that I learned during my research that I didn't include in the article straight out. At least not yet."

"You do want to write more about this, I hope? People upstairs are expecting a couple of more installments, at least."

"I do, but I think I'm going to have to be careful, Ned."

"What do you mean?"

"I didn't want to worry you, but I've been getting some disturbing letters and emails."

"Disturbing?"

"Well, scary, I guess."

"Threats?" Ned asked.

"Yes." Tiffany squirmed in her chair.

"Credible threats? Can you tell me what they were, Tiffany?" Ned asked, sounding anxious.

"I don't think they're credible, Ned. If I did, I would have reported them to the police. They look to me to be intimidation."

"By whom?"

"I have to assume the threats are being sent by people who have a vested interest in the device industry, don't you think?"

"I guess so. But who, specifically?"

"Don't know. The messages didn't give anyone away. They have all been succinct and to the point. 'Back off or else.' Don't explain the 'else,' but I can guess."

"Do you think Sterling is behind any of it?"

"I doubt it. Too obvious. My guess is that one of the doctors or hospitals that are making a lot of money may want to scare me off."

"I'm worried about you, Tiffany. Maybe you *should* report this to the authorities."

"Let's wait. I haven't gotten anything in the last few days. If they start up again, I'll let you know."

"Have you spoken with Gilbert about this?"

"God, no! He'd have a fit. He's got enough on his plate right now."

"What's up with him?"

"The hospital is crawling all over him. They're already nervous about losing referral. Wait till they see my next installment when I talk more about my sources."

"Of whom Ray is the most prominent."

"Yup."

"Does he care about getting named in the articles?"

"He's OK with it. He's still fuming about all of the crap he's had to swallow and wants to fight back, especially against the state medical society."

"And he wants people to know who's throwing the punches?"

"For sure. He figures his days in this area are numbered anyway. I just hope he's ready for the backlash."

Which was the precise reason Philip and Dorothy decided to call Gilbert. After Tiffany's first article, the Philly papers and other media outlets had picked up on the story, so by midweek it was hot news. Philip heard it on the radio around the same time that Dorothy read about it on the internet, and both arrived home on a Tuesday evening, anxious not only to talk about the article but to decide whether Philip should intervene. They chose to wait until after dinner, baths, and bedtime stories for Emily and Erin, who were pleasantly tired and off to sleep almost before the lights went out.

"So what do you think?" Philip asked, pouring himself a second scotch on the rocks while Dorothy finished her first glass of white wine.

"I finally got to read the entire article this afternoon," Dorothy said, taking a stool at the kitchen counter across from Philip, their favorite configuration for evening conversation. "I'm not sure if this Tiffany person is a good reporter and how much of what she says is substantiated, but she's good at stirring the pot. There was a lot of material in there that she was fed by someone in the know."

"And you think it was Gilbert?"

"What do you think, Philip? Doesn't it sound familiar to you?"

"I guess so, but she didn't actually name Gilbert, did she?"

"Not yet, but the paper announced she's going to be coming out with more articles, and she plans to get into specifics."

"So he's going to be in harm's way?" Philip asked.

"I think so. It's hard to say what the repercussions of this will be, but I can't believe his hospital and the medical community up there are going to give him a parade for whistle-blowing and destroying their referral business."

"What should I do?"

"Call and warn him to restrain Tiffany Springer. Or get away from her now, before it's too late."

"Really?" Philip replied, surprised by Dorothy's firm and unqualified answer.

"Yes, really. He's your friend and former student, and he's walking into a potential hornet's nest. If he's alerted and lets it happen too bad for him. But I think you need to give him a heads-up."

"Let me think about it, Dorothy."

"Whatever. But I don't see much to ponder here, Philip. If I were you, I'd call him right now."

"Now?"

"The next installment of her series may be coming out soon. They probably plan to do Sunday articles to maximize readership, and I don't think they're going to dawdle now that they've seen how fired up people are. He has to decide soon if he wants to shut her down before she gets into the weeds and starts naming names. Call him now, when he isn't working, and you have a better chance of getting him on the phone."

"Now?" Philip repeated, trying to decide whether to take Dorothy's advice, which was seldom, if ever, wrong. "OK, now." Philip acquiesced after seeing Dorothy's stern expression. He picked up his cell phone off the kitchen counter. "How about if I put him on speaker so you can hear both sides of the conversation?"

"Fine, Philip, but I'm not going to say a word. This is your party."

Philip punched in the number and placed the phone back on the middle of the counter.

Three rings later: "Hi, Philip. What's up?"

"Hello, Ray. How are you? Is this a good time to talk?"

"Perfect, actually. I'm in my car on my way to pick up my date for dinner."

"Ray, I'm calling about the article in the Allentown paper last Sunday."

"What about it, Philip?"

"The woman who wrote it used a lot of material that I suspect you supplied her with."

"So what if I did?"

"Ray, I know you're angry about the situation up there, but going public with a local reporter may not be the best approach."

"What *is* the best solution, Philip? As you'll recall, educating and going to our professional societies were your last two suggestions, and neither worked out very well, did they?"

"Ray, I don't pretend to know the answer. But I'm pretty sure this isn't it."

"You went public with your finding years ago—you know, about unnecessary pacemakers?"

"I published the scientific data. I didn't go directly to the papers, Ray. It's much different. Believe me."

"But you were attacked by your peers, pretty viciously, if I remember. Different means but the same end."

"Ray, you won't be able to control what this woman says about the situation and about you, in particular. This is just too risky, in my opinion. As your friend, I suggest you back off, and tell Tiffany you're not going to help her further. Insist that your name not be used in her articles."

"Thanks for the advice, Philip. I'll take it under advisement, as they say."

Philip looked across at Dorothy, who shrugged and then, surprising herself, chimed in.

"Ray, this is Philip's significant other, Dorothy Deaver. I don't believe we've met."

"Hi, Dorothy. Philip didn't tell me you were on the line. No, we haven't met, but Philip speaks very highly of you."

"Thanks, Ray. He knows better than to do otherwise. You probably know that I'm an attorney with a lot of health care law experience. Forgive me for butting in, but this is important. I have no question that what you and Tiffany Springer allege has some truth to it. Industry has been playing fast and loose with regulations regarding product marketing for years, and they'll continue. Writing an exposé about it is fine, and maybe it will do some good. My concern is that Tiffany is aggressive and not terribly savvy—a bad combination that leads to overly aggressive reporting."

"Tiffany is a good reporter, Dorothy. What she is saying in the articles is true. Doctors are taking advantage of patients, and it has to stop."

"I'm sure Tiffany is doing her job, Ray, but remember—she's protected by the First Amendment, and her newspaper will take care of her. You, on the other hand, have no such protection. If Tiffany goes way out on a limb and uses you as the excuse for her accusations, you *will* be vulnerable."

Silence for several seconds. "Vulnerable is an interesting word, Dorothy. It's exactly how I've described patients who've received devices they didn't need or operations that were unnecessarily complicated to line the pockets of the doctors, hospitals, and the companies that Tiffany is going after."

"We understand your mission, Ray," Philip interjected. "We're simply warning you to be careful and not ruin your career—and your life, for that matter. Your patients and your students need you."

"I appreciate that, Philip and Dorothy. I really do. I promise to give it more thought. I'm pulling into a parking lot now, so I have to say goodbye."

Philip shook his head at Dorothy, judging that Gilbert had no intention of heeding their advice, but he had nothing more to say. "Take care of yourself, Ray, and call us if we can help in any way."

"Sure thing, Philip."

"Well, that was a waste of time," Philip said after the call ended.

"I don't agree, Philip. If and when the shit hits the fan in Allentown, you'll at least know that you called Ray and warned him to back off. If you hadn't done that, you'd feel horrible."

"Swell. I can feel real good as poor Ray swirls around the toilet bowl on his way to infamy or worse."

"Lots of bad things happen in this world, Philip. People attack people with half-truths all the time. You can't stop them, no matter how hard you try."

"I guess this one feels fixable to me, if only Ray would listen."

"Right, Philip. If only."

Dorothy swiveled her stool, climbed off, and headed for the bedroom, trailed closely by her hounds. "Going to get under the covers, let the doggies warm my feet, and read some real fiction, Philip," she said over her shoulder. "Care to join me?"

15
CHAPTER

Sunday mornings at the Sarkis/Deaver household were like no other. At Dorothy's insistence, forbidden were the frantic routines that marked every other day of the week, even Saturdays. There would be no work for either of them, and no school, of course. But also prohibited were sports activities of any kind for adults or children or any activity that would require jumping out of bed to prepare for a frantic rush to some godforsaken neighborhood that happened to include a soccer field. Their agreement was firm and time-honored. Philip, the morning person, would get up with the dogs and the kids and let Dorothy sleep late, in exchange for an afternoon nap for Philip while the TV played his sporting event of choice. The children, upon awakening, would be allowed to watch television while they had a leisurely breakfast that Philip prepared with gusto. The doggies would have a mini-romp at the local park, and nothing more would happen until Dorothy shook off the cobwebs with a cup of French-press coffee that Philip would have waiting for her. The routine was set in stone, and serious repercussions awaited anyone who dared to break the rules.

So when Dorothy was jolted from her bed early that particular

Sunday morning, she was not at all pleased. And what she heard that woke her from her slumber made it almost impossible for her to fall back to sleep. Angrily throwing off the covers, Dorothy stormed out of the bedroom and into the kitchen, where Philip was hunched over his computer, head in his hands, muttering obscenities, ignoring the dogs who had climbed off the sofas to give Dorothy their customary tail-wagging, good-morning greeting.

"Philip, what the hell is going on out here?"

"This is unbelievable."

"Yes. I gather that something *is* unbelievable since you've been using that word in a loud voice for the last several minutes. Which is why I'm standing here instead of asleep in our bedroom."

"Sorry," Philip mumbled.

"Sorry? Come on, Philip; you know the rules. Quiet out here so I can sleep one damn day of the week. Is that asking too much?"

"No, you're right," Philip said, still focused on the screen in front of him.

"What's so friggin' important that you lost your sensibility over it?"

"The second installment of the Tiffany Springer exposé was published in the Allentown paper this morning, and it's already all over the internet."

"Are you kidding me? That's what got you all excited? I hate to break this to you, Philip, but I really don't give a rip about Tiffany and her vacuum-packed boyfriend. You told him to be careful. It's on him if he didn't take your advice."

"Either he didn't listen, or she's out of control because she has taken this to a new level."

Realizing that her sleep was over, Dorothy shuffled over to the coffeepot and poured herself a cup, adding a little cream as she hoisted herself onto a counter stool.

"OK, Philip, it's clear that you're not going to be quiet until you fill me in on the article, so let's get it over with. What did airhead Tiffany Springer come up with this time?"

"It's worse than before. First of all, it's obvious she doesn't understand the medicine or the science. She's blurring the indications and making all kinds of mistakes about what's in the guidelines for pacemaker and defibrillator implantations."

"For example?"

"Our professional organizations love to put out guideline papers to explain to doctors what good studies have shown but also how experts in the field interpret those findings. They make specific recommendations about what's appropriate, what's not, and what's questionable but permissible. For example, nobody argues about putting a pacemaker in a patient who's had a blackout because their heart rate was very slow and not putting one in a patient who has a slow heart rate but no symptoms, like an athlete. The questionable case would be an elderly person with a fainting spell but without a clearly slow heart rhythm. Springer's assuming that those questionable cases are wrong, which inflates the numbers of supposedly unnecessary pacemakers dramatically. And she's applying those metrics selectively to doctors and hospitals she wants to attack. She's doing a lot of damage."

"Anything else setting you off?"

"She's not making general accusations anymore, like she did in the first article. Now, she's specifically naming hospitals, doctors, and companies. She's drawing black and white lines without any shades of gray. There are good guys and there are bad guys, and no one in between."

"She's just asking for a lawsuit."

"Seems that way. I can't believe she's smart enough to have a bulletproof case against all the people she's naming. I hope her paper has a good umbrella insurance policy."

"Who's going to go after them?"

"The big device companies. They have to."

"And what about Ray?"

"He's in there. A good guy, of course. The person who decided to come forward and who was rebuffed by his own hospital and by the state medical society."

"Oh my God, Philip! Are you in there too?"

"Fortunately, no. There is a reference to an expert who was asked to examine a number of the cases to determine medical need. The article also talks about an attempt to educate the docs up there with a case conference run by someone described as a key opinion leader, but they didn't use my name."

"Thank God for small favors. That would have been ruinous."

"I know and not something I could sidestep easily. I'm not out of the woods, though. I'm sure Tiffany will be asked about the unnamed expert, and who knows if she finally will cough up my identity."

"What are you going to do, Philip?"

"How about nothing? I warned Ray and it didn't make a dent. I'm not wasting any more time on this."

"Philip, I wish I could believe you."

"No, Dorothy. I'm pretty firm on this. As long as they keep my name out of the stories, I'll be silent."

"Yeah, yeah. We'll see. I'm going to take a nice hot shower and try to wake up. Are the girls OK?"

"Perfect. They had pancakes with syrup and milk and are now knee-deep in the Cartoon Network."

While Philip did keep his promise of silence, the rest of the cardiology community was buzzing about the high-profile articles that, within a few hours of publication, had been disseminated around the country. It was the main topic of conversation in the hallways at NorthBroad, as well as at the lunch tables. Even non-cardiologists were engaged, asking questions and wondering how so many bad things could be happening in a region so close to several major medical centers, perpetrated by many of the people they knew and trusted. When asked by his peers if he knew about the scandal, Philip feigned ignorance, a stance made more difficult because Gilbert had been one of his prized trainees.

"What's the inside story, Dr. Sarkis?" Marwan Baschri asked as they stood at the scrub sink, getting ready to start a catheter ablation case on Monday morning. "Did those guys upstate really take a bribe and put in devices that people didn't need?"

The question immediately got Philip's attention. He looked over at the fellow, wondering if the question was idle chatter or if somehow Philip's name had been attached to the fiasco.

"What do you know about it, Marwan?" Philip asked.

"Nothing more than what I read on the internet this morning. And of course, I remember Dr. Gilbert from when he brought his patient here in a helicopter. Sounds like they're really going after the docs up there, and I was just wondering if you think they did anything wrong."

"There are always shades of gray, Marwan, and newspapers are printed in black and white."

"That's what I thought. I'll bet a lot of those cases were close calls, and the newspaper worked hard to make it sound like the docs are criminals."

"Scandal sells newspapers, Marwan," Philip said, anxious to change the subject. "Now, tell me what you know about this case we have this morning and how you think we should go about this procedure."

Monday morning at the *Allentown Times Herald* was tumultuous.

Ned's office was overrun by attorneys and upper management, who were plotting the best way to handle inquiries that were pouring in from all over the state. Highest priority was given to phone calls from the offices of US congressmen and senators, who wanted to respond to the scandal to assuage and impress their constituents but who needed to know the strength of the case before going too far out on a limb. Next came the personal injury lawyers, trolling for the names of patients who might have been harmed, in the hope of beating their competition to the punch in filing class action litigation. And then the blitz of calls from attorneys representing the device industry, getting ready to file subpoenas for source documents as they considered whether or not to take legal action against Tiffany and the newspaper.

Things finally began to calm down by late afternoon. Tiffany took advantage of the lull to park herself in front of Ned's desk and put her stocking feet up on his desk.

Ned sat forward, looking at her over his half-frame reading glasses. "Haven't seen this place so lit up since 9/11."

"I wasn't around for that one, Ned. Still in high school."

"Lots of things get people pretty excited, but there's almost nothing like a good old-fashioned medical scandal to get their attention."

"Why, do you think?"

"Just about everybody has to see a doctor, and everybody wants to think that their doctor is the best there is. You kinda have to. Confidence in your doctor is important to the healing process, I think. When someone implies that there are doctors who are not just stupid but also evil and cunning—well, it sets people off."

"Sort of like the priests abusing young boys."

"Exactly. It's called the it-coulda-been-me syndrome."

"So the thing about my story that hooks the public is the evil doctor angle."

"I think so. Everyone assumes that big industry is evil. They count on their doctors to protect them and to do the right thing. When they don't, people start paying attention."

"So I should focus on that in the next parts of the series?"

"I would make it a heavy emphasis. The readers will understand individual stories better than statistics. You definitely need more of that in parts three and four."

"Will do."

"But you should also keep digging on the industry side. They're going to come after us hard, and if we can't prove that our allegations are truthful or at least supportable, our insurance companies won't be happy, and neither will the people who run the syndicate."

"And who pay our salaries. I get it. I have a lot of work to do."

"I'll be staying in the office late this evening. Wanna order take-out?"

"Nah. My task this evening is to bring my prime source deeper into my confidence. I need him to drill down, if you know what I mean," Tiffany said.

"Lucky him."

"It's a tough job, but somebody has to do it."

"Just remember what I told you: focus on the individual cases, and don't worry too much about statistics. Case vignettes will rope in the average Joe and make him or her want to buy more papers. Obviously, you'll make sure they're properly redacted so no patient gets hurt."

"Oh, I think there's going to be a lot of hurt, Ned. Don't you?"

When Tiffany arrived home, she made a point of tidying up her usually-messy apartment and taking a shower and washing her hair to make ready for Gilbert's arrival. As Ned had pointed out, Gilbert was going to have to help her come up with a few outrageous cases to pull on the heartstrings of her readership in the succeeding issues. She needed details that Gilbert might not want to cough up unless properly motivated. Tiffany's philosophy was that the fastest way to a man's heart was via his genitals.

And to most properly grease the slide, Tiffany had used a secure source to purchase a fresh supply of recreational drugs. A snort and a puff during foreplay would not only enhance the sexual experience but likely would loosen Gilbert's tongue and make him more likely to expound on the cases Tiffany wanted to extract.

Gilbert arrived on time, as usual, hauling a couple of bottles of champagne to celebrate Tiffany's enormous success. The wine was hardly opened and the cocaine only barely snorted before the two were ripping away at each other's clothes as the four-legged monster steered its way into Tiffany's bedroom, collapsing heavily on the bedcovers. Tiffany wasted no time ridding herself and Gilbert of their underwear and guiding his member into her vagina. Ray's orgasm was quick, leaving Tiffany unsatisfied. While he lay on top of her, she wondered if he was going to make an attempt to help her to orgasm, as he usually did, but instead, he rolled over on his back, swinging his arm over his head.

"What's the matter, Ray?" Tiffany asked, doing her best impression of a person who cared.

"Tough day at work."

"How so, Ray?"

"It's bad enough that I don't have much to do and sit around my office all day. Referral has really dried up, and the hospital is making sure I know I'm the reason. Now, I have to put up with dagger stares from just about everybody at the hospital."

"Have they threatened to fire you again?"

"One good thing about having your articles out there is that they can't do that. I've spoken with a friend who is a lawyer. Since most of the devices that may have been implanted unnecessarily were for Medicare patients, he thinks there's going to be a federal investigation at some point. Which makes me a potential whistleblower. It's not official yet, but the hospital can't take the chance of getting into hot water with the feds by firing their accuser, so they have to keep me on the payroll."

"At least you're making a living. And maybe you can hire an experienced attorney who can help you turn that whistleblower thing into some money in your pocket."

"I hope so. Most of my salary is incentivized. Without cases and procedures and patients, I'll be lucky to be able to pay my rent next month."

"What can I do to help?"

"Believe me, you've done enough," Gilbert said.

"You were the person who wanted me to take this on. You wanted me to go after those people, and you got me started on the project."

"Yes, I did. But I didn't expect you to go off on people like you did. You've implicated a lot of institutions and companies and provided enough specifics to keep investigators going for a long time. Not to mention inviting lawsuits."

"It's what I do, Ray. I had the full backing of my editor at the newspaper."

"And I'll bet you aren't done."

"Not by a long shot. I have plenty of ammunition for at least a couple of more articles. I have the green light to get them into print within the next month."

"I guess I shouldn't be too concerned. I can't imagine what you have that will get me into more trouble."

"Ray, I've tried to make you look like a good guy, right? As the articles progress, I'll develop that theme even further. Isn't that a good thing for your career?"

"If I wanted to be the new Dr. Oz, maybe. But I have no plans to be a circus entertainer. I just want to take care of my patients and be a good doctor and make a reasonable living."

"And you can't do that?"

"I doubt it. Even if I leave Allentown, my reputation will follow me. The medical community is pretty close-knit and not kind to people who attack it, especially from within. Oz did it and is the laughingstock who will never be able to be a real doctor again."

"I'm sorry, Ray. I guess I should have anticipated this."

"Why? That's not your job. Let's face it, Tiffany: your stories are meant to titillate, not educate. And that's what you've done so far."

"How about if we change the focus for the last two parts?"

"How would you do that?"

"Instead of attacking the doctors and the hospitals and the companies, let's go over to the patient side. Explain what all of this has meant to them."

"You mean, individual patient stories?"

"Why not? Readers would love it, and it would personalize what has happened here. It isn't only about the money but human suffering. Betrayed trust. And how you, Ray Gilbert, tried to help these patients deal with the adversity. Wouldn't that play well and reestablish you as a doctor's doctor?"

"I guess so. I'd have to think about it, but it might help to put a different spin on the story."

"Surely you have a few patients who have been harmed or potentially harmed who would be willing to tell their stories."

"I do. Finding them is not a problem."

"We can interview them together to make sure I understand the medical part well and that I tell their stories straight. And they can remain anonymous, if they wish."

"I kind of like the idea, Tiffany. It would put a better face on things and help me and the patients."

"No question. But we have to work fast. Ned, my editor, wants the last two installments on the newsstands by the end of the month."

"If I can use your computer, I can get into the system at work and get phone numbers and call some people this evening."

"Well, not so fast, Ray."

"I thought you said this was a good idea and that we needed to get started soon."

"It is, Ray. A grand idea, really, and we'll get on it first thing in the morning. It's just that … I think we have a few other things to accomplish this evening right here in my bed."

"You mean—"

"Of course that's what I mean, silly. After all, you had your jollies. Now how about if you put that remarkable tongue of yours to work where it really counts?"

16

CHAPTER

With a thick folder on his lap, Ned Armbruster sat quietly in a well-cushioned armchair in the waiting area outside the publisher's office, looking at his smartphone and trying not to be nervous. After the publication of the medical device articles, life at the paper had become a lot more interesting. Though he had anticipated a good deal of blowback, Ned was amazed by how vehemently the public had reacted to Tiffany's exposé, doctors and patients taking sides in a debate that was heating up fast. He had expected a summons to the publisher's office, expecting that it would come this particular morning, after the latest and most incendiary part of the series had appeared.

"I shouldn't be worried about how he is going to react," Ned had muttered to himself during the elevator ride upstairs. "Phineas has been all in with this from the beginning. He gets it. Or I think he does."

Phineas J. McCoy was the seventy-five-year-old veteran publisher of the *Allentown Times Herald*. He liked to think of himself as an old-school news guy. "You know I don't have blood in my veins," he would tell his favorite phlebotomist at the local hospital.

"I know," Alicia would say. "It's red ink, right?"

And Phineas would nod and offer a rare smile because life hadn't been the same for him for the past eighteen months. Not since his doctor had called him with the grim news that the results of his bloodwork that particular morning, as part of his annual physical examination, were not normal. The conversation was imprinted in Phineas's brain.

"You have leukemia, Phineas."

"Blood cancer?"

"I'm afraid so."

"How bad is it, Doc?"

"Hard to say, Phineas, until we do some tests, but I called one of our hematologists and she looked at the blood smear. She says the pattern looks like acute myelogenous leukemia."

"In English, Doc, if you please."

"It means that one type of white blood cells is produced at an abnormally fast rate. We call them blast cells, and they're taking over your bone marrow and replacing normal cells that allow you to clot and to fight infection."

"And makes me anemic?" Phineas asked, knowing the answer was the explanation for the unusual fatigue he had been experiencing the last few weeks.

His physician went on to describe all of the tests Phineas would need, including insertion of a needle into his hip bone to withdraw some marrow.

"Then what?"

"Chemotherapy to knock out the blast cells."

"Which will also wipe out my normal cells, right?"

"And make you pretty sick and susceptible to infection. It's going to be tough, but if you respond, you might be a candidate for a bone marrow transplant at some point."

"Even at my age?"

"Depends on how well you respond to the chemo. You've been a pretty healthy guy. If we can find a suitable donor, you have a chance."

So for the past year and a half, Phineas had been poked, prodded, invaded, and sickened by the myriad treatments that comprised the modern approach to acute AML. His doctors were happy with his response and the fact that he had finally had a remission, but they were pessimistic about a bone marrow transplant, the path to cure the disease. Phineas, a widower of ten years, had no children, and his siblings were either too old or too sick to be considered as donors. Though his name had been entered into the pool to find an unrelated donor, his age put him low on the list, unlikely to get the phone call he so anxiously awaited. Because without new bone marrow, the likelihood of a recurrence was high, and the next time around, Phineas would have a much lower chance of responding. And immunotherapy, the revolutionary approach to AML that was so widely publicized, was not available to a seventy-five-year-old.

But Phineas's brush with death and his potentially imminent demise had a remarkable effect on his judgment as a publisher. Though still responsible to the usually conservative board of the newspaper, Phineas was now more inclined than ever to take chances and be creative and to be less concerned about the consequences. "What are the bastards going to do to me that's worse than AML?" he wondered whenever he became concerned about the consequences of a story he authorized or approved, especially when he looked at his decimated body in his full-length bathroom mirror.

Under Phineas's enlightened leadership, the previously stodgy and centralist *Allentown Times Herald* had taken a decidedly leftward swing, championing causes like abortion rights, gay and lesbian freedom, environmental protection, and gun control. Phineas no longer felt compelled to hide or disguise the liberal tendencies he had harbored for years. He decided that the Allentown public—indeed, the nation and the world—should be treated to a dose of liberalism and concern for the common good. His wisdom and experience helped him plan and implement the changes so insidiously and quickly that before his board knew what had happened, a new path, a new philosophy of reporting, had been craftily charted.

Nevertheless, Phineas knew his board well. He understood that the conservatives would eventually catch on and oppose such an approach and work to have him fired for his impudence. Phineas was not quite ready for dismissal and didn't want to be remembered as the person who ruined (in their view) the *Times Herald*. The journalism business actually *was* in his blood, his father and grandfather having served in positions of prominence at the paper, dating back to the early twentieth century. They had impressed on young Phineas that the way to stay on top and to assuage a board full of businessmen was for the *Times Herald* to make money—a lot of it. Phineas's wager was that given the choice, the board would be swayed by profits and not by ideology.

And he had been right. Sales of the newspaper soared locally, and internet hits multiplied as Phineas carefully sequenced articles addressing important issues of the day. As much as he hated the man, the election of Donald Trump had been a godsend. After stating the facts of an issue, like an executive order that extended ocean drilling, Phineas could easily justify a contrapuntal article or editorial, crafted by an intellectually superior individual who knocked the stuffing out of Trump's moronic tweets and attracted readers on both sides of the issue like bees to honey.

It was in this context that Phineas first reviewed Ned Armbruster's proposal for an exposé on the device issue. If this idea had come to McCoy's desk two years before, he would have vetoed it without much thought. He would have argued that it was way too inflammatory and that it would undoubtedly provoke a host of lawsuits. But in this new era in which he placed the public good first and invited controversy, Phineas not only approved the series but felt compelled to meet with Ned to offer suggestions and constructive criticism; today's session was the latest installment.

Though inclined to be provocative, it would be unfair to say that Phineas was reckless. In anticipation of a vigorous response from several stakeholders and before he gave his final approval, Phineas met with his legal staff and laid out the issues the paper would likely have to deal with after publication of the complete series. Though a few voiced concern, the consensus was that the benefits outweighed the legal risk. Newspapers expected to get sued and many times benefited from the publicity that legal action engendered. Articles like Springer's would draw fire. As long as the stories contained a scintilla of truth, the courts would protect the fifth estate, as it had from time immemorial.

After a ten-minute wait, McCoy's secretary indicated that Phineas was ready for Ned and that he should proceed into the inner sanctum. For all of his tendency to be a hands-on publisher, Phineas maintained a very private existence at the newspaper, rarely venturing out of his office, while inviting few to meet with him in person. He even used a separate entrance to and from the parking garage to avoid the hoi polloi. Though this behavior wasn't new since the leukemia diagnosis, it was now exaggerated.

Widowed and not at all interested in the opposite sex, Phineas had nevertheless remained very conscious of his appearance. The leukemia and its hideous treatment caused him to lose a third of his body weight and all of his hair. He was gaunt, pale, and bald and, to his mind, thoroughly unpresentable. He sat on the sofa in his office seating arrangement, in khakis, a blue button-down shirt, argyle socks, and penny loafers, topped off with a Phillies baseball cap. He didn't rise to greet Ned or shake his hand but gestured to an armchair across from the sofa. Ned seated himself while placing a folder gently on the coffee table between them.

"Thanks for meeting with me, Ned. Would you like a cup of coffee or tea?"

"No thanks, Phineas. Had my caffeine fix already."

"That's one of the things I had to give up. Just gets my GI tract in an uproar that it doesn't need."

"How are the treatments going, Phineas?"

"Pretty good, I think. I'm officially in remission, so they have me on what is called 'suppressive therapy' that's supposed to lessen the chance of a recurrence. Who knows? I just do what I'm told."

"Any news on the bone marrow transplant?"

Phineas shook his head. "Nada. I even offered to put up some money to see if I could bribe my way up the damn list and was properly rebuffed. So here I sit."

"But you've been happy with the treatment at Allentown Medical Center?"

"So far. I do wonder if they might pay a little less attention to me after the articles we've published."

"I thought Allentown came out looking pretty good, especially the physician there who helped expose the problem."

"I guess so, though it didn't do anything for their referral volume. But that does bring me to the reason I called you up here, Ned. Tell me—what's your take on the reaction to the articles?"

"There are a lot of perspectives, Phineas, as you can imagine. The general public received it well. I think they like medical stories, especially scandalous ones, so newspaper sales and internet hits when the articles appeared were phenomenal. All-time records."

"I've been reading the letters to the editor. What's your take on them?"

"Again, what you would expect from the public. Outrage from the device industry and doctors, confirmations from personal experiences, calls for legislative action, and a lot of the usual nonsense from people who look for any excuse to hate other people."

"Have any other papers corroborated our story?"

"There have been a few copycat pieces, primarily in small- to medium-sized markets. Most of it anecdotal and poorly substantiated. I've got them in this folder."

"It's important to track follow-on pieces from other places, Ned, for obvious reasons."

"Right. It will help our lawyers. I can't say that anyone has taken on the device industry quite as directly as us. The small fry are happy to go after doctors and hospitals that have smaller legal arsenals."

"Our legal staff tells me that they have been peppered with requests for information from firms representing device companies and a few of the hospitals named in Tiffany's stories," Phineas said.

"Not a surprise. What do they want to know, Phineas?"

"The usual—identities, foundation, sources. All the stuff we can't and won't give them voluntarily."

"Until they subpoena the information."

"And we'll still deny access, with the usual arguments."

"Will they go further, do you think?" Ned asked.

"Who knows? It all depends on how hard their businesses are affected."

"I hear the hospitals may be hurting."

"They need to put that rumor out there to justify their outrage and make the case for economic hardship. Do you really think that losing a couple dozen device implants is going to seriously harm their bottom line?"

"Probably not, unless patients decide that they don't want to go to their local hospital."

Phineas smiled, putting his feet up on the coffee table. "My belief is that won't happen. People don't want to travel far for medical care, Ned. Look at me, for example. I could have gone to a fancy place like Sloan Kettering, but I stayed here. People like their community doctors. And for those who do venture out of their catchment area, when they get sick in the middle of the night, they're going to be right back to their local emergency room. Only this time, they won't be known, and their care will become hopelessly fragmented. The hospitals know all of this, so they'll blow a little smoke at us but won't be too worried."

"I guess you have a point, Phineas."

"And don't forget public amnesia. People forget about this stuff quickly. There's so much happening in the media and so many sources are competing for their attention that the public can't stay focused. Look at gun violence. Three days after a mass shooting, everyone forgets to be pissed off about the fact that our legislators haven't gotten off their collective ass and done something obvious, like banning automatic weapons."

"I agree. I haven't been too worried about the public outcry. It's the doctors and device companies I'm concerned about."

"Doctors? Are you serious?"

"We've had a number of calls from professional organizations, concerned that we've impugned physicians."

"So what? Do you really think that any of those organizations has its shit together enough to actually do something? They're a joke and a half, Ned. They've done nothing to defend or help their constituencies in obvious situations. Did they help enact malpractice reform, or stop the insurance companies from ratcheting down physician fees, or convince administrators to let up on needless regulation? They sat on their hands then, and I don't expect them to pull their fingers out of their asses now to do anything in this complex case."

Ned had no response. He could only add his agreement, impressed with how thoroughly Phineas had thought through the problem.

"But I will concede that our principal threat is the device companies, Ned. Specifically, Sterling. But let me ask you a question. Do you think any of the other companies will come after us?"

"Depends if they're pulled into the scandal."

"My recollection is that Tiffany, dear soul that she is, was carefully directed to steer mostly clear of other device companies, was she not?"

"Yes."

"And did she obey her instructions?" Phineas asked.

"She did. Well, she didn't in the first iterations of her articles, but I edited them carefully to distill out most of that other stuff."

"So there should be little motivation for the big companies to get riled up."

"Like I said, a lot of people are now on the chase, and I can't be certain that one or more of them won't uncover some of the big company's unsavory practices."

"Because you believe them not to be blameless?"

"Understatement. From what Tiffany learned, they're all in it up to their earlobes. Sterling was maybe more aggressive, as the new kid on the block. But there would be plenty of muck to rake if anybody chose to go there."

"But we don't, right, Ned? Which means that the large companies should not only leave us alone but give us an award for helping to sink their new competitor."

"I guess so. I included some letters from their counsel in the folder. I don't think they'll be giving us a trophy any time soon."

"Blowing smoke is all. I'll go through everything you have there and forward the most relevant stuff to our legal team for them to chew on. Have we gone over all of the tangible threats, Ned?"

"No. There's another problem that I need to discuss with you, Phineas, and I can't say I know how to handle it."

"Shoot."

"Death threats."

"Against Tiffany?"

"Yup. She told me about a few she received recently."

"Credible?"

"Who the hell knows? Some of them are from cuckoos trying to get attention. But a few have been a bit scarier. From someone who may be watching or stalking her."

"Uh-oh."

"It gets worse. Some of them have included her source, Dr. Gilbert. Whoever's doing this knows they're having an affair, spending a lot of intimate time together."

"That I didn't know and should have, Ned."

"Agreed. It's a big mistake for them to be screwing, and it's my bad for not telling you about the threats as soon as I found out—a few weeks ago."

"What's her attitude?"

"She wants to ignore them. She believes it's just some crazies and that it will blow over. She definitely doesn't want to go to the authorities."

"Do you agree?"

"Not sure, Phineas. Part of me sides with her because getting the authorities involved would turn this into a real mess. If their affair is made public, people may believe that the story is a hoax, concocted by a doctor with a hard-on for a hot reporter. And it discredits our story, turning it into a tawdry love affair."

"On the other hand, if you're wrong, and the threats are serious—"

"Tiffany and her boyfriend may be in real danger."

"This is a curveball, Ned. Let me think on it. In the meantime, talk to Tiffany again and see if she has changed her mind about going to the police. We would never stop her. *That* would be wrong. Also tell her to cut Gilbert loose right now. I think she's used him for all he's worth anyway."

"Agree fully on both counts. I'll sound her out and keep you posted."

"And I'll do my reading and thinking—as long as this damn cancer doesn't suddenly get worse."

"I'll be saying a prayer for you, Phineas. I can't imagine what this paper would be like without you."

"Thanks, Ned. As long as I can stand up, I'll be here for the paper."

Ned stood to leave but detoured to hold out his hand to Phineas, who grasped it in both of his and looked at Ned with tears in his eyes.

Ned turned to leave the office, hearing nothing more than a sniffle and a cough as he closed the door behind him.

17

CHAPTER

Gilbert slept alone the Sunday night after Tiffany's most recent article appeared in the *Allentown Times Herald*. Tiffany had made an abrupt decision to leave town to visit her parents in Pittsburgh for the weekend, explaining that it had been a long time since she had seen them. Unaware of the death threats she had received, Gilbert merely suspected she was tired of the media attention and didn't want to face the flack her most recent words on the subject of corruption in the medical device industry would summon forth, at least not at close range.

"Be careful what you wish for, Tiffany," Gilbert had wanted to tell her, never actually saying the words he knew would throw her into a snit. Tiffany could run, but she could not hide.

It hadn't been a good sleep for Gilbert. He had been awakened several times with nightmares, none of which required Sigmund Freud to interpret. They all involved him, and sometimes Tiffany, being forced by a dark figure to walk on a tightrope that stretched out over a vast chasm, the bottom of which was heavily populated by flesh-eating demons who looked up with bloodshot eyes, waiting impatiently for their prey to lose their balance and fall into their clutches so they could rip them apart.

Gilbert was dreading his morning appointment on this dreary Monday: a follow-up visit with his new attorney. Tiffany had finally convinced him to seek legal counsel to help him handle the blowback from her exposé, and to see if the whistleblower aspect of the case had legs. Ray had consulted with friends and colleagues, scouring legal directories until he had come up with the name of a personal injury attorney he thought he could trust. It had taken several days for Gilbert to summon up the energy to call Nicky Toscano for that initial appointment.

Gilbert had been prepared to take an immediate dislike to Toscano. Though universally lauded as highly competent and successful, Gilberthe would be be just another smart-ass lawyer with an attitude. Even worse, most of Toscano's work was for plaintiffs. And even though Gilbert had been assured by people he trusted that Toscano was a man of principle, the idea that he had made a small fortune taking physicians to the woodshed was difficult for Gilbert to swallow. His appearance didn't help. From photos that Gilbert had found on the internet and what others had told him, Toscano was a little guy who did everything he could to compensate for his small stature, including body building, dressing expensively, and making sure his jet-black hair, sculpted goatee, and manicured nails were trimmed perfectly, no matter the occasion.

What Gilbert couldn't know, at least not yet, was that Toscano's law offices were like his appearance—meticulously maintained. Toscano insisted that all the associates and paralegals he brought into his solo practice maintain their offices and desks in perfect order. Nothing out of place or askew. Never.

And similarly, the client cases and files. Toscano was a stickler for details and was known to go off on a rant if a page was out of place in a brief or a word misspelled in a motion. "Crazy man," his underlings were known to call him—behind his back, of course—all the while grudgingly respecting the man for what he had been able to accomplish in his short career.

Because Toscano arguably was the toughest personal injury attorney in the Lehigh Valley. He had acquired that reputation not by trumpeting claims on TV commercials and not by exploiting his underlings, but by the din of hard work and dedication. He never stopped or rested or took a vacation. And he never complained or backed away from the sixteen-hour days that were his routine. And he didn't suffer employees who weren't willing to put it all on the line and work just as hard as he did, which is why turnover at his firm was rapid and legendary. It wasn't that the people he hired were lazy; Toscano just burned them up, and when they broke down, he tossed them away and brought in fresh meat.

Toscano was not interested in niceties. He considered small talk or getting-to-know-you conversation to be bullshit and refused to indulge. His manner was so gruff that it turned off many prospective clients. Toscano didn't care. His record spoke for itself. Winning cases was everything, and if a potential client needed stroking or psychotherapy, "Let the fucker go see Dr. Phil," he would say sarcastically to anyone in earshot, including the sniffling client.

When Gilbert had called Toscano two weeks ago to ask him if he would be willing to meet, Toscano's reaction had been immediate and positive. He had read Tiffany's initial articles and was intrigued. He knew that legal action would be brought by several parties but figured it would be handled by in-house counsel at the device companies, the hospital targets, and by the newspaper. He had salivated over the idea of representing an injured party—for the publicity and the money it might generate—but assumed he would never get a taste. When the call came, he was pleased to tell Gilbert he would consider representing him for a negotiable fee, pending a meeting at Toscano's office.

Gilbert had arrived at Toscano's lair for that initial meeting feeling anxious and vulnerable. He had asked Tiffany to accompany him, but she too quickly pointed out that their being seen in public together, particularly visiting a prominent attorney's office, would do neither of them any good. Gilbert knew it was an excuse. Tiffany liked him, but she wasn't about to fight his battles for him. She had enough action of her own.

Fortunately, Gilbert only had to wait a few minutes before he was ushered into Toscano's office. Gilbert had assumed it would be palatial and was surprised to see that it was carefully but modestly furnished with a clean desk, comfortable chairs and a sofa, and a few prints and certificates to decorate the plain walls. A window behind Toscano's desk provided abundant light and a view of a couple of deserted warehouses and garages, shuttered years ago during Allentown's economic decline but recently purchased and under renovation.

"I enjoy that view," Toscano was known to say. "It reminds me that my timing was perfect." Meaning that Toscano's decision to hang a shingle and invest his career in Allentown had occurred just at the moment when his hometown had begun its renaissance. From a time when it was the butt of jokes and stinging song lyrics from the likes of Billy Joel, it had used its central location, natural resources, and the energy of its citizens to rise from economic collapse, capture new industry, and revitalize its business community. And with a surging population of Generation Xers and millennials came the need for medical care and legal assistance, just as Toscano had forecasted when he had surveyed his opportunities after graduation from Penn Law. Solo practice may have scared some of his classmates, but for Toscano, it was the only option.

As was his custom, Toscano was well prepared for that first meeting with Gilbert.

"Let's get started, Dr. Gilbert," Toscano began as he ushered Gilbert to a seat on the sofa. Toscano took his place in an armchair and weighed in immediately. "I know what your problem is."

"Do you really?"

"Yes. You're here because you've been on a crusade to stop certain doctors and device manufacturers from putting unnecessary pacemakers and devices in unwitting patients. When you were stymied by your hospital and by your professional organizations, you made a decision to go public with your accusations. Tiffany Springer published a series of articles in the *Allentown Times Herald* in which you were a named source, and you're worried that your employer is going to cashier you and that you might get sued by the parties she has identified. How's that?"

Gilbert was impressed. "I'd say you pretty much nailed it, Mr. Toscano. Except for that part about my employer. I've already been put on notice. I'm history at my hospital—unless, of course, I somehow manage to pull a rabbit out of my hat and recover the referral base I seem to have lost."

"Which is unlikely, given the fact that the doctors that Tiffany is attacking were your primary source."

"And everyone else in the world is angry with me for whistleblowing."

"Interesting choice of words, Dr. Gilbert. Because one of the ways we're going to help you is by finding out how much of the device abuse that occurred affected Medicare patients."

"Federal whistleblower statutes, right?"

"Precisely. If we can achieve that status for you, not only will your job be protected, but there could be a huge windfall."

"Which is why you gave me an appointment so quickly."

"Fair enough, Dr. Gilbert. I always prefer to have all of the cards on the table. By the way, can I call you Ray if you call me Nicky, as I prefer?" Toscano hated his given name, Nicholas, and gone out of his way to get people to use his nickname. Besides, to Toscano, *Nicky* sounded colorful. A name to remember.

Gilbert smiled. "Sure, Nicky."

"OK. You know I'm a successful lawyer and that this firm has flourished—and was flourishing even before things turned around for this region. Why? Because I'm not only a good lawyer but a good businessman. I don't take loser cases. They either need to be potential moneymakers, or they need to raise the profile of this firm. Yours has the potential to do both. The bonus here is that you're doing the right thing. If those doctors were doing what you say they were doing, they deserve to get it up their rear ends. And I'm just the person to represent you. So you see, there are many reasons why I decided to see you here so promptly, and why you should agree to hire me as your attorney."

"I don't have much money, Nicky."

"I figured that, Ray. I took a little peek into your private life. Don't worry; I haven't gotten to your financials yet, but I understand why you're strapped. Like I said, I think this case has the potential to be a big-time win for you and, thus, for me. So I'll agree to an initial minimal hourly fee in exchange for an eventual contingency agreement."

"Which means?"

"That if and when you recover any money from the feds for blowing the whistle, I get a significant taste."

"Significant being ..."

"Forty percent."

"More like a gulp than a taste, Nicky."

"Another thing you'll learn about me, Ray, is that I don't negotiate. When I put a number on the table, it's firm. Take it or leave it."

"I want to get this over with, Nicky."

"Of course you do, Ray. And you don't want to work with a lesser lawyer and significantly reduce your chances for success. So shall we get started? This is what I'd like to do: give me a couple of weeks and your permission to examine everything about you and this case. You'll come back here, and I'll tell you exactly what the situation is and how we can proceed. I promise there will be a way forward, no matter what. I just don't know which tactic I need to pursue to get us where we want to be."

And so the first meeting had ended. Now, on this dreary Monday morning, Gilbert was on his way back for the follow-up meeting with Nicky Toscano that he was anticipating and dreading at the same time. As Toscano had emphasized, he would be brutally honest with Gilbert and would leave nothing out, just as Gilbert desired—or thought he did.

When he returned, Nicky's private secretary led him immediately to a conference room down a short hallway from Toscano's office. Nicky was seated at the head of a long table, flanked by two of his young associates, whom he introduced as Lucas and Katie, fresh-faced twentysomethings who had helped him "explore the wonderful world of Ray Gilbert." Gilbert took a seat next to Katie, who nodded her hello.

"I hope you don't mind having Lucas and Katie here. I wanted to include them in our meeting in case you or I had any specific questions they could answer from their research. Believe me, Ray; they have been all over this thing."

Gilbert blushed. "I hope they weren't disappointed."

"In what, Ray?" Toscano asked. "Look, this isn't about impugning you or your work. This is about understanding the strengths and weaknesses of your case, strategizing our approach, and anticipating how and where they may come after you. So get over yourself. Everyone has skeletons. Yours are no worse than anyone's."

Lucas and Katie remained silent, showing no reaction to Toscano's preamble. They clearly understood their place in the discussion and were prepared to be discreet.

"Let's get started with this," Toscano said, sliding a folder across the table to Gilbert. "First of all, I need you to sign the retention agreement. It has all the stuff we talked about last time, including my initial fee and the contingency clause."

"Do I get to read it?" Gilbert asked.

"Help yourself. The clock is running, Ray, and I have a full schedule today. The longer you take, the less time we'll have to do important business."

Gilbert scanned the document, pretending he absorbed the details; he signed two copies and handed them back to Toscano.

"Perfect. I'll give you an executed copy when we're finished. Now, onto important stuff." Toscano gestured to Katie, who passed another folder to Gilbert. "This dossier includes everything we needed to know about you, Ray. Stuff about your parents, where you went to school and did your training, and details about your private life."

Gilbert opened the folder and began to skim the dossier. "And what did you conclude?"

"There's nothing to *conclude*, Ray," Nicky answered. "I told you this is not a judgment but an investigation. Katie, can you capsulize our findings, please?"

Katie spent the next ten minutes reviewing their findings, with

Gilbert listening expectantly, waiting for the inevitable recounting of the undoing of his private life. Katie was kind, electing not to get into the details of the many affairs that had ruined his marriage prior to his wife's death, his torrid relationship with Liz, or the other women he had slept with over the last three years. But she did specifically name Tiffany Springer as one of his bedmates, since she and Toscano considered that relationship to be a potential Achilles' heel.

"The plaintiffs will imply that your relationship with Tiffany was the explanation for why she decided to go after your targets so vehemently and without justification or evidence, Ray. I'm sure you know that. They will also use your affair to challenge the truth of the articles. They will imply it was all just pillow talk."

"Of course," was all that Gilbert could say.

"And your other affairs will just make the whole thing more lurid. Pattern of behavior. So there you are. What else, Katie?"

"We did find some things that will play well on your behalf, Dr. Gilbert," Katie said, attempting to mollify. "You've done good work in the community for a long time; your patients adore you, as do the people you've trained; and you have lived modestly."

"But we're going to have to deal with your reputation as a ladies' man," Toscano interjected, returning to the brutal facts. "Let's move on to other materials, shall we?"

Over the next hour, the three attorneys took turns summarizing the contents of several files they had built over the past two weeks. Each dealt with a different aspect of the case, from hospital procedural volume statistics, to literature and guideline reviews concerning indications for device implantation, to device company business reports. In each case, Lucas or Katie would take the lead, providing the meat of the data, leaving Toscano to offer his perspective, especially how each of the briefs would fit into his firm's strategy and the likelihood that the data would affect any potential litigation brought against Gilbert. Gilbert was provided with an exquisitely organized report folder for each section and advised to maintain its confidentiality at all costs, but he was admonished to read each one thoroughly and to respond as soon as possible to Toscano's legal team.

By the end of the session, Gilbert's head was spinning, but Toscano was laser-focused, as usual, and in control of the entire matter.

"Look, Ray. This is a lot to absorb. We know that. What we need you to do is go through the material carefully and call out those things you believe are the most important. For example, we saw a recent article from Scandinavia that was published in the *New England Journal of Medicine* that said that putting defibrillators in certain kinds of patients didn't do any good. What do you think about that? Is it something we should rely on? Was it pivotal in your thinking about this issue or not?"

"You need my perspective."

"Precisely. We're just dumb lawyers, and we'll never understand the medical issues as well as you do. As we go forward, we have to carefully marshal our arguments so we can persuade a jury, if it comes to that. They have to be convinced that you acted intelligently, with reason, and with the best interest of patients firmly in mind. Does that make sense? And even more important, can you do it?"

"I think so. At least I can give it a shot."

"Good, Ray. That's all I can ask. But now for the tough part."

"Go ahead."

"No more sleeping around. You're going to be watched by several different groups, and you can't afford the scandal. We also can assume that these people will be trying to get information, and we don't want any more pillow talk either. You can date people if you like, but you had better know who they are ahead of time."

"I understand."

"And no more Tiffany."

"Really? Not even if I'm careful?"

"No such thing as careful now, my friend. Too many sharks in the water. And I'm afraid you won't be able to resist that little boost you get from the cocaine and weed."

"How did you find out about that?"

"Seriously, Ray? You think that kind of thing is hard to discover? And if my investigators could uncover such things, how much more dirt do you think a professional firm hired by a large drug company will unearth?"

"There's nothing more to know, Nicky; I swear."

"Save it, Ray. I believe you, but you'll be seen and probably photographed when you're completely unaware. And Tiffany will draw even more scrutiny. They'll know about every boil on your butt. So I suggest you back off immediately."

"I'm supposed to see her at my place tonight."

"Cancel it, Ray. The stuff in the latest article puts the focus right on you. You have the attention of a lot of people right now."

"Is this permanent, Nicky?" Gilbert asked, somewhat piteously, surprising the lawyers, who had thought the Tiffany thing was just a sex opportunity.

"At least until we see where we're headed," Toscano answered. "Things may die down eventually."

"Do you really think so?"

"It won't be in the best interest of the hospitals or the device companies to keep this thing going. So unless we choose to literally make a federal case out of it—and we very well might—they're going to want to put it behind them and hope that people simply forget."

"Public amnesia."

"Happens all the time. But at this point, it's way too early to speculate. I see no reason to do anything until we see what action your hospital takes. Hopefully, they'll also let things just settle down and keep you on."

"I have no delusions about that, Nicky. It's just a matter of time until I leave."

"Which is fine, as long as you do it on your terms and not theirs. And that they don't try to sabotage your chances to find another job and a place to live. That's where I come in."

"I already feel better about things, knowing I have someone like you on my side."

"That's why they call us *advocates*, Ray," Toscano said, smiling for the first time since their meeting had begun. "I suggest we wrap this up for today. Take the files with you, study them as I said, and we'll meet again next week. My secretary will get you on my calendar at your convenience, and she'll coordinate with Lucas's and Katie's schedules as well. And she'll give you a copy of your agreement for your files."

Toscano stood, signaling the end of the meeting. He shook hands with Gilbert and escorted him to the conference room door. "And try not to worry too much, Ray. The way I see it, we will not only get you on the right path, but we might even be able to get you a little nest egg in the process."

After the door closed, Toscano turned around and walked back to the head of the conference room table, where Lucas and Katie were standing, also waiting to be dismissed.

"This is complicated," Toscano said, as much to himself as to his associates, who nodded approvingly to anything their boss had to say. "The key is going to be keeping his chestnuts out of the fire while figuring out how aggressive to be with the whistleblower thing. It's going to be a real high-wire act, any way you look at it. Hopefully, we can help that schmuck keep his balance."

18
CHAPTER

Ned Armbruster paced anxiously around his office, twirling a pencil in his left hand like a drum major marching to a John Philip Sousa cadence. "Where the hell is she?" he muttered to himself, a question he had posed several times to his secretary, Norma, several assistants, and anyone else he came across. The answer from all of them had been the same. Tiffany had informed everyone that she was going to see her family in Pittsburgh. According to her parents, she had stayed at their house over the weekend until Monday midday, when she had said her goodbyes and started her five-hour drive back to the Allentown area. She was due in the office early this Tuesday morning to begin a round of meetings with Ned, the publishers, and newspaper attorneys to deal with the deluge of requests and inquiries after publication of the most incendiary of her series. Phineas had ordered Ned to put it all out there at their latest meeting.

"I want you to tell Tiffany to continue to name names," he had told Ned, as Tiffany was putting the finishing touches on her latest installment. "Only those for whom you have good information, of course. We don't want to be reckless. But it's time to finish this exposé with a flourish. We want to finger all of the people who were harming patients. We don't want anybody to go to jail, necessarily. We just want them to stop fucking around and get their colleagues to be careful. That's the tack I want to take."

Ned said he understood and would pass along McCoy's instructions exactly, like the good soldier he was. But what he didn't tell Phineas, and later on would sadly regret, was that he was beginning to suspect that Tiffany's research was sloppy, to say the least. On those few occasions when he had taken the time to examine source documents and compare them to what Tiffany had written, it was clear that she was taking liberties with the facts. When she didn't know something, she didn't admit it or dig deeper but made assumptions that, at times, were unfounded. For example, Ned asked Tiffany to provide more details about kickbacks. How much money was involved, and how was it paid out and to whom and when? Tiffany's responses were uniformly vague, assuring Ned that she had all of those facts but didn't want to weigh down the articles with deadly details.

To this point, Ned had been able to satisfy himself that her overall conclusions were correct and defensible and that the industry had clearly attempted to manipulate physicians with aggressive marketing schemes. Impugning individual physicians and hospitals, however, escalated the risk substantially. And if Tiffany's facts were as distorted on these accusations, as they had been in earlier installments, the newspaper could find itself in a very awkward position.

In the end, Ned had decided to wait to see what Tiffany actually wrote. With a strong bias to publish and after getting his marching orders from Phineas, he had given a green light to the latest installment with only minor edits. Now, when the shit was clearly headed for the fan, Tiffany, her laptop computer, and the files and documents they needed for their defense were nowhere to be found.

"Goddamn Tiffany!" Ned exclaimed each time Norma informed him that she had been unsuccessful in her attempts to find the reporter.

"I've tried everything, Ned. I've called her cell a hundred times and emailed and texted her as well. She usually answers quickly, even when she's traveling. I also asked her family to call her friends out in Pittsburgh, thinking she may have stopped by to see one of them on the way home. I called her condo manager, and he told me her place is locked up, she didn't answer her door, and her car is not in her space. I don't know what else to do."

"What about that idiot boyfriend of hers?"

"You mean Dr. Gilbert?"

"Yes, Gilbert. How many idiot boyfriends does she have?"

"I don't know. I called his office. He's not in today."

"Then call his cell phone."

"I don't have his number, and his office said they don't give out cell numbers for physicians."

"They're afraid patients might actually be able to get through to ask them questions."

Norma shrugged. She was young and relatively new to her job and not yet ready to deal with Ned's sarcasm.

"All right. It's too early to file a missing person claim, so I guess we'll just do the best we can. Do me a favor and see if you can get into Tiffany's computer here at work. If you can, search to see if she has any files on her hard drive that relate to this device series she's doing."

"I'll have to get IT to do that, sir."

"Whatever, damn it. Just get it done quickly. I'm in a corner here, and Phineas is going to start getting feisty if I'm not able to help our lawyers with some hard facts."

"Understood," Norma said, backing out of the office, as if Ned were royalty who couldn't see the back of one of his subjects, and wondering if a transfer to another executive at the paper might be a good idea.

Gilbert's absence from work that Tuesday didn't go completely unrecognized either. The electrophysiology lab staff called his cell and his office line several times.

"He has a couple of cases down here," the laboratory supervisor explained to the secretary that Gilbert shared with five other doctors.

"Are they urgent?" the secretary asked.

"Of course not. Ray doesn't do important cases anymore. One's a tilt table test, and the other is an elective cardioversion for some gomer who's in atrial fibrillation. He can do them both in a half hour. The problem is, they came in as outpatients so they're prepped and sitting in our holding area, and the families are in the waiting room."

"Can someone else do the cases?"

"If I give these cases to someone else and Ray shows up, he'll eat me for lunch. He needs the income, and let's just say he hasn't exactly been knocking it out of the park recently."

"OK. I'll try him again in a few minutes and tell him to call you if I reach him."

But Gilbert never surfaced that day, and neither did Tiffany. Ned's anxiety mounted by the hour, but he managed to get through the day without pushing the alarm button. He fell asleep at home only after a generous dose of bourbon and arrived at work on Wednesday, convinced that Tiffany would be at her desk, offering some lame excuse as to why she had disappeared.

So when he saw her empty desk and blank computer screen, he went directly to Norma and asked her to call the newspaper's security office. "Tell them this involves one of our reporters. And make sure they know it's urgent," Ned needlessly stipulated. Norma was well aware of the seriousness of the situation. Ned had someone on the line within seconds.

"One of our reporters is missing," Ned started.

"Tiffany Springer, sir?"

"How did you know that?"

"Heard some rumors that she was MIA. I figured her boss would be worried about her, given the situation, sir."

"Well, then, Sherlock, you understand why this is a priority."

"I do, sir. I assume you want us to contact the authorities."

"This isn't *Casablanca*, damn it. Call the police, and tell them to find her."

"They'll want to talk to you, sir."

"Whatever. Just get them on the trail while it's still relatively warm."

"Roger that, sir."

Ned hung up, shaking his head at the *Smokey and the Bandit* language the security people insisted on using. He reminded himself to direct his anger appropriately. The rent-a-cops the newspaper employed weren't expected to be anything more than the frustrated police officers they were, and they weren't very helpful in this kind of situation. They mostly tried to keep the buildings secure and theft-free. Company policy said to call them first for incidents at the paper, but missing persons was way over their heads. So why give the poor schlep a hard time?

The police who arrived at the newspaper a half hour later weren't much better—two uniform cops who were probably more comfortable with directing traffic than finding a missing reporter. But once again, Ned persevered and answered their pro forma questions, promising to provide Tiffany's personal information so that her family could be informed and interrogated. While Norma went into Tiffany's contacts and jotted down the phone numbers and addresses of family, the officers reviewed the procedures with Ned.

"We'll take this information and spend the next few hours making phone calls, sir. If nothing turns up, we'll pass the case on to our detective squad, and they'll intensify the search. If they don't find anything locally, they'll put out an all-points. We'll find her, sir. Don't you worry."

"Alive."

"Sir?"

"I want you to find her alive."

A smirk from the younger of the two officers. "Oh, I think she'll be alive, Mr. Armbruster. I've been on the force for ten years, and I can't remember a missing person in this jurisdiction being found dead. Unless it was from natural causes. And I gather Ms. Springer is a young, healthy person?"

"She is. And I hope you're right, Officer," Ned said, refraining from reminding the officers that no one had placed herself in as much jeopardy as Tiffany had, with an exposé that the entire country was talking about.

The officers left, and the waiting began. By the end of the business day, the police informed Ned that they had not been able to contact Tiffany but had notified her parents and siblings, all of whom lived in the Pittsburgh area. Her parents were planning to drive to Allentown immediately and wanted to help in any way possible. Tiffany had not told them she planned to stop anywhere, and there were no reported fatal car accidents along the turnpike she would have used for the return trip. In addition, the police had obtained permission from Tiffany's parents to enter her apartment, which they did using a key from the condo office. Not only was it empty, but it was in perfect order. The mail piled up in her box confirmed that Tiffany had not used the place since she had left for Pittsburgh. With the routine inquiries over, the uniforms were turning the case over to detectives, who would surely be in touch with Ned soon.

The next morning at nine o'clock, two men in cheap suits showed up unannounced to speak with Ned. As soon as they produced their badges, Norma understood and asked them to have a seat for just a moment while she made sure that Ned was ready to see them. Within seconds, Ned popped out of his office, walked over, and extended his hand.

"Good morning, gentlemen. I'm Ned Armbruster. You're here about Tiffany Springer."

"Yes, sir. My name is Patrick Burgoyne, and this is Danny Ramos. Mind if we talk in your office?"

"Of course," Ned said and led the two through the door and directed them to a couple of armchairs in front of his cluttered desk. He only had a moment to size them up and saw little to distinguish either of them. Burgoyne—obviously the senior, graying hair slicked back from a forehead that was just a little too big for the rest of his pock-marked face. Ramos—looking like his Hispanic name, brown eyes and dark features, with a well-maintained goatee.

Burgoyne started in. "Mr. Armbruster, we just got this file from our uniforms late last evening, so we haven't really dived into it yet. But we will. We just wanted to get your perspective on this case before we expand the search for Tiffany Springer beyond her family. I know you're worried about her—for obvious reasons."

"Yes, Detective, for very obvious reasons."

"Do you suspect foul play in this case?"

"Yes, I do. Tiffany had received some death threats."

"When was that, Mr. Armbruster?" Ramos asked.

"A couple of weeks ago."

"Because of the articles she was writing?"

"Yes, I believe so."

"You believe so? Were they emails? Did you see the messages?"

"No. Tiffany didn't show them to me. She just told me about them."

"She had no idea who sent them?"

"I don't think so, although according to her, they obviously came from someone who had a stake in the medical device scandal."

"We need to see those emails, Mr. Armbruster. Can you access them?"

"We had our IT people go on her computer here yesterday, and they couldn't find anything to help us find her. I think she carried many of her files and her personal emails on her laptop, which isn't here."

"And she was allowed to do that?"

"No, but reporters around here do as they please. We don't come down on them for it, as long as they password-protect the computer and sensitive files."

"Were there any other threatening messages? Like letters or such?"

"She didn't tell me that. We went through her desk and didn't find anything. You can check her apartment, I guess."

"We plan to do that after we leave here. Is there anyone else we should contact as we begin our search for Tiffany?" Ramos asked.

"I didn't know Tiffany well enough to meet her friends. There is one person you do need to contact, though. A physician named Ray Gilbert."

"The guy at Allentown General?" Burgoyne asked.

"You know him?"

"No. But I've been reading Tiffany's series right along, and that's the guy she says fed her the information that helped her crack the case, right?"

"Yes."

"How friendly were they, Mr. Armbruster?"

"Let's say very close."

"They were having an affair?"

"I think so," Ned said, hoping to keep from looking like a complete idiot.

"And do you know where Dr. Gilbert resides?"

"No, but you should be able to call him at his office."

"Anyone else you suggest we talk to?"

"No, but feel free to interview her colleagues here. Norma, my secretary, can give you the names of the people who know her best in the newsroom. They might be able to give you a lead."

"Thanks, Mr. Armbruster. We'll get on this and keep you posted. If anything else occurs to you, please call us at this number." Ramos handed over a card.

And so began the routine police investigation of Tiffany Springer's disappearance, an investigation that took three days to complete and that was solved by a cleaning lady.

Who, in this case, was a sweet, diminutive Portuguese lady named Isabel, whose job it was to clean the rooms at the Little Town Motel, situated on the outskirts of Bethlehem, Pennsylvania. The irony of the name was lost on most of the clientele, who weren't interested in the ambience. What attracted them was the remote location and the absolute discretion of the manager and staff, who understood their business model and adhered strictly to the rules of engagement—cash preferable to credit cards, the statements of which might be subject to spousal inspection; no interruptions under any circumstances; and rentals for hours, days, or weeks, with the option of foregoing maid service for the sake of absolute privacy. Which was why the scene in room 235 went undiscovered for as long as it did.

"Mr. Jimmy, I need to talk to you," Isabel said to her fat manager, who, on this particular day, like most others, was seated in his office, feet up on his desk, surveying a wrestling magazine.

"What is it, Isabel?" he said in his most dismissive tone. "Did we run out of toilet paper again?"

"No, sir, we have plenty of that—this week."

"Then why are you bothering me during my lunch break?"

Break? Isabel thought. *That would mean that this lazy shit actually did some work, which he never does.* But Isabel knew better than to crack wise with Mr. Jimmy, who made sure that any transgressions on Isabel's part, including silly requests for a living wage, would be a good excuse for him to call the immigration police, something Isabel knew she and her family couldn't let happen.

"It's room 235, sir."

"What about it, Isabel?" Mr. Jimmy leaned over his belly to look at his desk ledger. "Paid up for three weeks. You're supposed to leave it alone whenever they put a privacy sign on the door. Which, as I recollect, they did."

"And I leave alone, Mr. Jimmy, I promise. But it smells bad."

"Did you open the door, Isabel?"

"No, sir. The front window is open a little, and I get a whiff. Smells like something is rotting in there, Mr. Jimmy."

"Seriously?"

"Come see for yourself."

"This better be for real, Isabel, or I'm going to be pissed."

"Come, come, you look in window."

Which is not exactly what Jimmy did. Because the stench that came out of the window of room 235 turned him on his heels and blew him back to his office, where he wasted no time in calling the police. The precinct receptionist took the information, including the aliases of the room's renters. The call didn't take long. No use asking for information about the renter. The police and everyone else in Allentown knew all about the Little Town Motel and the purpose it served. The likelihood that whoever was in the room had used a real name was low.

"Don't do anything until the squad car gets there in a few minutes," the dispatcher said.

The uniforms pulled up about twenty minutes later and went to the office. Jimmy filled them in with what little he knew, and together, they walked over to 235. They knocked loudly and called out the names of the renters before asking Mr. Jimmy to use his master key. What the uniforms found when Mr. Jimmy opened that door, with Isabel crouched behind him, would occupy the crime scene unit for the next several hours and the police for weeks.

The room was a mess—clothes and empty food containers thrown around the room, without a major surface spared. A man and a woman lay dead in the king-size bed. They were uncovered and naked; two used condoms were perched precariously on the bedside table. They were facing each other, locked in a mortal embrace, with heads thrown back as if struggling to disengage at the moment of their departure from life.

Time of death was later estimated as at least two days prior to their discovery, judging from the rigidity and lividity of the bodies. What killed the loving couple wasn't going to take a genius to figure out. Judging from the pills, reefers, and injection paraphernalia on the bedside table, the lovers had likely gone a little too far in their attempts to enhance their sexual experience, a supposition that was readily and easily verified by the toxicology test results a few days later. That, together with no other obvious findings at the autopsies ordered by the medical examiner, made the cause of death pretty clear.

As was confirming the identity of the unfortunate couple. Not only had both been on the missing person's list for the past two days, but they had abundant personal information in their possession, in addition to the cars that were parked outside their room at the motel.

When Ned got the call an hour or so later, he dropped the phone and fell back into his chair. His intense sadness and his guilt over losing a young colleague and mentee were mixed with an ironic reflection that Tiffany's series would reverberate farther than she ever could have dreamed. Any follow-up installments would have to be written without her, but her messy death ensured that her exposé would be the most spectacular story in the history of the *Allentown Times Herald*.

19
CHAPTER

anny Ramos was sitting at his desk that Friday afternoon, staring intently at his computer. He was reviewing information that had been gathered about Springer and Gilbert, trying to come up with a clue as to the reason for their disappearance. "If I can figure out why, finding them will be a hell of a lot easier," he had said to his partner, Patrick, several times over the past couple of days. The couple may have gotten themselves into a whole lot of trouble, but this was Allentown, for crying out loud. People got killed here, but it wasn't as common an event as it was in Harlem, where Danny had grown up and made his bones. Which was one of the principal reasons he had let his wife convince him to move to Pennsylvania. She was in constant fear that Danny would get shot working his detective job in Harlem. So when the recruiters had called, she talked him into moving, using every argument she could marshal, including better schools for their two kids, affordable housing, and access to the outdoors, none of which the city could provide.

Danny had to admit that she had been right, on most counts at least. Allentown was a better place to live, but it was also boring as hell. Danny immediately missed the New York buzz and the constant crime activity that made his job interesting. It wasn't unusual for him to be working four or five murders simultaneously. And the beauty of it was that they were usually solvable because the motives weren't complicated, and neither were the criminals, who were usually stealing to fuel a habit of one kind or another. Stupid enough and desperate enough to leave behind clues that were easy to find and follow. A high close rate made Danny look good and feel good about himself. It also helped propel him to senior detective in record time.

Allentown had some of those same crimes and criminals, but the number was far less. People whacked people now and again, but they did it for a wider variety of reasons and with much more refined methods, making Danny's job harder and less fun. This case was a prime example.

"Do you think this missing Tiffany girl was murdered, white bread?" Danny had asked Patrick that morning during their drive into the office.

Burgoyne lived a little farther east of the city and picked up Danny whenever the wife said she needed their car. "Why do you have to call me that?" Patrick asked, pretending to be annoyed.

"'Cause that's what you are. White and soft, right?"

"Yeah, but I don't call you spic. That would just piss you off."

"It would. But who said the word is fair? I can call myself a spic if I want, but you can't. For the same reason that black people call themselves the N-word, but that word is poison for anyone else."

Patrick smiled and nodded. Danny was right. And he admitted—to himself, at least—that he liked his partner, which had been a surprise. Burgoyne had gone ballistic when his captain had called him in months ago and told him that he had a new partner who was a Hispanic refugee detective from Harlem.

"I don't need or want a partner, sir," Patrick had retorted. He was still smarting from the sudden death of his good friend and long-time partner, who had died of a heart attack while chasing a suspect down an alley, just a few months before Danny arrived.

"Too bad, Patrick," his boss had responded. "Everybody needs a partner, and Ramos looks like a good egg to me. So give him a chance."

And damn, if the captain hadn't been right. A new partner was exactly what Patrick needed, and he had enjoyed getting to know Danny and helping to break him in. And it didn't take long for Danny to warm up to Patrick and start bantering, as they were this morning. Danny showed a sense of humor and family values that Patrick admired. Patrick enjoyed the interplay, using humor to suppress the racist feelings he had inherited from his bigoted father.

"You didn't answer my question, white bread," Danny said, agitated. "Do you think that Tiffany got offed?"

"That's certainly possible. She got a lot of people pretty stirred up, and I'm sure they wanted to shut her mouth. But—"

"But what?"

"If that was somebody's intention, why did they wait until she wrote and published so much of her story? If they wanted to kill her, why not do it sooner? And what about her boyfriend? Where is he in all of this? Doesn't make a whole lot of sense. The simplest explanation is that they just took off together."

"I disagree. Too many things against that theory, like why didn't she pack up her stuff and take it with her if she was leaving town? And why not tell her boss at the paper so they wouldn't call the police?"

"You have a point, but I'll bet Gilbert talked her into it. They did it on the spur of the moment, just to be cool, and they're going to show up somewhere soon, giggling about how much trouble they caused."

"Could also be a stunt," Danny countered.

"What do you mean?"

"More publicity for the articles if the reporter suddenly goes missing, even if she surfaces in a few days. People get off on that suspense shit."

That early-morning conversation continued without a firm conclusion, and they left things unresolved after they hit the office, each going off to chase down clues, calling contacts and colleagues. So when Patrick walked into Danny's cubicle later that day and interrupted his computer research with a confused look on his face, Danny had no trouble figuring out why.

"They found Tiffany, didn't they?" Danny guessed.

"Yup, and Gilbert too. Let's go find out what happened. I'll tell you what I know on the way. Ain't much, but it doesn't sound good at all."

The drive to the Little Town Motel took about fifteen minutes, during which Patrick informed Danny that the couple had been found dead, including what little he had been told by the uniforms who had responded to the call. By the time they reached the motel, they were both eager to get into the room and start looking for clues. But being seasoned detectives, they remembered to take care of business first.

They spoke to the uniforms who were stationed all around the parking lot, reminding them to keep the nosey public off of the premises. "Crime tape is a good start, but you'll see that people won't pay attention."

Next, they began to dispatch other patrolmen to interview everyone on the premises. "Some of them won't want to tell you their real identity, for obvious reasons, but make sure you identify all of them. If they're cooperative and don't know anything, just get what you can and cut them loose. If you suspect they know something, come get one of us, and we'll question them here or take them to the station."

Patrick and Danny reserved the manager's and the cleaning lady's interviews for themselves. "Tell them to sit tight, and we'll get to them as soon as we go over the scene," Patrick told the officers who were stationed outside the office. He knew that this situation was going to attract the brass, including Captain Detweiler, and he wanted to get as much done as possible before he had to start answering their questions.

After donning gowns, gloves, booties, and paper caps, Patrick and Danny made their way into the room. The smell was overwhelming, explaining why most of the crime scene technicians had masks on. Danny and Patrick opted for handkerchiefs over their noses as they walked carefully around the bed.

"What's your take?" Patrick asked Joe McAnulty, the crime scene chief who had been summoned soon after his people had arrived.

"Very complicated, Patrick. To be honest, I don't know for sure what happened to them. The obvious answer is that they overshot the runway with drugs and managed to off themselves."

"You mean both of them screwed up?"

"Exactly. Hard to believe that they both overdosed by mistake. I guess it's also possible that one of them murdered the other and then committed suicide. The killer would have had to time his or her own overdose so he or she could get on the bed and cuddle with a corpse. Pretty creepy and also a little hard to believe."

"Or—" Danny started to cut in.

"Or somebody murdered them and made it look like an overdose. If that's true, this was a very professional job because we haven't found anything that looks like violence or force. No marks on either body, no blood, and no signs of forced entry."

"So the murderers would have had to break in here, maybe while they were asleep, and inject them with something that would have put them down quickly, without a struggle and little noise."

"Yup. Both of them have a couple of holes in their arms that look pretty new."

"If that's the case, the murderers would have had some way to know they were both using."

"Something like that. The fact that they were users will make our tox analysis pretty worthless, unless we come up with something in very high concentration or a product that the loving couple here wouldn't have had access to."

"That's unlikely. He was a doctor, remember."

"First things first," Joe cautioned. "Let's see what they have in their blood, and then we can try to figure out if this was recreational drugs gone bad or a very well-thought-out assassination."

After Patrick and Danny satisfied themselves that the crime scene was secure and in good hands with Joe, they shed their protective gear and went outside for an update from the uniforms and the other detectives, who had filtered over to lend a hand. They learned that, as expected, none of the occupants had heard or seen a thing. No one had seen Gilbert and Springer arrive or leave for food or use their cars. As far as they could tell, the couple had rendered themselves invisible for this little adventure.

Mr. Jimmy, on the other hand, was willing to answer questions. Most of what he said was irrelevant, but at least he knew something of the couple. This was the first time they had used the place. They paid for several days up front, telling him that they wanted to keep their stuff in the room, undisturbed. They brought in food the first night they were there, and then he didn't see them again. He figured they were in there because their cars hadn't moved for three days. They had a DO NOT DISTURB sign on the door, so he had told Isabel to leave some towels outside the door but not to knock. The towels were still out there when the police arrived.

"It was the smell that made me call the police. Man, I'm a hunter, so I know when an animal is rotting," Jimmy explained.

"Good work, Jimmy. You can go about your business, and we'll let you know if we have any more questions," Patrick said as he walked away, wondering how many times Jimmy had looked the other way when criminals did their criminal thing at his establishment.

"We have a lot of work to do, partner," Patrick said as the detectives walked toward their car.

"You can say that again. There's a bunch here I don't understand, Patrick."

"I agree. Like what the hell were these two pretty-well-off people doing at this fleabag of a motel? They each had a pretty nice place to shack up."

"Unless Tiffany was convinced that someone was after her."

"Somebody who also knew about her boyfriend and where he lived."

"In which case, getting out of town for a while—until whoever was coming after them backed off—may have seemed like a good idea."

"Or they were using this place until they could arrange a real relocation, someplace where they couldn't be found."

"Right. We need to get the phone records from that motel room and from their cells."

"And their computers, to see if they booked a long trip to a warmer climate."

Over the next several days, Patrick and Danny worked just about every angle they could think of to try to understand what had happened to the tragic couple. They interviewed family, coworkers, friends, and anyone who had had contact with either Ray or Tiffany in the days and weeks leading up to their deaths. They learned a good deal about the couple, their personalities gradually becoming manifest, like an old Polaroid photo slowly gaining definition.

Gilbert's life was medicine and women, both of which he pursued passionately. And on each front, he had interspersed success with mind-numbing failures. Clearly a brilliant and caring physician, he pissed off his bosses fairly often and suffered the consequences, his path to promotion blocked by vindictive and jealous foes who delighted in his failures. And though he had no problem attracting women, he had illustrated an amazing inability to establish a real relationship with any of them. Except for Linda Vespucci, a Wilkes-Barre beauty, whom Gilbert had met during her employment as a nurse in the coronary care unit at Gladwyne Memorial where he had trained.GMH. She moved with Gilbert to Allentown, where shortly thereafter she became pregnant, dying suddenly at home before the baby was born. It wasn't long after her death that Gilbert was spending time with Liz and several other women he met at bars. He thought he had rediscovered true love with Tiffany but, unfortunately, never had a chance to find out.

Tiffany was not much different. Her passion was journalism, so she had eschewed the idea of a relationship with a man until she established herself as a first-rate reporter. She used men for lots of things, including sex and information, and then discarded them after she had extracted what she needed. Her relationship with Gilbert had started the same way. Ned Armbruster believed she was screwing Gilbert to get as much information out of him as she could. But people who knew Tiffany and spoke with her before she died, including her family, believed that Tiffany had finally found someone she cared about. If that were true, and Tiffany really was attracted to Gilbert, Patrick and Danny thought that Tiffany might have considered leaving Allentown and beginning a new life with him.

As interesting as the details of Ray's and Tiffany's lives may have seemed, Patrick and Danny both knew that the case was going to rely on physical evidence. The coroner eventually had to determine the cause of death, and if it was drugs, how they had been administered. It was their meeting with Joe at his office that finally cooled their ardor about the case.

"Guys, I'm sorry to tell you that the only thing we know is that they both died from a massive heroin overdose. The levels were off the charts. They had some cocaine and weed for sure, but it was trivial compared to the opioid levels."

"Self-administered?" Patrick asked, already knowing the answer.

"Like I said at the site, they had holes in their arms. I have no way of knowing if somebody did it to them, or they did it to themselves. If someone got to them, it was done ultra-professionally because there were no traces of anyone else having been in that room. No strange fingerprints, footprints, forced windows. Nothing. On our recommendation, the coroner is finished with the case."

Patrick and Danny left McAnulty's office shaking their heads, knowing that their investigation could continue and probably would, but the trail was getting cold, and the truth of what really killed Ray and Tiffany might never be forthcoming.

"What a piece-of-shit case," Danny muttered that evening as Patrick chauffeured him back to his home.

Patrick understood what Danny meant. "I know."

"Patrick, my instincts are telling me that those two didn't both shoot up too much heroin."

"I agree, although it happens all the time, Danny. People get hold of heroin; they're naïve and stupid, and they don't know how much to use. Those two were probably neophytes."

"Then why heroin? They were probably getting off real good with some weed and some blow, so why the hard stuff?"

Patrick shrugged. Despite their best efforts in the hours since learning about the heroin, they hadn't been able to identify a source or a supplier, so they couldn't determine how easy it would have been to purchase or how the couple could have bought enough to kill themselves.

"Captain Detweiler doesn't want us to stay on this case much longer, Danny."

"I know. The chances of finding anything at this point are pretty small."

"High-profile case, Danny. They want people to believe that we have worked the case hard until—"

"Until amnesia sets in."

"Right, until the public moves on and doesn't give a shit anymore."

"Which is likely, because I don't see any big-wheel politicians screaming about the scandal."

"No, Danny. That's not going to happen either. Everyone who has a stake, except the poor goddamn patients, wants business to go back to usual. The big device companies employ a ton of people and pay a lot of taxes. The hospitals in this area are the main employers, and the public doesn't want to believe that their doctors are evil. So they think it's time to bury the case and not let a murder investigation that has no hope of succeeding keep the Springer articles alive."

Silence, as each of them processed what they had just vocalized and knew to be the bitter truth.

"So what is your wife serving for dinner, Danny?"

"Why, Patrick? You wanna eat with us? Where's Beth?"

"She took the kids to a movie. Tired of waiting for my ass to do something with the family."

"Then stay and have dinner with us. Maria is making meatloaf. Easy-peasy."

"I might just do that, Danny. Thanks. And maybe we should start archiving some of the case files tomorrow morning," Patrick added, hoping that dinner with his new partner and his family would make him feel better about striking out so very miserably on the Gilbert/Springer case.

20

CHAPTER

News of Ray Gilbert's death didn't reach Philip until the next day. Philip had completed his customary early-morning flip through the *Philadelphia Inquirer*, which he insisted on having delivered to his door every day. "I like the feel of the paper in my hands" he had retorted when Dorothy pointed out that the rest of the world got their news on the internet. When was Philip going to enter the twenty-first century? But that particular day, he missed the story of the death of Gilbert and Springer, which had been relegated to the bottom of page three. It also hadn't made it to the "all news, all the time" radio station that he listened to every morning on the way to work. The station spent more time on traffic, weather, and sports than real news. "Stale news, all the time," Dorothy remarked every time they got into Philip's car together, to which he only shrugged.

So when, on their Saturday rounds, one of Philip's first-year cardiology fellows mentioned that an Allentown cardiologist had died the previous day, Philip feared the worst. He took out his smartphone and, feigning a patient phone call, excused himself. When he was out of the group's earshot, he googled the story, something he did know how to do electronically.

The shock made Philip's knees buckle. He sat down on a stool in the nurses' station while he read the brief description of what the police had discovered at the shoddy motel in Bethlehem. The principal focus, of course, was Tiffany, now famous for her exposé, but the story contained information about Gilbert, the other person found dead, and some background about his medical career. Omitted were many of the crime scene details, but the story did mention heroin overdose as the probable cause of death. "The investigation continues," the story ended.

Philip gathered himself, knowing that he was going to have to complete rounds in the cardiac intensive care unit before dealing with Gilbert's death. As he had done so many times in his career, he forced himself to focus on the task at hand, blocking out, as best he could, the awful news and its implications while he listened to a hapless intern recite, in idiotic fashion, all of the "pertinent negatives" in the review of systems of a patient Philip didn't know and didn't need to.

An hour later, with the patients seen and treatment plans mapped out for each, Philip retreated to his small office, closed the door, sat at his desk, and called Dorothy.

"Philip, don't you answer your emails?"

"I was on ICU rounds."

"Then you don't know what happened to Ray?"

"Actually, I do. One of the fellows told me, and I googled the story. What do you know?"

"Probably not much more than you. I caught a snippet on the internet this morning and then read the *Inquirer* story."

"They said something about finding drugs in their motel room?" Philip asked.

"Yes, but not much detail about that. Is there somebody you can call up there who might be able to give you more information, Philip?"

"There may be. I just have to figure out how to get in touch with her."

"OK. I'm at the office, but text me when you know something. In the meantime, I'll see if I can get more information from my friends who work up in that area."

"That'd be great, Dorothy. I'll see you at home, midafternoon, after I read cardiograms and get everybody tucked in. Have the whiskey ready. Going to need it."

Philip hung up feeling a little better. He was always relieved to have Dorothy's opinion about anything important. She was uncannily right about so many things that he had come to rely on her knowledge and intuition. Figuring out what happened to Gilbert was important to Philip, whose own curiosity had been known to get him into deep trouble. This time, maybe he would be able to gather information while keeping himself out of harm's way.

Philip swiveled around in his desk chair, turned on his desktop computer, and began to scroll through contacts to the Gs but to no avail. For some reason he had neglected to add Liz Gold's name. Then he remembered that he sometimes added seldom-used phone numbers and email addresses to the file of the person who was his principal contact. In this case, it would be Ray Gilbert, and, to his relief, the cell phone number he needed was in the notes section of Gilbert's file.

Philip wasted no time dialing the Allentown number from his office line, hoping for a human voice and not an automated message.

"Hello?" the voice said nervously. "Who's this?"

"It's Philip Sarkis, Liz."

"Dr. Sarkis. Good to hear from you. I guess you heard the terrible news?" Liz said in a quivering voice.

"Yes, I did. I'm calling to say how sorry Dorothy and I are and to see if you know any of the details."

"Details? I don't think anyone has figured out funeral arrangements, if that's what you mean."

"Well, not exactly. I do hope to get up there for the services, but I was wondering if you knew what happened to Ray."

"What happened is that slimy bitch seduced Ray and turned him into a drug addict. They stupidly injected themselves with a shitload of drugs and managed to kill themselves."

"That's what the media is implying but probably too early to know for sure. I was hoping you could explain a few things."

"Like what, Dr. Sarkis?" Liz asked, her anger and frustration just below the surface.

"Do you know how long they were using drugs?"

"How would I know? Ray has been acting weird at work for the last few weeks but there was a lot going on in his life. Everyone knew he was having an affair, but I never saw him high at work. Just tired a lot; I thought he was depressed."

"So you wouldn't have any idea if or when they started using narcotics."

"No clue. I never thought to look carefully at Ray's arms when he was in the lab, which wasn't very often anymore. No one else who scrubbed in with him ever said anything about it either."

"You said he was depressed. How bad?" Philip asked.

"You mean was he depressed enough to kill himself? And Tiffany too? Or did they end it all together? I can't buy any of those theories, Dr. Sarkis. Ray was too much of a positive person to feel that sorry for himself. And too kind to take someone with him, even though I would have loved to kill that slut myself."

"I understand, Liz. It must have been tough for you to see him at work."

"Tough doesn't describe it, Dr. Sarkis. I got to the point where it was making me physically ill. I decided last week to resign as of the first of next month."

"Where are you going?"

"Don't know yet—just away from this place. Noah and I have been talking for a while about relocating to someplace warm. I resisted because of Ray. I foolishly thought he would get tired of Tiffany. I finally began to get serious, not only about quitting but getting as far away from this place as possible. We have a few things lined up in California and Florida. I suspect we'll be in a warmer climate soon."

"Liz, I'm so sorry."

"Don't be sorry for me, Philip," Liz said, suddenly switching to his first name. "I did it to myself. I wasn't satisfied simply to work with the guy. I fell in love and had an affair with him. My husband, whom I still love by the way, found out and got hurt, and now Ray's gone because neither of us had the courage to make a permanent commitment to each other. He let Tiffany into his life, and the rest is history. A sad story that I can't change or fix. So, time to move on."

"I hope it all works out for you, Liz. I guess I'll see you at the funeral in a few days? Maybe we can talk more there, if you want," Philip offered.

"I'm not sure I'll be there, Philip. It's too upsetting, and it'll just rub salt in my husband's wounds if I cry my eyes out over my ex-lover. And I don't want to embarrass Ray's family either."

"You know, Ray never talked about his family."

"Ray has been estranged from his parents for years. He didn't want anything to do with them, and vice versa. His sister, Darlene, lives out west. She moved away after they graduated, and they didn't keep in touch much at all after Linda died. The police called them all yesterday. Hopefully, they'll attend the funeral. It's going to be a pretty barren event, I'm afraid."

Philip rang off and then set out to finish his distracted workday, anticipating getting an earful from Dorothy after they both had a chance to reflect on what already had been a very eventful morning.

Philip's arrival home was the usual tumultuous event—dogs barking, kids screaming, Dorothy scurrying about, trying to do housework while preparing dinner for everyone. Philip was immediately put to work, helping Emily and Erin with their homework, which this evening consisted of a reading assignment for Emily and an art project for Erin. Each relished her task. Emily, the older and more cerebral of the two, loved books of all kinds, while Erin, who Dorothy insisted had the largest right brain in the family, loved music and art and appeared to have talent for both. By the time they settled down to spaghetti and meatballs, Emily's and Erin's favorite, things had calmed down enough for Philip to ask Dorothy about her day.

"I had a bunch of meetings, mostly on the phone, but I did manage to speak with a couple of colleagues up north about the Gilbert thing. I've got some useful information for you."

"Which we'll get to when little eyes are closed."

"Of course, which should be happening pretty soon. You want to put them down or do the dishes?" Dorothy asked.

"Seriously? You're giving me the choice?"

"I know you love to put the kids to bed. I'm a little tired of reading the same storybooks every night. So why don't you go ahead and get them ready for bed, and I'll tuck them in before they go to sleep."

It didn't take either of them long to complete their tasks. Emily and Erin were worn out after an enthusiastic visit to the playground with their nanny. They were almost relieved to get into bed and have their daddy get them under their covers and read them a story. Dorothy was able to stack the dishwasher and wash the pots and pans quickly and meet Philip at their bedside to kiss the girls good night. They finally convened on the sofa in front of their gas fireplace, with glasses of cognac in hand.

Philip was anxious to fill Dorothy in on his conversation with Liz and keen to hear what she had found out from her Allentown friends. After listening to Philip's news, Dorothy nodded.

"What you got from Liz is consistent with what I heard. Tiffany's newspaper stories were based, as we know, to large extent on what Ray had told her. Word on the street is that this was not a new MO for Tiffany. Many of her sources required, shall we say, her personal touch before they delivered the goods. Ray was an easy mark. He was alone, depressed about his job, and in a bad predicament he had created for himself."

"So people up there assumed that Ray and Tiffany were an item."

"Yes. But I don't think anybody was surprised or concerned about it. What they did talk about was how pissed off people were at her."

"Do we know who, exactly?"

"The hospitals and doctors who were named in her articles and also device manufacturers."

"Pissed enough to do something about it?"

"I don't know, Philip."

"I mean, why would they wait to kill Tiffany until *after* she published the most damaging parts of her series?"

"You think people who are compromised and scared make good judgments?"

"And why kill Ray too?"

"Because he helped to rat them out?"

"So are you telling me that your friends up there believe this is a murder case?"

"They're just saying that Tiffany underestimated how much she lit up a lot of powerful people. Remember, Allentown isn't exactly Beverly Hills. It's been a depressed area, and the health care industry is very important to the local economy. Putting that in jeopardy to go after a Pulitzer prize would be considered selfish."

"Do the police know about all this? From what Liz told me, it sounds like it could be just a drug overdose."

"I have no idea, Philip. Not our problem."

"But if the cops who are on this case are idiots and don't have an inkling about a strong motive for murder, they could end up walking away from the case."

"First of all, they would really have to be stupid not to get that thread, Philip. Tiffany was a local celebrity, and everybody knew she was in the middle of a big scandal."

"But what if they don't?"

"Where is this going, Philip?"

"If someone murdered Ray Gilbert, they need to be caught and punished."

"I'll drink to that, Philip. But I hope you're *not* saying what I think you are."

"And what would that be, Dorothy?"

"That somehow you're going to make sure that whoever did this is going to get what's coming to them."

Silence, while both pondered the obvious, until Dorothy finally exclaimed, "Philip, have you completely lost your mind?"

"Dorothy, you know how I feel about Ray."

"Philip, I understand. Ray was your mini-me—sensitive, bright, caring. And I understand that he got caught up in a mess up there, and he tried to do the right thing. And it's possible that somebody made him pay for doing what he did."

"He didn't do anything wrong!" Philip protested.

"I agree that he attempted to get his superiors and the authorities to pay attention and got stonewalled. But his decision to go public was ill conceived, especially when he picked Tiffany as his mouthpiece. She was unstable and dishonest, and she used Ray to tell her things she could use as a weapon."

"The essential fact is that devices were being placed unnecessarily up there."

"But was it with malicious intent, Philip? Did you read her articles carefully? Did the doctors up there really mean to harm patients, or were they just stupid and gullible at the same time? Do you actually know the answer to that question?" Dorothy asked, sipping her cognac.

"No."

"And are you convinced that the companies had a policy of bribing doctors to put in unnecessary devices or to push business one way or another? Or were the sales representatives up there naïve? How much influence did they exert? There's a big difference between taking a doc out to dinner or a hockey game and stuffing his or her pockets with cash."

"I know that, Dorothy. We know the companies are nice to us so we pay attention to them."

"Come on, Philip. That's why they hire pretty women and handsome men. Good-looking people are much more likely to attract and keep your attention. So that's the background that Tiffany chose to ignore and Ray failed to impress on her. Without that context, it's pretty easy to jump to the conclusion that whatever was going on up there was illicit."

"But didn't Tiffany have more evidence than that?"

"Read the articles carefully, Philip. Tiffany may not have been a good researcher or a particularly honest person, but she knew how to spin a story. Beyond the silly dinners and sporting events, she had absolutely no proof that doctors were bribed or influenced to do the bidding of the device companies. Everything else in her article is carefully worded innuendo and assumption, to titillate the reader to want to read the next installment. And to make it worse, she used Ray viciously. His quotes never lead off any topic. She starts by painting a picture and then uses Ray's comments in snippets to support her contentions. She took much of what he had to say out of context to make an argument."

"And Ray let her get away with it."

"Apparently. He was with her to the end."

"Why did he go along?"

"Hard to say, Philip. I suspect he had been angry and frustrated for a long time. He was convinced that patients weren't getting the best care, and he couldn't get anyone to listen to him. Tiffany's exposé changed everything. Not only were people listening, but they were providing affirmation. Scandal sells well. You can always come up with a few rotten apples who do awful things to make your point."

"Ray was effectively vindicated, so he chose to ignore the obvious issues with Tiffany's articles?"

"Precisely, and he paid a dear price. He was going to have to leave Allentown, at the least, and who knows? Somebody might have finally decided to shut him up before Tiffany got to the real issues."

"There was more to learn?"

"You betcha. I don't know where she was going, but the questions that Tiffany never answered and possibly would have were how pervasive, how systematic, and how intentional these bad practices were and are."

"So I'm right. There's a lot more to learn."

"There is, but you're not the person to do it, Philip. There are just too many facets for you to examine, and, I'm afraid, if this was payback of some kind, you could put yourself in danger. Promise me you aren't going to play amateur sleuth again."

"You're right. I have enough on my plate right now."

"You sure do, Philip, including those little girls in there. You have a lot to lose here, so you have to back off. Because if you don't, I'm not going to be as forgiving as I've been in the past. I'm not going to live through another nightmare of a case, and I'm not going to risk my life and my girls' safety. Do you understand?"

"I do. I promise that I won't pursue this further."

"No contact with the media or with Gilbert's family or friends, and no calls to the police with one of your lame theories. You swear."

"I swear."

"Good," Dorothy said, rising from the sofa. "I'm going to get ready for bed and read my book. And get a good night's sleep. I suggest you do the same."

"On my way," Philip said, the wheels in his head already turning.

21
CHAPTER

Dick Deaver's life had been transformed. A few years ago, in the space of about three months, he had gone from curmudgeon boss, notorious playboy, and inveterate workaholic to doting grandfather, considerate male companion, and pleasant supervisor of his thriving private detective firm. Dick relished his new self, hardly able to remember those bygone days when he had trolled bars for fresh conquests to assuage the loneliness that his ridiculous lifestyle and grumpy demeanor had brought him. He had been emotionally isolated; his daughter, Dorothy, was the only person in whom he could confide and then only on certain subjects. Which made her relationship with that Philip Sarkis character even more difficult for Dick to countenance.

He not only mistrusted Philip for the dastardly deeds Dick was pretty sure he had perpetrated, but he envied Philip for the tenderness that Dorothy so freely afforded him. Dick had gotten used to having Dorothy all to himself after his beloved wife had died. Though Dorothy professed equal affection for her father, Dick had convinced himself that their special relationship was lost because of Philip, never to return.

But then Ursula came along and stole Dick's heart. A gritty New York

City artist with a mind of her own, Ursula reminded Dick that he could and should share his life with a contemporary and allow his daughter the freedom to show her love in a different way. And what better way to do that than to offer her father the gift he always wanted but would never admit: grandchildren. Emily and Erin stormed the emotional fortress that Dick had constructed when Dorothy left the nest, knocking down every barrier so that Dick's love spewed forth like water through a giant hole in a dike. And try as he might to sustain an air of aloofness with just about everybody else, Dick couldn't restrain himself in the presence of the grand-girls, hugging and kissing them at every opportunity, bending his aging, squeaky knees to get on the floor and play their games, relishing every moment he spent with them in a way that he never thought possible. Gradually and inevitably, Dick's affection for the "mighty mites," as he called them, and his tender relationship with Ursula turned him back into a happy man, much like the one who had met and married Dorothy's mother those many years ago.

Though he knew he could never fully trust Philip, he was determined to do better on that front as well. He also realized that sustaining a meaningful relationship with his grandchildren and his daughter meant that Dick would have to figure out a way to get along with his pseudo-son-in-law. Under Ursula's tutelage, Dick had implemented several coping mechanisms that seemed to work, at least most of the time. First, Ursula had convinced Dick to respect Philip's career choices. He should avoid referring to Philip's descent in the academic community, some of which was clearly self-imposed, but instead engage Philip about his job and show some sympathy when Philip pointed out, as he frequently did, how difficult the practice of medicine had become. Dick also had to stop asking about marriage prospects. It was fine to be concerned about his daughter's future and security, but he had to concede that the choice not to formalize their relationship had been mostly Dorothy's, who was almost as wary of Philip's escapades as Dick had been. And perhaps most important, Dick had to adhere religiously to the most important grandparent directive: never, ever criticize parents for any child-rearing judgment, no matter how wrong it seemed. As long as parents loved their children and attempted to do what was best for them, grandparents needed to remain quiet, with the firm but tacit understanding that raising children is anything but an exact science.

So far, Ursula's counseling had been effective. Philip and Dorothy were delighted to have Dick visit regularly, made even more special when he brought Ursula along. By focusing on the children, Dick avoided the hot buttons that had plagued his earlier interactions with Philip. So he was a bit surprised when Philip pulled him aside during preparations for one of their Sunday afternoon dinners.

"Dick, I've been having some problems with our grill on the back deck," Philip announced, while Dorothy and Ursula were prepping their meal. "Would you mind taking a quick look at it? Weather's getting better, and I'm pretty sure we'll want to start cooking out more."

Dick's reaction was to glance toward the playroom, wondering what Emily and Erin were up to.

"The girls will be fine for at least a few minutes," Philip said. "They're playing with their Barbie dolls."

"Sure, Philip," Dick replied warily, suspecting that there was another agenda. "Let's take a look at your grill."

"I grabbed a couple of beers. Might as well enjoy the weather," Philip said, heading for the glass slider, Budweisers in hand.

"OK, Philip, what's the problem?" Dick asked as the slider closed.

"It's not about the grill," Philip said as he took the cover off the Weber and pretended to look at the ignition mechanism.

"Seriously, Philip? This is the best ruse you could come up with? You know more about grills than I do, and you've never asked me any handyman stuff before. So what's on your mind?"

"Come over here, Dick, and pretend you're looking at this thing," Philip said, keeping one eye on Dorothy, who was presently intent on chopping vegetables. "I need you to look into a case for me."

"A case of what?"

"A death that I think could be murder."

"Really? Around here?"

"Allentown area."

"Does this have anything to do with that newspaper reporter and doctor who overdosed?"

"Yes," Philip said, sneaking another peek at Dorothy, who was setting the table. "Look, Dick. I need your help with this, but it's really complicated. I didn't want to cold-call you. And we can't have this conversation now. I just want to know if we can we set up a meeting."

Dick was reluctant. In addition to accepting her coaching about his behavior with his family and staff, he had promised Ursula he wouldn't let Philip pull him into another dangerous case. Ursula saw those cases as land mines that would complicate his relationship with Philip and, in addition, anger Dorothy, who was violently opposed to Philip's amateur sleuthing. Dick came to believe that Philip had finally learned his lesson and would not want to place his family in jeopardy. He shook his head at his own naiveté.

"Philip, I thought you were finished with this stupid stuff."

"I am, Dick. I promise. I have no intention of getting involved with this case. All I want you to do is a little gentle inquiry. There are good reasons I can explain when we meet. I just can't do it here and now. It would take too long."

Dick paused, fingering the red button that, when pushed, would ignite the grill, pretending it didn't work, in case Dorothy happened to look out on the deck. Despite his years of dealing with Philip's "adventures," he *was* intrigued about this case. The device scandal and the death of the reporter and her doctor boyfriend had been in the papers for days. The facts and the publicity had gotten Dick's investigative juices flowing to the point that he was now going to do something he would eventually regret for the rest of his life.

"All right, Philip. Set up lunch for this week sometime, and you can lay out your issues."

"Thanks, Dick. I really appreciate this."

"Don't thank me yet. I didn't say I would do anything. But just in case, is it OK if I bring along someone from my office who can help keep me out of it? That's *if* I agree to help."

"Fair enough, Dick," Philip replied. "As long as you can guarantee that whoever it is knows how to be discreet."

Dick nodded, somehow managing not to sarcastically remind Philip that discretion was integral to his business model.

"Now let's pretend that you fixed the grill and get on with our dinner," Philip suggested, an invitation that Dick wholeheartedly accepted.

Sunday dinner was as pleasant, as always, although Dick couldn't stop wondering if his daughter suspected Philip and him of conspiring. If she did sense duplicity, her demeanor didn't betray her. She and Ursula enjoyed the evening, as they always did.

Philip was able to free himself for lunch two days later and called Dick's office to set up the meeting. They decided on a deli in the Fairmount section, about halfway between NorthBroad and Dick's downtown office. Philip was the first to arrive and asked for a booth near the front window. Within a few minutes, Philip watched Dick drive up and parallel park his car at a meter. A smallish, younger man, dressed in well-pressed khakis, maroon V-necked sweater over a white shirt, and highly polished penny loafers, emerged from the passenger side and followed Dick into the restaurant, where they quickly spotted Philip.

"Philip, this here is Al Kenworthy. One of my top investigators. Al is particularly knowledgeable when it comes to medical issues."

Philip rose to shake Al's hand. "I've heard a lot about you, Al, but I don't think we've ever met."

Al had a good smile. "No, we haven't, but I used to work with Dorothy. When she was a student, she spent time in our office. We worked on a number of cases together. Smart lady."

"And didn't you do some digging for us on some medical cases a few years back?"

"Yup, I sure did."

"And you got some pretty impressive results, as I recall."

"I enjoy research, Philip, especially on the medical side. Not a lot of people know about all the work that goes on behind the scenes, but research is one of the most important things our firm does. I take a lot of pride in my work. It's not as exciting as field work, but it's critical nonetheless."

Philip nodded. From what Dorothy had told him, Al was a relentless investigator who never failed to get to the most important facts of a case, no matter how long it might take or the lengths he needed to go for the details. And as everyone in the firm knew well, Al had a chronic crush on Dorothy that motivated him to dig even harder for a case that Dorothy cared about. Philip smiled, wondering how helpful Al might be to the man who had stolen Dorothy away from him.

He didn't have to ponder that question very long because Al Kenworthy came out of the gate in a rush, hardly waiting for menus to be delivered, before launching into what he had already learned about the Tiffany Springer affair.

"Dick told me about the case yesterday, Philip," Al explained. "I spent last evening trolling through multiple news sources. I wanted to be up to speed today. It's quite a story."

"I'm acquainted with some of it, but I don't think Dick is, so why don't you sum up what you learned, Al."

Al held forth for the next half hour, pausing only for small bites of his Reuben sandwich or sips of ice water. Philip and Dick used those infrequent pauses to ask questions. Hardly necessary, given the lucidity and completeness of the Kenworthy dissertation, in which he outlined, point by point, what Tiffany Springer had uncovered, how she had synthesized the information, and who she had eventually fingered as the bad guys—people and companies that had been complicit in selling pacemakers and defibrillators to hospitals that were implanted by doctors in patients who may not have needed them.

Philip listened intently to the presentation, made so logically and orderly that for the first time, he felt he had a good grasp of the entire story. Philip was particularly excited to hear the few factoids that Al included about Ray Gilbert and his role in the Springer exposé. The fact that Al had gathered little substantive information about Gilbert himself reflected the fact that he had relied on media reports for his research and hadn't yet interviewed anyone with direct knowledge of Gilbert's relationship with Tiffany or his motivation to help her.

"Do you plan to talk to anyone up there who knew Ray and Tiffany personally?" Philip asked.

Al sat forward, excited by the idea, but before he could answer, Dick interjected, "Al's job is to research the case, Philip. That's what he does best; in fact, better than anyone else at my firm. We need to let him finish that, as he'll describe in a few minutes. Until he does, it's pointless and maybe even dangerous to do personal interviews and such. That's something I'll have some of my other people take care of—that is, if we go that far."

"That's great, Dick," Philip said, relieved to hear that Dick was at least open to taking a deeper dive.

"But we want to keep a low profile, right, Philip?" Dick asked.

"Exactly, Dick," Philip said. "For obvious reasons."

"I do sense that there's a lot more to the story, Philip," Al said as he bit into his Reuben.

"I'm sure there is, Al. What do you propose to do next?"

"Now that I understand the storyline, I have to take a careful look at the facts that generated Tiffany's story. That will involve looking at the book of business for Sterling and its competitors in that region of Pennsylvania, where she said the bad guys were doing their thing."

"Are those records difficult to obtain?'

"The financial statements won't be too hard. A little tougher will be hospital implant volumes. That will involve some gentle hacking, which used to be a lot easier before hospitals and doctors' offices started putting in better firewalls and security screens."

"HIPAA?"

"Exactly, Philip. You know this stuff better than I do. To be compliant with federal regulations, the hospitals had to show they were at least making an effort to protect patient information. There are still isolated breaches, but unless there's a major screw-up, the hospitals are able to cover it up and not disclose it. Because if they do—"

"Major fines and the possibility of jail time," Philip said. "We have to take computer-based courses on all of that crap, and they spend a lot of time telling us about the dire consequences of a data breach."

"Which is the most absurd thing, because 90 percent of those violations are caused by administrators, not by doctors."

"I believe it," Philip said. "One of our HR people just gave away personal information on about ten thousand employees with one keystroke because she got a phishing email that said our CEO wanted the data."

"Crazy, right? Most hospitals don't have fail-safe mechanisms in place to keep that nonsense from happening until it happens. Which is why I hope I won't have any trouble getting hospital data on pacemaker and defibrillator volumes for the period in question."

"Won't they have locked those data down, given the publicity?" Philip asked.

"We're talking about hospital IT departments, Philip. Pretty much bottom of the barrel when it comes to expertise. I don't think our computer people will have a problem."

"Do you think the hospitals will have those data broken down by implanter?" Dick asked.

"Yes," Philip answered. "Hospitals use data like that all the time, mostly to look for opportunities to save money."

"How does that work?"

"Pricing always varies among vendors," Philip explained. "Usually not by a lot. Vendors don't want to get into a price war. But if a hospital is using a large volume of a particular device, the savings from using a pacemaker that costs only a couple of hundred dollars less can add up."

"And there's no difference in quality?"

"Companies are always coming up with new bells and whistles to justify a higher price," Philip said, "but the reality is that they make very little difference in patient care or outcomes."

"But how would the purchasing drones at the hospital know that?" Dick asked.

"They don't, which is why smart hospitals bring doctors into their committee meetings to help them decide on the best and most economical purchasing approaches."

"Why would doctors care?" Dick asked.

"They can be incentivized by raises that reflect cost savings, or they can get kickbacks," Philip answered.

"Aren't kickbacks illegal?"

"They are, unless the hospital goes through a process to put gain-sharing into place," Al said.

"What's that?"

"The government's way of allowing doctors to profit from cost savings. It's complicated but legal, as long as it's done according to a precise formula," Al explained. "And since the government wants that process to be transparent, financial records are in the wind. So that's how I'll be able to gather information about the volume of implants for each of the vendors and each of the doctors in those hospitals upstate."

"Amazing lack of forethought," Dick observed.

"Yes. Dick did explain to me that Ray Gilbert is the reason you're interested in the case. And I admire you for caring about your friend. But the first step will be determining if Tiffany had her facts straight."

"Don't you think those facts are pretty obvious?"

"They seem to be, Philip," Dick answered. "But remember what Mark Twain supposedly said: 'It's not what you don't know that gets you into trouble. It's what you know for sure that just ain't so.'"

"So you don't believe that Sterling or other device companies were pushing physicians to do the wrong thing?"

"Maybe, Philip," Al replied. "But do you think Tiffany Springer got it entirely right and that there really was criminal behavior? Or could this have been just a few dumb-asses doing the wrong thing for the wrong reasons? Remember, she had a pretty big ax to grind. She was looking to get famous and maybe make Gilbert rich, so the worse she made Sterling look, the better her chances for notoriety."

"Fame that ultimately got her and Ray killed," Philip said.

"We aren't anywhere near that conclusion, Philip," Dick reminded him.

"And I fear we never will be."

"Like Dick and I have told you several times now, Philip," Al concluded, "let's just take this one step at a time."

22

CHAPTER

Dick Deaver arrived at his agency office the next morning at his customary nine-thirty. He was not and never could be a morning person. He had tried very hard when he was young to be an early riser, like the bosses he admired. It had taken him a long time to realize that his biological clock worked best when he slept until at least eight o'clock and gave himself enough time to wake up with coffee, check out the news, and take a proper shower before dressing. Not that he wasted time; his schedule was tight. Having a beard saved him a few minutes of preparation, time that he that he used to pester Ursula whenever she stayed at his place, now a much more frequent occurrence as their relationship blossomed.

Which it did, despite Dick's continued insistence that he was a confirmed bachelor, never to remarry after the untimely death of his first wife and Dorothy's mother, whom he had cherished. Insidiously—and seemingly unintentionally—Ursula continued to insinuate herself into his life with more frequent visits from New York. Her pottery business was gaining momentum, with several stores in the Philadelphia area requesting permission to retail her products. "Is Ursula targeting the

Philly market for romantic reasons?" Dick asked himself frequently, as he felt himself pulled into a relationship that he had underestimated from the start. Beginning with a state of relative indifference, Dick now found himself craving Ursula's company, counting days until he would see her again at his place in Philly or hers in New York.

Dick's secretary, Anita, greeted him as she always did, with a cup of hot tea, just a little more caffeine to jolt his brain into play. As he took his first sip standing at her desk, Anita briefly reviewed his itinerary for the day, reminding him that Al Kenworthy would lead things off in just a few minutes. Dick was surprised. He thought he had adequately charged Al at their meeting with Philip the day before. He couldn't possibly have finished all of the research that Dick had suggested.

It wouldn't take long to figure out what Al was up to. Almost before Dick's computer was fully booted, Al appeared in his open doorway, a stack of folders under his arm, smiling nervously. "Can I come in, Dick?"

"Sure, Al. Let's sit over at the conference table so you can spread out."

Al found a chair and began to lay files out in front of him. Dick joined him, teacup in hand. Dick saw that Al was a little rumpled, with bloodshot eyes.

"Beverage for you, Al?"

"No thanks, Dick. I've had quite enough caffeine over the last several hours. I wanted to get to you early so I can start making plans."

"Plans for what, Al? I thought we laid out your tasks yesterday."

"You did, Dick. You were very clear. So I decided to get started last night. I was able to access the records from several of the hospitals and the practices up there and to go through their device implantation numbers. Turns out that there was a definite upswing over the last two years."

"Across the board?" Dick asked.

"Not exactly. I would say there were maybe three hospitals that really kicked up their numbers. What's interesting is that those three hospitals had a few different cardiology groups on their staffs."

"Did any group outgrow the others?"

"Not really. All of them seemed to increase their implant numbers over the same period. The increases were impressive, Dick. In some cases, the number of devices going in doubled or tripled. And it wasn't just pacemakers and implantable defibrillators. It looks like those practices were doing more coronary procedures too."

"Using what? Stents?"

"Yup, and artificial heart valves. Pretty much everything in the device companies' product lines."

"Now the big question: which of the companies was responsible?"

"All of them," Al said quickly, having anticipated the question.

"Really?" Dick asked.

"I know. That's why I'm here. If you just look at volumes, all of the companies did very well at those three hospitals over the years in question. It was like watching a horse race, Dick. Sterling was clearly the front-runner up there, but once they got ahead, the other three closed the gap and nearly pulled even. The pattern was repeated several times over the last few years."

"Why?"

"That's what I want to know and what we need to find out."

"How do you propose to do that, Al?"

"We have to go to the source and ask some pointed questions. Specifically, did the companies put any policies into play that would have led to this pattern, or were other forces at work?"

"This gets back to who's responsible for what we assume to be unnecessary implants?"

"*Assume* is the operative word, Dick. Tiffany's articles were long on innuendos and short on proven fact. On the other hand, if we find evidence that the companies were complicit, and Tiffany had enough evidence to expose them—"

"They would have had the clout to shut her up—for good."

"Precisely. But we're going to have to approach this very carefully, Dick. If they're as evil as this makes them seem, they aren't going to enjoy having their pants pulled down."

"I meant to ask you, Al—who's *we*?"

"I talked to Doug Eisenberg this morning. He's willing to help me with the interviews."

"So you want Doug Eisenberg to assume some false identity and go to these big companies and try to get them to tell us why their sales volume went through the roof at a few shithole hospitals in Butt-Fuck, Pennsylvania?"

"Pretty much. Except I need to go with him."

"And why is that?" Dick knew that Al was busting a gut to become one of his field agents and not just a backroom hacker.

"Because I know the case better than Doug ever could. And if we don't go in there with our facts straight and our false identity airtight, we could get this firm into plenty of hot water."

"Al, I hate to break this to you, but that's true for almost all of the covert operations this firm carries out."

"This one is more complicated, Dick. First of all, if we're going to visit four different companies as government surveyors—which is our best bet, by the way—we'll be expected to know an awful lot about medical devices. I'm knowledgeable about that stuff from previous cases I've worked on. Doug isn't. And this kind of interrogation is usually carried out by two agents, not one. So Doug is going to have to take another person with him. Why not someone who is familiar with the background of the case?"

Dick paused to reflect, chin on hand, elbow on desk, staring at Al. *A good soldier,* Dick thought, *who someday will need to get his feet wet with door-to-door work. Why not now? Why not this case?*

"OK, Al. I approve. Prep Doug, and submit a request to HR so you can get your travel and hotels. But let me be clear. Doug is the lead. He gets to make the introductions and do most of the talking—got it?"

"Absolutely, Dick. I know I'm still learning this stuff. I just want to have the chance to grow in my job."

"I agree, Al. It's a good strategy, and expanding horizons is how I've kept good people in my firm. But what has to be clear is that you and Doug will not force the issue. I want you to come back here with a scouting report after you meet with these companies, and I'll decide what to do next and with whom. Don't go off the game plan."

"I promise, Dick. Doug and I will check in with you for final instructions before we leave, hopefully in a day or two."

Al departed, leaving Dick wondering, once again, how and why he had let his idiot boyfriend-in-law get him embroiled in a case with so much potential downside for Dick and his firm.

Over the next two days, Al worked closely with Eisenberg, first prepping Doug to bring him up to speed on the case and then to strategize and make plans for their interviews. After considering several alternatives, they finally decided on a ruse in which they would pose as federal auditors charged with keeping track of payments from CMS to hospitals and companies for devices used for Medicare patients. As such, they naturally would be looking for abrupt alterations in the pattern of usage by individual physicians and hospitals and would be entitled to ask for explanations for perturbations—that is, if large, unexplained fluctuations were actually identified.

Al phoned each of the four major device companies on their list, advising the regulatory departments at each of the reason for their visit and making it clear that the appointments would need to be expedited to meet the deadlines for the report from his bureau. None of the four flinched, each representative desiring to be fully cooperative. Since all four were located in the Minneapolis-Saint Paul metropolitan area, the birthplace of modern pacing, travel logistics were relatively easy. Their interviews could be completed in a couple of days.

While Al did the scheduling, Doug took on the task of creating photo IDs for the two of them, not a trivial matter, given the extra measures put into play to discourage forgeries since 9/11. Fortunately, Dick's firm was highly experienced in such matters. In addition, since the IDs would be presented to civilians, the chance of any kind of challenge was considerably reduced. They also went online to obtain the names of a couple of agents of similar age and looks to use as aliases, just in case the companies went to the trouble to check.

With Dick's permission, Al purchased first-class upgrades for himself and Doug so they could confer in relative privacy during the flight west. Following their arrival in Minnesota, they continued their conversation over a light dinner before retiring and agreeing to meet early the next day for breakfast before their first visit, probably the most important of all—Sterling Medical Devices.

Neither Doug nor Al was prepared for the building at which their Uber driver dropped them at 9:00 a.m. They had anticipated lavishness but were greeted by stark simplicity. The headquarters of Sterling Medical Devices was housed in a squared-off, five-story brick building with double-paned glass doors that led to a modest lobby, fronted by a desk, behind which sat a pleasant African American woman in a blue blazer.

"Good morning, gentlemen. Welcome to Sterling. How can I help you?"

"We here to see Mr. Adair in regulatory," Al answered, not able to refrain from looking around the lobby for a passage to the real device headquarters.

"Are you looking for something in particular?" she asked.

"Is this the entire headquarters?" Al asked.

"Yes, it is. Did you expect something perhaps grander?" she asked.

"Frankly, yes. I thought this was a pretty big and successful firm," Al explained.

"It is, Mr. ..."

"Goodyear."

"Mr. Goodyear, this is a good company doing well, but it's managed, shall we say, frugally."

"No frills."

"Exactly. Employees are treated fairly, but nobody, not even the CEO or the board, is killing it."

"Where's the rest of the company?" Doug asked.

"Manufacturing is in Puerto Rico."

"That's the whole thing?"

"Like I said, frugal."

"Can't wait to see the rest of the place," Al said.

"And you will. After you show me your credentials, sign our log-in, and I give you a badge, I'll call Mr. Adair's office, and they'll send someone down here to escort you upstairs."

Al and Doug waited in the lobby until they were greeted by a pleasant, plain-looking, big-boned blonde woman, who introduced herself as Bobby Adair's executive assistant. She led them to the elevators, filling the waiting time with small talk about the weather and their flight. Al probed, trying to understand the company's hierarchy. He was able to confirm that Mr. Adair reported directly to the CEO and was responsible for all regulatory issues. As such, what he had to say about policy would hold considerable weight.

Adair wasted no time in greeting his visitors, walking through his open office door, sticking out his hand, and exclaiming with a pronounced Southern drawl, "Hi, I'm glad to meet ya. Bobby Adair. And you must be Mr. Goodyear."

"I am," Al answered, sizing up Adair. Friendly smile, side-parted black hair, in good shape, not anxious or on edge. "And this is my partner, Mr. Albert James. Thanks so much for meeting with us on short notice."

"Damn happy to do it," Adair said with a little too much enthusiasm. "Why don't we go into my office, and you boys can tell me just exactly what you need from me."

Al surveyed the modest office—windowsills crowded with family photos; old but well-maintained furniture, including two chairs in front of Bobby's desk in which Al and Doug parked themselves.

As rehearsed and as stipulated by Dick, Doug took the lead and explained that a recent audit had uncovered a curious uptick in implant volumes in central Pennsylvania that the auditors, first of all, needed to confirm with an examination of Sterling's records, and then they wanted some opinions from Adair as to the reason.

"Well, I can certainly save you boys some time and tell you that your audit is probably correct. We noticed the very same thing over the last several months."

"You did?" Al interjected, drawing a sideways glance from Doug.

"Yes, indeed, we did."

"And what did you do about it?" Eisenberg resumed.

"Nothin'," Adair said.

"It didn't concern you?"

"It did at first, especially when those newspaper articles came out, implyin' that there was some dirty dealin' goin' on."

"You mean Tiffany Springer's exposé."

"If that's what you want to call it. Seemed like a mud-throwin' party to me. But yes, that was part of the motivation to go lookin'. But to be honest, we track volumes carefully and are always tryin' to reconcile what we see."

"How did you reconcile this one?"

"Easy. As you boys will see, the uptick we saw in Nowhere, Pennsylvania, is somethin' we've observed in lots of other places in the country. When we normalized the data usin' what we thought were expected changes over time, we didn't think there was anythin' to be concerned about."

"Why the fluctuations?"

"We're a relatively new company. Doctors are inclined to try us out, and if they like us, they swing a lot of volume our way—at least for a while. But this industry is built on leapfrog technology. As soon as they can, our competitors catch up and pass us—or make it look that way— and volume shifts again. We take the long view, boys, and are less upset by short-term movements."

Al sat quietly, thinking, as Doug asked a few more exploratory questions. In a few short minutes, Bobby Adair had thrown more light on the alleged pacemaker scandal than Tiffany Springer had been able to do with months of her so-called research and feature-length articles. Al knew that he and Doug were going to finish their round of interviews with the other device companies on their calendar and that those companies were considerably more profitable and manipulative. But he sensed that the conclusions they were bound to reach when they finished their investigation and did their own analysis would likely resemble what Bobby Adair had told them in four or five sentences.

Two days later, Al and Doug made their report to Dick in their Philly office. Dick sat across the conference room table from the two men as they spread out the diagrams and charts they had generated during their flight home. The figures tracked implant volumes for the four companies and, for the most part, conformed to the patterns that Adair had outlined at their initial interview.

"So let me get this straight," Dick said. "From what you were able to find out, device volumes did go up a lot in central Pennsylvania, but you were able to convince yourselves—or some guys and gals convinced you—that none of these fluctuations was unexpected."

"Correct," Doug answered. "I have to say I was still skeptical after we talked to Sterling, but the patterns looked very similar for the other companies. Just not as striking."

"And you think that this just happened and that nobody was doing dirt up there."

"That can't be ruled out, Dick," Doug admitted. "We were kind of at the mercy of the people we interviewed. After all, we couldn't compel them to open all of their books. If we tried and they said no, we would have been stuck. So we had to play nice and take what they gave us."

"That's exactly my concern," Dick said.

"Not sure how we can resolve this, Dick," Doug offered.

"Only one way. Somebody has to go up to Nowhere, Pennsylvania, and do some active snooping. Talk to the locals, especially the docs and the pacemaker salespeople, and find out what the hell was going on—something I'm sure that lazy reporter never bothered to do herself."

"Could be hazardous, Dick. If someone did a dirty deed, they might not take kindly to our poking the bear."

"What choice do we have, Doug? If we accept the fact that the whole thing was due to volume fluctuations, Gilbert and the reporter were idiots and had it all wrong. Which makes their deaths senseless or, even worse, irrelevant. Or we probe further and try to figure out what made them suspicious enough to write an exposé that possibly got them killed. What's your pleasure?"

"You're right, Dick. Some local snooping is definitely in order. I'll repack and head on up."

"Not so fast, Doug. First of all, you've been introduced to multiple company people who could blow your cover up there. And you're right; there could be some danger to this. Since I've pursued this at the request of my daughter's boyfriend and not for profit, I don't want to place anyone else in jeopardy. I better do this myself."

"Are you sure, Dick?" Al asked. "How about if I go along and at least give you a little cover?"

"I don't need cover, Al. My goal here is just to pressure-test what you learned in Minnesota. If I can do that and find a reasonable explanation for things, I'll drop the investigation and high-tail it back here before you can blink."

Al nodded, grudgingly agreeing that Dick had it right. With just a few hours of old-fashioned meet-and-greet detective work, Dick was likely to garner what he needed to either continue or to halt the investigation and to get some closure for Philip and anyone else who cared about the miserable deaths of Ray Gilbert and his lady-friend reporter.

23
CHAPTER

O f all the things Dick had done to make a living in his life, his favorite, by far, was being a detective. Not the kind he had become, sitting behind a desk and moving his men around like so many chess pieces, supervising investigations, and being strategic. But a real gumshoe detective like the kind he used to watch on TV when he was a kid. The kind who got to meet clients and suspects, pressed the flesh, and looked people in the eye and asked them tough questions. The detective who solved cases that everybody else had given up on. That was the most fun of all and, unfortunately, the part that Dick got to do the least.

"You're the victim of your own success, Dick Deaver," Ursula would tell him when he was in any kind of mood to listen to her. "You're good at what you do and people know it and want you to solve their cases. You couldn't possibly work every job yourself, so you have to be a good supervisor and keep your people properly aimed at the target."

Dick would grunt disdainfully, not wanting to acknowledge that Ursula was correct, as she usually was. But that never stopped Dick from always looking for opportunities to hit the road himself, to get his hands dirty. He had to pick his spots carefully because he had a business to run. And even Dick had to admit that his skills were no longer as honed or his reflexes as sharp as when he had started out years ago. On the other hand, he did have the advantage of years of experience to make up for at least some of the accumulated rust.

To begin the Springer/Gilbert investigation, Dick reread all of Tiffany's articles, focusing on persons who Tiffany had identified as persons of interest. Though she didn't always name actual names, the detail she provided did everything but post a photo of the alleged villains. Her ability to describe the medical issues that brought them to her attention convinced Dick that Ray Gilbert had been doing a lot of talking and that, without his expertise, Tiffany's articles would have fallen as flat as a pancake. How could you finger a doctor for putting in an unnecessary pacemaker if you didn't know what a pacemaker was, what it was expected to do, and, most of all, which patients should get one?

Dick made a list of several people he might want to talk to during his investigation and turned it over to Al Kenworthy to gather contact information, and as much dirt as he could find without making direct contact with them, be they family, friends, or colleagues.

"I put them in order of importance, Al," Dick said when he handed over the list. "I expect that the first two or three will provide enough information to get to the bottom of what happened. But you can look up the others, just in case I hit a wall."

Within a couple of days, Dick was armed and ready to travel north. His secretary booked a room for him for three nights at the best hotel in the Hazelton area, central to the facilities and the offices Dick would visit. After conferring with Al and other colleagues, Dick decided on a risky but effective identity: a Medicare fraud officer. As the funding agency for Medicare, CMS had broad authority over several aspects of device manufacturing and marketing, including fraud and abuse. Though a CMS officer could not pursue and arrest a person suspected of committing Medicare fraud, it was not uncommon for an agent to refer the case to a federal bureau—specifically, the FBI. This identity would fit well with the work that Al and Doug had done in Minnesota. If they had returned to their agency with any residual concerns, the next step would have been an investigation by Medicare Fraud and Abuse. If anyone at the local level had been warned about an investigation by Bobby Adair or others at the home office, Dick's arrival would make perfect sense.

Dick's team was able to prepare a suitable identification document for Richard Ratner, Dick's alias. Anita, using a burner phone, called a few of the intended targets to set up appointments, and soon thereafter, Dick was on the Northeast Extension of the Pennsylvania Turnpike.

Dick was fairly certain that Sterling was the key to the controversy, and the sooner he could talk to the person in charge of the central Pennsylvania sales region, the sooner he might be able to figure out what had happened. Unfortunately, that person, Robert Helge, was attending a national sales meeting and wouldn't be back in town for two days. Rather than waste time, Dick chose to interview a couple of chief executives of hospitals who Tiffany had fingered as profiting from an increased number of device implants. First stop, Saint Anselm Hospital, a friendly-looking, medium-sized community hospital in a rundown area of Hazelton.

Hearing that a Medicare officer was on the doorstep for an unscheduled visit got the anticipated reaction. He was quickly ushered into a finely appointed boardroom and made welcome by a senior secretary, who asked if he had a beverage preference.

"I'm fine, thanks," Dick answered. "I'll just wait until Mr. Beamon can join me."

"He'll be right in, Mr. Ratner. He's just wrapping up another meeting."

Or calling the hospital attorneys to find out what he should do when he comes in here, Dick thought. Which was spot on, as Mr. Beamon entered the boardroom accompanied by two younger people. *Lawyers*, Dick thought. *How unique!*

"Mr. Ratner, it's a pleasure to meet you. I'm Dave Beamon. I've asked a couple of my colleagues to join us. This is Debra Friedman and Dan Blasingame from our legal office."

Dick stood to greet them, shook hands with each, offered a bogus business card prepared just for this occasion, and sat down, trying not to smile at the predictability of it all. All three looked fit and well dressed, and they smiled hard to hide their anxiety.

"Mr. Beamon, I'm sure you're wondering why I'm here," Dick began. "First, I want to reassure you that we have no reason to suspect wrongdoing by anyone on your hospital staff. And we don't want to launch a full investigation. We have limited resources, and there are better places to spend our time. However, we believe that the Tiffany Springer articles about cardiac implants are a potential problem, so we're interviewing key individuals at institutions that she named in her series to see if we can figure out what led to her suspicions of wrongdoing."

Beamon took a deep breath, relieved to hear that the hospital was not in hot water but still concerned that a fraud officer had popped in for a chat. "Let me say we were as surprised as anyone that we were named. At the time of Ms. Springer's death, we were trying to understand what had happened ourselves. We couldn't find evidence that anyone had done anything wrong."

"So you went back and looked at your pacemaker and defibrillator numbers and didn't see a blip?" Dick said.

"Yes. Our total implant numbers did go up over the period that Ms. Springer reported on. But everybody saw an increase in this area, as best we can tell. There was also a shift in volume for a few months to Sterling that was easy to see, but that movement was evening out over time."

"Do you know why?"

"We heard rumors that doctors were being treated well by Sterling, but we didn't have any details. We talked informally to a few of the physicians and couldn't come up with anything definitive."

"Was pricing comparable?"

"Pretty much. Sterling had a few bargains on bulk purchases that we were happy to take advantage of, but there was no windfall for us. We'd be happy to show you the financials, if you wish."

Dick had no intention of taking Beamon up on his offer. He wouldn't know how to examine those records, and he didn't want to look foolish. There was only so much he was willing to do for Philip, and embarrassing himself and risking his cover wasn't one of them.

"Did you notice any other device purchase or use trends over the same period?"

"Not really. There's always a small amount of flux from month to month, but volumes, compared to the same period a year ago, looked about the same."

Dick knew that he had gotten what he needed. He asked a few more perfunctory questions to make his appointment look legitimate. "Mr. Beamon, this has been most helpful. Chances are, I won't have to bother you again, but I may be back to you with a few more questions."

"We're happy to cooperate, Mr. Ratner. We have nothing to hide. Our hospital takes great pride in our integrity and service to our community. If you do come up with something that looks suspicious, we'd sure like to know about it."

Dick left with the distinct feeling that Beamon was telling the truth. He might have to circle back to look at the actual financials with help, but for now, he was satisfied. He called Anita on his way to the parking lot.

She had three more hospitals lined up over the next day and a half, but after Dick finished with the second and heard a nearly identical story, he decided to postpone the others. There was no reason to risk exposure when all he was going to hear was something about a temporary shift in volume that clueless Tiffany had apparently escalated into a scandal of Watergate proportions for the purpose of selling newspapers and becoming famous.

Dick used his afternoon off to drive through the mountains of central Pennsylvania, enjoying the lush scenery and the spectacular vistas. No, the Poconos weren't the Rockies, but they had their own brand of natural beauty that Dick appreciated, especially since it was so close to home. Dick finished off his leisurely drive at an all-you-can-eat family-style restaurant that had the best fried chicken Dick had ever tasted. He arrived back at his hotel room, pleasantly tired and ready for a good night's sleep.

The next morning, Dick called Robert Helge while sipping a coffee in his hotel room. He was sent to voicemail, but his call was returned within a few minutes. Helge sounded anxious.

"This is Bob Helge."

"Hi, Mr. Helge. This is Richard Ratner. I believe my office called you a few days ago to set up a time to meet?"

"Uh … yeah. They did. I just got back from Orlando. Sales meeting."

"Yes, I heard. Is today still OK for you?"

"I think so. What do you want to talk about?"

"This has to with pacemaker and defibrillator implants in your region over the last several months."

"Really? What about them?"

"I would prefer that we have this conversation in person. I'm staying at the Hazelton Inn on Broad Street. Can you meet me here, say, around 10:00 a.m.?

"Uh … that should be OK."

"Great. I'll meet you at the registration desk, and we can have breakfast in the lobby restaurant."

"Fine. Do I need to have a lawyer with me?"

"I doubt it. You're not under any kind of investigation, and I couldn't charge you with anything, even if I wanted to—which I don't."

"OK, Mr. Ratner. See you at ten."

Dick had found a photograph of Helge on the company website, so he thought he knew what to expect at the registration desk. What he didn't anticipate was Helge's size. He was well over six feet tall and weighed at least 250 pounds. He walked with the kind of limp ex-football players have after years of knee trauma, but he was well dressed in a blue serge suit, white shirt, red power tie, and black loafers. And a face that let you know he had downed his share of beer over the years.

Dick met Helge in the lobby, flashed his bogus ID, and shook his beefy hand. They walked to the nearly empty restaurant, where they were escorted to a table by a window. The waiter offered the buffet that Dick figured had been sitting out for at least four hours. Instead, they ordered from the menu, Dick deciding on coffee, juice, and a pastry, while Helge ordered the belly-filler breakfast, his anxiety somehow fueling his appetite. Dick started the conversation as soon as the orders were taken.

"Mr. Helge, I know you're busy, so let's just get to it. Do you mind if I tape our conversation? It's only so I don't have to take notes. Nothing you say here will be on the record."

Helge hesitated and then shrugged. "Got nothing to hide, Mr. Ratner."

Dick took out a cheap tape recorder and put it on the table between them and turned it on. He had no real use for the tape; he used it as a ploy to get people to pay attention and answer questions carefully and truthfully. If the target refused, that was helpful too.

"As I said on the phone, I work for Medicare. We're carrying out an investigation as a follow-up to Tiffany Springer's articles. I'm sure you're familiar with them."

"Oh yeah. I know all about them."

"Then you understand that, without using your name, she implicated you in the scandal."

"She did."

"Have you had a chance to read the articles in their entirety?"

"Almost all of them. They made me want to puke, so I had to stop."

"So you had a negative reaction to what she had to say."

"I told you; they made me physically ill."

"Because they were untrue?"

"Look, Mr. Ratner—"

"Call me Dick, please."

"If you call me Bob. Dick, this is complicated. Let me give you some background so you know where I'm coming from. I was a poor kid, growing up around here. Coal mining dried up, and a lot of our families had to scratch around to make a living. My parents wanted me to go to college, and it never would have happened without football. Fortunately, I was a pretty good offensive lineman in high school and got a full boat to go to Penn State. I made second team All-America my senior year and tried to play pro ball but eventually found out that I just wasn't good enough. After 9/11, I got all worked up about terrorism and enlisted in the army. I lasted all of two years before I realized what a friggin' mistake I had made, so I got out.

"Problem was that I had no idea what I was going to do with my sociology degree after the army. Medtronic was hiring sales reps at the time, and they thought I was perfect for the job—and not because of my education. I was a local celebrity from my football days, which meant that docs would let me into their offices to meet me, and then I could convince them to use the latest product. And it worked. Except as the years went by, people forgot who I had been, so I no longer had that edge, and my sales fell off. Medtronic didn't fire me, but they started talking about a transfer to who knows where. My wife couldn't have that. Her parents are from around here, and her mom and she are, shall we say, joined at the hip.

"Along comes Sterling, a new device company. They're looking for people with my experience. They offer me a district manager position. I jump at it and sign up before reading the fine print. It says that my district will have a sales quota, and if we don't make target, our pay will be pretty much shit. Now, Dick, I grew up disadvantaged, scrapping for anything I could get, so I was *not* going to let those assholes screw me out of my earnings. So I went to work. I came up with, like, a million ideas of ways to convince the docs up here to use Sterling. Let me emphasize—they were all legal. I didn't give kickbacks or anything like that. I'm talking about making friends with the docs and their office staffs and hanging out. Most of the time, we'd go to a ballgame or a show. They would pay their own way, but they depended on me to get good tickets and line up a place to eat afterward."

"So you just befriended them?"

"Pretty much. Me and the sales guys and gals. Now remember, Dick, these docs up here are not the smoothest people in the world. They're almost all immigrants, they don't dress too well, they don't speak English well, and this is Hazelton, for Christ's sake. They feel isolated. All I did was treat them like human beings, and they responded like I figured they would."

"And they used your devices."

"Hey, Dick, don't make it sound like we were implanting crap. Sterling has some good devices. All we did was make friends. So if you had a choice of four devices, and your good friend was selling one of them, and it was just as good as the others, what would you do?"

"Did they put in more devices than were necessary because you and your salespeople were their friends?"

"I ain't a doc. No way could I answer that question. But for sure, we never asked them to do anything like that. We did go into the operating room and helped out with unpacking the devices and making sure they had the leads and other stuff they needed. From what I could see, it looked like most of the patients had a good reason to get a device."

"How long did this go on, Bob?"

"It's still going on. The damn thing is that these people ended up being likeable. They're funny, family-oriented, hard-working, good people, Dick. I have to say that I learned a valuable lesson in all of this. Don't judge a book by its cover and all that."

"So have the other companies caught up with Sterling?"

"Hell, yeah. They did the same thing we did. They made friends and treated the docs and their families well. Now, there's no reason to pick Sterling all the time. And to tell you the truth, I feel better about it. The community up here is much happier, and I think the patients are getting better care. I'm not saying it's perfect. There are still a few cases where you look at them and go, 'Shit, why did he or she do that?' But it's a process that will need to go on for a long time before we get it perfect, especially in places like this. These docs are isolated from mainstream medicine, and there aren't a lot of people looking over each other's shoulders like there are in academic programs."

"Bob, I hate to ask you this question because it's probably out of line and really none of my business. Call it idle curiosity, but some other people may get around to it. Do you have an alibi for the night that Tiffany Springer and Ray Gilbert died?"

"You're right, Dick. Your question is out of line, and I shouldn't need to answer it. But I will. My wife and I hosted a dinner party that evening for some of the implanting docs and their spouses at our house. Paid for by me, and we did it because we enjoy their company."

"So a lot of people up here who might have had a motive to hurt Tiffany and Ray were in the same place at the same time?"

"Yes, and, ironically, you're the first person to ask me that question."

"Tiffany didn't bother to ask you anything?"

"As far as I know, Springer never showed her face up here or talked to anyone she crapped on in her articles. Don't you think she should have taken the time to find out what we were about before throwing bombs?"

Dick dropped his head, abashed by how poorly Tiffany had done her job. She had fallen upon a few cases of apparent abuse and then tried to indict an entire community of physicians, hospitals, and companies. And she had used a clueless, horny doctor to help her make it look authentic.

After saying goodbye to Helge and checking out of his hotel, Dick made his way south to his Philly home. He marveled at how much he had learned in a few interviews, including a half-hour breakfast at a hotel in the middle of God's country, talking to an ex-jock who had lived the story. If only Tiffany had spent a little time doing the same damn thing, maybe she would still be above ground.

24
CHAPTER

Dick sat on the living room sofa in his bathrobe, taking in the view from Ursula's apartment. *Not too shabby*, Dick thought. Actually much nicer than Dick had expected when Ursula had announced she was tired of her old place in Manhattan and wanted to move. At first, Dick had foolishly assumed that Ursula could be talked into relocating to Philadelphia so they could be closer. As much as he enjoyed his weekends with Ursula, the Acela was wearing on him. He was tired of sitting on crowded trains next to rude strangers, who insisted on consuming large, fragrant, and juicy meals, while Dick was forced to suppress his hunger until he arrived at Ursula's apartment and dinner was prepared at "Ursula speed." The trips home were no better; Dick always was unhappy to leave the woman he had come to cherish, knowing that their next rendezvous might be weeks away.

But Ursula had other ideas. Her plan wasn't to leave the Big Apple but to upgrade her New York digs. A wealthy aunt had died and left her enough money to buy an apartment overlooking Central Park, complete with a balcony and large picture windows that afforded a spectacular view. Dick's consolation prize was to rise before Ursula, prepare French press coffee, and take in the park scene while he mentally processed his latest cases. *People-watching at its very best,* Dick thought. No end to the diversity of people and their activities, each enjoying the sunny, cool morning at the city's oasis.

Not surprisingly, his musings this morning were about the Springer/Gilbert case. He had returned home from his trip to northern Pennsylvania more convinced than ever that the couple's deaths had not been in retaliation for Tiffany's exposé. There simply was no one he had identified or interviewed who had the juice or a reason to plan and execute such a dastardly crime and leave no evidence. Tiffany's story affected hospitals, physicians, and medical device companies, none of which was regularly in the business of killing people who pissed them off or of hiring hitmen to do the job for them. And if Dick's interviewees were correct, the downturn in business that Tiffany's stories had caused was just a temporary nuisance that would get better quickly, as long as all parties kept their mouths shut. Killing the story's reporter would only throw gasoline on the fire. It was not the smart move, and stupidity was not an attribute Dick had yet discovered in his people of interest.

Dick's flight of ideas was abruptly interrupted when Ursula plopped herself down on the sofa next to him, cup of tea in hand. "That was one of the best night's sleep I've had in weeks," she announced. "I always rest better when you're here, my dear."

Dick smiled. "Glad I have that effect on you."

"You were pretty lost in thought there, sailor. What's making the wheels spin?"

"The Springer/Gilbert case."

"Right. You told me about that one. You were going to do some interviews on-site, as I recall. What happened with that?"

Dick summarized whom he had talked to and what they had told him, before asking Ursula what she would conclude.

"Sounds to me like Tiffany was an airhead and that her exposé was ultimately a dud. Sound and fury, signifying nothing, as Shakespeare would have said."

"That's my take as well, Ursula. Not only was the exposé a bust, but I can't see any of the accused marshaling the resources to kill her and her dupe. Assassins are paid well because they don't get caught, and we didn't find a money stream."

"So your next move is obvious, right?" Ursula asked.

"You mean back off?"

"You certainly could do that, and no one would fault you. Except maybe Philip. Or you could change the focus of your investigation."

"To Gilbert."

"Precisely. Is it possible he was the target, and Tiffany was collateral damage?"

"I thought about that back at the beginning but dismissed it. Other than the targets of the Springer stories, who would have been motivated to take him out?"

"Beats me. But isn't that what you do for a living? Find a motive and then drill down on possible doers?"

"Sometimes. Depends on the case," Dick answered.

"Well, it seems to me that this could be one such case. You need more information about Ray Gilbert before you can begin to look for people who might have wanted to kill him."

Dick nodded. "I knew there was a reason I fell for you. Not only are you beautiful, but you're smart as hell. I will definitely pursue that thread on Monday when I'm back at the office."

"Beautiful and smart, eh? Did you forget another important attribute?"

"Sexy?"

"Before we get dressed and do brunch, how about if we examine that aspect of my persona? I have just the thing."

"And what might that 'thing' be, Ursula?" Dick teased.

"You mind is always in the gutter, Dick Deaver. I guess that's why I enjoy your company so much."

Each Monday morning, Dick called a meeting of his senior managers and detectives to review the status of their active cases. It was his way to keep hands-on without micromanaging, a fault to which he was prone but one that he realized could demoralize good workers. After his weekend with Ursula, he moved through the agenda, saving the Springer/Gilbert case for last. He summarized what he had learned during his trip and then solicited opinions from some of his most trusted people. He was surprised that all but one had basically shrugged and recommended backing away from the case. The sole exception was Al Kenworthy, who went last.

"I'm not surprised, Dick. When I researched this case, I wasn't able to identify anyone who was likely to commit murder."

"Not in their DNA?"

"Something like that. And if this was a double murder, it was professional and would have cost a bundle, right? And when I researched

Tiffany, it was pretty clear she was a loser who finally had found a bone to chew, but I didn't find any skeletons in her closet that would have led to this."

"So what are you saying, Al?"

"Double murder. Check out the other victim."

"Bingo. And for agreeing with me, you get the privilege of not only doing the background stuff but heading up to Allentown to lead your first investigation."

"Thanks, Dick," Al said. And to his surprise, the remaining twelve people in the room gave him a round of applause.

"Looks like you have some fans here, Al," Dick said when the hubbub died down. "Start the ball rolling, and talk to me when you have all of your ducks lined up. You can set up interview appointments and pick your partner for the trip. How long do you think you'll need to put this all together?"

"I should be ready to travel by the end of this week and have all of the interviews in hand within ten days," Al replied.

"That would be fine," Dick said before adjourning the meeting, already feeling better about the approach that Ursula had suggested and Al had ratified.

As usual, Al was punctual. By midweek he had prepared a case synopsis, sent a copy to Dick for his review, and scheduled an appointment to discuss his findings. He requested that Doug Eisenberg be allowed to attend. Doug already knew a lot about the case and was going to be Al's partner selection for the next set of Allentown interviews. Dick greeted his men and seated them around a small conference table in his office, with notepads, pens, and bottled water at the ready. Al quickly started in.

"First of all, Dick, I went back and looked through my notes to make sure I didn't miss anything about Tiffany that might be relevant. And I didn't. She was a mediocre reporter and hadn't been involved with any high-profile, high-risk cases before this device thing. She was a party girl and slept around a fair amount but had no long-term relationships before Gilbert. She used recreational drugs but in smallish quantities and had no outstanding debts to dealers that we could find. Most of her family is in Pittsburgh, and her visits there, or theirs to Allentown, were infrequent."

Dick only nodded.

"Doug and I spent most of our time on Gilbert. I'll skip over college and medical school because it was a big fat nothing. Squeaked into medical school, where he was in the middle of the class. Internship, residency, and then cardiology fellowships at reasonable places. He never intended to do anything other than practice and make money. Met and married Linda Vespucci when he was in training. She was a nice Italian girl from Wilkes-Barre, an only child, who went to nursing school here in Philly and then took a job at Gladwyne Memorial, where Gilbert met her. Quite attractive; they made a handsome couple. They got married, and she moved with Gilbert to Allentown, when he took his first job. She worked as an OR nurse for a couple of years but then quit to take care of her sick parents. She brought them down from Wilkes-Barre to a nursing home in Allentown. Not exactly a five-star place, so Linda spent tons of time taking care of them. She wanted to move them to the house she and Gilbert had bought, but he nixed that idea. Pissed her off pretty good."

"What was Gilbert up to while she was taking care of Mama and Papa?"

"Mostly chasing skirts. Not sure if Linda knew it before he put a ring on her finger, but the guy was a sexaholic."

"Huh?"

"That's right. And his problem started in high school, apparently. Got a couple of girls pregnant and was almost lynched before his daddy bailed him out with payments to the angry families. I guess he eventually learned how to use a condom because I couldn't find another baby trail or evidence he was treated for STDs."

"STDs?" Dick asked.

"Sexually transmitted diseases. And that's not because he was abstaining. He was going after almost everything in every hospital he worked in. Boyish good looks with lots of charm. And marriage didn't make a dent. In fact, it might have increased his sexual appetite."

"Any clues from that activity?"

"Not much. Gilbert was careful not to screw married women—or at least not married women who would rat him out. And he generally didn't linger. A couple rolls in the hay and onward to the next conquest. Except for one."

"Who was ...?"

"Elizabeth Gold, his nurse practitioner."

"Seriously?"

"That was obviously a colossal mistake, and for some reason, it took him a fairly long time to realize it. Liz not only worked with him, but she's married to a jealous nutcase named Noah. Gilbert had to know that Noah was going to find out, and Liz should have been able to warn him that Noah would go off the chain when he did. And it all happened just that way. Lots of screaming and yelling and crashing outside their house. As far as I can tell, it never came to blows."

"Someone you and Doug will be visiting?"

"For sure. Number one on our list."

"Did Gilbert and the nurse finally break up?"

"Tiffany took care of that. Whether it was the drugs, the sex, or some spell she cast over him, Tiffany totally turned Gilbert's head. He abandoned his other sexual escapades once he got involved with Springer. Liz was given her walking papers and was none too happy to go into that good night."

"That will be interview number two."

"Correct."

"Gilbert became monogamous with Tiffany. How did he manage to spend so much time with her? Wasn't his wife suspicious?"

"Wasn't married while he was with Tiffany. Let's back up. Linda's parents both died in the nursing home within a couple of weeks of each other. Linda then turned her attention to creating her own family. Gilbert obliged and got her pregnant. She was twelve weeks into her pregnancy when she died suddenly. They did an autopsy, but the results were never made public. Gilbert hired a lawyer and got them sealed. Since Linda had no immediate relatives, he said he didn't see the point in releasing the information that her friends might find distressing. The argument worked. Nobody asked. So I got nothing."

"Come on, Al. You never have nothing. And even if you did throw snake eyes, you wouldn't admit it."

"OK, you got me. I do have a way in, but it needs to be handled delicately."

"Shoot."

"Linda didn't make many friends, but there was one person she played tennis with, in whom she may have confided. I want to talk to her to see if she knows what happened to Linda."

"Interview number three."

"Right."

"So you're ready to go?"

"Yes, and if it all works out, I should have something for you in a couple of days."

"Have you guys planned an alias?"

"How about life insurance company investigators trying to determine if Gilbert's policy should be paid off."

"Pretty good, especially given the suicide possibility," Dick pointed out.

"It may be a little flimsy, but who will we be talking to here? A teacher, a nurse, and a housewife. I doubt any of them will question this approach. And the beauty of my idea is that ID is a snap. Practically off the shelf."

"OK. Just be careful. As I keep telling everybody, this is not a life-or-death case. I'm doing it to appease my faux son-in-law."

"But now you're hooked, aren't you, Dick? You need to know."

Dick looked down at his hands, knowing he was caught. "Get the hell out of here, and go to work."

Al and Doug rose and left the office smiling, knowing they had hit the Deaver target.

Al and Doug felt like they had the road trip thing sorted out. They understood each other's preferences and habits and shared a number of important attitudes; most important was getting the work done efficiently and quickly so they could get out of town before they were discovered. The longer they lingered, the more likely that targets might connect. If people put the dots together, they could nab the duo and ruin the investigation.

They decided to talk to Liz first. Noah was the more volatile and most likely to go to the authorities. If Liz had any smarts, she might be able to keep him from going crazy, a higher probability than if they approached him cold. Al called Liz from the car to let her know why they needed to talk to her and to arrange a time. Getting Liz on the phone was not as easy as Al had hoped. She was paged multiple times before she finally answered and didn't sound pleased to be disturbed.

After lying about the reason for their interview, Al asked the most sensitive question. "Ms. Gold, we know that you and Dr. Gilbert were having an affair. What we'll want to know from you and your husband is if he might have harmed himself because of your relationship."

"Or been harmed?" Liz countered.

"Yes, that too."

"I can answer both questions for you right now. And it's an emphatic no! Ray was well over me when he died, and I was over him. I had made peace with my husband, and we moved on. There was no reason for revenge or recrimination. Ray never would have killed himself because of me. Never!"

"That's good to hear, Ms. Gold. Would you have a problem if we stopped by and talked to your husband directly to get his take on this?"

"Is that really necessary? I've hurt my husband enough."

"We understand," Al said. "The interview will be brief. We are just trying to cover all bases."

"I guess it's all right, as long as you don't dwell on the affair."

"Would you mind calling him to let him know we're on our way and what we need?"

"That's a good idea. Noah has a temper, as you probably already know."

"Exactly what we wish to avoid," Al replied. "Most grateful for your help."

As he hung up, he looked over at Doug, who could only take a big breath and grit his teeth. This was going to be uncomfortable.

The Gold residence was a pleasant surprise. Instead of the poorly cared-for shack they had envisioned, they found a neat, two-story colonial on a quiet, tree-lined street in neighboring Bethlehem. And they were greeted at the door by a diminutive, well-kept man in khakis, a cardigan, and a neatly trimmed moustache, looking exactly like the college professor he was supposed to be.

"Liz told me you were on your way. Please come in."

After seating his guests in the living room, Noah asked, "Can I offer you a beverage?"

"No thanks," Al answered. "We won't take much of your time. We just wanted to get your perspective on the Ray Gilbert matter."

"I'm in the middle of grading papers, and marks are due in the dean's office tomorrow morning. Liz and I want to get this behind us so we can get on with our lives, so I'll be brief. Ray Gilbert was a bad person. He seduced my wife and many other women and thought nothing of using them like sex toys. Most of them he discarded quickly, but he kept Liz on the hook longer than most for his convenience—until I found out about it. I would like to think that my temper tantrum in front of our house had something to do with cooling his ardor, or maybe it snapped Liz to her senses, but as far as I can tell, that was the end of the shenanigans. Liz and I have made our peace, and I'm content."

"So ..."

"If it was murder and not suicide, it wasn't me. I'm not the killing kind. And I seriously doubt that Liz's leaving him unseated him to the point of killing himself and his latest girlfriend."

"Mr. Gold—"

"I hate to cut you off, but I'm not going to answer any more questions for you or for anyone else. You're just going to have to take what I said and believe it."

Noah rose from his armchair, signaling the end of the meeting, and Al and Doug dutifully followed his lead and made their way to the front door.

"Here's my card, Mr. Gold," Al said as he presented his bogus business card. "Call me if anything else occurs to you, OK?"

"Fine," said Noah as he closed the door with a bang.

Doug and Al walked to their car, holding comments until they were on the road.

"Hard to argue with either of them, Al," Doug observed.

"To be honest, I didn't think we needed to worry too much about them. Our next interview is the most important, but that's not until tomorrow morning. What do you say we find ourselves some grub and then head over to our luxurious motel accommodations?"

The food they found at a local eatery was plentiful, if not delicious, and was washed down well with a couple of sixteen-ounce drafts that helped sleep arrive just a little faster. They rose early, had a light breakfast at a nearby diner, and arrived at the home of Trudy McMoody at the stroke of nine.

Trudy arrived at the door in exercise clothing, showing off an athletic body topped by a pretty face. "Just got the kids off to school, and I have a tennis appointment at ten, so let's get to it, shall we?" she said. She led them into her kitchen and seated them at the table. They agreed to black coffee that she served in cups that didn't match; then she scurried about, putting dirty plates and utensils into the dishwasher. "You guys have questions about Ray Gilbert's death, right?" she asked over her shoulder.

"Yes," Al said.

"I hardly knew Ray, but Linda told me a lot about him."

"We're interested in anything you can tell us," Al said.

"I only knew Linda for a year or so. After her parents died, she joined my gym, and we started working out and playing tennis together. Sometimes we'd go out for breakfast or lunch, and we became friends."

"She confided in you."

"Yes. She didn't have anyone else. Just that asshole husband of hers."

"Asshole? Why?" Al asked, trying to sound naïve.

"He cheated on her all the time, and she knew it. After her parents died, she had no one else in the world, so she clung to him and put up with his nonsense."

"Must have torn her up," Doug offered.

"That's an understatement. She was depressed as hell but couldn't figure a way out. She got pregnant because she thought she could get his attention or maybe grow her own friends, but it only made things worse. He was super-pissed off about having children, so when he wasn't screaming at her, he left her alone more than ever."

"Was she getting professional help?" Al asked.

"Off and on. She couldn't stick with it, so she would go long periods with no one to talk to, except me. Plus, she didn't want to take antidepressants while she was pregnant."

"Were you around when she died?"

"No, damn it. We were away on vacation. First one we'd taken in years. She called me a few times, obviously very unhappy, and I talked to her, but I couldn't be there for her."

"Was there a history of heart disease in her family?"

Silence, then, "Why do you ask?"

"Her death was sudden and was called a heart attack."

"Her heart was under attack all right but not the way you think."

"Are you saying she died of a broken heart?"

"You could say that."

"How does that work?"

"Are you guys on the level? Do you really not know what happened?"

"That's why we're here."

"This interview isn't being taped, right?"

"Absolutely not. You can search us if you like. We don't have a recording device."

"I really need to get this off my chest. It's tearing me apart. But I'll deny telling you what I'm about to tell you."

"Please, We'll be discreet."

"My husband works in IT at the hospital and has access to medical records. If he got caught looking at patient records without permission, he would not only be fired but could be prosecuted. This is a big deal. He and I decided that we needed to know what happened to Linda. Don't ask me why; we just did. The autopsy records were sealed but were placed in her electronic medical record."

"Why?"

"It was a mistake. The report wasn't supposed to be in the chart, but it was, buried in an obscure section where only my husband would have looked. Just another in a long list of things that the electronic medical record has done for medicine. Makes whatever you want to find damn near impossible. But I can tell you with confidence that Linda didn't die of a heart attack."

"What was it?" Al asked, barely able to hide his curiosity.

"Wait here," she said as she left the kitchen. They could hear her climb the stairs and then descend a minute or two later. "Here. Take this, and use it any way you need to. Just never, ever tell anyone where you got it, or my husband will kill me." Trudy handed over a copy of Linda's autopsy report.

Al and Doug looked at each other and then at Trudy, who had tears in her eyes.

"Read it, and you'll see. She took an overdose of sleeping pills and killed herself and took her twelve-week-old fetus with her."

Trudy started to sob; emotions overwhelmed all of them. She didn't need to tell Doug and Al that the interview was over and it was time for them to leave.

25
CHAPTER

Al and Doug wasted no time after their return to Philadelphia to arrange a sit-down with Dick. Both were pleased with the outcome of their foray into northern Pennsylvania. They had had to extend their stay to probe the Vespucci family; Linda's suicide left open a few other possibilities they needed to explore. But they had gathered enough information in anticipation of Dick's questions, so they were ready for the intensive debriefing that was Dick's custom.

They convened in Dick's office, circling his desk. Dick sat back, tea mug in hand. "All right, boys; let's have it."

Dick listened intently to the narrative, interrupting only to ask questions. He raised his eyebrows a few times and saved his most surprised facial expression for Linda's suicide.

"So that's why you were a little late getting back."

"Yes," Al replied. "After seeing the autopsy report, we hoped somebody would be able to give us more background. We talked to a few other people who knew her."

"How did that work out?"

"Not so great, boss. She had no family to speak of, and almost no friends, other than Trudy."

"Were you able to get hold of any other records or legal documents?"

"Sealed tight as a drum. We tried to strong-arm a couple of clerks at the courthouse with a phony story about a federal investigation, but they told us we would need a subpoena just to get in the door. They wouldn't even tell us what documents were listed."

"You think Gilbert intentionally hid the cause of death?"

"It makes sense. Linda had a modest life insurance policy. If it got out that she was a suicide, he wouldn't have gotten a payout."

"Could Gilbert have persuaded some estate attorney to commit insurance fraud?" Dick asked.

"Who knows what was going on up there? I mean, we couldn't find a shred and we weren't going to ask the police how they closed the case. It looks like someone with clout went out of their way to wipe the slate clean."

"Any idea who might have done that?"

"Not a clue, boss. We couldn't find anybody who knew her well enough to stick their neck out and risk tampering with evidence. The entire investigation of her death and the autopsy are unavailable. And no one up there seems to be the least concerned about it."

Dick looked down into his empty coffee cup, lost in thought. Doug and Al knew they needed to be quiet and wait for Dick's next comment, which hopefully would include his decision about what to do with this miserable case.

"Boys, I think we're done with this dog. We've spent more than enough time and resources on it as a favor to Philip. I'll talk to him this afternoon and fill him in. Put this one in a file, and we'll move on."

"I have to agree with you, Dick," Doug said. "We hit a wall, and breaking through it is going to take a lot of muscle. My suspicion is that we won't find much on the other side anyway. She killed herself and her baby. If somebody got really pissed off about Gilbert causing it, we can't figure who that might be."

"Good. Then we're in agreement. You boys take the rest of the day off, and go play golf or something. You earned it."

Dick decided to call Philip and invite him to lunch. Better to deliver the news in person than to try to explain his dismissal of the case on the phone. Philip was a pain in the ass, but Dick knew he was smart and would have lots of questions that would be easier to answer with some form of alcohol in hand.

And to make sure that his martini would be as cold and as dry as possible, Dick asked Philip to meet him at the Union League. This famous city social club was perched at the top of a flight of circular stairs on Broad Street, a stone's throw from city hall. It had been one of the last bastions of white male domination in Philadelphia, home to some of the city' most prominent businessmen, lawyers, and politicians and host site for presidents, starting with Lincoln. Until it was forced to enter the twenty-first century. Under new and "enlightened" leadership, the club decided to admit minorities and women, at least those who were educated and moneyed enough to appreciate the us-versus-them philosophy that was so central to a club that had no real purpose, other than an excuse for a good meal.

Diversification, or a shallow version of it, had allowed people like Dick, who had scoffed at the idea of joining such an anachronous organization, to pursue membership in good conscience, with the excuse that it was a convenient place to meet people and that it was good for business. Dick had even managed to steer the League toward public works and had been honored for his success with the homeless who populated the streets of Center City. Such efforts allowed people as liberal as Philip and Dorothy to break bread there on occasion without a red face. It was just a short ride on the Broad Street subway from NorthBroad Medical Center, Dick was happy to remind Philip, who would have arrived at Dick's table on time but for an old Union League tradition.

"Where the hell were you, Philip?" Dick asked as Philip made his tardy entrance and sat at the table.

"I was downstairs, arguing with the Neanderthal at the front door."

"About what?" Dick asked a second before he discerned the answer. "They wouldn't let you in without a jacket, would they?"

"Precisely," said Philip. "Who wears suit jackets to work at a hospital anymore?"

"So that abomination you have on is not yours?" Dick said, referring to the ugliest plaid jacket he had ever seen.

"Wouldn't be caught dead in this piece of crap, Dick. I think they deliberately keep ugly jackets in their closet down there to embarrass outsiders."

"There's been a lot of discussion about doing away with the rule, but—"

"There are enough effete snobs to keep it the way it is."

"All organizations have their good and bad points, Philip."

Philip sat back and took a deep breath. "OK, Dick. I don't want to argue with you about the social value of the Union League. Get me a class of Chardonnay, and I'll complain no more. At least not today."

"Already ordered and on its way, Philip. Along with my martini. I also ordered you the clam chowder and the chef's salad. Both real good and highly recommended."

They spent the next few minutes catching up, focusing mostly on Emily and Erin and their latest high jinks. Dick could never get enough of the girls, who had bonded with him in a way Philip and Dorothy had never anticipated. He greedily accumulated photos that he carried in his wallet and showed to anybody who cared to look. He also framed them to decorate every nook and cranny of his office and apartment. He was a different man when he was with them or talked about them. So when the conversation shifted to the subject matter of the meeting, the Gilbert/Springer case, it was as if a switch in his head had been thrown. Dick's demeanor and tone changed abruptly.

For the next fifteen minutes, Dick methodically reviewed what he and his team had learned about Gilbert and Springer. Though he had a dossier on the table, he didn't refer to his notes while he related chronologically and with great detail the story of their relationship, from its inception to their deaths. He then listed the several possible reasons for and the cause of their deaths, first those that related to Tiffany and then to Gilbert. He concluded his presentation with Trudy McMoody's blockbuster revelation that Gilbert's wife, Linda, wasn't taken from him by natural causes, as Gilbert had intimated to Philip, but by her own hand, killing not only herself but also their unborn child.

Philip was thunderstruck. "I had absolutely no idea, Dick. Ray told me nothing about how his wife died."

"Nobody else knew either. And to tell you the truth, the guys I sent up there would have walked right past it as well, if it hadn't been for Trudy's husband having access to information he had no right to see. He essentially committed a felony. So Trudy isn't in a position to share that information with anyone else. Frankly, I'm surprised she opened up to Doug and Al."

"This raises a lot of possibilities, doesn't it, Dick?"

"It does, Philip. Al and Doug explored most of them as best they could. They had to be very careful because they had no business with that seminal piece of information—Linda's cause of death. But from everything they gathered so far, we have no way to connect her suicide with what happened to Ray and Tiffany."

Philip reflected as he sipped his wine. "So now what?"

"That's why we're here, Philip. As far as I'm concerned, we're done. But before I close the case file completely, I wanted to make sure you knew the facts and agreed. This is, after all, your case."

Philip smiled. "It's not like I paid for your help, Dick. You did this as a personal favor, and I truly appreciate your kindness. Seems to me that I have no right to ask you to persevere, especially since it looks like you hit a dead end."

Dick was surprised by Philip's reaction. "I'm glad you're of that opinion, Philip. I really am. I don't want to disappoint you, but I don't have the resources to stay on this case. It would take a major investment of time and money, and the overwhelming likelihood is that we would still draw a blank at the end of it."

Soup was delivered as Philip continued his musings. Dick sipped his martini while greeting friends and acquaintances who walked by. They finished their salads, having returned to incidental conversation, now centered on Dorothy's developing plans for the girls' birthday parties, rapidly approaching.

"Pony rides, amusement park, or swim party," Dick marveled. "What choices. Those little girls have no idea how lucky they are to have you guys as parents."

"And you as a doting grandfather, Dick. The girls love you."

"I really appreciate your reasonableness about this case, Philip," Dick admitted. "I was afraid you would feel frustrated."

"I get it, Dick. Like I said, thanks for making the effort."

Dick smiled, feeling as fulfilled as he had in a while. And he owed a lot of his satisfaction to a man he hadn't favored for his daughter but one who was possibly changing his stripes. Dick hoped so, because this guy was clearly going to be around for a while.

Philip felt distracted for the rest of his day at NorthBroad. He stumbled through the fellows' outpatient clinic, letting his young charges make management decisions that he might not have made himself but with which he couldn't find fault. He was anxious to conclude the day and have a chance to seek Dorothy's advice about a situation he shouldn't have cared about as much as he did. Why did Ray Gilbert matter so much to Philip?

As luck would have it, his drive home was complicated. An accident on Roosevelt Boulevard, not an uncommon occurrence, had traffic backed up, so Philip had to bail out onto surface streets. By the time he parked his car and opened the front door in Narberth, the girls were so "hangry" that Dorothy was two glasses of wine ahead of him, her patience stretched to its limit.

"Why are you late, Philip?"

"Traffic."

"Traffic, huh? I didn't see anything on the local news about an accident."

"What can I tell you? I would have texted you, but you know what they say."

"Yeah, yeah, I know. Don't text and drive. Did it occur to you to do an old-fashioned hands-free phone call? As I recall, that car you drive has Bluetooth, does it not?"

"Hmm … does it?"

"Never mind, wise-ass. Go get washed up. Dinner is ready. Actually, it's way past ready."

Philip decided to forgo any further bantering. It wasn't going to change Dorothy's mood, and he wanted to have a serious conversation with her about the case. He would hold his tongue and wait until the girls were in bed, which they were able to manage close to the usual time. Philip and Dorothy then settled down at the kitchen island with cups of decaf tea, their latest unwinding formula after a long day.

After the exchange of mundane information from the day, Philip jumped in. "Dorothy, there's something I need to talk to you about."

Dorothy burst into tears. "Finally, Philip," she said between sobs.

"Why are you crying? I know I should have filled you in before, but it's not something you should be sad about."

"Really, Philip? You don't think our relationship is important?"

Philip was gobsmacked. "What on earth are you talking about?'

"Where were you at lunchtime today?"

"Why do you want to know?"

"Your secretary said you had a lunch date but wouldn't tell me with whom."

"I did."

"Why didn't you answer my call to your cell phone?"

"I was at the Union League and had to turn my phone off."

"The Union League? Pretty damn fancy. Who did you have lunch with, Philip?"

"Your father."

"My father? He didn't tell me about having lunch with you."

"Does your father report to you about everybody he lunches with?"

"Of course not. But you're my partner, the father of my children."

"We didn't want you to know about it."

"Know about what, Philip?"

Philip had his opening. Time to come clean. "He and I have been working on the Gilbert case."

"What do you mean, *working on?*"

"I prevailed on him to put some time and resources into an investigation to see if we might find out what happened to Ray and Tiffany."

Dorothy's expression immediately brightened. "Thank the good Lord!"

"You wanted us to chase the case?"

"I don't give a damn about the case, Philip. I was convinced you were cheating on me, just like that asshole Ray Gilbert," Dorothy said, wiping tears from her eyes.

"Cheating on you? Seriously?"

"You've been distracted, Philip. And spending more time working or whatever. You've left the room to take phone calls and write notes that you have been careful to stick in your pocket. What was I supposed to conclude?"

"That I was having an affair?"

"How was I to know my father was the person you were hanging out with? I was worried that Gilbert fixed you up with one of his cheap girlfriends when you were up there. I wanted to confront you but could never get up the nerve. I kept making lame excuses for your behavior while being scared to death you'd found somebody to replace me."

"I'm so sorry, Dorothy. If I had known, I would have spilled the beans a long time ago. I should have known better than to try to keep things from you. You're just too damn perceptive." Philip rose from his stool to give Dorothy a long, firm hug. Deep breaths and a few moments of silence before Philip held Dorothy by her shoulders and looked into her eyes. "You have to be nuts. Nobody could ever replace you in my life. You're the best thing that ever happened to me."

Dorothy sniffled a bit and then said, "You might as well tell me what you've found out. It would be a shame to use up all of this emotional energy for nothing."

"That's where I started," Philip said, reseating himself at the island.

"I wanted to tell you what your father's guys came up with and then ask you for your opinion about what, if anything, to do next."

Philip summarized the results of the investigation, emphasizing the most dramatic development—the discovery that Ray Gilbert's pregnant wife had committed suicide.

"At the end of the day, Doug and Al couldn't come up with anyone who might have killed Tiffany. And at the same time, they suspected that Ray's infidelity drove his wife to kill herself, but they couldn't identify anyone with the motive or the means to do something about it?" Dorothy asked.

"That's what they reported back. I think your dad pushed them pretty hard and was satisfied there was nothing else to learn."

"Dad knows his guys and his stuff, so it would be hard to argue with him. But—"

"But your dad was doing this as a favor to me."

"Right. And pro bono cases are never handled as aggressively as paid cases. It's just human nature," Dorothy explained.

"So your question is whether he kept the pedal to the metal."

"Or let up because he's a good businessman who knows when to cut his losses."

"He never really believed in the case in the first place, probably because I was the person who brought it to him."

"Maybe, but let's try to keep personal feelings out of this, Philip."

Philip nodded, relieved that Dorothy had decided to put aside her own anxieties about his behavior and focus on the facts of the case.

"What do you think I should do?" Philip asked.

"There's very little you can do, Philip. If my father and his people came up dry, it's unlikely you can do better. And this was a police investigation, so you can't afford to attract a lot of attention to yourself. Besides, there's still a very strong possibility that Ray and Tiffany did it to themselves, intentionally or by mistake. They weren't necessarily murdered."

"I know Ray, and I just can't believe he would have been that evil or that stupid."

Silence, as Philip waited expectantly for the conclusion he hoped Dorothy would reach—on her own.

Finally, "My father usually keeps a master file with notes from the field agents and his edits superimposed."

"He had a dossier with him at the Union League, but he didn't open it."

"I'm not surprised. He's the master at remembering details, even in a case with so many moving parts."

DEATH BY YOUR OWN DEVICE

"What's your point?"

"Can you get that file for me? It will have a lot of good information in it."

"Are you kidding? If I were to tell him his darling daughter needed his right ear, he would rip it off and give it to me."

"Yes, but you have to be careful. We don't want to hurt his feelings by implying he didn't get the job done. He's meticulous about his work."

"You're right. I'll just tell him you were curious about the case and wanted to read the file."

"Philip, here's my offer. Get me the file, and let me review it. My only goal is to look for a hole or a glitch or a wrinkle that my father and his guys may have overlooked. But let's be clear. The chances of this working are very small."

"I know."

"If I come up empty, you agree to accept the suicide theory. And if I do find something, I have absolutely no intention of following up on it myself. You can choose to drop it or to take it back to my father, who can pursue it if he wishes. And that will likely depend on the strength of the evidence."

"Right. I understand."

"And you'll promise me—no, you'll swear on the souls of your children—that you will under *no* circumstances get involved with this case yourself. No super sleuth, no caped crusader, no Colombo."

"OK, I get it."

"You had better get it, buster, because I mean it. If you screw this one up, I'm out of here with the girls. Period. No discussion. I'm doing this to help you without getting in hot water, and you aren't going to make a fool out of me. Understand?"

Philip did understand, better than he ever had. His principal emotion at that moment was relief that Dorothy had trusted him enough to accept his explanation of what was clearly aberrant behavior. And that she believed in him and was willing to put some of her precious time into a case that held no interest for her personally but one that had affected Philip so much that he had been willing to enlist the aid of her father, who had never shown Philip the respect he thought he deserved.

Philip cared about what had happened to Ray Gilbert, despite his ridiculous dalliances, and if someone had targeted him for an ugly and premature death, Dorothy was up to the challenge and willing to help—but, as she had made abundantly clear, only to a point. And the consequences of crossing that line would be dire indeed.

237

26
CHAPTER

Dick was a little surprised when Philip called him and asked for the Gilbert/Springer dossier. He had already passed it on to Anita with instructions to file it away with other unreconciled cases on the odd chance that more evidence or information might come to light. Resurrecting a case happened once in a blue moon, but its rarity didn't dissuade Dick from maintaining an enormous file room. Whenever an unwitting young associate asked if Dick ever considered putting all of that information on computer files, Dick scoffed. "Evidence is meant to be on paper. Scrolling down a computer page is not the same as combing through a paper file. Now get out of my face before I fire you." Being old gave you some rights, Dick figured, like being stubborn and kicking butt once in a while but just for fun.

Philip stopped by Dick's office on his way home from work and double-parked outside his building. Double-parking was an art form in Philly, and one that everyone, including the cops, accepted as routine, as long as whoever did it remembered to get back to their car quickly and to smile nicely at whomever they had blocked in.

It took Anita only a few minutes to find the file and bring it to Philip.

"Now, Dr. Sarkis, this is our original. Would you like me to Xerox a few copies for you?"

"That's OK, Anita. No need to trouble you. The only person who'll be looking at the file is Dorothy, and she'll take good care of it."

"Oh my, Ms. Deaver," Anita said. "I remember when she worked here before she went to law school. She was the very best and so responsible. But it's been ages since I've seen her. How is she?"

"Doing well, Anita. She works in a small firm now but enjoys her work, and the girls keep us busy."

"Yes, Dick talks about Emily and Erin all the time. He's quite in love with those little tykes."

"And they with him, Anita. Anyhow, thanks for the file. I'll get it back to you in a few days."

Philip placed the dossier on the front seat of his car. He found a parking spot only a few steps from their house and carried the brief, along with his briefcase, from his parking space to their front door. When he entered, Dorothy was sitting at the kitchen island, answering emails on her phone. Without a word, she pointed to a tumbler with a giant ice cube she had placed on the counter next to her.

"Thanks, my love," Philip said as he put his coat and the brief on a table by the door and headed for the cabinet they used for spirits. He selected a bottle of twelve-year-old Macallan and poured himself a small amount. "Just a wee nip," Philip said. "I want to go easy this evening. I have to read electrocardiograms later, and that is best done in a relatively sober state."

One of Philip's jobs was to over-read EKGs that were carried out on the various units at NorthBroad and then interpreted by the fellows in training. His corrections provided feedback that helped them learn how to interpret the complex tracings, an integral part of cardiology practice. But the work was tedious and required full concentration, something Philip wouldn't be able to muster after a second cocktail.

"I do have a present for you, however," he said to Dorothy.

"Oh, how lovely. What's the occasion?"

"Just my never-ending devotion to you."

"Cut the crap and tell me. Oh, I know. My father's file."

"Once again, your perceptiveness astounds me."

"Cut the flattery. It won't get you any more than I promised. I just have to figure out the best time to dive into it."

"The Heart Rhythm meetings are in Chicago next week. I'll be gone for a few days."

"That might be a good time, depending on what Emily and Erin are up to. Maybe I can sort out some things to keep them busy. I just need a block of time to go through the file."

"I'll leave that up to you. There's no rush. What's done is done. The only question that remains is why?"

"Yeah, I got it. Now on to the more immediate problem. What are we going to serve our monsters for dinner?"

Philip left for Chicago on a Saturday morning, annoyed that his professional association insisted on having meetings on weekends, time that he cherished at home. They were bowing to the practicing doctors, who didn't want to give up office and operating time and patient revenue by being away during the week, something that Philip, a salaried physician, couldn't have cared less about.

Dorothy was able to call in a few favors and arrange some "away" playdates for the girls for Saturday and Sunday afternoons. It really wasn't hard. Everybody loved E squared. They were always well behaved and played well with all of their friends, which meant that the friends' parents had an opportunity to do house chores while lightly supervising the happy munchkins.

Dorothy retreated to the office that she and Philip used when they worked at home, followed, as usual, by Rocky and Meeko, who each had their own dog beds where they could nap while Dorothy worked. Within seconds, they were both on their sides, out cold, snoring seemingly in synchrony, making Dorothy smile, as they always did.

Though there was only one desk, there was enough cabinet space to store their things so they didn't clutter the desktop and get in each other's way. She opened the dossier on the empty desktop and began with the summary that Al Kenworthy had dictated after he had completed his investigation. As usual, it was well written and easy to follow. Al liked the chronological approach and methodically cataloged everything he and Doug had found, beginning with the early lives of Ray Gilbert and Tiffany Springer. Dorothy used the summary to focus on some of the details she found particularly important or interesting, including Gilbert's marriage.

By the time she had gotten through the summary and some of the supporting documents, Dorothy's intuition began to kick in. Whether because of Al's bias or what he had learned, or because of Dorothy's naturally suspicious personality, she began to move away from the Tiffany Springer theory. Her exposé had the familiar shocking aspects that would attract a national audience. The public loved to hear about rich, famous, or influential people who screwed up, especially if they intentionally hurt others for their own gain. Endlessly fascinating were the travails of politicians who were caught stealing money intended for poverty programs. Or priests, charged with maintaining the spiritual health of their flock, assaulting children to satisfy their perverted sexual needs.

Here, Tiffany told the story of sophisticated physicians, who had taken the Hippocratic Oath, seemingly intentionally cutting people open and inserting hardware they didn't need for the purposes of lining the physicians' own pockets, while their hospitals and the device industry either turned a blind eye or colluded with them.

But because such scandals were commonplace and reported on a nearly continuous basis by a voracious, multiheaded media, their effect was rarely durable. Within days, if not hours, reporters seeking their share of the limelight would have moved on to the next scandal or massacre or natural tragedy. Interest was bound to wane quickly and without retribution, as long as the targets kept their mouths shut and a criminal or civil case wasn't pursued. And in Tiffany's case, her newspaper had been careful to couch her accusations in such a way that it would have been quite difficult to bring any kind of legal case. Yes, the attorneys would rattle their sabers, but they knew that a long and costly litigation would likely yield little, all the while keeping the case in the public domain. Ultimately, that would be bad for business. Better to just shut up and let it all pass.

All of this caused Dorothy to agree with Al that it was hard to believe that any of Tiffany's targets had gone after her. They had neither the means nor the motivation. Move on.

Question number two for Dorothy: was there anyone else who might have wanted to kill Tiffany? Once again, Al's notes were critical. *Tiffany was an airhead,* she thought, *but if people were killed for their stupidity, we would all be stepping over bodies in the street.* As for angry lovers, Ray Gilbert was one of her few serious affairs. The rest were no more than one-nighters that went nowhere. People at her job didn't like her much because of her attitude about the truth being a convenience rather than a necessity for her stories, but pumping her full of drugs was not something they would have pursued to teach her a lesson in good reporting.

Question three: could it have been a suicide? Tiffany and Gilbert had their share of troubles but they were not overtly depressed. Quite the contrary. Tiffany was being heralded as the second coming of Woodward and Bernstein. Al had discovered Gilbert's consultation with the Toscano firm, and it hadn't been hard to infer that Gilbert was looking at a whistleblower windfall that would have put working hard as a doctor in his rearview mirror. Tiffany used drugs, and like most people who did, she had sleep and concentration problems, but she had too much self-esteem and a relatively bright future to put herself down. *Simply not possible*, thought Al, and once again, Dorothy agreed.

And finally, did Tiffany make a stupid mistake and overdose herself and Gilbert? Al had gathered enough information to suggest that Tiffany never went past weed and blow and then only in small quantities. Hard stuff, especially mainlined, had not been in her repertoire. An accident was something certainly to consider since it was the official cause of death but, in Dorothy's mind, an unlikely scenario.

On to Gilbert. A little easier to analyze since she already had some background from Philip. Al had listed most of the biographical facts and then went to describe Gilbert's behavior after his arrival in Allentown with Linda, his new wife. Dorothy wondered if either Gilbert or Linda had been under the delusion that he would be a more loyal husband once out of Philadelphia and in the more family-friendly Allentown. "Leopards don't change their spots," Dorothy said to her sleeping hounds. Meeko's head came up for a moment. She looked around expectantly, hoping that Dorothy had disturbed her sleep because she had treats to offer. When none was forthcoming, it was back to peaceful canine slumber.

Gilbert's prowling had done nothing but accelerate in his new small-town environment, where young, healthy, attractive women were plentiful, and a young doctor, married or not, was prime bait. He started at the hospital but quickly became acquainted with the best meat markets in town. It took a little while for Linda to catch on, stupidly accepting Gilbert's explanation that, as the youngest member of the group, he had the heaviest call responsibilities.

Within a few months, Linda knew that Gilbert was straying, but by that time, she was pregnant. Without parents or siblings, Linda was stuck. She endured her plight for several weeks until her depression became so deep that she killed herself, taking her fetus with her. "I don't want my daughter to go through the deep depression I've experienced," she had written in her suicide note, excerpted from the autopsy report. "We'll go to heaven together."

Dorothy paused. Linda had chosen not to point to Gilbert's infidelity as the reason for her suicide. Why not? Why had she elected not to ruin him with a terrible scandal that would have played well in the media?

Had she still loved him? Was she afraid someone might hurt him for what he had done?

But who? Al and Doug had extended their stay in Allentown specifically to answer that question and had come up with little more than what Trudy McMoody had given them. Nice person with a weird and unfortunate married name who also had shed light on Linda's state of mind. But when it came to other close friends or meaningful family, Al and Doug had come up dry.

Dorothy needed to stretch her legs, so she left the den and went to the kitchen to make a cup of tea. She stood at the stove, rolling what she knew about Linda Vespucci around in her head until it came to her. What was Linda's mother's name? Might that information help her learn more about this unfortunate woman?

Her obituary, Dorothy thought, as she hustled up the stairs to the den. Doggies still out cold. An hour or so before she had to pick up the girls. Plenty of time to find the document. And there it was, copied into the file by reliable Al. Daughter of Gerald Vespucci and Nicoletta Naccarella.

"Naccarella," Dorothy said out loud, once again stirring the hounds. "I recognize that name from somewhere. I know, I know! High school!"

And with that, Dorothy was off to the pull-down stairs that took her to the tiny attic they used for storage, searching for her senior-year high school yearbook. Found it in the box she used for memorabilia. Blow off the dust; page through the senior photos. And there she was. Terry Naccarella. Dorothy's classmate and close friend, until they went their separate ways for college. Terry had signed her photo, "Come visit me in Ann Arbor." Right, she'd gone to the University of Michigan, but Dorothy hadn't taken her up on her invitation. After a few listless letters, they had lost touch. Where was Terry now?

Dorothy fired up her computer and accessed her work desktop. From this vantage point, she could do all of the things she could at the office. Cool. Time for Dorothy magic. Within twenty minutes, she had everything she needed.

Terry had graduated from Michigan with a degree in geology and had gotten her master's and PhD at Penn State. She was now on the faculty at State College, Dr. Naccarella. Unmarried, no children, and with a dead, much-older sister named Nicoletta!

"Oh my God, is Terry really Linda's aunt?" Dorothy asked the doggies breathlessly.

Rocky was so excited that he barked, causing Meeko to jump about five feet out of her bed.

"Sorry, guys. Let a sleeping dog lie, right? Too late for that. Settle down. I have to talk to Terry."

A look at the clock quickly cooled Dorothy's jets. "Oh my. We have to pick up the girls. Come on, you two; take a ride with me. You've slept enough, and my phone call is going to have to wait."

Far longer than Dorothy had envisioned. The girls were a handful when they arrived home after their playdate. Too much sugar and too much excitement made it impossible to get them settled at their normal time. It was 10:00 p.m. before Dorothy was finally able to get back to the file, too late to call Terry. Tomorrow was another day when she could work on the case. "I hope Philip appreciates everything my father and I are doing for him. It's a real pain in the ass," Dorothy informed her pets, who were waiting at the foot of the stairs, quite anxious to get into bed with Dorothy to replicate their wonderful afternoon snooze.

Dorothy awoke refreshed on Sunday and, while sipping her first cup of coffee before E squared awoke, spent a few minutes making a list of questions for Terry, starting with establishing that she was indeed Linda's relative. She wanted to make sure she had her facts straight before bothering a busy person. She used her cell phone to call what she hoped was Terry's home number and was happy to hear a voice she recognized say hello.

"Is this Terry Naccarella?" Dorothy asked as politely as she could, hoping she wouldn't be mistaken for a telemarketer.

"Who's this?"

"Dorothy Deaver. I went to high school with a Terry Naccarella."

A moment of silence and then, "Dorothy, is that really you?"

"Yes, Terry, it is."

"How wonderful to hear from you! How are you?"

"I'm well. First of all, I want to say how sorry I am for losing touch with you so many years ago."

"Why are you apologizing, Dorothy. The fault is just as much mine."

"Maybe we shouldn't be so hard on ourselves. Life happens, right?"

"Did it ever," Terry said. "So many things to talk about. I'd love to have the chance to catch up with you."

"We'll make a point of doing that. I promise, and this time I mean it. But I called you for a specific reason, and I hope you can help me."

"Anything, Dorothy. I only owe you a million favors. You kept me afloat in high school, as you well know."

Dorothy smiled. Terry had had a tough adolescence. She was shy and didn't dress well. The irony was that she was quite attractive when she got her makeup and wardrobe right. Dorothy spent a lot of time pumping up Terry's self-esteem and positioning her for success at social events. It paid off. By the time they graduated, Terry's metamorphosis was complete—an attractive, kind person who had to beat the boys away with a stick.

"This favor is a little complicated. I'm an investigative attorney, and I've been asked to look into the deaths of two people in Allentown several weeks ago. One of them was a newspaper reporter, Tiffany Springer. The other was her boyfriend, Ray Gilbert." Dorothy paused, hoping for name recognition. It came quickly.

"That son of a bitch is dead?"

"Yes, Terry. You didn't know?"

"How would I? I haven't seen or spoken with him since the day we buried Linda."

"So Linda Vespucci *is* your niece."

"Was, yes, my older sister's daughter."

"Did anyone else in your family know Ray?"

"There isn't anyone else left in our family. My sister and her husband are dead, as I'm sure you know. I have no children, and Linda was an only child."

"I guess you were aware of Ray's, shall we say, dalliances?"

"Oh, yeah. Everybody knew about that. They were even talking about it at the funeral."

"So you went to Linda's funeral as well?"

"Like I said, not much family left. I felt like somebody had to be there."

"What else can you tell me about their relationship and marriage?"

"Linda and I talked on the phone every once in a while. I felt like I needed to fill in the mom stuff, even though I'm really not cut out for it. Linda wanted a kid really bad. It was Ray who wasn't so sure. She told me he practically forced birth control pills down her throat until she got the bright idea to substitute some vitamin D tablets in her pill case. Ray must not have been paying attention. Linda got pregnant quick, and apparently, Ray went ballistic. I don't think he actually struck her but came close. From that point on, Ray was mostly out of the house. When he was home, he just tortured her. It was past ugly. She became more and more depressed. And then—"

"They found her dead?"

"Yes. I felt terrible. I never saw it coming. I was afraid she might lose the baby, or leave Ray, or God knows what, but I didn't think she would kill herself and her unborn child."

"So you know her death was a suicide."

"I was one of the few people who knew, yes."

"I have a copy of the suicide note. Were there any other records or documents?"

"Ray kept just about everything. I suspect he sold her jewelry and anything else that had value. I met her friend Trudy at the funeral, who told me that Linda had given her a sealed box about a week before she died. She told Trudy that if anything happened to her, she wanted me, the sole survivor of the family, to have it. She gave it to me in the church parking lot."

"What was in the box?"

"Mostly family photos, diplomas, stuff like that. Nothing of any monetary value."

"Terry, do you still have that box?"

"Yes. Why?"

"Would you mind sending it to me so I can have a look? I promise to get it back to you quickly. I need to learn some more about Linda before I can put this case aside. I want to be sure Gilbert's death wasn't some kind of payback."

"Payback? By whom? Dorothy, who are you working for?"

"I can't divulge that, Terry. At this point, I have no idea if Gilbert was killed or died accidentally. That's why I'm looking for clues."

"I can't imagine how the box will help you. As you'll see, it's a bunch of junk. And as to retribution against Ray, it's only little old me. And as much as that prick deserved to get it, I'm not a killer. But what the heck. Just make sure it doesn't get lost. It has a lot of sentimental value."

"I understand. I only need a quick peek. And like I said, I promise to be back to you soon about a mini-reunion. A drive to State College would be easy and fun. If I have time, I'll even drive the box back to you."

Two days later, the box arrived, sent by special courier, not an overnight delivery service. Terry wasn't kidding about its value. Philip arrived home around the same time, but Dorothy decided to hold off on briefing him about the case until she'd had a look at the box's contents. While Philip unpacked, Dorothy took the package out the back door to her car and put it in her trunk, figuring it would be easier to open and explore at her office without having to worry about Philip getting into it.

Dorothy's Wednesday was front-loaded with a million calls and mini-meetings, but the afternoon was relatively free, a good opportunity to examine the contents of Terry's box. Her enthusiasm was quickly squelched. Terry had been right. The box contained family photos and mementos, nothing that provided an apparent clue about Linda's suicide.

Crestfallen, Dorothy absentmindedly paged through Gilbert and Linda's wedding photo album. It had been a fairly large wedding, judging from the size of the guest list, perhaps a couple of hundred people. As an only child, Linda had been given a first-rate event at one of Philadelphia's nicest venues, no expense spared for food and drink. *So much money wasted*, Dorothy thought. In the unlikely event she ever gave in to Philip and got married, it was not going to be like that. Simple was the way she would want it, money saved for many more important things than a blowout.

There were dozens of pictures of every phase of the wedding, from bridal party preparation all the way through to the couple's departure for their bridal suite. The photography team had been very thorough, taking time to capture photos of the guests at every table. Dorothy examined each one, looking for Terry. Would she be able to recognize her after so many years? Did she still wear glasses? Was her hair still brown? Had she shed her baby fat? Surely, Linda's only aunt would have been featured in some of the photos.

And then she saw them. Seated together, their wives on either side, arms around each other in a brotherly embrace. Each with a smile a mile wide, holding up champagne glasses to toast the bride and groom. Dorothy started to shake, heart pounding, goose bumps on her arms, sweat breaking out on her upper lip.

"No, it can't be. Please, God, tell me I'm dreaming," she said to no one in the office. It didn't matter. She knew it was true—and that her life could once again be in their hands.

27
CHAPTER

Dorothy was shaken in a way she hadn't been for years, struggling to process what she just had discovered. The Romanos—again. How many times was she going to be involved in a case that Vincente and Giancarlo had something to do with? Granted, their tentacles spread out across the entire state and even beyond its borders, and she understood how powerful they were in the Italian community. But this was just too much. Friends of the Vespucci family, invited to their only daughter's wedding. And Vincente had signed the wedding register as Linda's godfather, her frigging protector.

She had enough of her wits about her that she asked her secretary to hold all calls for the rest of the day and to cancel what few remaining meetings and appointments she had on her calendar. She sat in her desk chair, forcing herself to breathe deeply while she came to her senses so she could decide what to do next, if anything. This was not a new situation. At least twice before she had had to go to the brothers to find out if Philip had been involved in illegal activity. Nevertheless, she knew they were dangerous liars, and the prospect of seeing them again was making her skin crawl.

OK, Dorothy, gather yourself, she thought. *Make a good decision. There's a lot riding on this.* She took a legal pad out of her desk and began to list her options, with one column for pro and one for con.

First and easiest was simply to deep-six what she'd just seen. Pull the photo out of the book along with the guest list and sign-in register, shred or burn them, and tell Philip she'd hit a dead end. The upside was obvious. End of investigation and angst. But Dorothy's detective juices, her need to know, was still boiling and had brought her to this point. Plus, obfuscating seemed like a betrayal of any trust her father and Philip had ever placed in her ability and integrity. Blowing this off just didn't smell right.

Second, she could bring this information to her father and get his advice. That would be an exercise in futility. She knew exactly what he would say: go with option one, and forget about it. Too dangerous to proceed further. Dick would allow his heart to rule his brain, and fear for his daughter's safety would outstrip all other considerations. Of course, she had to consider the obvious danger, but again, if Gilbert and Tiffany were murdered, she owed it to them to find out who did it and why. Or did she?

Third, talk to Philip. She almost laughed out loud at that notion. Philip, the unguided missile. She was pretty sure he would fly off the handle and do something they would both regret. She wasn't going to talk to him until her ideas were mature, and even then, she would have to present them carefully to prevent a Philiplosion.

Fourth, she could take her suspicions directly to the police in Allentown. This option would soothe her sense of justice but had two distinct downsides. If the Romanos were involved and found out what she had done, they would likely kill her and maybe her family. Plus, Dorothy was not impressed with the quality of the detectives in that neck of the woods. They would have very little to go on. No physical evidence, no witnesses, nothing but a motive that looked thin, even to Dorothy.

Fifth, as she had in the past, she could go directly to the Romanos and ask them if they were involved. She knew they were inveterate liars, and they would have no reason to confess to her. And even if they did, their confession would be the end of the investigation. No one in their right mind would take what they said to the authorities. That *would* be suicide.

Finally, she could simply dump this on Terry Naccarella. It was her niece who committed suicide. Let her deal with it. Dorothy shook her head. Stupid idea. Terry would only succeed in getting herself in serious trouble. She didn't have the experience or the wherewithal to make the correct decisions. It was sending a Boy Scout out into a mine field.

Dorothy sat back, holding the pad up in front of her face, her eyes moving back and forth among the choices and their ramifications. *I can't decide*, she thought. *I need advice, but Philip and Dad will not be helpful. Who can I trust to give me good advice and remain discreet? I know! She's the perfect choice*, Dorothy thought as she scrolled through her cell phone contact list and began to enter the number on her cell phone. *I hope she has some time for me.*

Dorothy's drive home that evening was her opportunity to outline what she was going to say, or not say, to Philip. Fortunately, Philip was late himself, and so after Dorothy dismissed their nanny, she had time to treat herself to a rather large glass of wine that she downed while getting dinner ready for the girls. By the time Philip arrived, Emily and Erin were fed, bathed, and seated in front of a *Sesame Street* episode that Philip had taped for them. Dorothy was putting together a niçoise salad, using salmon left over from the night before. Philip poured a whiskey and sat on a stool at the kitchen island, conversing with Dorothy while she worked. They filled the time with small talk and reports of their day's activities. Although Dorothy decided to wait until after dinner to drop her bombshell, she couldn't help but tease Philip.

"By the way, I spoke with Ursula today. She says hello."

"What did she want?"

"Oh, I called her," Dorothy said breezily.

"About what?"

She had him. "I needed some advice about a case I'm working on."

"And you called Ursula? Hardly a legal expert."

"No but a lot of common sense. Dad bounces stuff off her all the time."

"What was the case?"

"Not much of a legal thing. One of those deals where there are many ways to skin the cat. Just needed somebody with horse sense."

"What am I, chopped liver?"

"Needed a woman's point of view, and she helped immensely," Dorothy said, now wondering if she should have opened up the can of worms before she was ready to deliver the full message.

"OK, you obviously aren't going to tell me everything."

"I'll give you more detail later. Let's get dinner on the table now. It's getting late, and I'm going to have agita if I go to bed on a full stomach."

Philip was not assuaged, not by any stretch. He spent dinner semi-sulking, answering Dorothy's questions about his day monosyllabically. Dorothy couldn't wait to finish the meal, clear the table, and get the dishes in the dishwasher. Philip didn't let her take her apron off before he was at her again.

"I really want to know what you talked to Ursula about. I have a feeling it has something to do with the Gilbert case."

"Pretty good intuition for a guy, Philip. Let's sit on the sofa, and I'll tell you what I learned."

With the dogs at their feet and the house quiet, Dorothy started in. She described how she had pursued Linda Gilbert's background and came up with her mother's maiden name, one quite familiar to her. And how she had found Terry, who had sent her the package that had turned the case so dramatically. And finally, precisely who had been seated at one of the tables of honor at Gilbert and Linda's wedding.

Philip's jaw dropped with each new revelation. By the time Dorothy finished, he was incredulous. "Let me make sure I understand. Your father's best investigators overlooked Linda's mother's background? And by sheer chance, you happened to go to high school with Linda's aunt?"

"It's not that unbelievable, Philip. Where I grew up and went to school, there were tons of Italians. Terry was one of my many friends, and I remember her because she transformed from a pimply-faced freshman to an outstanding senior. And she was such a good soul. I don't find any of that surprising."

"But the coincidences keep on coming. The Romano brothers reappear?"

"I thought about that. Also not surprising, given their reach and power. Giancarlo and Vincente are probably godfathers to hundreds of kids. What better way to make sure that your son or daughter is protected and given every advantage? And when your godchild gets married, no matter where or when, you go, and you make sure you're seen by the community—a reminder of their generosity and influence. It's just the way it works."

"What did you have to ask Ursula about?"

"You, mainly. I was in a quandary about what to do with my newfound knowledge. I was afraid that if I told you, you might go off half-cocked. I also thought about destroying the evidence and forgetting about the whole thing, but that didn't feel right to me. I also didn't have the stomach to go the Romanos myself. After we talked about it, Ursula and I agreed that you needed to be told. And that, if you agree, we should visit the Romanos together."

"Are you crazy? Why wouldn't they just kill us?"

"First, I think they respect us, and they like me. I've always been straight with them so they shouldn't be worried about exposing themselves. Also, they won't know where I placed the key evidence in the case and what will happen to it if I'm removed, so to speak. We go to them with the promise that we'll take this no further than Terry, the only remaining person in the family, so she can have some closure and is also protected from prosecution. I think they'll be OK with that. Family means a lot to them, obviously."

"I don't know Dorothy. I'm not at all enthusiastic about this."

"I don't expect enthusiasm, just cooperation. Come with me, make me feel less anxious, and we'll put this all aside after the meeting."

"Suppose I decline?"

"Unless you're willing to lock me in the cellar, I'll go myself, eventually. Terry was one of my best friends, and I'm willing to put myself on the line for her."

Philip shook his head. "Like I said, this thing is making me squirm, but if you insist, I'll go along. Just promise me it will end well."

"It will, as long as we do as they ask. I'll go ahead and set it up for later this week. Do you have anything pressing on your calendar?"

"Nothing more important than this. If I remember correctly, getting to their place is pretty easy, so I'll clear time whenever you say."

"I appreciate that, Philip. I'd also be grateful if you'd let me do the talking, at least at the beginning of the meeting. I need to frame the conversation carefully, and I don't want you interrupting my flow."

"Whatever you say, Dorothy. I'm happy to be your arm candy."

Dorothy sat in her office the next morning, smiling ironically. She didn't know if she should be pleased that her memory was sharp or frightened that she knew the phone number of two brutal mobsters by heart. Or that she remembered Roe, the delightful administrative assistant who seemed to enjoy Dorothy's visits so much that she looked forward to them. Because when the appliance store switchboard put her through to Ms. Wells, she used her sweet, friendly voice to say, "Why Ms. Deaver. How are you? The gentlemen told me that you might be calling."

"They did?" Dorothy said. She felt her airway tightening.

"Yes, they did. A few days ago. I was hoping they were right. It's been too long."

Too long, Dorothy thought. *Why? Is there some reason I should be visiting the Mafia on a regular schedule, like a dentist?*

Dorothy fought to recover her senses. "Yes, well, then would it be OK for Philip Sarkis and me to come in to meet with the Romanos? At their convenience, of course."

"Absolutely. They have some time this Thursday afternoon around two o'clock."

"We can do that," Dorothy said.

"Great. Let me double-check with the gentlemen to make sure they know that Philip—I mean, Dr. Sarkis—will be joining. If you don't hear back from me, we're on. Is this a good number to reach you?"

"My cell would be better. You should have that in your records."

"Indeed we do. And remember to get here a few minutes early."

"Of course," Dorothy said. *Need to leave time for a delightful strip search, the part of my visits I like the best.*

"Bye, Ms. Deaver. See you soon," Roe said before hanging up.

Once the appointment was booked, Philip and Dorothy realized that they would be lucky to get much of anything done while they waited through the morning for their afternoon meeting. Dorothy paged through some low-profile briefs and depositions. Philip was not on service, so he could pursue what he called "monkey work," stuff he could almost do in his sleep, such as reading or reviewing manuscripts. Anything creative was out of the question. Too much tension.

Philip told Dorothy that he would meet her at the Romanos' office, now in a separate building from the appliance store. The business continued to be successful, bucking the suburban warehouse trend that worked so well for the conglomerates. The Romanos maintained their loyal following with the promise of the best prices and service in the region, pledges they actually delivered on. After all, the appliance store really didn't need to make a profit. It was merely a front for their illegal businesses and a convenient money-laundering operation that maintained the Romanos' respectability. Slashed refrigerator prices and free service calls were just part of the cost of doing the *real* business.

Dorothy waited impatiently for Philip, who arrived five minutes late.

"Philip, are you out of your mind? You can't keep people like this waiting."

"Not my fault. The Broad Street line was backed up because of track work."

"You should have left more time. Let's go."

Dorothy led the way to Roe's office. "Dorothy, how are you?" Roe said, rising from behind her desk. "I was getting worried about you. You're usually so prompt."

"Philip ran into a subway problem. Roe, this is Dr. Philip Sarkis." Philip shook Roe's hand.

"So nice to meet you, Dr. Sarkis. I've heard a lot about you."

I bet she has, Dorothy thought. *A lot of it was probably heavily sprinkled with Italian swear words.*

"Let's get you two prepared. Shouldn't take a moment. We do have to move this along. The gentlemen have a conference call with the archbishop at three o'clock. Can't be late for that," Roe said with a laugh.

I wonder if the brothers want to have the cathedral named after them, Dorothy thought. *The Basilica of Giancarlo and Vincente. It has a ring.*

And with that, Roe led Dorothy down a hallway while directing Philip to a restroom, where he was met by a boyish clerk who looked more Italian than Al Pacino. The clerk smiled, apologized, and proceeded to frisk Philip, apparently just as interested in wires as in weapons. But he was efficient and polite, and the experience wasn't as unpleasant as Philip had feared. Philip even thanked him when it was over.

He exited the restroom and, reunited with Dorothy, was escorted to a modest-sized office. To the right of the desk was a small conference table, at which were seated two elderly men, both casually dressed. They rose when they saw Philip and Dorothy.

"Ms. Deaver. What a pleasure it is to see you," one of them proclaimed. "And this must be the famous Philip Sarkis. Dr. Sarkis, I am Vincente Romano, and this is my brother, Giancarlo."

Philip smiled and shook hands with each. "I'm happy to finally meet you both."

"Indeed," Vincente replied. "Please have a seat."

Philip had a few seconds to size up the brothers. Almost exactly what he had anticipated, having viewed their photos in many places over the years. Vincente—the older, gray hair with highlights combed straight back from a sloping forehead, piercing eyes, and a hooked nose. Giancarlo—some black hair remaining, the heavier of the two, but both in magnificent shape for their seventy-plus years. Both were well dressed but not ostentatiously. Dress shirts with open collars, finely pressed wool slacks, and soft leather loafers with fancy socks for their flair.

They all gathered about the round table. Vincente leaned forward on his elbows and began.

"Ms. Deaver, Dr. Sarkis, what can we do for you?

"Forgive me, Mr. Romano," Dorothy said, "but Roe Wells seemed to indicate that you were expecting our visit."

"Expecting is probably stating it a little too strongly. We know that you're a skilled investigator, and we anticipated that you might be perceptive enough to find Terry Naccarella after the police and even your father's investigators overlooked her. And she cooperated by sending you her box of goodies."

"Cooperated? You make it sound like she was in on this."

Giancarlo's turn. "Ms. Deaver, we have had frank conversations before; granted, not with Dr. Sarkis present. But let me remind you that nothing we say will be recorded. You will not repeat our words to anyone, and after you walk out of here today, you will do *nothing* about the deaths of Ray Gilbert, Tiffany Springer, or Linda Vespucci Gilbert. If you or Dr. Sarkis don't obey these instructions, there will be severe—and I do mean severe—repercussions. Understood?"

"Perfectly," Dorothy said.

Giancarlo turned to Philip. "Doctor, understood?"

"Yes, of course."

"Excellent," Vincente said. "Now we can speak freely. Let's start with the Naccarellas. They have been our friends for a long time. Nicoletta was such a sweet girl. We were ecstatic when she finally found herself a good man in Gerald Vespucci. They waited so long to get married that Nicoletta had a tough time getting pregnant. But oh my! Linda, my goddaughter. She was just so beautiful. Everyone fell in love with her. And so smart. She wanted to be a doctor but gave that up and settled for nursing. She was good at it, and her future seemed bright."

"Until she met that good-for-nothing, Gilbert," Giancarlo interjected.

"Yes, a very mean and selfish person in every respect. I am surprised he got to be a doctor. He didn't deserve an MD, and I'm sure his patients didn't deserve him."

Philip tried not to wince. Why was his own assessment of Gilbert so vastly different? What had he missed?

"But what could we do?" Giancarlo asked. "After all, she knew what he was like before they got married. He cheated on her like crazy, but we did a little surveillance and never uncovered any evidence of physical abuse. We are not avenging angels. We can't right every wrong."

"But we made one big mistake, Dorothy," Vincente added. "We failed to correctly assess Linda's mental situation."

"You didn't know how deeply she was depressed over Gilbert's philandering?" Dorothy asked.

"Precisely. We visited her infrequently, and when we did, she seemed fine. She was very good at hiding her emotions. We knew that about her from her childhood. We just didn't take it into account, and for that, we will be eternally sorry."

Almost in unison, Giancarlo and Vincente lowered their heads in contemplation, the silence broken by Dorothy's next question.

"How did you find out about Linda's death?"

"We have our sources. We called Terry to confirm, and she told us that Linda was pregnant when she left this world," Vincente answered.

"Terry Naccarella?"

"Yes, of course."

"You were in contact with Terry?"

"For years. We loved her as much as Linda. Though she was Aunt Terry, she might as well have been Linda's big sister."

"So you learned that I found her during my investigation."

"She told us. She was worried that she might get in trouble for fingering Gilbert. She told us that she was going to send you a box of Linda's personal effects. We suggested she include the wedding album and lists."

"So I would come to you, rather than leading the police to Terry."

"Precisely. And you did, and here we are!"

"And you're not afraid that we'll turn you in."

"There's always that possibility, Ms. Deaver. Either of you might have a crisis of conscience and report what you know. But exactly what do you know? Pretty much nothing. There is no physical evidence to link us to a murder, no witnesses, no accomplice to flip. I guess we have motive, but we aren't blood relatives so that's pretty weak. Balance that against the repercussions and what will happen to you after you do your duty, and we have no reason to worry."

"Just for fun," Philip cut in, "how did you do it?"

Giancarlo answered. "We don't do things for fun, Dr. Sarkis. In fact, we did nothing. We made the arrangements, and people with whom we subcontract took care of the details. I think you'll agree that they did a very professional job. And I believe you will also admit that the world is a better place without Gilbert. A scoundrel who not only drove his wife to kill herself but then stood to become a millionaire whistleblower to boot."

"And Tiffany Springer?"

"Collateral damage, I'm afraid," answered Vincente. "If we were going to mimic a drug overdose, she had to be there. And let's face it; she wasn't in line to be the next Mother Teresa. She was a whoring drunk who slept with people to get them to help her with her muckraking articles. Did she change the world with all of her garbage? Hardly. Like most newspaper slime, all she did was exaggerate a problem and get the public excited, without providing a scintilla of a solution. Good riddance."

"Have we answered all of your questions, Dorothy?" Giancarlo asked. "It's getting close to the hour, and His Eminence doesn't like to be kept waiting."

"I think we've covered everything."

"If you have anything further, please come back. We love seeing you, and now that we've met Dr. Sarkis—Philip, you're welcome here as well."

"And please don't forget us when you need your next major appliance," Giancarlo reminded them. "You'll get the employees' discount on anything you need."

"Thanks, Giancarlo and Vincente, for your time and your generosity," Dorothy said as she rose to leave. *And thanks for descumming the world,* she thought. *I just hope you can keep the good guys and the bad guys straight.*

Roe escorted them back to back to the Broad Street entrance. When they were on the sidewalk, Philip turned to Dorothy and shook his head. "Who would have ever believed that we would walk out of their office alive after finding out how two very dangerous mobsters took care of business?"

"Keep your voice down, Philip. The only reason we're still vertical is because we promised to accept what they said and to keep it a secret. You got your answer, and Terry is not going to be named as an accomplice in Ray's murder because of us. Now we have to be satisfied with what we discovered and put it behind us. Or else."

28

CHAPTER

"O r else what, Dorothy?" Philip asked as their conversation continued on the street in front of the Romanos' appliance store.

"Seriously, Philip? Did you have your hearing aid turned off in there? Do you want to google the word *repercussions*? Wasn't that a vocabulary word you needed to learn for the medical school admission test?"

"Maybe it was you who wasn't listening, Dorothy. Those two guys didn't kill Tiffany and Ray. They were killed by their local talent. Shouldn't those people pay for what they did?"

"And if somehow you did catch the murderers, they would never implicate the Romanos, right? Philip, you aren't making sense. No one is going to be punished for this crime—no way, no how. You have to accept that and move on, just as I warned you before we visited this place."

Philip pursed his lips in a way that indicated to Dorothy that he wasn't satisfied.

"You aren't willing to accept this from me. I understand. I'm just a woman who wants to protect her family. Before you do something stupid, why don't you talk to my father? He's up to speed on this case, and we need to brief him about the meeting anyway. Tell him what we found out, and see if he has a way forward. And if he doesn't, man up and move on."

Philip nodded. "Good idea, Dorothy. I'll do just that. In fact, this is as good a time as any. I have the rest of the afternoon off, so if he's around, I'll have that conversation right now."

"Wonderful. And while you're having your little man-chat, I'll go home to spend some time with the girls. Probably a good idea, because if their clueless father missteps, I may not have many other opportunities."

Before Philip could protest, Dorothy had spun on her heels and was walking briskly to the parking lot to fetch her car. Philip watched her for a few minutes, feeling frustrated and angry but at the same time pleased that there was someone in his life, someone quite bright and attractive, who sincerely cared about him and his welfare.

Frustrated by his bad experience with the Broad Street line, Philip elected to Lyft his way to Dick Deaver's office—a clean car with a courteous driver—arriving at his location in less than fifteen minutes. Philip decided not to call ahead and to take his chances that Dick was in his office and unoccupied. *Nothing to lose.* Finally, given the lateness of the hour, Philip was fairly sure he could convince Dick to share a drink with him while they chatted. After a cocktail or two, Dick would become a little easier to handle, maybe to the point of being downright cooperative.

Philip was in luck. Dick was behind his desk, reviewing a file, when Anita announced his arrival. Dick looked up, surprised to see his faux son-in-law. "Philip, what brings you downtown?"

"Your daughter and I had a meeting with some pretty remarkable people, and I wanted to fill you in."

"You have my attention. Sit down and talk to me."

"Better idea. How about if I buy you a drink next door at McGettigan's?"

Dick looked at his watch. "Hmmm ... it is close to four o'clock. What the heck? This stuff will wait, if you're buying."

"You bet. Let's go."

The tavern was uncharacteristically quiet, and they had little trouble finding a table next to a window that looked out on Broad Street. Service was quick, and before they had their jackets off, a martini for Dick and a vodka tonic for Philip had been delivered by an underworked waitress.

"This place will be jumping in about an hour or two, as soon as offices start to close," Dick said. "People use rush hour traffic as an excuse to linger a while at their favorite watering hole before heading out to the burbs and their lackluster lives."

"I suppose they could go to a gym and exercise," Philip said.

"A few do that, but the majority are pretty burned out and just want to escape into a glass. Anyhow, you didn't visit me to get my opinions on how people ought to handle job stress. You wanted to fill me in on a meeting you and Dorothy had. Does it have anything to do with extending your family?"

"No, Dick, nothing like that. I think we're pretty happy with the size of our crew, at least for now."

"And its quality," Dick reminded him. "Those two girls are pretty special. Any new photos?"

"I think we're up-to-date, although I have to say that your daughter wears out her smartphone with taking pictures."

"Memories, Philip. Someday that's all you'll have. Collect and secure them like gold."

"Good advice, Dick. Speaking of which, I think you'll remember the people we visited today. Quite well, actually."

"Who, Philip?" Dick asked.

"The Romano brothers."

Dick paused mid-sip. "Huh?"

"Giancarlo and Vincente send their greetings."

"How the hell did you end up with them?" Dick asked, not sure he wanted to know the answer.

"The Gilbert/Springer case."

"They were involved?"

"You could say that. In fact, they were the people who ordered Ray's and Tiffany's deaths."

"Why would they do that?"

"Long story, Dick, which is why I thought it would be best told with a little alcohol."

"Go on."

"First of all, you aren't going to like to hear this, but your guys dropped the ball."

"Al and Doug?"

"If they were the two guys you sent to Allentown. I know they might not have anticipated that Linda killed herself, but when they did find out, they didn't dig deep enough."

"What do you mean? I looked over their notes and didn't see anything missing," Dick said.

"Linda's maiden name was Vespucci, as you'll recall—they reported that. What they didn't know was Linda's mother's maiden name. Naccarella. Ring any bells?"

"No."

"Your daughter went to high school with Terry Naccarella. They were pretty close. Dorothy contacted her and found out that Terry is the younger sister of Linda's mother. Terry had stayed in touch with Linda's godfather, who attended Linda's wedding. Terry informed that person that Linda's death had been a suicide. And she told him why Linda killed herself."

"Let me guess—the godfather is named Romano."

"Vincente, to be exact. Dorothy found him and Giancarlo in one of Linda's wedding photos and made the connection."

"And Dorothy decided to go to talk to them?" Dick asked.

Philip nodded.

"Philip, did you know that Gilbert talked to an attorney about his case? A guy named Nicky Toscano. My guys talked to him, and he admitted he was disappointed he wasn't going to be able to cash in on fraud-and-abuse claims."

"Could Toscano have also ratted out Gilbert to the Romanos?"

"I don't know. My guys heard rumors that Toscano is tied up with the Mafia but couldn't come up with anything substantial. They thought the whistleblower issue wasn't a key to the case and dropped it."

"That's another place where they screwed up. Knowing that Gilbert was going to get a lot of money might have given the Romanos a little more motivation to push the Gilbert off-button."

"Easy to say in retrospect, Philip," Dick replied. "Did the Romanos have to murder Tiffany as well?"

"She had to go for a variety of reasons. They weren't terribly sorry about it, having convinced themselves that she was as slimy as Ray. They think they made the world a better place. Plus, they needed the drug cover story that Tiffany provided."

"So you told Dorothy you were cool with putting it all aside, and you decided to do me a solid by coming by to provide closure, right?"

"Not exactly."

"Damn right, not exactly," Dick said with a smirk. "You know you're going to have a hard time swallowing all of this crap, and you told Dorothy you wanted to talk to me to see if you have any alternatives, right?"

"Yes. Well, actually, it was also her idea. She thought you would convince me to put it all away."

"And you thought I might be a little more cooperative after a martini. You do love to manipulate people, don't you, Philip?"

"I prefer to think of it as facilitation."

"You can't bullshit a bullshitter, Philip. I know where this is going, and for your information, I'm not offended in the least. As a matter of fact, I'm flattered that you believe I could come up with a way forward when all paths look blocked."

"I like that spin, Dick."

"I also bet that I'm your last hope. Dorothy won't tolerate your shenanigans much longer, Philip. If you do an encore of the caped crusader in this case, I suspect you'll be eating dinner alone for a long time to come. That is, of course, unless I give you some leeway."

"I think you've summed it up well, as usual, Dick."

"Well, then. What do we have? The device scandal that kicked this whole thing off is forgotten. It's business as usual for the doctors, hospitals, and companies. The only thing Tiffany Springer accomplished was a few weeks of discomfort for some backwater hospitals and towel-head doctors. And a hassle for a device company that didn't deserve bad press but had plenty of lawyers and PR people to do damage control until public amnesia set in."

"Tiffany's yellow journalism made her the likely victim, a theory the police in Allentown still think is viable."

"Ironically, she drew the hayseed detectives off the track quite effectively. I doubt they'll ever solve this case without substantial help."

"From someone like me."

"Getting there, Philip. I do agree that the focus had to shift to Gilbert once we knew about Linda's suicide. And Al and Doug did go in that direction. What stymied them was that they didn't know about the Naccarella connection, uncovered by my brilliant daughter."

"I agree that she's amazing, Dick, but the Romanos intimated that Terry baited the trap. She made sure the critical photos were in the wedding album she sent to Dorothy."

"Why did she do that? She could have just shit-canned the whole thing, and Dorothy would have been at a dead end."

"She's the last surviving member of the family and was worried that Dorothy might make the connection between her and the Romanos. If she did, Dorothy might find out that Terry had set up Gilbert. Which she did. But she was sure that if Dorothy suspected that the Romanos were the murderers, and Terry was no more than an informant, she'd be much more likely to let it all go. For obvious reasons."

"It all goes back to the Romanos, and they made their position abundantly clear."

"Understated, as usual, but they convinced me there were going to be repercussions if they came under any suspicion."

"Plus, your case is weak, and good luck finding the actual killers. I wouldn't be surprised if it was the same outfit that killed those nurses up in Wilkes-Barre. Everything done perfectly, without a clue to be found."

"How about if we make an anonymous tip to the police?" Philip asked,

"Several problems with that, Philip. Tips are traceable, no matter how careful you are, and that would be very bad for you. The detectives might not even take it seriously. And what do you have to back up your suspicions? You have to remember that you're putting your trust in a bunch of investigators you don't know and shouldn't be expected to be first-rate. If they were, they wouldn't be riding a desk in Allentown."

"So I'm out of bullets."

"It's worse than you think, Philip. There's a lot of downside. Those monsters have several ways of ruining you. Hell, killing you might be merciful. They know about a lot of the things you've done in the name of justice, Philip—"

"I don't know what you're talking about Dick. Nobody proved anything."

"Don't be naïve, Philip. They don't have to prove anything. All they have to do is whisper in someone's ear, and you'll become a target for a variety of nasty crimes. Whether you did or didn't do them is immaterial. The investigation would destroy your reputation and drain your savings in defending yourself, and Dorothy wouldn't tolerate that nonsense too long. Then there's your family. There's no such thing as civilians in the mobster business. Cross the Romanos, and you put Dorothy, Emily, and Erin at risk. They don't have to murder them. All they have to do is take them away for a short time—or permanently—to utterly destroy you. They have dozens of ways of making you pay for an indiscretion, Philip. Shooting you in the head would be the most humane."

Philip sat silently, processing all that Dick had unloaded on him. Finally, "Thanks, Dick. This has been most helpful."

"You have to make a decision, Philip, and tell me what you plan to do. You owe me that much."

"Right now, I'm going to go home and talk to Dorothy some more."

"Good idea. Listen to her, Philip. She's a good person, and she's solidly in your corner."

"A lot to process, Dick," Philip said, rising from their table. "I'll pay the bill on the way out. Thanks again. We'll talk soon."

Dick looked out the window at the departing Philip, uncertain, as always, if his advice would be heeded.

Philip arrived home to the usual hubbub of dinner preparation and childcare. He was happy to quickly change into a comfortable pair of jeans and a T-shirt and to pitch in. He knew from Dorothy's demeanor that she would not be interested in a deep discussion of anything until they had completed their chores and were safely in bed, at the earliest. They both needed some decompression time, and the girls were nothing if not expert in taking their minds off anything other than *Winnie-the-Pooh*.

They finally settled under their covers, reading lights on, books in hand, before Dorothy asked the question of the moment: "What did my father have to say?"

"After he got over the Romano shock, he had a number of very cogent things to say about the risks of going further."

"You mean taking the case to the authorities."

"What else is there? I'm not quite ready to go to war with the Mob, and going public would just be a mess, as Ray learned the hard way. As your father pointed out, the Romanos have a boatload of deniability. And how would I ever be able to convince myself that anyone I spoke with wasn't somehow under their influence?"

"You couldn't, and, Philip, I'm afraid that also goes for the police. A substantial percentage must be on the Mob payroll. Talking to them would be like playing Russian roulette."

"They're so evil, Dorothy. I know they don't look it, but the Romanos are gangsters who prey on the public, taking advantage of so many people who can't fight back. They give discounts on home appliances to people while their children get hooked on drugs that the Romanos make available. Or they use the money they saved on a stove to rack up gaming debts they can never repay. And it's been going on forever."

"And Dr. Philip Sarkis, eminent cardiologist, is going to take on the Mob and make everything better."

"Sounds stupid, but I can't stand the idea that they killed Ray Gilbert and are going to get away with it."

"Philip, I don't understand this obsession with Ray Gilbert. What did he do for you that makes you so ready to forgive him for all of the awful things he did to his wife?"

"I feel that way about all of my students."

"That's a load of crap, Philip. OK, you spend a lot of time teaching them and helping them get jobs and all of that, but you don't hang out with them. They aren't your friends." Dorothy watched Philip's reaction and didn't like what she saw. "Oh my God, Philip! Did you have a relationship with Ray Gilbert?"

"What are you talking about?"

"You know—a guy thing."

"Are you implying that I had a sexual relationship with him?"

"He was quite the stud, and sometimes they go both ways."

"Dorothy, that's disgusting."

"It's come up before, Philip," Dorothy said, harkening back to Jimmy Chamberlain, the mechanic who may have had a reason to rig a truck to kill a bad guy who'd made the mistake of getting in Philip's way a few years earlier.

"That was your delusion, Dorothy, and that Scotty guy. Jimmy Chamberlain was a friend when I was growing up. We played golf together. I never had a homosexual relationship with him or with anyone."

"I'm sorry, Philip," Dorothy said, trying to be conciliatory. "I'm just trying to understand why the Gilbert murder sticks in your craw so much."

"He was a special person, Dorothy. I know he's been demonized for all the crap he pulled in Allentown, but the Romanos were wrong. He *was* a good doctor who took care of his patients. I saw him work hard to bail out sick patients. He was unselfish and gentle. The patients and their families loved him. I didn't know he was sleeping around when he trained with us. Hell, I can't believe he had the time. Something must have happened to him when he got to Allentown. I regret that I lost contact with him as we both got busy. But when we reunited, it was because he had a genuine concern about patients who were being harmed with unnecessary device implants. It was another example of his caring."

"Then why didn't the asshole care about his wife?"

"I have no idea. But it's one of the reasons I would love to see this case progress. For my own peace of mind, I need to know if his wheels really came off and why he became worthy of being murdered."

"I'm sympathetic to that, Philip, but, as I'm sure my father explained, to get to where you want to be would be a gigantic risk, not only with your life and career but mine and—most important—the girls. How can anything be worth that?"

"You're right, Dorothy. It just isn't realistic. I'm going to have to live with this and move on for the sake of all of us."

"Philip, I wish I believed you, but I'm afraid you're telling me what I want to hear. Let me put it this way: if you do anything—and I do mean *anything*—with this case, even reopening that infernal dossier, we're finished."

"Dorothy—"

"I know I've said this before, but the stakes were never this high and the implications never so great. The girls are people now, and they're aware of their surroundings. If you manage to turn this house, their refuge, into an armed camp, and if I have to worry about them every minute of every day, I'll never forgive you. And not only will I leave you, but I won't be bashful about telling the world about some of your previous adventures, like that attorney's dissection in Boston."

"You couldn't—"

"This conversation is over. I love you. I'm here for you. I want to spend my life with you, but don't cross me. If you do, whatever the Romanos have planned will seem like a company picnic compared to my wrath. Now, I'm going into the bathroom to brush my teeth and wash my face. When I come out, we will not talk of this further. Never."

Philip listened to Dorothy's electric toothbrush, using the buzzing noise to wipe his mind clean, as best he could.

29

CHAPTER

anny Ramos and Patrick Burgoyne had mostly moved on from the Gilbert/Springer case. Captain Detweiler agreed that it was time to file it under cold cases. In fact, Detweiler had been vigorously in favor of the double-suicide theory right from the start of the investigation. He had agreed, reluctantly, to let Danny and Patrick pursue a murder theory, even though there was hardly any evidence that the couple had been killed. Sure, there were plenty of people who hated Tiffany, but, as Danny and Patrick eventually concluded, none of them had the juice to pull off a highly sophisticated crime of this nature without leaving some kind of trail.

"I'm glad you guys are willing to pull back from the case," Detweiler said after summoning them to his office. "I'm getting a lot of flak from upstairs. They want us to come to a conclusion so they can put out a statement and get the media off their back for good."

"We appreciate your giving us some time, Captain," Ramos said.

"Actually, you're doing me the favor by sitting with me for a few minutes to tie this up. I've had a million things on my plate the last few weeks, and I've only been in this chair a few months. I read your reports and have tried to keep up to speed, but getting your perspective on the case is very important before I make a decision about its disposition."

"Sorry it took so long, Cap. We had to spend a fair amount of time doing background checks and such to make sure there wasn't anybody else who might have had a motive for killing Tiffany—or Gilbert, for that matter."

"Gilbert? You think he could have been the intended victim? How did you get there?"

"He was the initial whistleblower, as you recall, and a lot of people blamed him for feeding the story to Tiffany."

"Was there anything else that would have put him in the crosshairs?"

"Not really. His wife died during her pregnancy. We think there was an autopsy, but we couldn't get our hands on a copy. She was a loner and apparently had been depressed ever since she came up here with Gilbert a few years ago. She was a pitiful thing—not much of a family left and only a few friends. After we finally unraveled all of that, we were pretty sure that Gilbert was not the likely target."

"So if Tiffany or Gilbert wasn't the victim, what do you think happened?"

"All the physical evidence points to an inadvertent overdose. Tiffany probably got hold of some powerful shit and didn't realize it. She dosed Gilbert and then herself, and neither one woke up. Not a bad way to go, if you're old and ready. They were neither."

"This is all in your final report?"

"Sure is," Patrick answered. "I did most of the note-taking and scribing and wrote the report. Both of us polished it up."

"It's going to get a lot of scrutiny, and so are the three of us. Especially me, since I have to make the final decision to ice the case."

"I guess things are a lot more complicated here than they were up in Scranton, eh, Captain?" Danny said.

"No question. There were some pretty screwy cases up there I had to deal with, like that nursing agency fire, but I would've been happy to stay in that sleepy little job if not for my wife, who wanted a chance to live in the same town as her parents."

"And the promotion should help the finances, right?"

"Especially with three tuitions to pay. But so far, so good."

"We're glad you're here, Cap," Patrick said, polishing the apple. "We like the idea of having our ideas listened to and supported."

"That will continue to a point, Patrick. I walk a thin line between maintaining the police work at a high level and keeping the chief and the politicians happy. In this case, I think we've hit the right note."

And so it was with confidence that Patrick and Danny filed their final report. After all of the appropriate signatures were affixed, it was placed in a file that was boxed and shipped to storage, retrievable but only with a good deal of effort.

But only a few days went by before the call came that upset the applecart. They would learn later that it had come from a burner phone, purchased by a man with an alias and a false address. When Danny answered, the caller said he knew who killed Ray Gilbert and Tiffany Springer. And if the detectives wanted his information, they needed to meet him on the fourth floor of an Allentown public parking facility at midnight.

"Crackpot?" Patrick asked when Danny hung up.

"Probably. But why would he have waited so long to give us a bad lead? I don't think we can afford to just blow this off. Do you?"

"Hell no, man. It's just what I want to do in the middle of the night. Why not just tell us on the phone?"

"Maybe he's afraid of a trace. Or he wants to see our reaction—make sure we're serious. Who the hell knows?" Danny answered.

"Or maybe he's just a nut who's watched too many Watergate movies. Should we tell the captain?"

Danny shook his head. "We just put this thing to bed. It's too early to go back. Low probability of it coming to anything. Tell you what. Let's knock off early, surprise the wives, and have a quiet evening. I'll pick you up around eleven thirty, and we'll get this crap over with."

"Sounds like a good plan," Patrick said and returned to the rote work he had planned for the rest of the day.

Patrick had fallen asleep in a recliner in front of the TV when Danny pulled up and knocked softly on the door. Patrick startled awake. It took a few seconds for him to come to his full senses and open the door for Danny, while wiping the sleep from his eyes.

"I guess I conked out."

"Good for you. Now get your shit together. We need to get going. Don't want to keep Deep Throat waiting."

"Let me get my stuff. I assume we're packing."

"Damn right. This is not a situation I'm walking into unarmed."

The drive to the center of town was a speedy one, the road empty except for the occasional tractor-trailer taking advantage of easy movement through an ordinarily congested area. They pulled into the lot that, at this hour, had gates up and drove to the fourth floor, where there were no more than four cars parked; no one in sight. Danny looked at the clock on the dashboard: 12:05.

"Where the hell is he?" Danny asked.

"Maybe he's a real jerk who likes to pull cops' chains."

"Could be."

"Let's give him a few minutes to do our civic duty, and then we can bug out."

A minute later, they watched a figure emerge from behind a red Mustang that was parked in a corner of the parking lot. The closest light bulb had been removed so they could hardly make him out. Looked like he had sunglasses and a baseball cap, average build, maybe a beard.

Patrick and Danny got out of their car and walked toward him.

"That's far enough. Don't come any closer, and don't do anything stupid," the man said. "This is going to be a short conversation. I just want to pass on some information that may be useful to you. I'll answer a few questions, and then you're going to get in that car and drive home. If you do exactly what I say, you'll have a new thread of evidence to pursue in the Gilbert/Springer case."

Patrick and Danny nodded.

"Excellent. Now listen carefully, and remember what I tell you. You don't get to reach into your pockets to pull out a notebook or pen because I don't trust you. You have two brains; use them. I am sure you have heard of a couple of mobsters in Philly named Vincente and Giancarlo Romano. They arranged to have Ray Gilbert and Tiffany Springer killed. Vincente Romano was the godfather of Linda Vespucci Gilbert, and they blamed Gilbert for her suicide."

"She committed suicide? How do you know that?" Danny asked.

"Autopsy said so."

"We never found that report."

"It was sealed, and only a few people saw it. I can't tell you who."

"You're telling us that Mafia guys in Philly killed Gilbert and Springer."

"They arranged their deaths."

"Why did they kill Springer if they wanted Gilbert dead?"

"Collateral damage. And besides, it's not like she was a saint."

"Who actually did the killing?" Patrick asked.

"I don't know. It's your job to find out."

"Who informed the Romanos about Ray's affairs and the real reason for Linda's death?"

"I'm not prepared to tell you that."

"Then how the hell are we going to get them for the murders?" Danny asked.

"Like I said, that's your job. Go do it."

"Is there any physical evidence or witnesses who can tie the Romanos to the crime?"

"Not that I know of."

Danny was exasperated. "How do we know you're not just making this shit up? Maybe you have a score to settle with the Romano brothers."

"I won't lie to you. I'd love to see them pay for what they've done. But that's not why I'm here."

"What else do you have?" Danny asked impatiently.

"What else do you need, Detective? I've given you a way to solve two nasty murders."

"OK. Got it. If there's nothing else, we would like to get some sleep."

"I'm warning you. Don't fail to take advantage of what I'm giving you. You'll never have a better opportunity to put those murderers away."

"We understand, and we'll take this back to our team. Hopefully, we'll be able to do something with it."

"That's all I ask. Now, if you don't mind, can you please keep your hands in sight and get back in your car and drive away? Don't circle back and try to follow me or anything dumb like that. No crime has been committed here, so let's not create one. OK?"

Patrick and Danny nodded, backpedaling to their car. They were gone before the figure disappeared into the darkness.

Patrick and Danny did nothing but discuss what they had learned on the way home that night and during their drive to work the next morning. They agreed that what they had, if true, was potential dynamite, but both remained skeptical. They agreed that any decision about how to proceed was way above their paygrade. The first thing they needed to do was arrange a time to talk to Detweiler.

"My assistant said you had an update on the Gilbert/Springer case," Detweiler said as they seated themselves in front of his desk later that morning. "I thought we iced that case a couple of days ago."

"We did. But then we got a call yesterday and followed up on it last night."

Patrick went on to summarize their parking lot meeting and the information the unknown informant had given them.

Detweiler listened attentively, asking questions only when necessary, until Patrick was finished.

"That's quite a story, guys. Any idea who your informer might have been?"

"No, Cap. We decided not to follow him last evening or to snoop around the garage. He made some threats that we think were bullshit, but we didn't think there was any reason to put ourselves in harm's way. The guy didn't do anything wrong; there was no reason to take him into custody either."

"Did you, by any chance, record the conversation?"

Patrick put his head down. "No, Cap. That might have been a mistake."

"Not a big deal. I think you handled it fine. The question is, what do you think we should do next?"

"Not sure, Captain," Patrick answered. "The Romanos are a very powerful family in this state and in this area, especially, with a lot of friends. Taking them on without evidence is going to be difficult."

"While we were waiting to see you this morning, I did some research," Danny said. "The only person left in the Vespucci family is a woman named Terry Naccarella. She's a professor at Penn State. She was Linda's aunt, but her name never came up when we were looking into Linda's background. We'll talk to her, but I can't believe she had anything to do with this or that she's tied in any way to the Mafia. Without someone soliciting help from the Romanos to give them a motive, we have very little to go on."

Detweiler bit the eraser of the pencil had been twirling during their conversation, trying to decide the best course. "Gentlemen, I tend to agree with you. While this is all very interesting and worthy of a little more digging, I can't see how we can approach the Romanos with any kind of accusation. They'll simply deny involvement, which will leave us as empty as we are now, except they may go to our superiors, who will make our lives miserable."

Patrick and Danny looked relieved.

"Tell you what. Feel free to explore this case a little more if you like, but I know you have a lot on your plates, so you can't give it much time. Anything you learn, bring to me before anyone else so we can decide together what to do next. It's not that I don't trust you. I just don't think it would be fair to you to have a bunch of politicians come down on you for doing your job. I'm the one who has to take that heat, and I promise you I will."

"Cap, that sounds perfect. We have a bunch of other live cases to chase down anyhow. We'll keep our ears open and let you know if anything further develops, for sure."

The meeting ended with Patrick and Danny telling each other how lucky they were to have such a politically savvy leader. When his office door closed, Detweiler began fishing around in his desk for a cell phone he rarely used. He put it in his pocket and left his office, telling his administrative assistant that he needed to get something from his car. In the farthest reaches of the parking lot, he used the cell phone to call a number that immediately went to voice mail.

"Some fool tipped off two of my detectives last night. I'm sure you know who it was. I put the fire out for now, but something needs to be done before the cannon goes loose again."

That should do it, Detweiler thought after closing the flip phone. *Now back to work before somebody notices.*

Dorothy had witnessed this behavior many times, but it never ceased to amaze her. She wasn't a psychiatrist, but Dorothy was convinced that Philip was bipolar. After their final conversation about the Gilbert matter, Philip had gone into a deep funk. He dragged himself to and from work during the week, but he could do little else. He had no energy for the girls; he shirked chores around the house and sat for hours in front of the TV, watching mindless sports, resorting to watching drag racing and wrestling when there was nothing else he cared about. As if his depression wasn't enough, he was also super-irritable, going off the handle at the slightest provocation. Everything made him angry, from work matters, to the state of the economy, to the soggy newspaper on their doorstep. He found fault with anyone who crossed his path. He was even short with the girls, who finally learned to avoid him whenever they could.

Dorothy tried several times to help him, pointing out what his behavior was doing to his relationship with his coworkers, friends, and family. Even Dick and Ursula had canceled their latest Sunday dinner after they had been scolded by Philip too many times for their comfort.

So when Philip announced, a couple of weeks into his funk, that he needed to go to Washington for a two-day meeting, Dorothy was ecstatic to get out from under his cloud, at least for one night. The evening before his trip, Philip surprised Dorothy by packing calmly and quietly and not, as she had feared, by expressing outrage that he had to attend yet another worthless meeting.

While he was away, something hit the switch. Philip called Dorothy at her office and excitedly informed her he had extricated himself from the meeting early. He was on an earlier Acela and would be home in time to pick up the girls at school, to take them to the playground.

Dorothy knew immediately that the chameleon had changed colors, and Philip was going to be a different person altogether. By the time she arrived home, Philip was a whirlwind. He had entertained the girls so thoroughly at the playground that they had insisted on staying for over an hour. Philip had followed that up with their dinner preparation, baths for the girls, homework completion, and some storytelling before the obligatory thirty minutes of TV time. He had also planned dinner for the adults and had a glass of sparkling wine waiting for Dorothy. Before her coat was off, he grabbed her around the waist and gave her a huge hug and a kiss.

"I missed you," he whispered in her ear.

"And I missed you, Philip. For the last few weeks."

"You mean my bad mood."

"That's putting it lightly, Philip. You made Attila the Hun look like Mr. Rogers. What the hell is going on?"

"Just work stuff. You know. I let it get to me sometimes."

"I'm not sure I'm buying that, but I'm glad to see you more like your usual self. The girls need you to be their father, not their warden."

"I know. You're right."

"Philip, this has happened several times before. Do you think it might be worth seeing a psychiatrist?"

"You think I'm crazy?"

"Of course not, Philip. You're a doctor, and you know there are a lot of reasons why people have mood disorders. Maybe you should get some lab work too."

"I'll take your suggestions under advisement."

Dorothy looked at him askance.

"No, really, I will," Philip insisted. "I'll talk to Henry Wong about it. I'm overdue for a physical, so he can check it all out when I go in."

"Promise me you'll make that appointment, Philip."

"I will. See here?" he said, picking up a pen and pad from the kitchen counter. "I'm writing it down so I don't forget. Appointment with Henry. OK? Happy?"

"This is for you and for all of us, Philip. If you want to keep your friends and family, you'll get to the bottom of your mood swings so they don't keep happening."

"Roger that, Dorothy. Now, let's proceed with our cocktails. I can tell you about my trip, which wasn't as worthless as I thought it would be, and you can tell me about the cases you're working on. And then burgers on the grill."

And for the rest of the week and weekend, gone was the brooding, depressed Philip, replaced by an ebullient Philip, full of enthusiasm and good humor, considerate of Dorothy's needs, playful with the girls and the dogs, eating well, drinking moderately, seemingly as happy as he could be with the life he had found.

The Philip she had fallen in love with was back. Where he had been and why and how he had returned were mysteries Dorothy knew that she, or Henry Wong, or anyone else, for that matter, would never be able to answer.

30
CHAPTER

As the warm spring days stretched into early summer, Philip continued his upbeat attitude and good humor. On weekends, a constantly bouncy Philip was too much for Dorothy, to the point that she was constantly on the lookout for diversions that would get him out of the house—better with the kids and the dogs and best without her. It didn't take much to stoke his enthusiasm, and he hardly ever protested or made excuses, although he nagged her about accompanying him to wherever he and his merry band were headed. Dorothy used the work card as many times as she could, but on those occasions when she had no excuse and she was pulled into the party, she marveled at Philip's energy and his willingness to do almost anything to keep the girls and the dogs happy. Whether it was boarding the roller coaster or Tilt-A-Whirl at the amusement park, going to Chuck E. Cheese's for lunch, or sitting for hours on a bench at the playground or the dog park while the kids and the pups ran themselves to exhaustion, Philip was all in.

Philip's work, with all of its hassles and torments, forced some equilibrium and balance for which Dorothy was grateful. The hours he spent at the hospital absorbed his energy so that the evenings were relatively tranquil. The price she paid was that Philip continued to complain to her about all of the things he hated about medicine in general and academic cardiology in particular. And then there was NorthBroad, an institution that served a valuable purpose by caring for the poor and the indigent in a bad part of town, its importance ratified by the state legislature, which provided generous subsidies to make up for the revenue lost as the hospital cared for patients with advanced disease, most of whom had no capacity to pay their bills.

Philip was outraged that misguided leaders of the health care system insisted on trying to morph the university hospital into a tertiary care center. The truth, as Philip explained it, was that this was simply never going to happen. Affluent and even middle-class patients from the suburbs were afraid to venture into North Philadelphia for consultation, preferring the more genteel neighborhoods around Jefferson or the Main Line hospitals. The enormous salaries and research support money NorthBroad paid to subspecialty superstars to move to NorthBroad rarely eventuated in the expected patient and grant revenues. With each misstep, NorthBroad fell farther into debt and was forced to lay off support staff and nurses, which made care at the hospital worse than ever. The vicious cycle of deteriorating conditions and resignations was awful to watch, especially for someone like Philip, who was used to having his patients well cared for by a full set of experienced doctors and nurses.

So although he complained over cocktails, Dorothy detected a not-so-subtle difference in his attitude. While frustrated, Philip was no longer bitter and mean. He was able to put his pique aside much faster, steered on to happier topics by Dorothy after she was sure he had gotten most of the venom out of his system.

And by tacit agreement, while Philip was allowed to complain about work, he had to stop carping to their family and friends. Work and politics were mostly off limits at social gatherings. When Philip strayed there, Dorothy was quick to change the subject, making sure that he knew what she was doing by flashing him a toothy grin. The system worked well, as Philip reconstructed a number of relationships that they were again able to enjoy.

Philip even gathered enough emotional energy to call his ex-wife, Nancy, now living in California with her second husband, to insist on a visit with his two children from his first marriage. Now teenagers, they were content to keep up with Philip via an assortment of social media but had little motivation to get on the phone or, preposterously, to board an airplane and visit Philip. His few visits to California hadn't gone well at all. The kids were bored when they spent any time with him at his hotel or in a restaurant or mall, and he clearly wasn't welcome in Nancy's home. Far from acknowledging her part in the breakup, she blamed their divorce on Philip's affair with Dorothy. No matter that Philip pointed out that the affair had only been a one-night stand and that Nancy had abandoned him when he plummeted into a suicidal depression. Philip had finally given up in frustration and hadn't spoken to his ex-family for months. Nancy was surprised by the call.

The conversation was expectedly cool, but Nancy finally acknowledged that Philip had a point. If he was willing to make the reservations and pay for the airfare, she would tell the children they were going east. Philip promised to put together an itinerary for their visit that they would enjoy, including a visit to New York to see a Broadway show of their choice. Dorothy knew that it was his new positive attitude that had made the difference with Nancy and was proud of his forbearance.

The new Philip wasn't lost on Dick and Ursula either, whose visits returned to a regular Sunday schedule. Dick had quizzed Dorothy during one of the visits, when Philip had gone to the grocery store for ice.

"What's up with Philip? He seems like a changed man," Dick said.

"I'm not sure, Dad, but it's been a pleasant surprise. It started about two or three weeks after our visit with the Romanos."

"Do you think he finally came to grips with it all?"

"That would be unusual for Philip. I haven't seen him put too many things aside without resolving them somehow. At first, I worried he had gone after the Romanos, but we're a couple of months out now without a hint of an issue with the Romanos or the Allentown police."

"That's a good sign, I agree. I guess I shouldn't look a gift horse in the mouth. Just enjoy the new vibe and hope it endures."

"You aren't the only one who's grateful, Dad."

Because all of these positive developments had also spilled over into Dorothy's job. With more time available and less friction at home, Dorothy was able to bring a number of her cases to a positive solution, pleasing her partners, who finally voted her a full share in the firm. With that came more say about business development. Most important, Dorothy had a greater voice in the choice of cases she and the firm elected to take on.

Dorothy's five partners, all middle-aged men with families, were inclined to accept work if it had the potential to bring in large revenues. Though Dorothy didn't totally disagree with that approach, she also wanted the firm to do more cases for the public good. This might include pro bono cases but, even more important, reduced fees for people of modest or little means. She volunteered to take such cases at the risk of a reduced bonus, as long as it didn't jeopardize her base pay. To their credit, her partners agreed, effectively subsidizing her good work and preserving the camaraderie that had attracted Dorothy to the firm in the first place.

But Philip and Dorothy's life could never remain that simple. A week after her conversation with Dick, on a nearly dark Saturday morning, Philip was awakened by a blow to the back of his head. Startled, Philip spun around to come face-to-face with a large black head, staring menacingly at him. Philip blinked the sleep from his eyes until he was able to focus on the threatening figure—unblinking brown eyes, large nose, sharp teeth, foul breath, and a tick collar. Finally, a menacing bark that said, "Come on, Dad. Get out of bed. It's time."

Philip craned his neck to see the alarm clock. Six o'clock.

"Darn it, Rocky. It's too early. Go back to sleep for a few minutes," Philip said as he turned over and closed his eyes.

Whack. Another paw punch. *Rocky isn't kidding around*, Philip thought. *I bet he has to do his business. I wonder if I can get away with just taking him out front for a few minutes and then come back to bed.*

That thought was interrupted by the arrival of the second hound, Meeko, who had jumped on the bed, tail wagging furiously, expecting to join in the fun. The two of them were a formidable force, and Philip now knew that any hope of further sleep was gone and that his day was going to start earlier than he had planned. He got out of bed, looked out the window, and welcomed the light that was just beginning to filter though the blinds. "At least I'll be able to see where we're going," he said to Rocky, who remained on the bed, tail pointed directly up, ready for action.

Philip went over to Dorothy's side of the bed, where she slept peacefully on her side, oblivious to the dog attack he had just suffered. He adjusted the blanket to cover her shoulder and kissed her lightly on the head, happy that she was at peace, although he was more than a little jealous that she was going to sleep a bit longer than he. "But a deal is a deal," he said to Meeko, referring to his offer to be the dog caretaker when he was home on the weekend. After all, dog care, just like childcare, usually fell on Dorothy more than he.

Philip then started his weekend morning doggie routine. First into the small changing room to don a T-shirt and walking shorts, low-cut socks and sneakers, and Phillies cap. Out the bedroom door with the dogs, closing it softly behind him. Dog collars placed—each with name, address, and phone number, just in case—treats and poop bags for his pockets, leashes at the ready, and then out the front door for the short walk to the dog park. No need for phone or wallet. This next hour would be all about the dogs.

There was no better time for Rocky and Meeko. They were rested, with their dad, and on their way to one of their favorite places in the world on a morning that was not too hot and not too cold, perfect for doggie exercise. They pranced up the Narberth residential street, content to wait to do their peeps and poops until they were within the gates of the dog park and off the leash.

The walk was only a few blocks, including a stretch through a greenbelt that preserved the bucolic nature of a small town that was in the middle of the busy Main Line. The proximity of nature, combined with the easy accessibility of shops and restaurants in the quaint downtown area, made Narberth one of the most popular residential neighborhoods in the entire Philadelphia region.

Despite the early hour, the dog park already had a few regulars. Rocky immediately ran to greet his Labradoodle, Irish setter, and German shepherd friends. Meeko preferred to wander around alone, nose to the ground, looking for just the right place for her constitutional. Like all good dog parents, Philip watched both of them carefully, dutifully bagging their proceeds and depositing them in the designated container.

Next came exercise. Rocky, the youngest, played "chase me" with each of the other dogs in turn. Meeko preferred a more leisurely walk around the perimeter of the fenced park, occasionally requiring Philip's encouragement to complete the full circuit.

But there was a part of the experience that Philip liked very little: small talk with the other dog owners. While he recognized most of the supervising humans, he had never taken much of an interest in any of them. In fact, he didn't even know their names or what they did for a living. That meant that the conversation could have no real meaning. Just jaw flapping.

Fortunately, this particular morning, two of the owners appeared as tired as he felt. They sucked greedily on plastic coffee cups, using caffeine to pump life into their day. Only the Labradoodle's mom had any energy and an inclination to converse. The subject was too familiar: how much her man-made breed looked like Philip's Portuguese water dogs.

And how great it was that they didn't shed. And how wonderful that her dog got the good parts of two breeds—brains from the poodle; loyalty and affection from the Lab. *What a magnificent idea*, Philip thought. *Manufacture a new breed for your convenience.*

Philip merely smiled while the woman blabbed, nodding when it was appropriate, beginning to plan his escape.

"Jeez, look at the time, would ya? It's almost seven o'clock, for crying out loud," Philip said, looking at his watch. "Have to get back and get the day started. Lots of things on my honey-do list, if you know what I mean."

"Sure do. I have one waiting for my husband," she said with a laugh.

Good luck to him, whoever he is, Philip thought as he said goodbye. Meeko was more than ready to go, but Rocky was having too much fun and had to be roped in. He pulled hard on his leash in protest, but Philip was able to convince him that some treats would make up for the terrible loss of companionship he would suffer. Together, the three started for home.

Despite the time, the streets were still empty. Newspapers were perched on doorsteps throughout the neighborhood, the owners clearly taking advantage of the moderate weather to sleep in. And several households likely were beginning to make weekend visits to the shore and the mountains, putting a significant dent in street and road traffic throughout the area.

Street parking in Narberth was not common. Everyone had driveways and garages, so Philip did make note of a large black Suburban parked on the street next to the greenbelt. Through partially tinted windows, Philip could see that the driver was in the vehicle. *Somebody with money is probably going to the airport or train station this morning, riding there in style*, Philip thought as he crossed into the woods for the short trek to his street on the other side.

As the three souls made their way through the greenbelt, Philip was lost in thought, planning his day, when he heard a few twigs break behind him. He assumed a small creature was crossing the path, and, as he turned to see, someone forced him to his knees and put a bag over his head. Before he could yell for help, he was struck in the head with a blunt object and knocked out cold.

Dorothy awoke to the sound of someone knocking on the front door and ringing the doorbell simultaneously. As she shook off sleep, Dorothy assumed Philip had locked himself out again and was just being his usual impatient self. *Darn Philip*, she thought as she put on her robe and slippers. *I wish he would hide a key outside somewhere for this kind of thing.* She had suggested it multiple times. Philip simply had ignored her.

Irritated, she pulled her robe closed as she shuffled to open the front door, where she was greeted not by Philip but by two uniformed Narberth police officers, an odd pairing of a tall white man and a short Asian woman.

"Sorry to disturb you, ma'am. I'm Officer Cook, and this is Officer Li. We think we have your dogs in our car."

"Huh? Meeko and Rocky?"

"That's the names on their collars. Are you Mrs. Sarkis?"

"That's my partner's 's name, Philip Sarkis. We both own the dogs. I'm Dorothy Deaver."

"Well, Ms. Deaver, we found your dogs wandering around the greenbelt area, just up the street here. They had their leashes on, but there was nobody looking after them," Cook said.

"Philip must have taken them out early this morning. They go to the dog park on weekend mornings."

"They probably cut through the greenbelt on the way home, you think?"

"He almost always does. It cuts off two blocks."

"We looked around in the woods and the streets near the dog park and didn't see anyone searching for the dogs."

"Philip would never leave them alone. He's exquisitely careful with them. Something must have happened to him," Dorothy said, rapidly becoming unhinged.

"Hold on, Ms. Deaver," Li said. "First of all, is Mr. Sarkis's car here?"

"It's right there in the driveway, with mine."

"So he was on foot, and the dogs were still in the area, so we have a very good chance of finding him," Li said, trying to quell Dorothy's rising panic.

"Oh my God, do you think he collapsed somewhere?"

"Let's not jump to any conclusions," Cook said. "We haven't conducted a thorough search yet. How about if you take the dogs and settle them down, and we'll go back and hunt around some more. We'll call this in now, so if we come up empty, we'll be able to quickly widen the search."

Dorothy might have had a worse day in her life, but she couldn't think of one. The next fourteen hours were consumed by phone calls, conversations with police detectives, visits by Dick and Ursula and a few close friends, carefully worded explanations to Emily and Erin, and soothing words for the dogs, who wouldn't stop panting and pacing around the house, frantically looking for Philip, fully aware that something bad had happened to him and frustrated by not being able to inform their mom.

It wasn't until late in the evening, after she had dismissed her father, who had pleaded futilely with her to stay at his apartment, that Dorothy was able to finally sit down on the sofa with Meeko and Rocky, wine glass in hand, and sort out what had happened.

Philip was missing, and, for all of their reassurances, the Narberth authorities hadn't been able to explain his disappearance. They knew he had made it to the dog park, substantiated by the regulars who had seen him there, and he had left with the dogs, all looking fine. One elderly neighbor mentioned he had seen a large black car or SUV parked near the greenbelt when he went out on the porch to get his paper, but no one else had seen it arrive or depart.

"You guys are the only ones who know what happened to your dad. Can you make like Lassie on TV and show us what happened or where he went? Please?"

Meeko lay down and put her head on her paws in silent contemplation, while Rocky jumped onto Dorothy's lap, desperate to provide clues to get Philip back.

Dorothy would eventually lie down on the sofa with her hounds and succumb to a fitful sleep filled with terrible nightmares, none of them as awful as the reality she would confront when Sunday's dawn finally arrived.

EPILOGUE

They never found Philip, but it was not for want of trying. Dick Deaver had his agency put every project on hold while he sent out his minions to retrace Philip's last known movements, interview neighbors, and chase down clues. They were instructed to avoid the Philadelphia police, who had no choice but to work hard on the case after the public reaction to the local media reports. Hard to beat the drama of the mysterious disappearance of a prominent cardiologist, especially one with Philip's checkered history.

But despite their best efforts, neither the Philadelphia police nor the media discovered the most important feature of the case: the connection with the Romano brothers. There was nothing in the public domain that tied Philip to the Allentown scandal, and only Dorothy and Dick knew of the Romano brothers' involvement with the Gilbert/Springer case, among so many others over the years. Mere hours after Philip's disappearance, father and daughter had the talk that would forever seal Philip's fate and damn the investigation of his disappearance to failure.

They sat on Dorothy's sofa, each turning slightly to face the other, both on the verge of tears. It was the opportunity they had been waiting for since Dick and Ursula had arrived at Dorothy's home. Ursula, understanding the need for Dick to ask Dorothy some important questions, offered to take the girls out for ice cream.

"Dorothy, I have already put a bunch of agents on the case," Dick said. "I'm going to stay on this and work with the police as long as necessary."

"Thanks, Dad, but you know there's only a small chance that anybody is ever going to find him, right?"

Dick dropped his head, not wanting Dorothy to see the affirmation on his face.

"You don't have to answer, Dad. We both have a good idea of who did this, and if we're right, they're not going to make any mistakes."

"Did he provoke them, Dorothy?" Dick asked, choking back tears. "The last time I talked to him, we agreed that he would forget about Gilbert and move on. If he had done that, the Romanos never would have come after him."

"The obvious answer is that he just couldn't let the Gilbert thing go. I still don't understand why the damn case was so important to him, but then again, I haven't been good at figuring out much about what he does. Or should I say *did*."

"It's just crazy. He knew how dangerous the Romanos are and how far they would go to protect their family and those close to them."

"He did. But I think he believed he was smarter and could get away with defying them."

"So if he did rat out the Romanos to the authorities, wouldn't they have them listed as suspects in Philip's kidnapping?"

"Under normal circumstances, yes. But remember, the Romano tentacles reach out everywhere. If Philip did try to implicate the Romanos, he probably did it anonymously. I wouldn't be surprised if whoever he contacted was instructed by his or her boss to shit-can information coming from an unidentified person who was asking the police to take on a very dangerous family."

Silence while each considered the pivotal question that Dorothy finally vocalized.

"What do we do about the Romanos, Dad?"

"Two clear options, my daughter. You either tell the authorities about why you suspect them, or you keep quiet and let them get away with kidnapping your man."

"And killing him," Dorothy added.

"Probably, although we don't know that for sure. Maybe they just wanted to scare him."

"Really, Dad. You think they would take a chance that Philip, the nutcase, wouldn't find another opportunity to place them in jeopardy?"

Dick didn't need to answer.

"So we give it a few days. If Philip doesn't surface, do we let the Romanos get away with murder?" Dorothy asked.

"Under ordinary circumstances, absolutely not," Dick answered.

"But this is not usual. Right, Dad?"

"I shouldn't have to spell it out for you, Dorothy. The Romanos never would have gone after Philip if they didn't have us checkmated."

"By the girls."

"Yes, the girls and Ursula."

"No way around it?"

"Let's think logically, Dorothy. There will be no physical evidence that the brothers themselves did anything wrong. They are highly skilled at firewalling themselves and using agents to do their dirty work—loyal agents, who are unlikely to squeal. In the end, it would literally be our word against theirs. And not to forget that going after our family may not even be necessary. They have myriad political connections and the resources to hire the best legal help. Even if they let this go through the legal system, the chances of our prevailing would be small."

"And if we somehow overcame all of that—"

"I almost wish we couldn't because that's when we would be particularly vulnerable. They are not going to take losing lightly."

"Can't risk anything happening to our girls."

"No way. Ursula, Emily, and Erin are our future, our lives. Getting the Romanos is not going to bring Philip back."

"Oh my God, Dad. How did we get into such a mess?"

Dick slid over to sit next to Dorothy and put his arms around her. "You fell in love with a complex person, Dorothy. Somebody who cared about other people so much that he couldn't stand to see bad people go unpunished. It happened over and over again. It ruined his marriage and his career and finally destroyed his life with you and the kids."

"I warned him, Dad. I really did, every chance I could. But you and I made the mistake of helping him too many times. And this last time, he stepped way over the line."

"Afraid so."

"I loved him so much," Dorothy said through her sobs.

"I know you did, Dorothy. And so did the girls. He was a good father."

"What am I going to tell them, Dad?"

"For now, tell them he went on a trip. Let time pass, and then you can begin to give them the truth in small doses. Ursula and I will fill in the gaps as best we can. They're young and will get over it. You, on the other hand—"

"Never."

"You *will* pick up the pieces and make a new life for yourself. Lots of possibilities, Dorothy, after you have a chance to grieve."

"Thanks, Dad. I really appreciate your being here, but I need to be alone for a while."

"Understand entirely. How about if I shuffle up the street and meet Ursula. The kids should be ice creamed up and ready for some playground time. Shoot me a text when you are ready to have them back."

Dorothy managed a smile and a nod and a thank-you as Dick stood and left her alone on the sofa to contemplate what her life would be without her soul mate, the father of E squared. The man who drove her crazy but had made her life whole. The man she spent as much time loving as hating.

"Philip Sarkis," Dorothy murmured, "how dare you leave me?"